A SOUTHERN GIRL

STORY RIVER BOOKS

Pat Conroy, Editor at Large

A SOUTHERN

GIRL

A Novel

JOHN WARLEY

Foreword by Therese Anne Fowler

The University of South Carolina Press

For our daughter,
MaryBeth Warley Lockwood

IN MEMORIAM

"The stroke of death is as a lover's pinch, which hurts, and is desired."
Shakespeare, *Anthony and Cleopatra,* Act V, Scene 2

Barbara Nelson Warley
February 5, 1949–February 21, 2014

Published by the University of South Carolina Press
Columbia, South Carolina 29208

www.sc.edu/uscpress

Manufactured in the United States of America

23 22 21 20 19 18 17 16 15 14 10 9 8 7 6 5 4 3 2 1

LIBRARY OF CONGRESS CATALOGING-IN-PUBLICATION DATA

Warley, John.
A southern girl : a novel / John Warley.
pages cm.—(Story River Books)
ISBN 978-1-61117-391-8 (hardbound : alk. paper)—ISBN 978-1-61117-392-5 (ebook)
1. Adoption—Fiction. 2. South Carolina—Fiction. I. Title.
PS3623.A8624S68 2014
813'.6—DC23 2013032346

CONTENTS

Foreword vii
Therese Anne Fowler

Acknowledgments xiii

Prologue 1

Part 1—Confluence 5

Part 2—Rapids 145

Part 3—Flow 159

FOREWORD

John Warley and I first met at the South Carolina Book Festival a few years back. As we got acquainted over drinks and hors d'oeuvres at the authors' reception, I could easily see that he was an intelligent and thoughtful person. Soon after, I read one of his novels and saw that he was an excellent writer, too. But when he told me he was working on a new book about an adopted Korean girl told through the perspectives of not only the adoptive parents but also the girl's birth mother and the female Korean adoption agent, I worried that he'd bitten off more than he could—or maybe should—chew.

When a white writer tells the story of non-white characters, folks sometimes accuse the writer of cultural appropriation—as in, what business does this person have in telling those characters' stories? Similarly, there is skepticism in some quarters about how well even the most observant and well-intentioned man can write about women's experiences. These are reasonable concerns. Even though the story it tells is fictional, a good novel has to be authentic. It has to *feel* true. If it doesn't, the author—male or female of whatever ethnicity—has done a disservice to the book's characters, and even worse, to its readers.

A Southern Girl aims to be more than simply a good novel, however. As John explained to me, its story is an exploration of personal experience as accomplished through fiction. In 1978, John and his wife Barbara, already the parents of two healthy boys, decided (not without some conflict between them) to adopt a daughter from another part of the world—in this case, Asia, a region that many Americans of the time associated with communism, war, and brutality. In June of 1979, they brought home a tiny infant Korean girl and named her MaryBeth.

So all right, I thought. John knows something of what he writes. That's a start.

John gives his character Coleman Carter much of his own background, making him scion of a "South of Broad" Charleston family with roots nearly as deep as the most resilient of the city's grand old magnolia and oak and cypress trees. Now, certainly, any decision to adopt is fraught with risks. What can the new parents really know about the child's background, health, and mental capacity? How well, or how poorly, might the child integrate into the immediate family? What about the extended family? What about the community? All of these issues matter, but some prove to be more acute than others. Traditional Southerners to their core, Coleman, his parents, and the society they all keep could be the undoing of every good Coleman and Elizabeth hope to accomplish in giving this abandoned infant her first real home. Like John did, Coleman struggles to reconcile two powerful forces: his wife's admirable desire and determination to adopt a child from Korea, and his parents' not-entirely-unreasonable objections to any adoption at all, and particularly to this one.

Coleman is not, of course, the only one with worries, and here is where *A Southern Girl* really shines. We get his wife Elizabeth's earnest and poignant account of the journey. We see Jong Sim, the distraught but determined birth mother, as she does what most of us would deem impossible. We hear from Hana, the dedicated woman whose job it is to oversee the care and—in the best cases—adoptions of the orphaned or abandoned children in her ward.

As I began reading *A Southern Girl*, I was quickly caught up in the story, to the point of forgetting what I knew about the author, or even that I knew him at all. Instead, I was pulled into these characters' complex lives. With Elizabeth and Jong Sim and Hana and Coleman, I struggled with the practical versus the profound. I considered the problems and the benefits of birthright, tradition, opportunity, exclusion. I thought about loss and renewal and what constitutes family. I contemplated the questions of what we owe the people we care for and what we owe ourselves. I wondered how—or whether—Allie, the Korean born Southern girl at the center of it all, would come through her experience all right.

We are affected and shaped by many forces in our lives, and among those forces is the power of story. Here in your hands is one that I hope will move you as it has done me.

Therese Anne Fowler

ACKNOWLEDGMENTS

Writing a novel is a famously insular endeavor, yet any novelist who is circumspect will appreciate the debt he or she owes to those who nurtured, encouraged, and even criticized, if the criticism made for a stronger book. When the work has a prepublication life of twenty years, as this one did, the debts are particularly numerous.

I must begin, as all good novels begin, with inspiration. In June 1979, Northwest Orient brought us our daughter from Seoul, Korea. Mary-Beth's arrival enriched our family beyond measure. *A Southern Girl* is not MB's story, but to deny that she was the inspiration for this book would be foolish. Equally foolish would be my failure to express my thanks to her mother, my wife, Barbara, whose courage, determination, and foresight brought MB to us. And to her "other mother," whose name we have learned but whom we never expect to meet, thank you for your sacrifice in putting MB's future first.

In 1993 I moved to Mexico to write this book. Shortly thereafter, a courier delivered a large box filled with some of the best fiction I've ever read because it is some of the best ever written. Pat Conroy, my friend, Citadel classmate, baseball teammate, and now editor, had personally selected them at Cliff Graubart's Old New York Bookshop in Atlanta. Pat knew what I needed in Mexico, and my debt to him is long and deep.

Therese Anne Fowler's acceptance of an invitation to pen a foreword to this book thrilled me. She is as nice as she is talented, as anyone familiar with *Z-A Novel of Zelda Fitzgerald* will attest.

I owe a sacred debt to Jonathan Haupt, director of the University of South Carolina Press. His editorial suggestions proved invaluable, and it is not too much to say that this would be a lesser book without his cogent insights and keen recommendations.

Martha Price Frakes was a year behind me at York High School and has been a friend ever since. A bridesmaid in our wedding forty-two years ago, she has come back into our lives to provide timely encouragement and support. Thank you, Martha.

I wrote the first draft of the manuscript in San Miguel de Allende, aided by my tolerant amigos in the writing group there—Donna Meyer, Roy Sorrels, and the late Barbara Faith de Covarrubias. Moral support and sunset planning in Mexico came from dear friends Federico and Barbara Vidargas, along with the late, indomitable Dotty Vidargas. Margarite's Haiti room in the novel came courtesy of Anghelen Phillips, a longtime resident there. Haiti's loss is Mexico's gain. Mi amiga Nanci Closson furnished encouragement when it was needed, then and now.

A special group of Virginians comprises my early readers—Wyatt Durrette, Christine Williams, Janice Harvey, Betsy Miller, and Doug and Tadd Chessen—whose advice and support I will always value. The Honorable J. Randolph "Randy" Stevens proved himself an avid and discerning reader, in addition to being a constant pal from my Yorktown days. A grateful nod goes to lifelong friends Ralph DeRosa, Palmer Lowery, and Howard Smith, Virginia gentlemen all. I abandoned my law firm by moving to Mexico, leaving said law firm most unhappy, so I must give a huge shout out to those who stayed behind and endured—my excellent and understanding partner Michael Mulkey, my office manager Charlene Smyth, Barbara Ferris, Cindy Norcutt, Jennifer Tobey, and Judy Allmond.

My Citadel family has done what Citadel people do—stand by those who stood with them in the long, gray line. A crisp and by-the-numbers Tango salute to Paul and Beth Green; Mike and Pam Steele; Jay and Jane Keenan; Ed and Sally Steers; Holly and Lois Keller; DG and Janie McIntyre; Steele and Molly Dewey; Peggy Bowditch and her late husband, John, "the Bowd," whom I miss every day; Tom and Lynn Benson; Ed Murphy; Jim and Lynn Probsdorfer; Rich and Bunny Lloyd; John and Haley Sitton; Barry and Deanie Wynn; Clarkson and Mary Ann McDow; and Dan and Jane Brailsford.

To my Beaufort buddies, a giant thank you for your embracing me as you have—Pat and Sandra Conroy, Bernie and Martha Schein, the marvelous Patricia Denkler; Mike Harris; Trish and Van Irwin (who always manage to root for the wrong team); David and Terry Murray; Wilson McIntyre and the staff at McIntyre's Book Shoppe on Bay Street; Kit and Lewis Bruce; my M.D. Clark Trask and his lovely wife, Evy; Nancy and D. C. Gilley; the irrepressible John Trask III; Janelle and Bob Proctor; Wendy Wilson; Bill and Carol Carpenter; Teresa Bruce; Sean Scappelatto; Terry and Peter Hussey; Jack and Marilyn Sheehy; and Cathy and Mike Nairne. My classmate Scott Graber and his very talented wife, the artist Susan Graber, have shown unfailing and undeserved kindness. Wright's pointers Duke and Angie Hucks, Bob and Marylou Cullen, and Tom and Daria Paterson set a new standard for great neighbors. My roots grow deep in 29902, and you made Beaufort bloom for me.

To Toller Cranston, the remarkable and gifted Canadian artist who lives in San Miguel, I owe a special debt for his efforts in the months prior to publication.

By the miracle which is the internet, I "met" Lee Farrand on-line and found his blog, leeskoreablog.blogspot, both entertaining and an excellent source of information about Korea. Lee; his wife, Heather; and her parents, Min Jong-Hee and Jung Jae-Won, gave needed insight into Korean families and culture.

A Southern Girl is essentially about family, and family is essential. My love and thanks to the beautiful folks who have fostered my work—the Warley women, MB and Barbara; the Warley men, my sons, Caldwell, Nelson, and Carter; the spouses who make my children and me happy—Heather Partridge Warley, Drew Lockwood, Erin Gemma, and Nessa Snyder Warley; in-laws par excellence Bob and Jeanne Partridge, Nick and Shannon Gemma, Howard and Mary Anne Snyder, David and Christy Lockwood; and grandchildren Addie, Eli, Anna, Ellis, and Oliver. To my sister Shanny Satterstrom, my brother Rob Warley and his partner Jim Hare, brother Tom Warley and to the memory of our parents, John Caldwell Warley and Susannah Barnwell Warley. On Barbara's side, Chris and Ann Duplessis, Matt Langenderfer, and the Hutchison girls: Rachel Langenderfer, Barbara and Helen Hutchison, and the memory of their mother, sweet Beth—without you all, what's the point?

PROLOGUE

June 28, 1978

Dear Open Arms:

My name is Elizabeth Carter. I am a twenty-eight year old mother of two biological sons. This letter responds to Section 3(a) of your application: "State in five hundred words or less why you want to adopt a son or daughter from a foreign country."

No question on a pre-printed form has cost me so much sleep as this one. My husband, Coleman, has been asking me this exact question for months (although he wisely did not restrict me to five hundred words—he knows better). My answers have not convinced him, and worse, they haven't convinced me either. So I decided to put my desire in writing, in hopes that by the last period on the final sentence both you and I are persuaded that this adoption is best for everyone. If either of us remains doubtful, perhaps it was not meant to be.

I cannot address the question without telling you something of my early life. As you know from responses to other questions on this application, I was born in Topeka, Kansas, on July 14, 1950. As a child I attached no significance to that date—the middle of summer heat when no one felt like doing much and my friends were either at camp or traveling, so the few birthday parties I remember were poorly attended. In high school, I learned I was born on Bastille Day. I liked the sound of it. Peasants storming a prison to liberate people who should never have been there in the first place spoke to me. I searched for some ancestral tie to France, but never found one. My folks were of Polish and German descent, and their parents were the outer limits of their genetic curiosity.

So many of the girls I knew had parents just like mine: second generation eastern European, middle class, church-going, tax-paying, hard working. But somehow those families succeeded in areas where my family seemed predisposed to fail. My friends adored their parents, whereas I found mine rather stiff and removed. My friend Janet told me her three brothers were her best friends, but my two brothers just happened to live in the same house. I knew from visits to my friends at Christmas that certain traditions predominated, yet my family observed very few of those. In a real sense I grew up without the identity felt so strongly by those I spent my time with.

Things only got worse when I reached high school. I was skinny, flat-chested, and bookish; hardly the attributes that got a girl elected homecoming queen. I had a few girlfriends, but they focused more on boys than anything else. By the time we graduated, a couple of them were already engaged. I, on the other hand, couldn't wait to get away from Topeka, to run toward a special and exciting future that I was sure awaited me in some other place. I chose Hollins for college because it was in the East, had a strong English department, and promised some sophistication I hoped would rub off on me. My parents were none too happy with the price of tuition, but they reluctantly supported my choice. I filled out there, both physically and emotionally.

I first met my husband on a blind date, then again just before he finished college at the University of Virginia. He is a true son of the South, but without that sappy drawl I find grating to the ear. He is an only child, the "golden boy" his parents doted on, in much the same way he dotes on our two sons, Steven and Josh. He is an excellent father, which is why I have been surprised at his attitude about this adoption. I probably shouldn't be telling you he has reservations, but he does and I want to be honest even if it dooms my application; <u>our</u> application, because he has signed it despite those reservations. He says he doesn't think he can love an adopted child the same way he loves our biological boys. I think he is wrong. In important ways I know him better than he knows himself, and once he gets past his fear of the unknown, he will be a great father to her (we want a girl, as specified in response to question 2(c)). He also says a foreign adoption will upset his parents. He is probably right on that one, as his parents are old school and quite conservative. I've come to learn that in the South, blood is everything. But as I say, he will come around. Whether they will remains to be seen.

So I come back to my reasons for wanting this child. Part of it is altruism, no doubt. So many children are born into dire circumstances dooming them from birth. Rescuing one doesn't solve that, but if our family is in a position to help, we should do it.

Altruism aside, I sense that out there somewhere is an infant whose life will be radically altered for the better by what we do. I am speaking here beyond the generic benefits of a loving family to a child without one. My own upbringing came with a liberal dose of alienation, and I know firsthand how painful that can be. A child adopted into a strange culture in a land foreign to her birth may feel that same alienation, particularly here in the South. I can relate. I can ease that pain. I can make the difference. I know I can. Somewhere out there is or will be a girl who with my help will grow up safe and secure and with the same sense of belonging our sons feel. And with those advantages, she will soar.

I have used more than five hundred words, but this is too important to skimp. Please let us know your decision soon.

Very truly yours,
Elizabeth Carter

Part 1

CONFLUENCE

O, Captain! Is there golden shore
Beyond this golden sea?
And will those curving, spotless wings
Keep company with me?
I know, I know the land I seek
Lies far away to lee,
And we are sailing with the wind
Across a golden sea,
But tell me of the golden shore,
The world that is to be.
And will these saintly, angel wings
Be given even me?

ROBERT WOODWARD BARNWELL, SR.
"The Emigrant," *Realities and Imaginations*

1

Jong Sim

My sweet gardenia, today we will go into Seoul, a city I myself have never seen but one we can visit together. What a day we will have. Everything will be new, as you are new. Oh, do not worry about getting lost. Min Jung gave detailed instructions. This bus carries us to the edge of the city, where we will take another. The sights and sounds and the aromas will welcome us there. They will forever live in our pooled memory. Little flower, we will remember this day always.

Am I holding you too tight? It is because the bus lurches from side to side and hiccups when the potholes find the wheels, and at any moment you may be jarred from me. Can I loosen your *pojaegi?* There. You may move your arms for greater comfort. Your perfect little arms.

I have a surprise for you. Later. Surprises are best when you must wait for them. I should know. You yourself were a surprise. Imagine my happiness when the midwife held you up. When she cut the cord, you turned from blue to pink and you cried and I cried with you.

When we boarded the bus, the aunties in the front seat swooned when they saw your perfect skin, so like a peach. We cannot fault them for jealousy. Perhaps they have daughters who do not have your endless smile; the smile reflected in the pearl-backed mirror. Yes, I brought it with me. But I will bring it out later, because I must keep my eyes open for the tall sign with the green dragon. That is where we must get off to wait for the next bus. Min Jung told me three times: "a tall sign with a green dragon." I hope there is not more than one such sign, but she would have told me if there was a chance for confusion. She is such a good friend.

Are you warm, little one? Let me loosen your blanket. Better? The heat on the bus is set for winter, but today is so mild I may open a window. Min Jung said we must make this trip soon, as the mild weather cannot last. I wish the flowers were in bloom for you to see and smell.

Did I tell you the pearl-backed mirror was a gift from my mother? She must have loved me very much because to get such a thing she would have to have sold at least a pig or three goats. How she could have managed such an expense I do not know. She always looked and felt so special when she held it to brush her hair. I loved to watch her pause to turn her head first one way and then another. You would not have thought her beautiful, certainly not as you are beautiful, but when she held the mirror she saw herself as special. She would not let me hold it until I was ten for fear I might drop it. But, smiling, she held it for me, turning it at angles to show me all sides of my face and head. Her smile was like sunshine, but seldom did the sun come out because farming life was so hard for her. She always told me my life would be different, but it has not been so. Your father, Hyun Su, says our lives are Buddha's will, but I was taught that Buddha does not decide our fate. Your life will be different, of that you can be certain. How can I be sure? Ah, that it what today is about. You will see me keep a promise to you that my mother could not keep to me. My little angel, you will not farm.

The windows are so dusty and dirty that it is hard to see the beauty of this land. Let me clear a space for you to look through. You see those mountains in the distance? Lovely, are they not? This is the beauty of Korea, a beauty that you must remember.

Did you know you were born during the festival of *Dongji,* the shortest day of the year? Yes, it is true. That makes you even more special. The midwife was not pleased to be pulled away from the festival, but my time had come—our time had come—and we had paid her in advance. Hyun Su told her you would be a boy. He listened to Uncle Jae, as he always does when they drink their *soju* far into the night. Uncle Jae went to the *chom chengi,* the fortuneteller. So much for her special powers. I could have told them the truth. Your heart beat with mine. Your moods I recognized as my own. When I felt your restless stretch at sunrise, I stretched with you. When I cried, my belly swelled with water, or so it seemed. When I shook with fear, you trembled inside me. Shaking with fear is part of life here, where men rule with fists. Oh yes, I have felt those fists, but you will not.

Is that hunger I see? Very well, come suckle. You will need strength for the day ahead, whereas I need only to stay awake while you nurse, as the motion of the bus wants me to sleep. If I sleep, I could miss the green dragon, and then we would be lost. Here, take the breast. From their frowns, the two *ajummas* beside us do not approve, but today is about us and not them. And pay no attention to the bruise. It is a little better today as the purple is not so bright. Hyun Su's fist is no match for you and me. Women have other weapons. You will have beauty as a weapon. Learn to use it and you will never be defenseless. And you will be smart, like me, but without education I am not much more than the long-haired ox or the large udder cow. Such a life is this, when a dumb animal like me must . . .

But there it is. The green dragon. Hurry your nursing, little one, because we must get off here. Let me adjust your *podaegi* so you can ride in comfort on my back.

The city is near. Look at all the motor scooters, the cars, the buses on this road. Everyone in such an angry rush. Houses with rice paper windows and doors. Stalls selling salted squid, steamed rice, kimchi, and giant garlic—tastes you do not yet know. The people in the city must be very rich, like Min Jung, who drives a car and came to see us when you were only days old. Such a nice visit we had. We must believe her when she said that it is caring for her mother and her husband's father that prevents her from helping us, but of course she did help us by giving directions.

Now we must find a bus with this number. She wrote it down for me. The cars are passing by so fast; such dust everywhere. The green dragon is very tall. I am glad it is not real. The rest of the day is real enough.

I have brothers you have not met. Three brothers older than I. My parents felt so blessed to hang the red chili peppers from our gate. Sons are celebrated. Daughters are tolerated. It has been that way since our ancestors came to this land. You will be celebrated. How do I know? I just know, in the same way I knew you would be born a girl, no matter what Hyun Su or Uncle Jae or the *chom chengi* said. Now we must climb on this next bus, which has a number matching the one Min Jung wrote down. She said to sit near the driver, who will tell us where to get off. One hour to the Jongam police station, she said. She measures time in hours, by a watch. How modern Min Jung is. You will be modern, too. You will wear a watch and drive a car and never work in a field. Now sleep, for our trial is coming.

How tall these buildings are. I wish I could read the signs I see everywhere. Some are so big they would stretch from Hyun Su's house to the edge of the rice field, and so high off the ground they would look down on the cherry trees by the goat path. There is a large boy with a ball. And over there a smiling woman is stirring a pot. What is she making? Does she have a daughter to feed? And there are three men in white coats with something around their necks. It is all so confusing. The bus stops and begins again, so that I am beginning to feel as I did before she moved within me. I cannot be sick on the bus. The driver will put us out and then how would I find the police station with the high hedge? I do not think I can do this. But I must.

That was a very short nap, little one, but who can sleep with the cars and buses making all this noise and stopping for people who walk in front of them. The sun is high so we must be close. I want to get off this bus, yet I do not want to get off the bus.

Stopped again? The driver is pointing to the door. "*Komapsumnida,*" thank you. We are here, and there is the high hedge. There are the steps leading up to the olive door with the peeling paint Min Jung told me about. She has been right about everything. Such a good friend.

Here in the shelter of the high hedge, I must tell you things. I loved your father, but I loved him before we could be married. When he learned of my condition, he refused to marry me and beat me. He said I counted the days wrong. If I did it was a simple mistake, but one I cannot regret because it brought me you. I went to my mother. At first she insisted on *nak-tae,* abortion, but like the bad daughter I had become I defied her and refused. As I grew bigger, mother softened, and by the end, just before *Dongji,* she pleaded with her father, your grandfather, to let me keep you if you were a boy. But grandfather would not hear of it, boy or girl. "Impossible," he said. "She has brought shame to the family. Get rid of it." I asked the midwife to contact Min Jung, who brought with her a magazine from America, where everyone must be rich. It showed beautiful people living in castles. She said that you could be sent to America, to grow up with beautiful people and wear a watch and drive a car and not farm. She told me to bring you to this door, to hide in this hedge until no one is looking, and to set you down on the steps. That is why we have come to Seoul.

And now, my lotus blossom, my own sweet Soo Yun, I must leave you. Here in the shelter of the high hedge, we must say goodbye. You must not hate me for this. I am your mother, Jong Sim, and like my mother and her mother I must do what is best for my daughter. When I place you on the steps, you must raise your cries above my own so they will take you in. You are Soo Yun. It means perfect lotus blossom. Min Jung wrote your name and I have pinned it to your linen. Here is the pearl-backed mirror. I am putting it in your *podaegi.* When they take you in, they will find the mirror and know you are special. Min Jung said giving up the mirror is not necessary, but I must leave you with something more than a name. One day, in America, when you count hours on a watch and drive a car and do not farm, you may thank me. Be a good girl for your new mother.

Now, it is time. The steps are warm in the sunshine. Cry, yes, cry, and they will take you in. Listen to your mother. You must cry. Until we meet again in heaven, Soo Yun.

2

Hana

I am ambidextrous. Have been since I was six. I write, eat and throw with either hand. And answer the phone, which is how I remember the call from Jongam that afternoon. Superstitious nonsense probably explains this pattern I thought I had noticed, but for a long time the pattern seemed to hold: bad news came into my right ear because I answered the phone with my right hand. The death of my grandmother? Right ear. An auto accident involving my parents and sister? Right ear. My ex-boyfriend's *soju*-aided epiphany that we should see other people? Right ear. Conversely, my promotion to head of the ward? Left ear. The call from the hospital to let me know my parents and sister were okay? Left ear. The plea from my ex-boyfriend to disregard the call he made the night before? Well, you get the picture, which is why the call from Jongam stuck in my memory. Calls from the police station with news of yet another abandoned infant belonged in the right ear. With three infants in every crib, we had no room for more. My ward was rated for thirty children, ages six and under, and when that call came in we hovered near fifty.

I looked out the window to confirm what I felt in my bones; the unseasonably mild January day had deteriorated into something more typical of Seoul in winter. Darkening clouds promised snow. Wind blew newspapers along the sidewalk in front of the bank across the street. Pedestrians cinched up coats against the chill I was sure to feel the moment I stepped outside. Jongam is a fifteen minute walk, but Korean weather in its worst mood can make that mile feel like a marathon. I told my assistant to keep the lid on; that I would return within the hour and to make a space in the nursery.

As I approached the station, habit and muscle memory carried me toward the old door, its green paint peeling now that a newer one on the opposite side of the building had been put into service. I retraced my steps and entered. The room has a perpetual smell of old vinyl and cheap aftershave. The receptionist motioned me through to an office in the back. As I expected, given the late afternoon hour, Captain Oh sipped tea with his deputy, Chan Wook Park. The captain was a jaundiced man with a massive head, thinning hair and sickly skin. I had spent enough time here to get to know something about him. Nearing retirement, he rarely strayed from his favorite topics of conversation, his vegetable garden and the unfair treatment Jongam received compared with other stations. When I entered, he motioned me toward a chair without breaking off the sentence he was then in the middle of.

". . . so Sinmun-No and Ulchi-Ro, those districts get what they want," he said bitterly. "Extra manpower, new equipment, anything. But at Jongam, we get leftovers. Always leftovers." This theme never lost its appeal to the captain, who seemed to me to take little notice of and no comfort from the virtual absence of crime in Jongam.

Chan Wook Park, seated near me, said, "The door at least is new."

Captain Oh gave a dismissive groan. "If they could have found a used door, it would have ended up here."

Then I noticed a fourth person in the room. She sat in the corner, partly concealed by a filing cabinet. In her lap she held what could only have been an infant. On making eye contact, we both bowed our heads faintly as the captain described to his visibly bored deputy the layout of his garden.

"The snow peas in the first two rows, the corn sowed in the last row, the westernmost row, so as not to put other plants in morning's shadow when it eventually towers above them."

Chan Wook Park suggested the garden be oriented east and west, an idea the captain seemed to be pondering when a loud squawk from the woman's lap reminded the men of the business at hand. Captain Oh looked at me.

"This is Mi Cha. She found it by the old door."

Mi Cha looked to be about seventy, but with Korean women it can be hard to tell. "You should put up a sign," she said with a hint of contempt in her craggy voice. "She would have died had I not come along. She may still die. She is hot with fever."

Captain Oh, unaccustomed to being scolded, particularly by a woman, seemed to take this advice in stride. I later learned that Mi Cha lived nearby, a fixture in the neighborhood for longer than most remembered. She knew all of the policemen who worked out of Jongam Precinct. She used its doorway as liberally as she used her own, venturing over one or two times a day as a cure for loneliness and to deliver food for the men. She had perfected her memorable kimchi on the palates of three sons and eleven grandchildren, and the massive clay jar in which she stored it must have been bottomless. She lived alone now, but continued turning out her specialty in quantities adequate for the three shifts at Jongam, with whom she shared it compulsively. She had just returned from a six week visit to the country home of her middle son. In her habit of the last ten years, she turned up the walkway toward the old door, just as I had done.

I rose, crossed the room, and took a chair beside her. Together we stared down at the child, whose nicely proportioned face was florid with fever, her damp hair matted against the shawl Mi Cha had placed around her.

"I came in search of my dog," the woman said. "Mojo. He has never run off, and I thought one of the policemen might have seen him. It is a good thing the child was crying so, because I may not have seen her. I changed her just before you arrived."

At that moment the baby winced as if in pain and began to cry so loudly the men ceased conversation.

"Shut her up," Captain Oh ordered.

Mi Cha shifted the child from her lap to her shoulder, patting her back in rhythmic measure. The cries and their volume increased.

"Let me try," I said. At the instant of exchange, the child redoubled her cries. Her face, already flushed in the grip of fever, darkened to a pagan mask of crimson rage. Freed from the bunting, her hands gnarled into fists so compressed that they grew white from lack of circulation. Her cries came in waves, with each outpouring demanding new air from her lungs to fully register in pitch and amplification her complete indignation.

"Such anger, my little one, such anger," I said, placing one hand under the head while my other hand supported the body. I smiled, and I suppose she must have sensed new circumstances in my hands and voice because, whether startled or comforted, she fell silent.

"You have a knack," said Mi Cha.

"It will not last," I said. "She needs a doctor."

"What becomes of such children?" asked Mi Cha.

"She is very young. If she is healthy, she may be adopted by Americans."

"By Americans?" The old woman shook her head, and the scowl which crossed her face at that moment was one of disgust, but whether reserved for Americans, or for Koreans who gave away their offspring, I could not read.

The infant grew impatient with our conversation. The discussion of her future held no interest for one with needs so immediate. As she squirmed and fretted toward another outburst, I thanked Mi Cha and turned to Chan Wook Park.

"Let me sign for her and go. She needs medicine."

As Chan Wook Park searched for a release, opening and closing desk drawers in haphazard inefficiency, Mi Cha asked if anyone had reported seeing Mojo. Captain Oh, preparing to leave and walking toward his coat hanging from a hook near the window, halted in mid-step. "And where is Mojo?"

"Gone. I left him in the care of my neighbor while I was away. She saw him yesterday, and I was certain he would appear today. I was coming to ask your boys if they had seen him when I found this infant."

The fringes of the captain's brow converged upon the center, furrowing the area between his wide-set eyes. "Mojo missing. This is most unfortunate."

"He has never run off. I fear the worst."

"Do not lose hope. I will have the men look out for him." He turned toward Chan Wook Park. "Instruct the shift change to keep eyes open for Mojo. And the men getting off can watch for him on their way home. He is a fine dog. We need to locate him for Mi Cha."

"Many thanks, captain."

"We are like sons here, Mi Cha. What kind of sons would let their mother's dog stray?"

"You are very kind."

I pulled the child closer. Her heat radiated through me like a brazier. The captain's concern for Mojo was touching, but in a country that eats dog he unwittingly made a statement about girls such as the one in my arms—little female corks set adrift by who knows who to float about in an uncertain ocean, where the tide is always rising and the shoals are sharp and submerged. I am one of them—a girl, that is—and this is why I do what I do.

Chan Wook Park found the release and I scrawled a signature. I was almost out the door when Mi Cha called.

"I almost forgot," she said, walking toward me and slipping something from her pocket. "This mirror was wrapped up with her."

I caught a cab back, bypassing the orphanage and heading straight to the offices of Dr. Lee, who treated our wards. He ran a high-volume clinic, but always managed to find a way to move me to the head of a long line. As I lingered at his shoulder, he unwrapped layers of rough, cheap cloth until she lay naked on the table, a crude incision of the umbilical cord just beginning to heal.

"About three weeks old, I think," he said, bending over her. "A bit premature."

My eye caught the small rectangular paper pinned to the cloth. "The child has a name," I said, examining the Hangol. "Soo Yun." Dr. Lee took no notice, repositioning his stethoscope on her inflamed chest.

"I'll give you something for the fever," he said. "If she isn't better in a day or two, bring her back."

After slipping the paper on which her name was printed into the same pocket holding the mirror, I discarded her wraps and swaddled her in a surgical gown I promised Dr. Lee I'd return. Then I stuffed her into my coat for the walk to the orphanage, two blocks away. Looking back, I feel sure something changed in those two blocks. Most of the abandoned children came without names. The staff took turns naming them. As it was a task I disliked, I pulled rank as supervisor of Ward 3E and skipped my turn in the naming rotation. Some came without even clothes. This one had not only a name but a mirror, and I couldn't remember any of our foundlings arriving with a possession. From my brief examination of the mirror, it was hardly of the best quality, but if this child came from the impoverishment signaled by her crude clothes, her mother gave something up in sending it. Sending them.

A sucker for children, I told friends who asked that I took the job at Open Arms Orphanage eight years ago because I had always wanted fifty children and this seemed like the only practical way to have them. They were my life, as anyone who came to my pathetic apartment and met my needy cat, Bo-cat, knew. I was rarely at home, and not for the reasons most women twenty-nine were away. I hadn't had a date in over a year. Physically, I was what you would call "plain." I knew this and had reconciled myself to it. I blamed my parents for my boxy build, my flat chest, my rugby calves, and uninspired features. We can't all be movie stars. But if I was honest enough to admit my shortcomings, I stated with equal sincerity that I was one damn fine nurse. I could tell you the name of every child on my ward and their birthdays, whether those birthdays were real or the ones we guessed at. I knew their histories. I knew their fears and their favorite foods. I rejoiced when they left and I cried when they left. I also cried when they stayed, as so many did, until they aged into the next grouping, where their chances for placement diminished each year. It broke my heart to see a child without a family. But while they were in my care, they knew love and compassion and support. I couldn't give them everything, but I could give them that.

That little peanut inside my coat weighed barely two kilograms. Her lungs sought air by the thimbleful. Tiny Soo Yun with the mirror, whose fevered pulse I felt pumping up against me. What would become of her? I asked myself that question about each of my children, but I had not been at the home long enough to test my instincts against results. When I started on Ward 3E, the oldest children, now fourteen, were six. I projected wonderful futures for them, the way you do when you are young and idealistic and lack experience. With my help, each would become a ballerina, a tennis champion, a teacher, a doctor, a mother. Soo Yun was too young to forecast any such future. First, she had to breathe. Next, she must be adopted. Lastly, she must be inspired. Soil, water, light; the elements of survival, and without all three she may find herself, years from now, the drug-crazed landlady of a large-appliance box in the armpit of a sweltering city. Or perhaps a life spent shuffling home from a corner market in an afternoon drizzle of mediocrity, where the umbrellas will be all black, the faces yellow, the packages beige, where she will wonder if others are able to perceive color in a universe that for her holds no interesting contrast, and where the first arresting sound she heard was also the last, that of her mother's retreating footsteps. No. No. No. Not for Soo Yun with her mirror. I realize now that in that walk of two blocks, I reached an unknown and perhaps unknowable resolve that her fate would be different. She was special, but in what ways I did not yet know.

I arrived back at Ward 3E just before the evening shift, which consisted of . . . me. I often pulled double shifts, both because we had trouble staffing a facility like that and because I loved the work. Orphanage policy required a minimum of two adults during the day, but during the evening and at night, we could make do with one. And if another ward, stretched thin by vacations or illness, needed relief, I could work both. I know. I was obsessed.

I handed Soo Yun to my aide to be bathed, powdered and fed, then placed in the crib prepared by my aide in my absence. Preparation consisted of moving the other two infants occupying the same crib. The nursery had never been this crowded. If we got another call from Jongam, I would have had to take her home to sleep with Bo-cat. My office, otherwise known as the supply closet, was just off the ward. I slipped in long enough to put the mirror and name tag into a drawer. By the time I left at midnight, Soo Yun's fever had dropped and she appeared to be sleeping restfully.

Open Arms is an international adoption agency headquartered in the United States. My boss, Faith Stockdale, was in charge here. The next morning, a woman on Faith's staff photographed Soo Yun and interviewed me regarding anything I knew about her abandonment. Meager as it was, my account was placed in a new file along with the photograph, to be used as the basis for a temporary custody proceeding by the orphanage. Faith also compiled dossiers to be sent to prospective parents in the

U.S., where most of our children were placed. I made a mental note to speak to Faith about Soo Yun, but with Winter Open House just days away, I forgot.

We held Open House quarterly. It reminded the local patrons and churches that we appreciated their financial support and, frankly, that we needed more. Spring Open House, held before *chang-ma,* the rainy season, drew the largest crowds. Large turnouts reassured the children they had not been forgotten. Winter Open House generated the fewest visitors, but the work and preparation that went into it was the same. Our entire staff reported early. We stripped the beds and substituted clean sheets smelling of warm bleach. We draped the freshly made beds in the navy blue-and-white spreads reserved for special occasions. We used ammonia by the bucketfuls, giving the floors an antiseptic scrubbing. A local flower shop donated fresh flowers; carnations, gladiolus, and lilac brightened the room in festive contrast to the beige of the walls.

Since the oldest child on 3E was six, any Open House can and usually did degenerate into something close to a kiddie flash mob. Children ran up and down aisles, between and under beds, around corners at full throttle. Squeals of terror—usually happy terror—echoed as tag and "gotcha" erupted. We did our best to keep things from getting too chaotic, but kids will be kids and when they are being scrutinized for adoption, that is exactly what prospective parents want to see. I have visited orphanages where the children are made to appear rigid and lifeless. They feel to me like dog pounds where the animals have been drugged. The girls tend to be less rambunctious. With some exceptions, they spent their mornings outfitting their dolls in holiday garb and propping them prominently on pillows for the best view.

The nursery was separated from the beds of the toddlers by a windowed wall. For that Open House, our generous florist sent an arrangement of fresh-cut orchids in a vase bedecked with yellow ribbons spangled with glitter. I placed this by the nurses' station guarding the door. The nursery itself looked like it did on any other day.

At nine-thirty, the administrator of the home, Yong Tae Shin, inspected my ward. A retired military officer with a ramrod, dignified gait, a dark complexion, and a full head of silver hair, he gave my kids his standard speech.

"Our guests will be here shortly. Remember your manners. Those of you who have 'Projections' will kindly display them in the proper fashion. Be friendly to our guests. They are like family to us."

Yes, a family of sorts. Not like mine, of course. Not the kind that taped your school drawings to the refrigerator and made certain you got on the same soccer team as your friends and attended recitals when you barely knew the scales. But family in its own unique and desperate way.

As the administrator moved to the next ward, my children opened their lockers and removed papers, pictures and crafts, spreading them on their beds for maximum exposure. At ten o'clock, the elevator doors opened to deliver the first arrivals. Most of the guests came from Christian churches in and around Seoul. The overwhelming majority were Koreans, older people who mirrored the aging populations of churches generally, and with no link to or relationship with the children beyond this outreach program. Many were grandparents.

That morning's group appeared typical. Women predominated, with graying heads and wrinkled faces, clutching plastic bags of candy and fruit to be distributed over the course of their one-hour stay. They dressed in western clothes, frequently with crosses suspended on gold chains from their necks or pinned to lapels. A number were paired, arm in arm, as they fanned out. The children waited with an awkward, reluctant fidget, the way they might receive a distant relative determined to hug them.

I spotted the Parks, an elderly couple who had attended every open house since I'd been employed at the home. Mr. Park, a stooping, grandfatherly man with an easy smile, wore a dark business suit while his wife dressed in colorful traditional silks. Mr. Park held the post of senior warden of the largest Presbyterian church in Seoul and was among the orphanage's most generous benefactors. He rarely spoke on these visits, yielding to his quite talkative wife, but he tousled the hair of every child within his reach. I've been told the Parks have thirty-one grandchildren.

From the back of the elevator came two couples who drew my immediate interest. A man of medium height, slender build and rigid posture wore a military uniform, the silver bars of a first lieutenant shining on his epaulets. His wife, roughly of equal height in her heels, wore a pale blue wool suit with a vivid scarf and a broach of circled pearls over the breast. The other couple was older, perhaps late thirties or early forties. They held hands as they walked and murmured to each other. Both couples were Americans.

The visitors began to mingle among the children, who remained standing by their beds. Visitors initiated introductions. The children old enough to attend preschool practiced their responses for a week preceding each open house. They extended their hands, made their best effort at eye contact, then bowed slightly at the waist. Visitors had been instructed to return the handshake and bow as reinforcement to the child's training but to avoid hugging or other manifestations of intimacy on first contact. These opening moments always produced strain. Five and six-year-olds, particularly those experiencing their first open house, tensed with the approach of strangers and remained so for several minutes, as if their performance was being graded by unseen jurors.

Questions were tricky in this setting. Clearly, the child's background was latent with potential embarrassment. To combat the shoe-shuffling silence after introductions, the administration instituted a practice called "projections."

Projections allowed each child to express, by means of a creation, a symbol or an artifact placed at the foot of the navy blue-and-white bedspread, a measure of talent, ability, or interest. The beds displayed an eclectic collection of drawings in pencil, paintings in watercolor, baseball bats, sheet music, basketball sneakers, ballet slippers, library books, dolls, a flute, even a calculator exhibited by one of our six-year-olds who was precocious in math. We discouraged stuffed animals among the older children but permitted them to the toddlers.

After introductions, adults asked about the child's projections to further break the ice and to avoid questions that might lead to hard answers; life-claiming auto accidents, parents-consuming house fires, or careless abandonments. As a source of questions for visitors and pride for the children, projections eased and enriched open house. But, as I well knew, there was a darker rationale for this practice.

I made it a habit to greet visitors with polite efficiency, resisting my natural urge to be overly outgoing. There was nothing worse in this setting than appearing like a salesperson on commission. I teased the children, reacted when they teased back, and always tried to pan the room for a child who lacked a visitor.

As I approached the older of the two American couples, I signaled the interpreter on duty. After an exchange of names, the woman introduced as Mrs. Jennings related their reason for visiting. I recognized only the words "Korean" and "Pittsburgh."

My interpreter translated. "They have two adopted children, both from our country. They wish to adopt another. They are visiting from Pittsburgh and wish to select a child while they are here. She is most concerned that the child be compatible with the two at home."

I nodded, asking the interpreter, "What are the ages and sex of the two at home?" Mrs. Jennings, a plump woman with stiffly coiffed hair and an ample bosom, smiled pleasantly as I got my answer.

"She says they have boys, ages three and seven."

"And are they looking for a particular child?"

"They would like a girl, age four or five."

"Very well," I said. "We have many here. Let's take a stroll through the ward."

I steered the group to a cot on which a girl sat fingering her pillow case. A pair of old women had just departed. I approached the girl, reached down for her hand, and grasped it gently in my own.

"This is Eun," I said. "She has been with us for three years. She was five in November. Eun, this is Mr. and Mrs. Jennings from the United States."

Eun rose and extended a tentative hand to Mr. Jennings, then to his wife. Mrs. Jennings smiled. "What a pretty girl you are." The interpreter translated. "And what have we here?" She pointed to the jump-rope at the end of the bed.

The girl darted around the bed and seized the rope. "I'm the best. I can do one hundred without a miss." She stepped away from the bed and began skipping. The rope hit the tile with a rapid-fire "thwap" and her blue-black hair in a pageboy cut lifted on the sides with each descent. The Jennings looked at each other, then applauded. Eun let the rope slack to the floor. Then, slightly winded, she resumed her seat on the bed.

Mrs. Jennings beamed with what I thought to be excessive broadness—a bad omen for Eun. "That was wonderful." Then she paused. "What about the piano, dear? Do you have any interest in music? I just love music in the house."

Eun listened to the interpretation, then looked toward me before shaking her head. "I like to be outside."

Mrs. Jennings smiled again. "You're so right. Practicing inside on a beautiful day is just no fun, is it?"

No, it wasn't, Eun agreed as the Jennings again shook hands and moved on to the next bunk. More cots. More handshakes. More smiles. At the flute player, a girl with a narrow face and close-set, intense eyes, they lingered. For the first time, the Jennings raised the subject of their sons.

"And what would you think of having brothers?" Mrs. Jennings asked. The girl gave an imperceptible shrug and remained expressionless. The Jennings exchanged glances and moved on. At the next row, Mrs. Jennings saw a young girl hovering over the small electronic keyboard at the end of her bed. She studied the child, her head tilted slightly to the side, before turning to me. "What about that one? We missed her."

I had to be honest. "She has a brother here. He is twelve. We attempt to keep brothers and sisters together. If you were interested in both . . ."

Mrs. Jennings laid her hand on my forearm. "You're right. It would be tragic to separate them."

As the Jennings finished their tour, the American lieutenant signaled me. For some time, he and his wife had been seated in chairs lining the wall that separated the nursery from the dormitory area. He glanced often at his watch. Evidently, he had been waiting for the interpreter, who joined us.

"You're in charge?" he asked me.

"I am. This is my ward. May I be of service?"

The lieutenant introduced his wife. He was stationed at Eighth Army Headquarters, he explained, and had just received orders to return to the States. His shoes glistened in the glare of the fluorescent lights overhead and two battle ribbons adorned his chest. "The wife and I thought we'd like to adopt one of these little tigers."

"Boy or girl?"

"Don't matter. Young and healthy, that's all we care about."

His wife added, "Aren't they just the cutest little things you've ever seen?" The interpreter hesitated, unsure the remark was intended to be translated. Before she could decide, the lieutenant spoke.

"Where do you keep the little tykes?"

The interpreter stumbled over "tykes."

"Behind that wall," I said. "I am surprised you have not heard them." I led them into the nursery. They stopped first at a crib with an infant just awakening from a late-morning nap. As the lieutenant and his wife bent over him, the child broke into a grin of infinite grace, and a gurgling coo that has no earthly equivalent escaped his rounded mouth. The couple beamed.

The lieutenant looked at me. "How old is this one?"

"This is Tong Soon. He is five months old and healthy."

"He's a pistol."

The interpreter was familiar with this slang, but I was not. At the explanation, we all laughed.

"He's just too sweet," said the wife, her eyes fixed on the crib. She and the lieutenant had evidently talked of the need to remain objective, detached. But as she watched the infant's hand come to his mouth and his head turn to follow her movement above, I felt sure she pictured that baby in the nursery she would decorate when they got home. Her hand went down to seize her husband's.

The lieutenant remained businesslike. "Show us the youngest one you've got. We've read a lot about that bonding business."

I'm sure my face slacked. "Let me think for a moment." I panned the remaining cribs, cataloguing their contents, while my mind debated my instincts. "Over there," I said at last, "is the youngest." They walked to the crib most distant from the doorway by which we had entered.

"This is Soo Yun. She is perhaps three weeks old. We cannot be certain."

Soo Yun slept facing away from the four of us collected by her crib. A knitted cap protected her head. The lieutenant and his wife leaned to see her face.

"Can't tell much," said the lieutenant.

"She's sooo tiny," added his wife, glancing over her shoulder toward Tong Soon's crib.

"Yes," I agreed. "So tiny. That is because she has been ill. She will enter the hospital this afternoon for tests." She came to us ill, but the decision to send her for tests was one I made on the spur of the moment. Her fever had spiked again and I suspected pneumonia.

"Poor thing," said the wife, contorting her face in a grimace which I read as a studied and habitual response to bad news not affecting her directly.

"That's too bad," added the lieutenant.

"Would you care to wait until she awakes?"

The couple made eye contact. "I don't think that's necessary," he said. She nodded her agreement and asked if they could return to Tong Soon.

"Certainly," I replied. "He is an adorable baby with a sweet disposition."

That afternoon, when the last visitor had left and the ward returned to normal, I carried Soo Yun to Dr. Lee. He agreed that her symptoms had lingered too long. She would be taken for tests to the Korean Children's Hospital, a glass and steel tower in the center of the city. As I returned to my ward, I felt the full weight of the stress exerted by every open house.

During my first year at the home, I saw no similarity between my chosen profession and that of my parents, the restaurant. Business wasn't for me, or so I thought. But as time passed, I came to see that I too had cast my lot in a capitalism of sorts. To be sure, the home made no profit. It was heavily subsidized by the Korean government and the burden of its funding grew annually. But the home, like the restaurant, had a product.

"Life is business," I heard my father say more than once. Perhaps he was correct. As a girl waiting tables, I remember the expressions of customers who declined the daily specials. There was universality to those expressions, a collective inhale as the eyes narrowed and the forehead wrinkled and the lips pursed from indecision. "No," they would often say, "I will have . . ." I remember taking those decisions personally, as though it were not the bibimbop or bulgogi being rejected, but me. Later, I wondered if it mattered that the specials were verbalized. The printed menu lay flat on the table, but specials carried with them part of me; my voice, my enthusiasm, my sincerity. "No," they would say at last, "I will have . . . something else." Someone else.

For a scant instant, I saw that look today on the face of Mrs. Jennings. And worse, infinitely worse, I sensed that internalization of rejection in Eun, flush in the victory of her flawless rope-skipping. I had a ward teeming with daily specials, many so listless, so uninspired, so ordinary that they would never attract a customer. "Life is business."

The lieutenant and his wife apparently had decided on Tong Soon and filled out forms before leaving. I thought I heard them discussing names, but the interpreter had gone and I could not be sure. In my heart, I sang a song, a lullaby, for Tong Soon. The lieutenant and his wife seemed like good people. Their attraction to him had been immediate and heartfelt. Perhaps a perfect match, as sometimes happened. And who could say what lives, present and future, had been altered in the radiance of that angelic smile and that heavenly coo.

And I wondered if I did right by Soo Yun. I had to be honest, didn't I? My position demanded it. But by disclosing the medical concern at the outset, I had effectively sealed her in the security of the home. Perhaps that was my intent. Soo Yun was special. The lieutenant and his wife would make good parents to Tong Soon if it all worked out, and he would be fortunate to have them.

But they were not special.

3

Elizabeth

I fixed a nice dinner and I waited for just the right time to bring up THE SUBJECT because I knew Coleman wanted to avoid THE SUBJECT, which was the only thing I'd been able to think about for weeks, THE SUBJECT being the adoption of a Korean girl who may or may not even have been alive when we all—that would be Josh and Steven and Coleman and me—sat down to dinner that evening. Really, I felt like I was pregnant again, with that anticipation you get as the delivery draws nearer and you truly focus on the fact that one day soon you will have another little person in your life, and that feeling came over me all during the holidays and kept coming so that it was all I could do to address Christmas cards and stuff stockings and play Mrs. Clause to Josh and Steven. One night just before Christmas I was sipping some wine and was tempted to tack an old stocking to the mantel with a big question mark where the name should be, and I'll be the first to admit that was a bit obsessive but I get that way when I want something as badly as I wanted HER.

By the time we sat down to dinner that evening we had scheduled the appointment with Social Services for the interview, and that seemed a perfect segue from Josh's indoor soccer practice to THE SUBJECT, so I reminded Coleman in my sweetest and most diplomatic voice that the meeting with Monique Hunter was at 4:30 P.M. and that he needed to be there and when he rolled his eyes the way he sometimes does I knew we were going to have a words on THE SUBJECT we'd had quite a few words on in recent months and while I was under no illusions that he had embraced HER like I had, I thought I had brought him around so that if he was not totally convinced we were doing the right thing he was at least less convinced he could possibly talk me out of it and therefore had become reconciled to the idea. Did I expect him to be counting down the hours like I was or perusing catalogs of girls' clothing or scouting the neighborhood for girls that might be close to her age, whatever that age turned out to be? No. But did I want him to embrace the concept and then, in a day or two, embrace her? Absolutely.

Granted, some people will question my desire for an international adoption when we had two biological boys and could have more if we chose, my husband being one of those people. He had cross-examined me on THE SUBJECT several times and, being a trial lawyer, cross-examination was something he did well. But I thought I held my own, thank you very much, because I refused to concede the idea was some "altruistic daydream," a phrase he liked to use in these "discussions." I reminded him that tens of thousands of couples adopted children every year and that many of those adoptions came from places like Korea where strict social customs prevented adoption there. He acknowledged I had a point but countered with a supposition that most of those couples were childless or unable to have more children, and you have to watch him when he rebuts a hard fact with a supposition because lawyers get away with that far too often. I asked him point blank if he wanted a daughter and when he said he did I assured him that my way was the only way he was going to get one and he raised his voice to complain that I was assuming we would continue to produce boys, a supposition. I love turning the table.

The real reason he resisted was his parents. They live in Charleston, South Carolina, where Coleman grew up. Their political hero is Barry Goldwater, if that gives you any insight. Barry fucking Goldwater. Okay, here is an area where I have to plead guilty because I began dropping the f-bomb in college and have never been able to break the habit, and in New Hampton, Virginia, where we live, young women simply did not say such things in 1979 and you can imagine what the reaction would have been in Charleston if I ever slipped up there, which I'd only done twice. Maybe three times. I'm careful around the children, of course, because no mom wants to be called into a preschool teacher conference to be asked where her son could have learned certain words. Coleman says his parents consider me "liberal," which to them could mean a person who missed church one Sunday or who had ever in their life voted for a Democrat. I hold my tongue when we visit them, which we do regularly because it is important to Coleman and important that our sons know their grandparents.

So, back to my dinner. Coleman rolled his eyes when I reminded him of the meeting with Monique Hunter and that reminded me that we were not yet on the same page where the adoption was concerned and I suppose I might have yelled at him and he said he was playing golf that afternoon but that he would be there. One step at a time. As I did the dishes he came into the kitchen to nuzzle me and make amends. He is pretty good in the nuzzling department, and afterwards he bathed the boys and put them to bed and when he does that it can sound like World War III upstairs because he tickles them and gets them laughing at a time when they should be getting sleepy according to everything you read about raising children. But then they read a story and everything eventually gets quiet and I love that time when the house gets still and the boys are bathed and in bed and everyone is safe and accounted for. That is a secure feeling I treasure. That is what I want our daughter to feel when she gets here. Soon.

4

Coleman

In January 1979 I became the newest and youngest partner in Mahoney, Cauthen, Miller & Slade, P.C. Elizabeth fixed a nice celebratory dinner. She hardly cooked at all when we got married but has improved steadily since. I remember buying a better wine than we usually served; a token of my new, better-paid status with the firm. That I spent the extra two dollars at the Gourmet Garden over what the same bottle of Sonoma merlot could be had for at Food King troubled me not at all. From this time forward, I planned to breathe great drafts of the Garden's pricier air.

Elizabeth noticed the unfamiliar label, a shock of yellow, blue, and green shards like the sunset in another galaxy, although frankly any wine suited her. "Smells wonderful," she reported as she passed her nose over the rim of the crystal glass she held loosely by the stem.

"At these prices, it should," I replied, smiling and raising my glass. "To the future."

Josh was seven. He lifted his milk in a toasting gesture, his glass wobbling precariously. Steven, age five and seated opposite, mimicked his brother, sloshing milk onto the outer rim of his plate and placemat.

"Oops," he said meekly, glancing toward Elizabeth.

"Oops is right, sport," I said. "Get a sponge." As Steven retreated toward the kitchen, I winked at Elizabeth. "Kid's going to be a sloppy drunk."

"Coleman, please don't even joke about that. Josh, elbows off the table."

Steven returned, carrying a cloth. He approached his chair, kneeling in it to provide the extension his short arms required to reach the spill. His mother leaned toward him to whisper, "A sponge, dear. That's a dish towel." Steven nodded, then pressed the towel down onto his soggy mat and newly irrigated plate, daubing the milk and mashing his carrots simultaneously.

"Yuck!" Josh said as Steven guided the cloth between his roast beef and the mashed potatoes. "You got milk in your carrots. Gross!"

Steven stopped, guilt registered on his guileless face. "I don't like carrots."

As Josh made a mocking face across the table, Elizabeth spoke, her fork suspended over her plate. "We're still on for tomorrow, right? You haven't forgotten."

I nodded, not looking up. "Sure."

"You don't sound excited."

"Of course I am. I'm excited."

"I know what you sound like when you're excited," she said with a hint of sultriness, "and that's not even close."

She no doubt heard my sigh. "We're not going to start across that minefield again, are we?"

She brought her napkin to her mouth, dabbing her lips and eyeing me in silence until I felt the glare. "We're expanding our family and you're treating it like a flu shot. I don't want to do this if we can't do it together."

"We'll do it together."

"Then why are you exasperated?"

"I'm not exasperated."

Josh, following the ping and pong of this exchange, wanted to know the meaning of a word that came out something like "zackerated."

"Exasperated," I corrected. "It means put out, irritably fatigued, peeved." Josh giggled, putting his hand over his mouth. Steven followed.

I had to laugh. "Not peed, peeved. And I'm not exasperated."

"Then why do I feel like I'm breaking your arm? We talked it through, didn't we?"

"We talked it through, yes. Whether we thought it through is open to debate."

"I see. So now you think we shouldn't do it."

"I didn't say that."

"No, you merely suggested we were adopting a child without any forethought."

I buttered a roll. "Look, honey, I know how much you've put into this. I don't mean to throw cold water. It's just that the closer we get, the less sure I am that we should do this."

"Why? Give me reasons. We want a girl—"

Okay, I rolled my eyes. "You know why."

Elizabeth narrowed her gaze at me as she strained to modulate her voice. "Yes, I'm afraid I do."

"Don't start with the racist tripe again."

"I certainly will."

"Well, save it. You simply refuse to recognize the kind of hurdles an Oriental child will face in a town like New Hampton."

"An Asian child."

"Asian, Oriental—call her what you want. You know what I mean."

Steven spoke, his mouth full of mashed potato. "No fighting."

"We're not fighting, Steven. We're discussing."

"Sounds like fighting."

Elizabeth continued. "There will be prejudice. I'm aware of that. But there is already an Asian population here, even a Korean church. I think you're exaggerating." She let the words hang in the air. "That, or not being honest with yourself."

"And I think you're being Pollyanna. You see one of these little almond-eyed fortune cookies and want to bring one home. We're not talking about a kitten."

She stood, folded her napkin, and pushed away from the table. "You can be such a jerk, Coleman. I'm going to Social Services tomorrow as scheduled. If you care to come, the appointment is with Monique Hunter at 4:30."

We watched her disappear into the kitchen, the swinging door rocking on its hinges in her wake. Josh grinned mischievously as Steven turned back to me. "What's mom mad about?"

"She's mad because I'm a jerk." Steven nodded and resumed eating.

Dinner ended, but the air remained charged with a static discord. Clashing sounds carried from the kitchen. The boys toted their plates through the swinging door and soon, from the den, the babble of television intruded; a rerun of *The Waltons* with its attendant corn pone drawls.

I remained seated, staring at the far wall, looking without seeing and conscious of a miasma in my stomach that seemed to well up with every mention of this subject. I dislike conflict, barely tolerable when I can hold fractious clients at a clinical arms length but unendurable when my most personal relationships clashed. A need for reconciliation arises within me as reflexively as the miasma. Without the enriched atmosphere of familial harmony, I flounder, gasping like a trout on a dock. In the kitchen, shielded from my view by the swinging door, drawers opened and closed with a martial edge. I rose and walked into the kitchen.

Elizabeth stood at the sink, scraping dishes before setting them into the dishwasher. I approached from behind, clasping her waist on either side, and pulled her to me, bending slightly to rest my chin on her shoulder. "I plan to be there tomorrow," I said. "I've just been having some second thoughts." She remained rigid, scraping dishes. Lean, tapered muscles in her back and trapezius, so familiar from soaping her when we showered together, held firm against me.

"You made it sound as though we've never given it the first thought. Like I woke up one morning and decided to drink tea instead of coffee, and oh, by the way, why don't we adopt a child."

"I didn't mean it that way. Sometimes things come out wrong."

She reached for the frying pan and edged it into the soapy water. "And sometimes they come out like you mean them."

"Sometimes," I agreed, feeling her body soften as she exhaled. "Remember when you first suggested it? Steven was what, one?"

"He was walking. One, I suppose."

"Hard to believe that much time has passed."

"We weren't exactly prompt with the paperwork."

I released my clasp, stepped from behind and turned toward her, leaning against the counter.

"Is the home study the last hurdle?" I asked.

"They have to find a child."

"You still think Korean is the way to go?"

"The people at Open Arms say it's still the best source. India will open soon, they tell me, but we've waited too long already." She dried her hands and tossed the dish towel at me. "Thanks for the help with the dishes."

"Hey, I kept you company. Besides, you know the rules. I cook, you clean."

A reluctant grin formed on her lips. "But I did both."

"No wonder the boys complained of stomach pains."

"Very funny."

I put my arms around her, drawing her close. Sighing, she turned her head against my shoulder.

"I'll put the boys to bed," I said.

"That would be great. They've seen enough of me today."

In the den, I sat down on the middle cushion of the couch between my sons just as John Boy was saying goodnight to everyone on Walton's Mountain. "Goodnight, Mary Ellen. Goodnight, John Boy. Goodnight, Momma."

"Time for bed," I announced. "Who wants a ride?"

With Josh on my back and Steven in my arms, I started up the stairs. The boys knew that somewhere between step one and step eighteen, the upstairs landing, I would stagger uncertainly, as if to put us all at risk for a Biblical tumble backward. In that instant, each boy would glom to me instinctively. Josh would clutch my neck from behind with such tenacity that my windpipe would close. Steven, in front, contorted himself into a ball of hysterics, doubling his body mass and therefore his weight in blithe disregard of whatever laws of physics were at play on the stairs. Each knew the faux-stumble was coming because it always did, but guessing which step would serve as tonight's trip wire created the mounting tension I relished. I relished it for its power to make them cling to me, to depend upon me to ensure that the game was only a game, to guarantee their safety while creating the illusion of danger. I could feel their young bodies bracing for it, and with each step I climbed, the suppressed giggles climbed with us. On nights like tonight, when I remained sure-footed as high as step fourteen, the squeals of anticipation could not be muzzled, and the three of us began to laugh with an energy that threatened to destabilize the unit. At fifteen, Steven let out a happy roar that echoed downstairs. At sixteen, they shook and contorted so violently and so collectively that I feared losing my balance. At seventeen, a step from the top, I faltered, pitching forward with my upper body so as the fling the boys onto the soft carpet of the upper landing. In a heap we laughed until Steven reached for his fly, to manually restrain his excitement.

Elizabeth appeared at the bottom of the stairs, hands on her hips, posed. "What's going on up there?" she demanded, knowing full well. When no answer came, she shook her head, smiling.

After their baths, I read a story. I often changed the names of characters to "Josh" or "Steven" to bring them fully into the night's fiction. Warm bath water had calmed them, and the baritone of my voice acted as a sedative in damping down the frenzy of the stairs. They leaned against me, one on either side, their moist hair matted against their foreheads and sleep approaching. I smelled their newness, the aroma of virginal masculinity.

"Goodnight, Josh."

"Goodnight, Steven."

"Goodnight, Daddy."

Social Services filled a four-story building in the heart of New Hampton's inner city and, in the past year, overflowed onto two floors of an annex near City Hall. From 8 A.M. to 6 P.M., it was a labyrinth of pandemonium dominated by young mothers toting infants and trailed by small children struggling to keep pace. In offices off the main corridor, phones jangled incessantly. I was a few minutes late. By the time I arrived, Elizabeth and Monique Hunter were in conference.

Monique Hunter, a diminutive woman of perhaps twenty-five, had medium black skin and short hair. She sat behind her desk, bare but for one manila file folder, while Elizabeth sat opposite. I introduced myself and took the plain metal chair beside Elizabeth, feeling like I had walked in on a conspiracy.

Monique smiled pleasantly. "I think what you are doing is wonderful. I see from your file you have two biological sons. How do they feel about this?"

Elizabeth smiled. "I'd like to believe they're wildly excited, but in fact I don't think they understand much about it."

"Seven and five is a little young to grasp this," agreed Monique. "Perhaps as the big day gets closer . . ."

"Exactly. We've been talking about this baby sister for so long they probably think it's some kind of family joke. Sometimes I feel that way myself."

"This is my first experience with an international adoption. How do you go about selecting a child?"

"Our agency, Open Arms, will send us a dossier on a child who meets the profile we gave them."

"And what was that?"

"As young as possible—"

"For bonding."

"Yes. A girl, full Korean. That's it."

Monique opened her file. "Today, I'll ask a series of questions about your backgrounds, your families, your children. Routine stuff that will let me write a report that will assure your agency they're not sending this child into a den of Satan worshipers." She laughed lightly at a joke I felt had been rehearsed. "Then I'll need to visit your home, which I'm sure is lovely but I have to see it. It would be best if your two boys were there when I came. Shall we get started?"

From the folder she withdrew a packet of papers stapled at the corner. "I'll begin with family histories. You first, Mr. Carter." I shrugged agreeably.

"Your parents full names?"

"Coleman Edwin Carter and Sarah Robbins Carter."

"Both living?"

"Yes. In Charleston, South Carolina."

"Dates and places of birth?"

"My father was born June 15, 1908 in Charleston. Mother was born August 12, 1910 in Darlington. That's also in South Carolina."

Monique Hunter pushed her ballpoint in a flowing script, tilting her head as she wrote. When finished, she looked up at me. "The plantations along the James River are full of Carters. No connection, I guess."

"A direct one, actually. I grew up in the southern branch of the family."

Monique Hunter's eyebrows arched faintly as she made a note. "Parents' health?"

"Mother is healthy. Father is not. Some recent heart problems."

Monique Hunter inquired about siblings: "None." When she had filled in her blanks, she turned to Elizabeth, who crossed her legs and fingered the fringe of her jacket.

"And your parents, Mrs. Carter?"

"Victor Hetzel and Ruth Altenhofen Hetzel."

"Your mother is . . . ?"

"German."

"And can you spell 'Altenhofen' for me."

"A-l-t-e-n-h-o . . . I can never remember if it's one 'f' or two . . . one, I think . . . e-n."

"And their places and dates of birth?"

Elizabeth studied her lap, where she had worked a thread loose in the hem of her jacket. "Both born in Cincinnati. I don't know my dad's date of birth. Mom's is March something. She's fifty-eight, so that would make the year 1920 or '21. Around in there."

Monique continued writing. In the hall, a passing child stopped in the doorway and stared into the room. Monique rose and closed the door.

"I suppose I should know this stuff," Elizabeth said.

Monique looked up, her pen poised above the paper. "Don't worry. Many people don't know these things. We can nail it down later. Siblings?"

"Two brothers, both living, both married."

"Catholic?"

"Lutheran."

The interview continued. Monique Hunter proved thorough and professional. After she finished the backgrounds, she moved on to habits, interests, hobbies, church affiliation, and professional endeavors. She devoted time to our philosophy of parenting, relationship to our sons, and preferred methods of discipline.

"We're almost done," Monique announced, shaking the cramped fingers of her writing hand and glancing up at the clock mounted above the door. 5:00. "Each of you take a minute to tell me how you feel about this adoption. Mrs. Carter, you go first."

Elizabeth inhaled, clasped her hands together in her lap, and said, "We have been blessed with two healthy, beautiful boys. They have a loving, stable home. I want to give that same chance to a child who has little hope of ever having a family as we know it. I think this child, whoever she turns out to be, will be a wonderful addition to our home and give us a chance to share our good fortune."

Monique nodded. "As I told you earlier, I think it's super of you to take this on. Not everyone would. How about you, Mr. Carter? What are your thoughts?"

"The same as Elizabeth's."

My wife was not pleased with this dodge. "Don't gush so much."

"So what's left to say?" I demanded. "It's great. I'm all for it."

"That's not what you said last night. Be honest about it."

I did not look at her, instead holding the expectant gaze which Monique Hunter focused on me. "I simply expressed some reservations as to whether we had thought through all the angles."

Monique Hunter opened her mouth to speak. Elizabeth cut her off.

"Tell her about your theory. The trauma an Asian child will experience in an American family."

"Won't she?" asked Monique.

Elizabeth's tone softened. "Of course. But benefits outweigh liabilities."

"Why don't we hear your husband's thoughts on it."

"He's going to say he's thinking of her; that he doesn't want her to be the victim of the kind of prejudice that exists in this town."

Monique dropped her eyes toward the desk and smiled faintly. "Well, that's a subject I know something about, but why don't we hear it from him."

"I'm sorry, I'll be quiet."

I glanced at Elizabeth before turning back to Monique. "I'm trying to be realistic. I worry about her acceptance. Our sons can go anywhere. No limits. But I think she'll encounter some and those will hurt her and hurt us for her."

Monique nodded. "Have you told your families; parents, brothers, sisters?"

Elizabeth said, "I've told mine. Well, some of them."

I felt both women staring me down. "I wanted to wait until we finalized things."

"How do you think they will react?"

"My parents will have . . . reservations."

"About adoption or the international part?"

"Both. They're old school."

We scheduled the home visit for the following Thursday. Monique Hunter walked us to the reception area. "Just imagine," she said as we exchanged good-byes, "on the other side of the world, there may be a child with your name attached to her." Elizabeth clasped Monique's hand, buoyed by the thought. I checked my watch.

"I'm playing golf," I said to Elizabeth as Monique returned to her office. "Tee-off was at 5:15 and I'm late. See you at home." In the parking lot we left in separate cars.

I inched my late-model BMW into traffic, always heavy at this hour. The New Hampton Shipyard, the largest private employer in the state with a workforce exceeding twenty-five thousand, ended its first shift at 5:00. Within minutes thereafter, weary, muscled men emerged from the colossal enterprise, trudging down the broken sidewalks leading from the yard and dodging cars, vans, and pick-ups with the mechanical indifference of arcade targets. They shuffled across Tyler Avenue with their heads down, their lunch pails emptied, and the stubble of their beards scented with the acrid sweat of a full day's work in the hull of some submarine.

Behind these men until the next morning lay the shipyard, a riverside sprawl of machine shops, gangways, dry docks, piers, and warehouses spread out before the watchful eyes of big-boomed cranes, which stood like mammoth egrets facing into the wind. The yard boasted a long tradition of building large ships, "large" being a relative term expanding with the decades, so that Hull No. 1, an ocean-going tug called *Dorchester* commissioned in 1896, matched in scale and displacement the lifeboats on modern liners now being built for the Miami cruise trade.

Dominating the north yard were two drydocks, so cavernous that their simultaneous flooding appeared to lower the water table on the river bank. Into these floated tankers and warships scheduled for overhaul while newly commissioned aircraft carriers and submarines glided out of their watery incubators with the ease of an expert skier over fresh powder. Giant cranes of enormous strength straddled the drydocks, moving up and back on rails laid on either side of the pits. On certain afternoons, crowds of hard-hatted men, some with welding goggles hung about their necks and steel-toed shoes on their feet, would tilt a collective head skyward to witness the cranes hoist an assembled conning tower from the staging area, swing it high over the heads of the men who made it, and place it precisely onto the deck of a nuclear powered city. From a distance, silhouetted against a western sky, the cranes resembled some enlarged gym apparatus, like vaulting horses built for giants.

For as long as New Hampton had been a city, the ear-splitting shrill of the 7 A.M. whistle had been its alarm clock. Mounted on the top of the steel fabrication building, it summoned the first shift to work as the rest of New Hampton opened one eye. From the parking lots, cafes, diners, and newsstands along Tyler Avenue the workers hustled to punch the clock before the late whistle cost them pay. During fall and winter, a morning fog off the river sometimes veiled the yard, amplifying sound and dampening spirits. Those days must have dragged interminably inside the gates. 5:00 seemed unreachable. When the shift change whistle finally sounded, the craggy old jailer unbolted its gates and paroled its occupants, who dispersed onto the streets with thoughts of warm whiskey or a seat near the heater for the ride home.

The Riverside Country Club, my destination, lay seven miles upriver from the shipyard. Known simply as "the club" to its members, it took a parental pride in its golf course. I played occasionally; usually, like today, at the invitation of Dr. Ross Vernon, a general surgeon with an eight handicap and a past chairman of the Greens Committee. He was also my best friend and my client. Ross's wife, Carol, saw Elizabeth often, and except for Carol's efforts to recruit her into Mary Kay, Elizabeth liked her. We usually socialized with the Vernons at our home or theirs, but occasionally at the club, where we were not members.

I parked, extracted my clubs from the trunk, and after leaning against the car to change my shoes, I headed across the fairway in the direction of the fourth tee, where instinct told me Ross Vernon would be by now. On a bench near the blue tee I watched Vernon and another man putt out on number three. They replaced the flag and walked toward me.

"You're late," called Vernon, a rotund, friendly man with contact lenses and hands surprisingly meaty for his delicate work.

"You're right," I returned, rising to meet him.

"Coleman, do you know Ed Polling of Armstrong Securities?"

"Don't think I do," I said, shaking hands with Polling who affably assured me it was indeed nice to meet me as well. Polling impressed me as a serious golfer. His bag and clubs showed wear and his golf glove dangled from his back pocket with the insouciance I had come to associate with those who took three-putting personally.

My first impression firmed when Polling, with honors on the third hole, stepped to the tee and drove his ball two hundred and ninety yards at the dead center of the fairway. I caught Ross Vernon's eye as Polling watched his ball come to rest.

"Not bad," I said. "Pressure is my middle name."

Vernon smirked. "There's beer in my bag. Help yourself."

I topped my first drive—I usually do—sending it bounding down the rough on the left. Ugly, but the distance wasn't bad. Vernon then hit a very respectable drive thirty yards behind and to the right of where Polling's ball lay. I wondered why I played this game. I do not enjoy golf, and I enjoy golfers as a group even less, although Ross Vernon is an exception.

We shouldered our bags and ambled down the fairway, lined on either side by the dead leaves of winter. "Looks like a ten ball afternoon," I joked. For me, winter golf means lots of time looking for my ball in the woods. I glanced toward Polling to see if my comment provoked a smile, the kind of response that would leave me free to take the game as lightly as I pleased. But Polling's eyes were fixed on his ball, his mind focused on his club selection, his pace quickening into a martial gait, and he appeared not to have heard. I turned to Ross.

"So, how goes the cut and cure business?"

"About the same," he answered. "Couple of gall bladders in the morning, golf in the afternoon. The usual."

"Remind me," I said, "when I need surgery to inquire about handicaps. I want to die at the hands of someone who doesn't know a birdie from a bugle."

Ross Vernon laughed. "You can't equate golfing ability with surgical skill. The best surgeon in town wins the member-guest every year."

"Who is that?" I asked. As a club non-member, I know little of these intramural honors.

"Bill Hartsock. The joke around the scrub basins is that Doctor Bill can do brain surgery with a putter."

"I'm old fashioned. I like the ones who use scalpels and aren't in a hurry to get to the first tee."

"Not many of those left," Vernon said as we arrived at my ball. I checked my distance, took out a five iron, and dropped my bag behind me.

"Ross, you want to run up there and tend the flag for me. I hate it when I get off a two hundred yard chip and the flag deflects it at the last second."

Vernon grinned. "About twelve shots from now, when you hit the green, I'll take care of the pin."

Polling remained silent, as though playing alone. As I limbered up with my five iron, I felt the intimidation of Polling's stare. I approached the ball, whacked downward, and felt a surge of relief as the ball erupted toward the pin, landing just off the green.

"Nice shot," allowed Polling.

"Thanks," I acknowledged. "If I had any sense, I would call it a day now."

The light was fading. Shadows of the bare oaks and maples lengthened across our path. Vernon took a sweater from his bag and pulled it over his head. When we putted out, Polling had parred, Vernon had a bogey five, and I had shot six, which pleased me. At the next tee, Vernon popped a beer. Polling declined.

On the fifth hole, a par five, Polling and Vernon each bogeyed while I took a ten. "Could have been worse," I noted. At number six, I made a par three. "Now that's the Coleman Carter we've come to know and fear," I mocked. Polling actually smiled. As we followed our shots off the next tee, Polling walked ahead and I said to Vernon, "Where did you find this Polling? Is he one of your patients who suffered oxygen deprivation while you stitched him up?"

"He's my broker. Scratch golfer, as you can see. Not much at stand-up comedy, but good with the market." We watched Polling stride purposely toward his ball. "You're only going to get in four or five holes. How come you're late?"

"You're not going to believe it when I tell you." I had resolved on the way to the club to say nothing about the adoption, but I liked Ross Vernon. "Elizabeth and I had a meeting with Social Services." Vernon eyed me expectantly. "We're adopting a kid."

"No lie," said Vernon. "When?"

"Soon, I guess."

"You guess?"

"Well, it's not your straight adoption. I mean, we're looking at international adoptions. There's a lot of paperwork and then a child has to become available."

"What kind of child?"

"A girl. Korean, we think."

Vernon stopped and looked at me, expressionless. "You're going to adopt a gook?"

I had to laugh. "Gooks are Vietnamese. Don't you know your ethnic slurs?"

"My error," said Vernon, returning the laugh. "That's awfully brave of you. What do Josh and Steven think?"

"It's okay with them. Elizabeth is ecstatic. It was her idea."

"I can't believe she hasn't said anything to Carol. But you sound less than ecstatic."

"Frankly, I think it's dumb."

"Then why—"

"Don't ask. Anyway, we're doing it and I hope it makes Elizabeth happy, because I know two senior citizens in Charleston, South Carolina who are going to go ballistic."

"Your folks?"

I nodded. "My dad's been sick and this could push him over. I mean it. And mother still talks about my cousin who got a divorce, of all things, like she turned tricks on the church steps. Telling them won't be pretty."

"Sounds like trouble," Vernon agreed. "And Elizabeth expects this reaction?"

"I have no idea. We haven't discussed it. I doubt she has given it much thought from their standpoint."

"They don't get along?"

"They do, but it's a delicate truce easily broken by importing alien children into the family." I felt the tightening in my throat. I had said more than I intended. Still unsaid, but very much on my mind as I walked the fairway, now hidden in the murky stillness of dusk, was the impending pressure to love a total stranger like I loved those boys. I didn't see how that was possible. I just didn't.

5

Jong Sim

The trip back to my village was the longest of my life. Your cries followed me down the street until I stopped my ears. When I stepped onto the bus, the driver stared at me because I was looking at him, just standing there like a tree. He took the fare from some money I held, then pushed me toward the back. The people I passed must have known I had done a terrible thing because they looked at me like a criminal. All the seats were filled, but a kind auntie made a space for me. I tried not to think about you but instead about the cane machete with the rusty blade I put under my sleeping mat yesterday. It was not very sharp, but it was sharp enough.

You looked so helpless lying on those steps. I could still hear you crying though the bus had been many miles. I told myself they had found you by now, that you were inside the police station being changed and fed and smiled upon. You were on your way to America, I whispered, but too softly for the auntie beside me to hear. I did the best I could for you by giving you away. You would rather be with me than on a doorstep, but you were helpless. I was just as helpless in a world controlled by men and tradition. I gave away my child. I murdered you. I will murder myself, I had decided.

The temperature dropped. You would be cold, but it was warm in the station, where you surely were by now, being cradled by someone who had seen the mirror and knew that you were special. The auntie beside me was most kind, patting my hand like she understood, but she could not because I myself did not understand. At the sign of the green dragon I got off. The temperature had dropped more and the air was very cold so I shivered as I waited. The bus to the village was not crowded, and the few passengers did not notice me weeping in the back. If they heard me, they did not turn around.

That night I took the machete from under my sleeping mat with only the slightest scraping of its rusty blade against the floor. I did not want my mother to hear. I crept into the kitchen and crawled into the large tub used to render meat. There I curled up with my hands locked around my knees. My breasts throbbed, swollen with milk. They will give you milk but it will not be my milk and you will not like it. I sat in the tub a long time, holding the machete between my legs and waiting for the courage to force it into the very place where I felt your restless stretch at sunrise. My heart beat with love for you and hatred for myself, for my parents, for my grandfather, for Hyun Su, for Uncle Jae, for Korea. Why must I, who had nothing, give up something so precious? If I must give up what I love, so must they. I would enter the next life so they would know I loved you more than life itself. When they found me in the morning, stiff and cold in my own blood, they would suffer loss and know the depth of mine.

I turned the rusty blade toward my stomach and gripped the handle with both hands. I knew I must do it quickly, with one thrust, at the very moment when my courage surged and before I could change my mind. I waited for that courage. The house was silent and I wondered if I would break that silence by crying out at the moment the blade entered me. I placed the point against my belly below the navel. The point was sharper than I thought, and a trickle of blood came down between my legs. To get the courage I needed I thought back to grandfather's order to "get rid of it," as if my perfect Soo Yun was some foul smelling garbage, and to Hyun Su's fists when he accused me of counting the days wrong, but the courage would not come. My hate was not as strong as my love for you, and love is not a reason for suicide. Near dawn, I rose from the tub, my legs like jelly and the machete so heavy I could not lift it but only drag it along the floor. I returned to my sleeping mat, slid the machete under it, and slept, exhausted.

The first week of separation from you seemed endless. I forced myself into the fields where I worked to forget. I ate little, slept little, and spent myself harrowing fields that were nearly frozen. After a time I could not feel my feet or hands. If only my heart could be numb also. That week dragged into the next. Lying on my back at night, I memorized a mildew pattern on the ceiling, but I avoided a view of the tub through the kitchen door. The mildew pattern formed a map, with crooked roads leading to anyplace but where I was. I walked them until exhaustion brought sleep.

One night I woke up trembling from a picture in my mind—you at the olive door, your oval face, your tiny hands, your nursing lips, those sad cries. What happened to you? Did they take you in? They must have taken you inside because it grew so cold in the afternoon. Will they send you to America? Do you cry for me? The pictures in Min Jung's magazine were just pictures unless you went to America. You could not grow strong and wear a watch and drive a car and not farm unless you left Korea. It grew so cold that day. Did you freeze? I had to know. I could not spend years thinking about the better life I gave you unless I knew you were on your way to that life.

On a day of bitter temperatures, I again boarded the bus for Seoul. I wondered if they would arrest me at the police station for leaving my child. I did not care. Arrest and shame were nothing compared to uncertainty. I again found the high hedge. I walked up the steps where I left you and knocked on the olive green door. A light snow fell and I stood there a long time. I knocked again. Why did no one answer?

I turned and walked down the steps. As I reached the end of the sidewalk, two policemen came around the corner on Yulgong-No Street. I pointed back toward the door, but the patrolmen were in a rush and one of them made a motion with his arm like a circle. I went around the building and saw another door, newer with fresh paint. I knocked and heard, "It is open."

Inside, I saw a long counter with a phone, a stack of greenish papers, and a box for mail. The desk person, in a uniform, looked up from a magazine as I bowed and came closer.

"May I help you?" he asked.

"I am Jong Sim. I have come to ask about a child, an infant."

"Is the child missing?"

"Yes, the child is missing."

"For how long?"

"Four weeks, about."

"Four weeks? And you are only now reporting it?" He did not look friendly.

"Not exactly." We were alone in the room. "My friend brought her baby here."

The man smiled, but it was not a true smile. "Now I see. Your friend wants the child back."

"Not the child, but only news of her safety. If I could bring her such news it would mean much."

The telephone at the man's elbow rang. It made me jump. The man told the caller, "No, no, yes, no." Then he returned his attention to me.

"We often have babies left here. We call the home. Our records are sealed from the public. I can tell you nothing to tell your friend. I am sorry."

"Can you say she went to this home? Even that would comfort my friend."

"I can say that is what usually happens. But for a certain child, I cannot say."

I felt my legs weakening and my heart thumped so loudly I thought he must hear it. "But I must take some word to her."

The man turned in his chair and disappeared through the door behind the counter. A short time later, a fat man in a tight uniform came out. He said he was Captain Oh. He told me to follow him through a swinging gate to the rooms beyond. At the far end of the hall were boxes and large metal cabinets. Captain Oh pointed and said, "The old door." I followed him into a room with a desk.

He sat behind the desk while I stood in front of it. The room was very warm and I saw sweat on the Captain's yellow upper lip. He straightened some papers in front of him, already straight.

"So your friend brought us her child?"

"About one month ago."

"A girl, I presume?"

I nodded.

The Captain said, "Yes, always girls. What is the name of your friend?"

I looked at the floor. My knees were shaking. "Must I say her name?"

The Captain shook his head. "It does not matter. We cannot give information, with or without her name. Tell me, did your friend use the door you came through . . . or the old door?"

"The old door, perhaps."

Captain Oh frowned. "That is a problem. We no longer use that door. One month ago? No, that door was not in use at that time."

"The man at the desk said she went to the home."

"Sometimes, yes."

"And others?"

"Others are the ones we never know about."

My look told him I did not understand.

"Women leave their children at the door. We know this. They rely upon us to take them to the home. But we cannot be certain all the girls are found. Others may come along . . ." His voice grew softer. "Tell me, did your friend hide in the hedge to see the child taken in?"

"I . . . I do not know."

"Some do. I am told that is why our door is popular. They can watch from the safety of the hedge. But that will all change now because there is no hedge by the new door."

"My friend did not say." I felt faint. The heat of the room felt like a giant hand pressing down on my head.

"But clearly the answer is 'no,'" said the Captain. He looked very pleased with himself. "Or she would not have sent you to confirm such a thing. Am I right?" He smiled a true smile and folded his hands across his belt buckle.

"You are correct," I said. "Are you certain there have been no children brought to you from the old door?"

The Captain rocked in his chair. "There was one."

"One month ago?"

"I cannot remember. Time is elusive as you age." He stood up suddenly. "But if I could remember, I could not say. There are strict regulations, and I am nearing retirement."

I could think of nothing to say except, "I understand."

"But Mi Cha might help. She found a child at the old door not long ago. What I am forbidden to discuss she may share freely. It is up to her. The sergeant can direct you to her home."

"I thank you so much. My friend thanks you."

I left the station for the freezing air outside, glad to escape the heat and the uniforms. I carried a map drawn by the sergeant. It looked nothing like the mildewed ceiling at home. The wind and snow watered my eyes as I tried to shield the paper with my body. Near the bus stop not far from the old door I found a wall to flatten the map. Snow fell into my eyes and I had to clear them to see the map. The house I sought was not far, a short walk.

On the third knock the door opened and an old woman, an auntie, opened the door. She could not have known why I was there but it did not seem to matter. She told me to come in. I followed her to her kitchen, which smelled of cabbage and garlic. She said she had been chopping vegetables. I told her why I had come. She offered hot tea and took my coat. I liked her very much for her kindness.

"Oh, yes," she said as we sipped tea at the kitchen table. "I remember well. It was the day I lost Mojo, my dog." She paused, staring at me through tired eyes. "But the child belonged to you, not your friend."

I said nothing. The tea warmed my hands.

"I will not press you, child. I am a mother also. And this morning I spent two hours in this weather looking for Mojo. I would not have gone out into this cold for a friend."

I remained silent, but my eyes must have told the old woman what she knew.

"She was a quite beautiful baby, but fussy. Perhaps that was understandable."

"You are certain it was the same child?" I asked. "One month ago?"

"Quite certain. A newborn wrapped in a gray blanket. May I ask why you are seeking her?"

I sipped my tea. "Only to satisfy myself as to her safety. To know she is well and cared for will allow me some peace."

"You have not thought of regaining her?"

"No."

"That is best. What is done is done. And she will thrive at the home. The nurse told me such babies are imported by wealthy Americans. She will have a good life."

"You are wise," I said.

She laughed softly. "No. Merely old. Have I told you all you wish to know?"

"Yes . . . I suppose."

"You don't wish the name of the nurse?"

Of course I did, as she knew.

"Hana, as I recall. A plain woman older than you. She had a knack with the child. It is well you came soon after. Another month or two and I would not have been able to recall the nurse's name."

I rose to leave. "You have been very kind. Could you give me one more piece of information? Directions to the home; I do not know the city."

"I will direct you," said Mi Cha. "It is easy to find, and you will ask another if I refuse. But my advice is to stay away. You have done well by your baby. Leave her there. This is only my advice."

"I wish only to know she arrived safely at the home."

Mi Cha smiled at me as a mother would. "Search your heart fully, child. You do not yet know it."

I felt my face redden. "Thank you for tea. I hope you find your dog."

"The dog is lost. This is certain. Still, I search. It is better than the reality."

Outside, I walked head down against the wind. It was so strange to walk where no one knew my name or had ever seen me before. The buildings along the way got bigger with each block, but the home was not so big. I went inside and asked for the nurse by name.

6

Hana

Soo Yun's condition was as I had feared: pneumonia. Her time outside the door in the cold had left her vulnerable to pneumocystis carinii, a strain of pneumonia common here in Asia. It is fatal if left untreated, and several of our children have died from it over the years. But caught in time, properly diagnosed, and treated with Bactrim, a full recovery usually results. When I visited her two days after she was admitted, she slept peacefully in a room with six other infants. I missed her on the ward, visiting her each week for the duration of her one month stay in the hospital, the time needed for Bactrim to do its work.

On the day she returned to 3E, part of me returned with her. I really cannot explain why this was so. I have nursed and cared for hundreds of infants here over the years. I loved them all, but something about her left me hollow in her absence, and restored when she returned. When you see something that small fighting against odds so long, you cannot help but be inspired and to cheer for her. She nearly died outside the police station door. Had that old woman not come along, she would have. And then to be hit with a disease so commonly fatal seemed grossly unfair, like the gods ganging up on her. Some babies might seem doomed by such misfortune, but something told me these early tests would make her stronger. She needed to get stronger.

She was asleep in the crib when I reported for work that day. The hospital stay had added weight, put color in her cheeks, and eliminated any trace of her nagging croup. I picked her up and carried her to a changing table, where I stripped her soggy diaper. I had just positioned her on a clean one when I saw them—raw ugly scars. The larger was a wide scar beginning under the left breast and extending toward the back. I turned her over. The scar protruded with suture marks on either side, running almost to the center of her back. Where it passed under the arm, there was a second scar, about three centimeters long. I had never seen scars like this. Something far more serious than pneumonia must have been detected at the hospital. I sent for her medical record, fearing the worst.

To my relief, the record did not disclose the heart or lung surgery I was sure I would find. Only pneumonia, with a lung biopsy to confirm the strain. I called our infirmary. I asked Dr. Kim to come to 3E when he finished his work there.

"Butcher," I said to Dr. Kim, handing him the record.

Dr. Kim was new to the home and youthful enough to pass for a high school student. He rubbed his chin, devoid of facial hair, and examined her. "The incisions are indeed quite large. The smaller one for the drainage tube would have been sufficient. I do not recognize the name on the surgery notes. Probably someone new."

"And incompetent. The hospital will receive a very strong letter of protest."

"But the child is healthy and the scars will fade in time. They are of no great importance."

"You are most mistaken, doctor. They will prevent her from being adopted."

Kim drew back in surprise. "Oh?"

"She is damaged. Prospective parents will be unwilling to take a risk."

"But she is fine."

"It will not matter. You will see."

I didn't mean to take out my frustration on Dr. Kim. Soo Yun was not his patient. But I knew what this meant for me in my dealings with Faith Stockdale, the gatekeeper for every child who left or hoped to leave the home. If Soo Yun became labeled "damaged goods," she was doomed to a youth within a kilometer of where she now lay.

I knew Faith as my boss. She was a cheerful woman in her mid-fifties, with closely cropped hair, broad shoulders and the largest feet I have ever seen on a woman. I liked and respected her, but we were not contemporaries nor did we socialize outside of work. The woman I replaced on 3E, my mentor here, had been her best friend and told me all about her. Faith spoke fluent Korean. She arrived in the country at age thirty-eight as the wife of an army lieutenant colonel. Winters here are harsh, and their marriage did not survive their first winter in Korea, as her wealthy parents had predicted. I was told her ex-husband, Anthony Stockdale, remained bitter over an evaluation from his commanding officer at Ft. Bragg. He drank too much and he blamed Faith because he said she did not love the military and did not do enough to help him become a general. It was not the military she did not love, but rather him. His tour ended at the officers' club in an incident involving a captain's wife and a scuffle in the parking lot. By then Faith had resolved to leave him, to stay in this strange country, and to learn its language. Her grandfather's trust fund eased her transition to that of a single woman determined to prove to the people back in Connecticut that Choate and Vassar had been worth their investment.

Open Arms approached Faith on her forty-first birthday, a coincidence she took as a good omen. In the fourteen years she has worked here, she discovered much about herself. For instance, she realized with some embarrassment but no regret that her ex-husband had just cause to criticize her lack of commitment to his ambition. She also found within herself skills at organization and implementation that exceeded her own assessment of her abilities. My mentor said that on nights when Faith entertained herself with a book and a glass of sherry in front of a fire, she occasionally thought of her former husband and concluded that she stood the better chance of becoming a general.

Faith's career with Open Arms had been blemished by just two incidents, one minor. That incident, the minor one, caused only temporary embarrassment when a precocious three-year-old improbably escaped from a wristband identifying him as an adoptee who needed to be put on the bus, then the plane, for passage to America. The adopting parents stood expectantly at the airport gate while families around them greeted their new arrivals and the escape artist slept in Seoul. Faith, red-faced, made profuse apologies, offered to pay the child's travel expenses from her own pocket, and ordered the child put on the next available flight.

The other incident could not be remedied, by Faith or anyone else. Sohn was a bright-eyed toddler adopted by the Saunders, a couple in Nebraska who had no children. Sohn died within a month of her arrival in the home of parents who, in that short span of days, had made her the focus of their universe. When an autopsy disclosed a congenitally deformed heart valve, two doctors in Lincoln opined that the defect was detectable by routine x-ray, and that Open Arms' failure to diagnose an evident flaw had caused needless grief.

Open Arms anticipated a lawsuit, but the again-childless couple did not believe in compounding their pain by attempting to fill a human void with money. Faith's investigation revealed that Sohn had, in fact, been x-rayed, but a blur had obscured the valve at the critical point of focus and the doctor had neglected to order another, assuming the best when the history of that luckless child dictated assuming the worst. Faith delicately approached the Saunders about another child, but they declined.

I usually looked forward to these briefings, but I approached this one conscious of a moral dilemma. Soo Yun's surgery, a mere whisper to the shouts of the scars, had come after her dossier had been forwarded. Open Arms' policy required in such instances a "Medical Alert" be issued and forwarded without delay to the recipient of the dossier. Such prompt notifications of altered status preserved the agency's reputation for integrity in a business plagued by a history of lies, half truths and deceptions.

But in my experience, such Alerts were nearly always fatal to the child's hopes. The great distance between Korea and America forced prospective parents to rely solely on the information provided by Korean authorities through the agency. The Medical Alert bulletins screamed "trouble," and despite artful drafting conveying effusive reassurance, the news was always perceived as bad. No matter how detailed, they rarely answered all questions and concerns demanded by those alerted. Now infected by restless apprehensions, those alerted tended to resolve their doubts conservatively, invariably asking, in so many words and with a multiplicity of excuses, "Why take the risk?"

Subtle ailments—a history of colic, poor sleep patterns, delayed development responses—could be, and were, glossed over by the home in its efforts to place as many children as possible. But scars were another matter. My silence could imperil my relationship with Faith and the agency's reputation in Korea; my disclosure meant a dreaded "Alert," probably dooming Soo Yun's chances for early adoption, or any at all. In full knowledge of the poor choices available, I approached Faith Stockdale's office at the appointed hour.

Faith opened her door at the first knock, smiled in greeting, then motioned me inside. "How are you?" she asked, returning to her desk as I glanced down at her large feet.

"Very well, thank you."

"And the children on your ward?"

"Very well, also." I found myself sitting rigidly, formally. My body was telling Faith what I myself had not yet to decided to share. The words "all but one" formed in my mouth, but I pulled them back and instead reported, "Last night one of the children saw a mouse. The boys took up sticks to hunt it down. Some of the girls were afraid of it but wanted me to prevent the boys from killing it." I laid my elbow on the chair's armrest to relax.

"What did you do?"

I shrugged my shoulders. "I told the boys I would give a prize for the safe capture of the mouse, but no prize for a dead mouse. They put down their sticks and began constructing a trap from a box."

Faith smiled. "And the girls?"

"They, too, wish for the prize, so they are making a trap also."

"The mouse lives."

"We must all find a way," I said. I wished to steer conversation away from the children but as my relationship with Faith was built entirely on the business of the home, conversation on other subjects did not flow naturally. "What is the news from America?"

"Applications are up," Faith said, pleased. "I just received profiles on thirty-two families. The economy there is good and more couples are coming to view adoption as acceptable."

"That is very good news," I agreed, thinking of the sutures, ugly puncture wounds trailing out over the landscape of Soo Yun's chest, side and back like the most primitive tractor marring a virgin hillside. In a few months or years, they will all but disappear, but the damage will be done. She will be consigned to the home beyond infancy, and possibly beyond that.

On the desk before Faith rested a pile of folders. She moved them forward. "Take these with you," she instructed. "I've looked through them. They are typical, except we have one family willing to accept a child as old as fifteen, either sex. That is rare, as you know. Also, we have an opportunity to place a boy between five and eight with a handicap of the arms or legs. Does anyone on your ward qualify?"

"Possibly Chang Yong Ho," I replied, mentally inventorying my ward. "He is six, the oldest in my care. He suffered a slight paralysis on the left side in an accident."

"Perfect," Faith said. From a credenza behind her she picked up a slim manila folder. "And these are the children who have been matched to parents' specifications. We are awaiting the parents' decisions. Let's see. . . ." She read seven names, beginning with Suk Non Hee and ending with Soo Yun. "Any problems?"

"Yes, the last one," I heard myself say.

"Health?"

"Yes, but she has recovered. She is . . . fine."

"Good. Then perhaps the prospective parents will decide in time for the next flight."

I spied a small, framed photograph on the surface of the desk. Faith followed my eyes, and when she spoke her robust voice softened.

"That is Sohn. A most unfortunate child who died shortly after placement. It happened just before you began here, I believe."

"I remember people discussing it. I have never seen her picture."

"I keep it here to remind myself of my duties to parents who rely upon me to be their eyes and ears in the home."

"Perhaps," I countered, "you should put up pictures of those who are happily living with new families. That would require many frames and a larger desk."

The women laughed. "There are so many success stories," Faith conceded. "Still, I can't help thinking about Earl and Rebecca Saunders, in Nebraska. Those were Sohn's parents. In just one month . . . well, no point in reliving that."

"You were about to say that in a very short time they came to love the child. I understand that feeling."

"I know you do."

"I must get back to my ward." I stood, hoping that the love I expressed for children, all children, somehow compensated for my half-truth, and knowing that it did not.

I had just returned to my ward when the reception desk called. I answered the phone with my right hand, the unlucky one. Into my right ear the receptionist spoke of a woman in the lobby who wished to see me. "She declined to say why."

I entered the reception area from a stairwell behind the reception desk. I spotted a young woman standing alone. Approaching, I realized at once that I did not know her.

"I am Hana. You wish to speak to me?"

"You are very kind to see me. I have come from outside the city to ask about my daughter."

"Your daughter is here, at the home?"

"From what I have been told by others, yes. They say she is in your care."

"I have many in my care. Is there a name?"

"Soo Yun."

"We have a child by that name, but she was abandoned." My gaze was steady, and I did not blink.

The woman's head dropped and her eyes lowered to the level of my belt. "At Jongam. I am very sorry." Her composure slipped.

I took her arm and led her to a chair in a removed corner of the long room. "Sit down. You look very tired."

"Thank you." She sat, then withdrew from the pocket of her coat a small rag, with which she dabbed her eyes. "You must forgive me. The child was my first born. I could not keep her, but neither can I forget her."

I appraised the peasant before me. "She is a sweet child. Very healthy, and much bigger than when you . . . last saw her."

"Mi Cha, who found her, said that she could be put in the care of a good family. To think that she is happy would mean everything."

"I can say only that this is possible."

The young woman nodded, then put to me the question I felt sure she had come to ask. "May I see her . . . just for an instant?"

"The rules are very clear. We have her custody, and we cannot permit what you ask. I am very sorry. But perhaps it is better this way."

She looked doubtful in her silence, staring at her hands which twisted the rag. I eyed her evenly, fighting against being drawn into the pathos of her disappointment. After a time she said, still focusing on her hands, "But what if she remains here? Can I never see her again?"

"If you chose to come when the public is invited, I cannot prevent it. Open House will next be held in March, on the last Saturday. But I would urge you strongly against coming because it will make your life without her more difficult and because she may by then be gone to her new life."

She managed a weak smile. "You are correct. I must think not only of myself but of her. I will decide later, when I am less tired. Thank you for your kindness. Now, if you will direct me out of the city, I must go."

From the window I watched as she crossed the street to the bus stop. Minutes later she was gone.

7

Elizabeth

On the morning after Christmas, we packed the station wagon for the eight hour trip to South Carolina. I tolerated these as a rule, but dreaded this particular one because I knew I would be blamed for the adoption idea, and Coleman couldn't have been looking forward to it either because the time had come to tell his parents we were expanding the family and, "no, Elizabeth is not pregnant." I told Josh and Steven they could each take one new toy and they showed what I thought commendable restraint in limiting to three the number smuggled aboard in overnight bags.

When you marry a southerner, you get a husband, his extended family, a region with all its quirks (and there are many), not to mention historical legacies that brides from the Midwest like me know nothing of until long after they say "I do." It seemed so simple when Coleman proposed, when naïve me asked myself the question most brides ask: did I want to spend the rest of my life with him? I did not ask whether slavery was as cruel and heartless as is often portrayed (it was), whether the Civil War was justified (it was) or rightly decided (it was), or whether the evening meal is properly called dinner or supper. Who cares?

His parents, to name two, care very much, and that should tell you something about how this adoption news will be received. Adoption is a word in the southern lexicon, but it isn't used much except to refer to things like the "adoption of Articles of Secession" or "adopting the ways of our forefathers." To adopt, as in embracing as your own a child not related by blood, and taking over the care and custody of that child? That's pretty rare, as I am learning. Coleman's mother, Sarah, once told me she had a friend who adopted twins orphaned by the death of their widowed mother, but was emphatic in pointing out that her friend was a cousin of the deceased, so the bonds of family, while stretched, were not broken, as if a stranger stepping up to adopt those twins would have committed an act of perversion. This conversation took place just after Josh was born and long before I had taken any steps to adopt.

His parents live in a beautiful old home in the Battery area, on Church Street. In Charleston it is fashionable to live "south of Broad," the street that separates the elite from the rest of the world. You can't get much further south of Broad than Church Street without finding yourself in Charleston Harbor. I waited until the third day of what had been a pleasant enough visit to approach Coleman after breakfast. "Let's take a walk," I suggested. He agreed, but I think he knew what was coming.

"Why should I tell them?" he asked when we were safely distant from the house. "It's your idea. Why are you afraid to take responsibility for something you feel so strongly about?"

My pace increased, no doubt from nerves. "I'm not afraid. But they think I influence you. Coming from you, it will sound like our idea."

He said, "I hate to disillusion you, my darling, but they could read this news in skywriting over Charleston and know it was your idea."

"Oh, Coleman! You'd think I had suggested we make a porn video. It's just a child who needs parents."

"Have you ever heard my father discuss his time in the Philippines during World War II?"

"Yes, and it's narrow-minded and disgusting."

"I'm not defending it. I'm only pointing out what we're dealing with."

"I *know* what we're dealing with. That's why I think you should tell them. You're the golden boy. They won't attack you like they do me."

"Come on. When do they attack you?"

"If you only knew."

"Tell me."

"No. One crisis at a time. Trust my instincts. This is news you need to break."

"Yeah? Well, trust mine that we better be prepared to duck no matter who tells them."

By the time we returned, Coleman had resigned himself to being the messenger although clearly he wasn't happy about it. You can count on one hand the number of times he has disappointed them in his life. One time was when he married me, and another was when we decided to live in Virginia rather than Charleston. Of course, neither of them ever said they were disappointed in either me or Virginia—things don't work that way in their world. What isn't said is what I've learned to listen for.

In the hour before lunch, as Sarah sliced a ham and his father read the paper and the boys played on swings in the back yard, I looked at him expectantly, but he bore deeper into the novel I had given him for Christmas. When his father rose to get the mail, I walked to his chair and whispered, "What are you waiting for?"

"The right moment," he replied, as if this delay was part of some grand psychology.

"That's another way of putting it off," I said.

"Later," he countered, but lunch came and went with no mention of "it."

Immediately after Walter Cronkite's broadcast, his father, Coleman Sr., who everyone calls Coles, announced cocktails. "Supper" followed, served, as always, by his mother. Sarah Carter must have been a beauty in her day. I associate her with the same grace that pervades Charleston in springtime. My first visit here took place in April, before Coleman and I became engaged, and I remember how seductive I found the azaleas, the magnolias, the trumpet honeysuckle, the lush lawns and gardens afforded by the heat and humidity that is so much a part of lowcountry life and that Sarah Carter seemed equally to be part of, as if she had been raised in the rich loam of a mulched flower bed. I found she possessed a simple charm without being a simple person. She seemed to wear her personal virtue on her sleeve, not out of pride but because she lacked the guile to do otherwise, and had she any shameful failings she would have been equally incapable of concealing them. I learned with experience of her tendency to color things black or white, but I always sensed this sprang from an intuitive, rather than analytical, sense of how things were and ought to be. She told me she lived by her trinity: God, family and the sovereign state of South Carolina, in that order. I noted that Kansas didn't make that list, but it was impossible to take its omission personally since no state other than her own was included. A part of me admires anyone who, like Sarah, can divide the world and its challenges into black and white, yes or no, right and wrong, but I've always found things to be a bit more complicated.

At the other end of the table sat his father, a man I hardly knew at all, and I'm not certain Coleman knew him much better. He was shy, introverted to the point of enigma. Sarah said that stemmed from lack of social confidence, and I guess she should know. I've tried to engage him in conversation dozens of time, and the only time I succeeded was after he had a cocktail or two, as alcohol seemed to help him overcome his reticence. Given tonight's inevitable discussion, I was tempted to fix him a double in hopes he would embrace his fellow man a little more; maybe even throw his arms around the plan soon to be unveiled. It had to be tonight, as we were leaving in the morning. I will never forget the conversation which followed.

By supper's end, a scotch and water and a glass of wine had steeled Coleman to his task, so that when I cleared my throat, fidgeted in my chair, and urged him forward with eyes darting over the rim of my wine glass, he leveled his eyes at his mother.

"Mom, Dad, Elizabeth and I have decided to buy a gook."

I exclaimed, "Coleman!" but found myself smiling nonetheless. Anything to vent the pressure.

Sarah looked first at Coleman, then me, before laughing pleasantly. "You've decided to buy a what?" As the last to get any joke, she often bought time with repetition while searching for the punch line.

"A gook. That's a slang word for an Oriental."

"But I don't understand. How can you buy an Oriental?"

"Not buy one, exactly. Adopt one."

"Adopt an Oriental?" Sarah grew quizzical. "Why would you do that?"

Coleman avoided looking at me, then pushed some untouched peach cobbler around on his dessert plate. "We want a girl. We may never have one the old-fashioned way."

Sarah Carter stared at her husband as she might have sought the aid of an interpreter in a foreign land. "You're not being serious. Elizabeth, what is he talking about?"

Coleman took a pull on his wine, then looked directly at me. "Yes, Elizabeth, what am I talking about?"

I deliberately placed my dessert fork down beside my plate. I'm sure my face flushed. "*We* are talking about adopting an international child; a girl. Your son will fill in the details."

His father spoke, businesslike. "Coleman, have you lost your mind?"

Coleman shrugged. "It makes more sense than you think, because—"

"I hope so, because at this moment it makes none."

Sarah, shaking her head as if to clear it, said, "Back up, Coleman. Let me understand. You intend to adopt what child?"

"We don't know, Mother," he said. "We are going through an agency called Open Arms. They haven't identified a child yet. But there is no shortage of them in Korea."

"Korea! Why, I can't even imagine it."

His father spoke next. "They tried to kill me in World War II."

"Dad, be fair. Those were Japanese. Korea was our ally a few years back."

Coles Carter sniffed his contempt. "The Oriental mind is all the same. They come from a common genetic cesspool. They are vicious and merciless and heathen." At that moment, he pushed away from the table, the flair in his cheeks like rouge against his pale, sedentary skin. He turned and walked toward the stairs, which he climbed with an aggression audible through the carpet. Coleman looked toward me, staring down at my plate. He turned to his mother.

"I had a feeling this might upset you."

She lifted her plate and with her head down broke for the kitchen, from which no sound issued for several minutes. Coleman and I sat there. To avoid staring at me, he made circular impressions on the linen tablecloth with his fork while the clock above the sideboard ticked with what sounded like small explosions in the stillness. At length, we heard Sarah leave the kitchen and mount the stairs.

"Like I told you. A piece of cake," he said.

"They need some time to get used to the idea."

"Elizabeth, you're speaking of people who are still trying to reconcile losing the Civil War. I wouldn't look for any sudden conversions."

"I know they're conservative. They reacted about like you predicted."

Coleman shook his head. "Not really. I've never seen my father like that. Never."

"He's got to come around. Adopting a child is not something that tears a family apart."

He propped his chin on his fist to gaze at me directly. "You know that coffee table book written on Mother's family? The one that traces her people back to the boat? Have you ever looked through it?" I nodded. "How many Orientals did you see? That's what I've been trying to tell you. They're southern, and family means something here that it doesn't mean anywhere else."

"We're not going to back out."

"I wasn't suggesting that. Just be patient with them. They're getting older, and changes frighten them. Changes like this terrify them."

"Just promise me one thing."

"What?"

"You'll be firm."

"I promise," he said, although I sensed doubt as he said it.

The next day, Coleman arose early to pack the car. His father retrieved the newspaper from the driveway and read it over coffee. He turned the pages with more crispness than usual. The boys slept in, then wolfed down bowls of cereal before dashing off for a final bike ride. In the kitchen, over breakfast dishes, Sarah asked me to accompany her on a walk.

"We won't be gone fifteen minutes," she said, doing her best to sound lighthearted. I was not fooled, but saw no exit.

We left the house and walked down Church Street to the Battery. "I brought this heavy sweater but I certainly won't need it today," Sarah said as we sought a bench in the sunlight. I just waited.

"What I'm about to say," Sarah began, "will sound like I'm injecting myself into your personal business; yours and Coleman's. We've always tried to avoid that. I think we've been successful there, don't you?" I nodded, and I meant it. "It's hard, I don't mind telling you. It's hard when you see your children making mistakes you think they could avoid; making mistakes which your experience tells you they'll regret. Still, you have to respect their right to make them, hard as it is to keep quiet. You'll see this clearly as your boys grow up."

At that moment, her voice softened. Her tone turned reverential. "My parents, especially my father, were so strict with me. Why, I couldn't even choose my clothes or hairstyle until I got to college. I rebelled, I can tell you. I fought hard against restrictions I felt were totally unreasonable, although looking back, I can see I dug in my heels on the minor issues and did what they wanted on the major ones. But they were determined to 'bring me up southern,' as my father termed it. For so long, I had no concept of what that meant. I mean, every girl in Darlington grew up southern as far as I could see. It was only after I was married and moved around during the war that I began to understand a bit. By then I was in my late twenties, about your age, actually.

"The people out west and in New England, where we were stationed while Coles was teaching at OCS, were friendly, most of them, and very nice to us. But those people didn't have the sense of identity I felt with the South. You could tell it right away. Whenever I met someone I liked, I wanted them to come to Darlington, to meet my parents and brothers and sisters and aunts and uncles and cousins, to have a big Sunday dinner and cut the fool with everyone around the table. I actually invited some of them; they thought I was crazy, I'm sure, driving fifteen hundred miles to meet someone's relatives. The point is, those people were my identity. I belonged to them and they belonged to me. Are you getting warm? I can't believe this is December."

"It is heating up," I acknowledged. As much as I wanted this conversation behind me, I knew my mother-in-law would have her say and I had resolved to hear her out. More from obligation than desire, I said, "Why don't we sit under a tree?"

"I was thinking of just that," Sarah said. We crossed the park, stopping at a bench shaded by a mammoth, gnarled oak, surely old enough to have witnessed the firing on Ft. Sumter. Along the promenade railing, a couple passed a set of binoculars between them while nearby a man with a telephoto lens trained his camera on the island fortress in the harbor. Pigeons flapped about, indifferent to tourists.

"I was talking about identity," Sarah continued. "This child you are considering. I wonder what identity she'll feel in a strange land surrounded by people who are so obviously different."

"But what is her alternative?" I resolved to be patient. "The Koreans don't adopt girls. I would think it would be worse to be in a country where you look the same but are treated like an alien."

Sarah cocked her head slightly and stared ahead. "Well, I suppose you have a point. But dear, you can't save the world. What will she do to your family's sense of identity? You've your children to consider."

"Of course. We wouldn't do anything that would hurt the boys."

"Naturally you wouldn't, which is my point. You don't think it will hurt. You probably think it will be an interesting experience for them. But in time you will come to see what I have seen; that family is the most important thing on earth, and bringing a stranger into yours will be a disservice to you and to her. You'll see."

"Maybe," I said, turning away.

"Let's take a stroll around the square," Sarah suggested. We walked west, to the Ft. Sumter Hotel, then turned north. "You see these grand old homes?" she asked. "Some of the finest families in the world live here. People think they're snobbish, and I suppose they are. But their clannishness is an effort to protect what so many people in this country seem to want to tear down or dilute. I admire them for it. Coles grew up here, and he can walk into any house on the South Battery and be the equal of anyone inside. That's a valuable heritage that Coleman enjoys and your sons will too. But this child will never be a part of that world."

"Which may be a loss for them."

Sarah shook her head slowly. "I believe that's wishful thinking. There is another matter you should consider."

"What is that?"

"My son, your husband. I know this was your idea. He didn't need to tell me that."

"Yes, we guessed you'd make that assumption."

"If Coleman agrees to this, he's doing it for you. Deep down, he agrees with me. I know because of the way he was brought up. He can't divorce his heritage, no matter how hard he wants to please you. Perhaps it is unfair to put him in this position?"

"Coleman is a grown man. He can say no if he chooses. I'm not forcing this on him."

Sarah just smiled at that, a doubtful smile that said she didn't believe me for a moment. "Good," she said, reaching over to pat me on the arm. "You two talk it over. Pray over it. The right decision will emerge."

We returned toward the house, making small talk for the duration of our walk. I had known it would come, eventually but inevitably, to where we left it. I would be the culprit, manipulating Sarah's blameless son into a scheme he opposed and exposing Sarah's grandsons to the Red peril, which in Sarah's view had begun taking over America on the day the Japanese built their first transistor radio. "They've taken all those jobs from those poor people in Detroit. I'd rather die than drive a Honda." At the root of Sarah's xenophobia were the Communists, those tireless devils whose agent on earth was the Trilateral Commission. And the list went on: Robert E. Lee and Barry Goldwater were defeated but right, a woman's place was in the home, "separate but equal" was "a sound policy which should never have been abandoned" and mankind took a giant step toward eternal damnation when the Episcopal Church approved the new Book of Common Prayer.

I perfectly understood my impatience with Sarah. We disagreed on everything from abortion to Vietnam, from cooking vegetables (Sarah cooked broccoli for forty-five minutes, until it was literally beyond recognition) to toilet training. On the other hand, she possessed an elusive quality which drew me to her even as I had not been drawn to my own mother. It went beyond our mutual interest in Coleman, for Sarah loved her son uncritically and without reserve while I had come to a point in my life that I couldn't say that, although I had said it when we married and thought I meant it. Marriage has taught me how difficult it is to love another person, any person, uncritically, and logic tells me it must be just as hard for anyone to love me that way. I'm convinced Sarah sees Coleman as perfect, rationalizing the imperfections as you might choose not to notice a tiny crack in your favorite mirror. Love for a spouse can't be that way. You see the flaws, and he sees yours. The trick is to look past them, to the compensating qualities that brought you to him in the first place. I've even come to recognize my own flaws, at least some of them. I'm judgmental, for one, with little patience for those who disagree with me, particularly when they can't back up whatever it is we disagree on. Uncritical love is a rare commodity, reserved for children I suppose. My love for Josh and Steven mirrors Sarah's love for Coleman, and soon I will bestow that same kind of love on a child that may or may not have been born. Coleman says he isn't sure he can love an adopted daughter that way. I'm betting he can, and that he will experience that sooner than he thinks. Sarah? Will she love her granddaughter as she loves her grandsons? I wonder.

As we approached the front door, Josh came bounding out of the house. "Mom, Grandma!" he yelled, nearly tripping as he reached us. "You should see Steven! Blood everywhere. His whole head is blood, blood, blood!"

I froze. "Josh, what are you talking about?"

"Steven's head. He fell down on his bike and he couldn't see after that because he had blood in his eyes and everywhere."

My heart raced as I felt my knees and legs weaken. I grabbed Josh by his shoulder. "Where is he?"

"Daddy and granddaddy took him off. In the car."

"Where were they going?" I demanded.

"Someplace to get the blood out of his eyes. You should have seen him, mom. I got some on my hands."

I looked down. The sight of the red smears sickened me. "Oh, God. Get in the car, Josh. Sarah, where would they have gone."

"Well, I'm just not sure," said Sarah.

"Well, get sure!" I screamed. "Let's go find them." I got behind the wheel as Josh and Sarah entered the passenger side. I backed wildly down the driveway, narrowly avoiding a car parked on the street, threw the shift into forward, simultaneously hitting the gas and spinning my tires on the cobblestones. With a death grip on the wheel, I maneuvered through the neighborhood. Sarah held Josh as he explained, yet again, how much blood covered Steven. "Josh, please!" I pleaded.

Sarah, refocused, gave directions to the emergency room as her eyes widened and the speedometer climbed. We jammed on brakes at a traffic light that stayed red for minutes, causing me to first pound the wheel in frustration, then gun the car through the light, still red. I almost collided with a bread truck, avoiding disaster only by a sudden swerve onto a sidewalk. At the hospital, I pulled into the ER lot, parked so as to fill two spaces, and threw open my door. "Wait here," I called as I slammed the door. Seconds later, I entered the building.

My father-in-law sat in the reception area, his eyes focused on the magazine in his lap.

"What happened?" I demanded.

"Oh, just a little accident," he said calmly. "Steven fell off his bike."

"But the blood!"

"He cut his forehead, but a few stitches should do it, according to the doctor. Coleman's with him." He nodded toward the double doors.

I found them in a harshly lit cubicle cordoned off by a green curtain. On the table lay Steven, his eyes open and riveted on the white-coated man hovering over him. On the other side of the gurney stood Coleman, who looked up from the intricate work being done on Steven's forehead.

"Hi, dear," he said cheerfully. "Looks like we're going to get a late start on the trip home."

Steven started to turn his head toward me but was restrained by the doctor, whose fingers bracketed the child's forehead as his thumb and forefingers did the work. I knelt beside, holding his hand and whispering words of comfort as the doctor cautioned him against sudden movements.

"You wouldn't want me to make a mistake and sew your nose shut, would you?" Steven's eyes widened momentarily until the laughter of the adults, even mine, reassured him.

Ten minutes and four stitches later, the doctor announced he was through, but wanted Steven kept still for a time. I thought it best to drive

Sarah and Josh, still waiting in the car, home while Coleman waited for Steven to be released. On my way to the parking lot, I offered a ride to my father-in-law, but he declined.

8

Coleman

While I didn't look forward to our time in Charleston, knowing the tempest that would ensue when we broke the news, I always enjoyed the trip itself. Holiday traffic in New Hampton receded as we crossed the wide expanse of the James River, cold and foreboding with choppy whitecaps stretching to the Chesapeake Bay. An hour later, as we entered North Carolina, the excitement of the trip gave way to fatigue, and I found myself the only one awake. I count the solitude of a long drive, unmarred by radios or conversation, among life's simple pleasures.

I glanced at Elizabeth, dozing against her headrest, remembering that my second view of her had been in profile, like this one. In a larger sense I had been attempting to profile her ever since. Beyond the complex chemistries that explain mutual attractions, I sensed in her certain strengths and sensitivities I felt I lacked. I told her as much on our honeymoon.

"Yes?" she said. "Like what? Name them and don't leave any out." I hit her playfully with a pillow but she persisted. "I'm waiting." We were in Barbados, still in bed at three in the afternoon.

"You have . . . intuition," I said. "You trust your instincts more than I trust mine. I'm too analytical."

"Are you saying I'm not analytical?"

"You pay more attention to your passions. I wish I was more that way."

"You've been doing alright in the passion department for the past three days."

"You know what I mean."

We met, or re-met, as it turned out, in May 1970. She had been up all night, as had I. The month before, U.S. forces based in Vietnam had invaded Cambodia, seeking to destroy guerrilla bases in an area called the Parrot's Beak. Four days later, amidst antiwar outrage, the Ohio National

Guard shot and killed four students during a protest at Kent State. Riots swept campuses of the nation's top universities. I was in my senior year at the University of Virginia. The very last thing we needed tossed into our academic bunker, a bunker filled with seniors worried about the draft, sophomores angry about everything, and wannabe revolutionaries who would eventually go to business school, was the hand grenade unpinned when William Kunstler, a New York attorney who had achieved national notoriety by his defense of the Chicago Seven, and Jerry Rubin, a Kunstler client and a platoon leader in the antiwar army, came to Charlottesville to give a speech. They packed University Hall, otherwise used for basketball, and worked the crowd into a maniacal froth. Rumors abounded that some building or feature of Mr. Jefferson's academic village would that night be sacrificed on an altar of revolution; that only by fire could the righteousness of the peace movement be sanctified.

Many opposed Kunstler, Rubin, their entourage, and their politics. Many more recoiled at the thought of torching the living history the Rotunda represented. A call went out for student volunteers to stand guard that night against any act of vandalism directed at university property.

I volunteered. Like so many with whom I would soon stand on that same lawn to take our degrees, I cursed the war for its toll, its ineptitude, its strategic schizophrenia, its mushrooming divisiveness, its monumental waste. But the war was in Southeast Asia, and I was there, in lovely Charlottesville, where every student feels, in varying degrees, the presence of Mr. Jefferson. I listened to all the zealots spouting quotes from the great man himself, quotes that they insisted justified and even encouraged the kind of revolt they felt part of, the "tree of liberty" to be liberally watered with the "blood of tyrants" like LBJ. All well and good, I thought, but not at his university, on his grounds, at the cost of his magnificent architecture. And not on my watch. Perhaps, I reasoned, if approached by anarchists set on destruction, I could talk them down, distract them, convince them that a target more replaceable was somehow more suitable.

They assigned me to one end of Cabell Hall's portico. With another student I did not know, I manned my barricade, drinking black coffee from a dented green hunting thermos and talking with curious students who ambled by with fresh gossip but no hard facts. One rumor held that Rubin, at that moment, was massing a mob at a student crossroads known as "the corner." Another: that Rubin and Kunstler had gone to dinner at the Farmington Country Club and retired early. By 3:00 A.M., the coffee was cold, the grounds quiet, and a humid chill had settled over the lush mall leading to the Rotunda. My companion yawned, stretched, declared victory and left, abandoning me within shouting distance only of the hardcore cadre stationed at likely targets. At dawn, I spotted a group of five or six people advancing toward me. My pulse quickened as I sought to make them out in the dimness. I heard a female laugh, and from it reasoned that these must be doubtful arsonists, so I spoke. One woman offered the fact that they had come from another college to hear Kunstler, then stayed for the prospect of witnessing some historic havoc—Beach Week with a conscience. They traded rumors each had heard, not for their truth or falsity but for their aberrance. By now, it seemed plain that the campus would survive. What had happened became less interesting than all the things that could have occurred.

The women began walking away just as the sun rose behind Monticello and the first beams of a new day followed them through Cabell Hall's colonnade, and at the moment I told myself I had seen the last of them, that my twelve hour shift defending Mr. Jefferson's Lawn had ended and I could get some sleep—at that instant she had hesitated, offering me a momentary view of her profile. She fell out of step with her denim-clad comrades, then turned to me, squinting into the sunrise, and said, "I know you." I tried to place her, but four years had passed and much had changed since 1966, and at that moment she looked vaguely like every coed I had met during that brooding era.

"Elizabeth Hetzel. Hollins?"

Then I remembered. As she faced me, testing my memory and squinting into the morning coming up behind me, I mentally sheared off the tangle of curls framing her lovely face to summon her image as it must have appeared to me on that blind date our freshman year. "Sure," I said. "We went to Tony's. You ordered pizza with pineapple on it. I didn't know they put pineapple on pizza."

"Not bad," she said, grinning. Then, turning back to her friends, she urged them to go on; she would catch up. We talked for two and a half hours. I learned things I must have learned on our blind date but forgotten. And, I learned she had arresting eyes I did not remember. Bands of welcoming brown were set off by harder bronze flecks seemingly embedded, like mica glinting in the light. By the time we had made a date for later in the week the sun was well up and I craved sleep at any price.

I glanced at the rear view mirror at my sons, our sons, their heads canted inward on a common pillow. Josh favored his mother in appearance, but had my mellow disposition. Steven seemed the reverse. Their births mirrored their development; Josh, long and labored and Steven, shorter and to the point. Heredity's irrefutable markings at the chins, the noses, incipient eyebrows. With shallow breaths, nostrils flaring faintly, and their brows unfurrowed by a single care they slept, their trust in me complete.

By the time I turned onto the interstate they were awake, playing a car game that awarded points for cows counted and deducting them for cemeteries passed. A mileage sign, confirming progress south, renewed my dread of the impending announcement. I tried to recall if the subject of adoption had ever come up with my parents. Did they ever consider adopting a sibling for me, their only child? I doubted it. The lone reference to adoption I could remember involved a cousin, orphaned by a house fire and taken in by a cousin more distant. While I had no basis to believe my parents disliked or disapproved of the concept, I knew it would strike them as a strange, even bizarre commitment for parents who were neither childless nor forced by circumstances to assume other parents' responsibilities. The very idea would be as foreign to them as an announcement that I was leaving Elizabeth and our sons to join the priesthood–noble enough, but under the circumstances a form of mental imbalance.

Elizabeth, on the other hand, always traveled with certain angst on visits to family, hers or mine. Holidays, in particular, depressed her, for reasons I never fully understood and she articulated vaguely, with adumbrated explanations like "not happy times." When I pressed, she withdrew, a morose distancing. In days preceding them, I watched her steel herself against whatever demons preyed upon her, and for a day or two into the visit she held up, bright-eyed and spirited. But it didn't last, and her moods became cloudy, overcast. If she felt heightened angst at this trip's agenda, it didn't show.

We stopped for fast food. The boys fought over french fries while Elizabeth doctored her coffee with her standard three sugars and two creams.

Entering South Carolina, we drove through rural towns, where shoppers walked Main Streets in search of sales and overhanging strings of red and green Christmas lights swayed in the wind.

Sixty miles from Charleston, we entered the Francis Marion National Forest, a thirty-mile stretch of unbroken isolation. A two lane road divided pines tall enough to throw the roadway into deep shadow by mid-afternoon. Here, the boys always wanted to sing, and I agreed. I grew up with the Kingston Trio and Brothers Four and remembered four or five of their ballads I intended to pass down. In full voice and errant pitch we sang, "This is the story 'bout Eddie-cochin-catchinarin-tosanearin-tosanokin-samma-kamma-whacky Brown." When we reached the last line, "Took so long to say his name that Eddie-cochin-catchinarin-tosanearin-tosanokin-samma-kamma-whacky Brown . . . drowned," we burst into laughter, always. Then it was on to *MTA* and *Blue Water Line* and the rest. One day our grandchildren will be learning those words from an off-key driver and I hope to live long enough to hear them.

Thirty miles beyond the forest, the air turned identifiably coastal, hinting of salt marsh and dried oyster banks. We crossed the high twin humps of the Cooper River Bridge, then turned down East Bay. Elizabeth gathered her things before pivoting for a quick visual inspection of the boys, crowded against the rear doors in anticipation. One last turn and I felt the familiar rumble of the cobblestones on Church Street, then saw my home, an antebellum, piazza-lined house a block from the Battery. Mom and Dad met us in the driveway.

Dad was a willowy man two inches taller than me. Even now, at age seventy, black hair predominated his head and eyebrows, and only with the onset of his illness had flecks of gray appeared. At the cheekbones, a network of blood vessels near the surface gave his skin an artificial robustness, belied by the sallow hollows in the cheeks themselves and the absence of color from his lips. A downy film of gray whiskers told me he had not shaved that morning. He had lost weight since my last visit, but his movements were sturdy, his handshake firm.

I hugged Mother and stretched my legs as the others exchanged greetings.

"That drive doesn't get any shorter," I said as Josh hugged his grandmother.

"How did you come?" asked my father, and I, who always came the same way, related it again to him, who put the same question to me after every trip.

That evening, as Elizabeth talked in the kitchen with Mother and the boys rediscovered the magic hidden inside the games drawer of the old sideboard, I retreated to the piazza off the upstairs den, leaving the French doors open. The wooden swing at the far end groaned under my weight. I pushed back, raised my feet, and felt a puff of salt air brush past me as the swing commenced its pendulum. Above, the "s" hooks at the end of their supporting chains creaked against the eye bolts augured into the ceiling as the harbor, faintly visible through the palmetto tree at the opposite end, appeared, then disappeared, with my line of sight. Winter stillness pervaded the yard below, so that while the unseasonably balmy temperatures suggested the monotone serenade of cicadas, no sound competed with the metronomic clicking from above. I breathed in, filling my lungs with the saline humidity that was as much a part of my boyhood as the maple bed in my room or the Little League trophy on my bookcase.

Out of the silence came footsteps in the hall. Looking right, I saw through the window beside the swing the outline of my father in the hallway leading to the den. "Dad! On the piazza." Moments later Dad's silhouette appeared in the doorway.

"Peaceful tonight," he offered, paused as though uncertain of whether to cross the threshold.

"Can't beat it," I said from the recessed darkness of the swing. "You would think that with us being near the same water a few hundred miles north the air would be the same, but it isn't."

My father made no reply. The overhead clicking seemed amplified in the lull.

"It's good to be home," I said.

"I saw Barron Morris a few days ago at a Christmas party. He asked about you. Wanted to know how you liked your practice and whether you had ever given any thought to coming back here. He said to call him next time you're in town."

"I'll do that," I said, mildly intrigued by this overture from one of Charleston's premier attorneys. An inspiration seized me to tell my father the answers to Morris's questions, but before I could begin Dad turned and walked away, so that light from the den again filled the unobstructed doorway. Perhaps Dad sensed what was coming; sensed that I was about to embark upon the kind of personal disclosure that, in the rare occurrences of the past, left my father silent, unable to respond and embarrassed by it. I gave the floor a forceful thrust and continued swinging.

On the day before we were scheduled to return to Virginia, Elizabeth pressed me to broach the issue at lunch, but lunch came and went as I grew steadily more impatient with my own apprehension. I had felt more relaxed in front of juries in death penalty cases. To kill time, I read a novel and then wandered aimlessly about the house. I grew up here, and all about me were the remembered relics of my youth: furniture, photographs, lamps, baseball and football pennants. I lingered at a photograph framed above my dresser. There was my childhood friend, Philip, grinning from the seat of a new bicycle. Philip died in Vietnam, while I was in law school. I took a nap. The afternoon waned.

I know my "buy a gook" comment at supper took Elizabeth by surprise, but we share a dark sense of humor and I needed something to counter the tension I felt building. Mother set such a nice table in honor of our last night. She shuffled in and out of the kitchen, mumbling to herself as she brought rice and cauliflower, snap beans and coleslaw, ham and artichoke pickle. Her disorganization was legendary, but she possessed the gentlest soul I had ever encountered. It was not unusual to find, in the kitchen after a sumptuous meal, a prepared dish on which she might have invested an hour's labor, only to forget to place it on the table. On such occasions, she laughed at herself along with everyone else, proffering explanations for her absent-mindedness which provoked ever more laughter. People sensed, with the barest exposure to her, that anything said to her in anger or pique would hurt her beyond rejoinder, leaving the tormentor wounded by his own sword. I prized her congenital tenderness and testing it, as I would momentarily, disturbed me deeply.

I knew generally Dad's attitude about Asians. Over the years, and especially during Vietnam, he made comments that evidenced a finely honed racism. His hawkish support for what we were doing there had nothing to do with the rights of South Vietnamese to live free from Communism. He didn't much care what system they lived under or, truth be told, whether they lived at all. His rationale for putting men and money over there, and possibly his only son, found its footing in the need to stand up to the Chinese, who he was convinced aspired to world domination. A classic domino theorist. But his expression at supper of disdain for all Asians shocked me. Voicing his most heartfelt feelings, on that or anything else, shocked me. Maybe he felt ambushed. Neither he nor Mom had a clue this was coming, so I was prepared to allow them some latitude in their response. The extent of Elizabeth's charity I would learn later.

Mother, on the other hand, followed the unwritten script to the final line. Ladies do not vent in public. They pick up dishes with dignity and adjourn to another room. She could not have cared less about the domino theory. For her, millions of slant-eyed yellow people in the Pacific, all dedicated to making her a war widow three years into her marriage, said all she needed to know. Her particular xenophobia ran to anyone living outside the South, and the emotion was not hatred or even dislike. She followed the Christian mandate to love thy neighbor—she just loved her southern neighbors more. For her, southerners were a breed chosen by God to represent all that was good and true and decent in the human race, and non-southerners, "some very nice people," she would allow, simply fell short of that standard. When I became engaged to Elizabeth, she took solace in Elizabeth's southern college education, but deep down she was asking the question that always obsessed her: "Who are your people, dear?" I once asked Mother if she had been disappointed I had not married a woman from the South. She hesitated, weighing her words, before telling me in a tone close to professorial that the choice of a mate involved a host of considerations, geographic origin being but one of many. I knew she didn't really mean that, and she knew it too. But by then Josh and Steven had come along, and grandchildren will bridge more divides than any force on earth. Then, as an afterthought, she said, "Your father and I never insisted on a girl from Charleston. There were charming girls in Columbia, too."

As if the adoption discussion were not crisis enough for one trip, Steven fell off his bike and cut his head on the morning we were to leave. Elizabeth arrived at the hospital as they were sewing him up. He'll be fine, the doctor assured me. The small scar will fade in time.

Dad and I drove home in silence. Steven rested his temple against the back seat, seemingly spent from his adventure. Before the station wagon came to a stop, Elizabeth emerged from the house to escort the patient inside. Clinging to her arm, he walked slowly and with his head down toward the house. I would have been with him but for Dad's comment as I turned off the engine. "Let's talk a minute."

I did not move because I could not move, so totally arrested by what would have passed, between others, as a routine overture. Unlike Elizabeth, who had anticipated the lecture she had received from Sarah that morning, I expected silence. But I saw now, in my father's grip on the door handle, his rigid body braced as if expecting some jarring impact, and his refusal to look at me directly, the very anguish which would render this moment, for me, indelible. For the first time, Dad's mask of anonymity slipped an inch, just enough for me to glimpse the pain behind the four simple words he had just uttered. Small wonder he hadn't spoken them more often or, to my memory, ever. His discomfort spread immediately across the space separating us physically, so that without consciousness I gripped my door handle, as if bracing.

I had seen, in the faces of witnesses at trial or deposition, an insecurity that bore some of the markings now exhibited by Dad's awkward stiffness and his effort to modulate his voice, and I had assigned that discomfiture to the intimidation which looms over one in stressful, defensive surroundings when confronted by another for whom that same environment is as relaxed as an overstuffed chair in the den at home. Growing up, we discussed politics with informal ground rules more appropriate to a confessional. No interrupting, no raised voices, considered regard for the other's opinion. But even these "arguments" occurred when Dad had armored himself in the mail of alcohol. He was not an alcoholic when measured on scales of frequency of use or quantities of consumption. By only one such measure could he have been, arguably, addicted, and that was his helpless dependency in the face of personal interaction or confrontation. Alone, he needed no anesthesia of the spirit, but venturing beyond his mental and emotional borders required the courage found in a cocktail and without it he stood at the edge of crowds, covered by a carapace of introversion, as hard and impenetrable as an oyster.

Looking straight ahead and still gripping the door handle, he cleared his throat. "If, ah, you and Elizabeth decide to go through with this idea of yours, what . . . ah, will you name her?"

I stared evenly at his profile. "We picked out Allison for a girl years ago, but of course we haven't had a chance to use it."

"I meant the last name."

"Carter. What else?"

Dad turned toward me, and on his face he wore a florid look of undisguised rage, his features contorted into a twisted malevolence that caused me to look away. "You're going to give our family name to some slant-eyed nobody. Unbelievable." He jerked at the handle, sprang from the car, and slammed the door behind him. He had marched up the walk almost to the house before I realized I had not taken a breath since the word "nobody."

I remained in the car, my breathing returning to normal as I relaxed my grip on the door handle and my heart rate slowed. I stared at the front door as if expecting Dad, against all logic and experience, to return. Instead, Elizabeth emerged from the house carrying clothes. Together, we packed the car in silence. Sarah alone kissed us goodbye, gave the boys candy for the ride home, and stood in the driveway waving until we turned out of sight.

In the late afternoon, as the car left the brooding desolation of the Francis Marion National Forest, I turned down the radio and, prompted by a sadness that had been with me since our departure and had deepened with the distance from Charleston and the moodiness of the forest, said to Elizabeth, "Why do I feel like I just left my parents with a dozen dead roses?"

"What an odd thing to say. They'll get over it—you said so yourself. They'll be mad for a few days until they've had a chance to get used to the idea. Don't worry about it. I'm not."

I fell silent again. Dead flowers, perhaps suggested by the moss hanging ghoulishly from oaks. The image wouldn't leave me. I had felt their anger, yes, but beyond anger, suffering, from a wound I had inflicted. The world made less sense to me than it had four days earlier. It was as though some fundamental law of physics had been breached in the materialization of suffering out of thin air. Matter had indeed been created. By what? Not the birth of a child but the mere prospect of an anonymous child in a country I wasn't positive I could locate on an unmarked map. How was that possible? It seemed in remoteness the equivalent of an American catching a cold across the Atlantic from a sneeze, not by a European but the ghost of a European. And now, because of some spirit once removed, I had carried those dead suffering flowers to South Carolina.

It didn't have to be this way, I decided. If matter could be created, it could be destroyed. I could stop this process before it went further. But doing so meant bringing the dead flowers back to Virginia and delivering them to Elizabeth. No matter what I did, someone I loved would end up holding those flowers.

I thought about it all the way home. Crossing the James River Bridge late that night, I very much needed to hear the reassuring strains of *Samma-Kamma-Whacky Brown,* but Elizabeth and the boys were sleeping soundly and I did not wake them.

9

Elizabeth

Like most people, I do some things because I want to and a lot more because I have to. The midwinter ball at the Riverside Country Club is always for me a "have to," because the crowd it drew consisted of many of the same people we saw all the time, only for this they dressed up. I'll bet a committee of women started it as an excuse to wear their fur coats, which they do even on the mildest evenings, and you could count on Sandra Hallet sporting her sable—a fucking sable—like we lived in Moscow, and you could count on me getting slightly drunk when I saw her because the I've-got-more-money-than-you bitch drove me up a wall. I went because it was important to Coleman, or he said it was.

It had been a month since we left Charleston, and while we hadn't heard from his parents I felt sure they had calmed down by now, resigned to the idea and maybe even a little excited at the prospect of another grandchild, the last they will have if I had any say in the matter, which of course I did.

I needed a dress for the midwinter thing, so I stood in my closet going through my better dresses one at a time, trying to remember the last time I wore what and whether the same people would have been there and the odds were good to the point of certainty that they had been. Another reason I hated this ball was that it always brought up the old argument with Coleman about becoming members, which he was very much in favor of and I had zero interest in. The club was all white (no Jews, either) and the wait staff was all black. This was not a coincidence, because the kind of bigotry practiced at Riverside was the subtle kind passed down through generations. Coleman said no minorities ever applied, and I didn't doubt it because who wanted to be the Lone Ranger at that picnic? But don't peg me as some high-minded altruist, because the simple truth is I'm not a club type of person, which is why I turned down the Junior League soon after we arrived, and if you think that didn't wad the panties of every member you don't know New Hampton because I got no fewer than four telephone calls asking if I'd made a mistake, checked the wrong box by mistake, the last caller telling me no one had ever refused membership. I heard Coleman come into the room just as I was deciding on a dress.

From inside the closet I said, "I really have nothing to wear to this thing, but I refuse to spend a lot of money just to please these people."

"Elizabeth, you say 'these people' like they're lepers."

"You know how much I love country club functions. You would think they would get sick of each other."

"I want you to try to be a little more charitable where the club is concerned."

I came out of the closet, a black silk dress draped over my arm. "Why should I?" He sat at the bedroom desk, a pencil in hand and the monthly bank statement spread before him.

"Because this could be important to our future. These midwinter balls are the traditional stockyards where members get to inspect new meat on the hoof, so to speak."

"I told you before I don't want to be a member of the Riverside Country Club. Surely we can find better uses for the several thousand dollars a year we would have to pay in dues, not to mention the initiation fee. What do you think of this dress?"

"You know I love that dress."

"Have I worn it lately? I can't remember."

"You wore it to the Cancer Society Benefit last year. I spilled a drink on it."

"That's right. Oh, there it is. I'll get it cleaned tomorrow. Where's your tux? I'll take it, too."

"Behind the door of the closet. Let's get back to membership in the club."

"Do we have to?"

"First, we don't pay initiation or dues, the firm pays. Second, the firm expects us to join. We're on Donald and Cynthia Mahoney's invitation list, and when the firm's rainmaker puts you on his list, it's more than an invitation. And it means we'll be asked to join unless you get drunk and moon the orchestra."

I sat down at my dressing table, fingering earrings in the top drawer of the mahogany jewelry box he gave me on our fifth wedding anniversary. "Well, I can't be expected to moon the orchestra sober." I glanced at him and grinned playfully, but he wasn't amused.

"I'm being dead serious, Elizabeth. I have to practice law in this town and to afford such luxuries as food and shelter I've got to go where the clients go. Like it or not, that means the club."

"But there are so many lawyers in it already."

"It doesn't matter. It's a base we need to touch. I don't make the rules, I just try to play by them."

"I'm going, aren't I? I'm outfitting myself more than thirty minutes before we walk out the door. That should tell you something."

"You have a point. Just please make an effort on this. It's important for all of us; you, me and the children."

"I'll do it for you, but I don't have to like it."

Coleman tossed aside his pencil. "What's not to like?" he demanded, his voice rising. "It's a party, for God's sake. You know, people dressed up, food, drinks, laughter, dancing. Most people have fun at that sort of thing."

My voice rose to meet his. "You grew up with 'that sort of thing,' as you put it. It makes me uncomfortable, like people are judging me. Besides, they're narrow-minded and exclusionary."

He stood, crossed the room with an angry stride and closed the door. Wheeling, he said, "Don't be troubled by gross generalities."

I shrank back momentarily, caught off-guard by the force of his reaction. "Not all of them, of course. But quite a few. Besides, are there any blacks in the club yet?"

"Now we're getting somewhere! This is all wrapped up in your bleeding heart liberal tripe that will one day force our sons to marry Eskimos to prove their egalitarian upbringing. The club has no black members because no blacks apply. It has no Jews because the Jews have their own club that looks down its nose at Riverside. Why are you turning a simple party invitation into an ethnic litmus test?"

"I said I'd go." If Sandra Hallet is there, I'll scream.

The next day I had coffee with my dear friend, Betsy Miller, who listened patiently as I predicted that spring would bring new life into my home and my marriage. I'm sure I sounded more hopeful than certain.

Betsy wasn't so sure, and said so. "The last time I brought it up he changed the subject."

She and I have been best friends for as long as we have lived in New Hampton, and it was only to her that I could impart the doubts I found myself suppressing. Slim and smart, Betsy has been mistaken for my sister more than once.

Mid-morning sun filtered through the breakfast room. Betsy brought her cup down firmly, as if to punctuate a thought just completed. "What you need is a face. For this baby to become a person instead of an idea."

"You think?" I said. "If he doesn't like the idea . . ."

"I'm not talking about him."

"I can hardly sleep now I'm so eager."

"I see that," said my friend, "but you'll need more. I loved being pregnant, but once Jessica was born I realized that for nine months I had been wrapped up in becoming a mother, which is not the same as being wrapped up in your child. Of course, it only takes .5 seconds to make the switch, but you know what I mean."

I nodded at a distance, newly conscious of a truth that had been lurking, waiting for a conversation like this to be seen in full light. The idea of adopting an Asian child held me in a certain grip; would the grip of the child herself be as strong? I narrowed my eyes. "Why are you complicating my life?"

Betsy laughed. "Me? Would I do that? Don't answer."

"Is this payback for some sin I'm unaware of?"

"Hell, no," she replied. "I'll let you know when you've sinned. It's the only way to keep score."

Perhaps it was the karma of that coffee that brought an envelope from Open Arms in the afternoon mail. I opened it expecting correspondence, but instead found an infant looking up at me from a passport size photograph, a blanket pulled to her waist concealing all but her head and arms. A small, red pull toy rested at her side. "Soo Yun," said the paper to which the photo was attached, along with a brief description of her as having a pleasing face, a pleasant disposition, and normal bowels. And that was it, the sum total of the information upon which we would check a block at the bottom: yes or no.

I called Coleman's office, but he was in court and I had to settle for his secretary's promise that when he returned she would tell him to come home immediately. I paced the living room, the paper in my hand, looking at Soo Yun every few seconds and staring at the two boxes at the bottom: yes or no. Every woman knows the potential significance of those two words, but in this context they loomed larger than any two words I'd ever read. Yes or no, one or the other, and no matter which I checked I knew that lives, hers and ours, would be forever altered by the choice, and altered not just for decades but for generations. For the first time I felt overwhelmed. One sparse paragraph of information on a child we'd never met to decide the futures at stake in such a decision. The lottery of procreation is one thing, because at least you've had a choice in your mate even if you have none as to which of his sperm wins the race to your egg, so you accept, love and embrace the random result as ordained by God or chemistry or fate. The inevitability of it all is more comfort than most parents acknowledge; the fact that your son or daughter is the way they are depends, at least at the beginning, on a biological card shuffle, and you willingly play the hand you are dealt. But this!!

I was still pacing when I heard Coleman's car in the driveway. By then I knew her face as well as I knew his, and while it might sound like an exaggeration—okay, it does sound like that, even to me—I thought I could have picked her out from thousands of others. Something in the way she stared up at me, a connection that wouldn't dissolve no matter how many times I looked away. I danced with excitement as he entered the foyer and I threw my arms around his neck.

"Yes," I said. "We need to check yes." I showed him the photo, still clutched in my hand. "Meet our daughter, Soo Yun," I said.

He stared at her for a few seconds. "She looks like your Uncle Mort."

I slapped him playfully on the arm. "You idiot. Tell the truth. She's beautiful."

His eyes grazed over the printed page to which the photograph was affixed. "Soo Yun . . . healthy . . . presumed to be of full Korean parentage . . ." He flipped the page, then looked lamely at me. "Is that it?"

"I guess so."

"Open Arms didn't exactly bog us down in detail."

"It doesn't matter," I said, staring at the picture. "She's perfect. I want to call Open Arms today."

"No. When you call, if you call, we're going to do it together. This is a huge decision."

"But what are we waiting for?"

"For me," he said. "I haven't heard a word from my folks. I need to go down there to talk with them. Alone."

"I see," I said, sliding the papers back into the envelope and feeling the wind escaping from my balloon. I turned, but he caught my arm and pulled me back.

"Elizabeth, have you noticed that I take being a father very seriously?"

"Of course."

"I'm a good father. Admit it."

"You're a excellent father."

"And I want to be that to all our children. I want to want this child. Do you understand?"

"Yes," I answered, nodding. "Just please don't take too long."

I suppose it was naïve of me to think he would dance up and down as I had done, but I did a lousy job of hiding my disappointment. When he returned to work, I braced the photograph against a perfume bottle on my dressing table, where I could glance at it as I went about my afternoon routine, pausing periodically to stare at features pleasantly symmetrical, the eyes lively (which could have been a startled reaction to the flashbulb), the face ovoid, the chin recessed, the mouth rounded as if caught in mid-word. Her wrists and hands showed the delicate bloat of recent birth. At one angle I thought I saw in her arms, extended slightly toward the camera, a reaching motion, but the same view moments later failed to reproduce the effect, suggesting I had seen only what I wished to see. I glanced down to the envelope, aware that in the distance that separated our house from the mailbox by the road, in the span of time required to boil an egg, I had taken in this infant, enfolded her in arms which, once locked, would defend her. And though I trusted my instincts at moments when my reason occasionally lapsed, in the minutes after opening the envelope those two competitors teetered in a precarious equilibrium more characteristic of Coleman, and for the first time I asked myself how the maternal love which flowed out to Josh and Steven in a profuse current from within me —how love like that could attach itself to a one-dimensional object delivered by the postman. Could a black and white image not much larger than a business card vault the years I had spent diapering, bathing, pampering, feeding, training, nourishing, disciplining my sons, to magically arrive on an emotional plateau on which rested all I had within to give? Coleman had a point. I would have lavished the same devotion on the picture of any child Open Arms sent, and for the good of all perhaps I should slow down. Conserve my heart's capital.

I telephoned Betsy. "I took your advice."

"Of course you did," Betsy replied. "But what did I advise?"

"You said to get a face to go with the idea, and today it arrived. Wait until you see her, Betsy. I can already picture her in the nursery."

"Can't wait. I'll be right over."

The evening after the arrival of Soo Yun's dossier, we drove to the club's midwinter ball, through the club's wide wrought iron gates and up the serpentine lane leading to the clubhouse. As seen from the parking lot, the club is not imposing; a contemporary, one story facade, too elongated to be a residence. The river bank on which the building had been sited drops precipitously so that the majority of the building lies submerged beneath the first level, as clearly seen by those approaching from the James River or from the gentle slope at the river's edge up to the clubhouse. From the river, as opposed to the road, the buildings and surrounding grounds match in grandeur and grace the magnificence of their setting.

"You look stunning, my dear," he said to me as he parked the car and I checked my makeup in the mirror behind the visor.

"I don't feel stunning, but thank you anyway. Well, here goes," I said as I reached for the door handle.

He reached for my near arm and held it lightly by the wrist. "Look, I know your heart isn't completely in this, but let's just have fun."

"Let's do," I agreed, but without much conviction.

Coleman checked our coats while I greeted Ross and Carol Vernon, two of only a handful of people who knew of our adoption plans. Coleman joined us. Carol and I enjoy how he and Ross love to taunt each other, and they wasted no time tonight.

"Counselor," Ross said, "let me be the first to tell you how positively ridiculous you look in that tuxedo."

"Why, thank you very much, doctor. But you have a regrettably short memory for a fat man. I borrowed this from you last year and had it taken in by a tailor who sews about as well as you do."

"Hard to imagine," said Ross. "Why don't we get a drink and talk it over."

They left for the bar, which was perfect as I couldn't wait to show Carol Soo Yun's photograph. She smiled the way you do at pictures of babies, but I saw a certain hesitation too, as if she was expecting someone who looked like me. She tried to hide it, but it was there; the faintest . . . shock. I guess that is something I'll have to get used to, and it is understandable in a place like New Hampton, where families tend toward the traditional, to say the least. She asked me about a name and I said Allie, looking back at the photo to make sure Allie fit Soo Yun, and it seemed a perfect fit to me. Just about then Coleman and Ross came back with our wine.

On the dance floor, Coleman and I danced before switching partners with Ross and Carol. I wish I'd stayed with them, but eventually we all separated in the press of the crowd and the "good-to-see-you's" so that I was alone and defenseless when the inevitable happened: Sandra Hallet approached. I replenished my wine from the tray of a passing waiter and readied myself for the boredom it would be my fate to endure. We all have a look that feigns interest, and I put on mine. Some people notice when you're really just listening to be nice, but Sandra was not that type. I could have been filing my nails and she would still have gone on about her "exhaustive" afternoon in New York, shopping for a prom dress for her daughter, Megan. I nodded and gushed at the appropriate spots, but this monologue bored me senseless, and the cad in me wondered why, with all her money, she couldn't dress more stylishly. Her husband had made a fortune in a chain of convenience stores, and she rarely let anyone forget it. As Sandra took me from one store—"Expensive, but not much more selection than you find at Minor & Renns"—across Fifth Avenue to the "cutest little boutique you have ever laid your eyes on," I saw Coleman coming to rescue me. By then I'd had another glass of wine and was feeling it. Sandra's face was beginning to fuzz over and her words starting to slur, or maybe those were my words. At any rate, I was terribly glad to see my husband and needed no urging when he slipped his arm through mine and reminded me of his promise to have the sitter home at a reasonable hour, a lie but one I was delighted to benefit from. "Thank you," I whispered as we crossed the floor toward the cloakroom.

We left by the south entrance, facing the river. On a circuitous walkway leading to the parking lot, we paused. A chilly breeze off the James swept over us, clearing our eyes of accumulated smoke. We breathed deeply, drawing the bracing air into our encrusted lungs before exhaling the closeness of the evening. I leaned into him, pulling the collar of my coat around my chin and ears. Overhead, the moon hung in marmoreal isolation, its land beams silhouetting the ghostly limbs of barren trees and its river beams refracting, pale and cold, into a shimmering mosaic among the whitecaps on the river. Coleman turned me, drew me in, and kissed my ear. My face inclined, the moonlight in my eyes. He kissed my lips, then whispered, "I signed you up for the club's public relations committee. You don't mind, do you?"

I grinned and kissed him back. "Nope. We can ride over together when you come for meetings of the Greens Committee." We laughed together as we turned toward our car.

The following morning, Coleman left early with the boys for a soccer game while I slept late. When they returned at noon, I'm certain he could tell I'd just gotten up, and with a hangover. I was in the breakfast room, a cup of coffee and an aspirin bottle beside my newspaper.

"A little too much sherry last night, my dear?" he asked, grinning. I hate it that Coleman enjoyed total immunity from hangovers.

I glared at him over the local section. "Oh, shut up," I said with pseudo anger. "It's not fair. You feel great and I suffer."

"It's totally fair," he said. "I drank modestly while you guzzled grain alcohol from a boot."

"Sandra Hallet does that to me. Every time she starts in on another one of her trips to New York, which is every time I see her, I run for the bar. I guess I should be more assertive and just leave, but she follows until she inflicts her quota of pain. How did the game turn out?"

"We won, three to nothing."

"Congratulations, coach. How did Josh play?"

"Very well for the five minutes I let him in the game."

"Your own son. How could you?"

"He's only seven, and he still gets our goal mixed up with theirs. I know coaches who consider that a handicap. Any coffee left?"

"A fresh pot."

"Good. I'll get a cup and then we'll talk." He returned moments later, set his cup on the table, and looked at me expectantly, until my gaze shifted from the newspaper.

"Something on your mind?" I asked. He said something about some conversation he'd overheard at the party last night, but even with my hangover it didn't take me long to realize where this was headed so I can't say I listened with much attention. I had felt this coming, and here it was. He opposed the adoption. He didn't want to go through with it. He had decided to check the "no" box on Soo Yun's dossier.

"Fuck you," I said, or words to that effect. I don't remember exactly. My head hurt.

10

Coleman

When my secretary told me I'd had an urgent call from Elizabeth to come home, I feared something had happened to her or one of the boys. So her joy when I walked in was a relief. I'd rarely seen her so excited. To see the photo I had to take it from her. That old bromide that all babies look alike? Well, not if they are Asian and you are not.

I drove back toward my office in the Pratt Building, a ten story building a dozen blocks from the main gate of the shipyard. Idling at a traffic light on Tyler Avenue, I tried to recall the face in the picture but could summon only a turbid montage of infant features, vaguely universal but for the crescent eyes, so preternatural. But Elizabeth had gazed at the photo with the precise maternal intensity with which she had peered over the bars of cribs, watching her sleeping sons. Dissuading her from this adoption was going to be doubly difficult now that a name and face melded with her instincts, and if it could be done at all, I needed to do it. How to tell her?

In the weeks following our visit to Charleston, I spent some time trying to assemble pieces of a puzzle that simply didn't fit. In the beginning,

I assumed it was this child who did not fit. An orphan of unknown origin imported to a family with whom she could be expected to have not a material thing in common, biologically, culturally, or historically. A stranger to be presented to my family and relatives, most of whom shared atavistic foreheads and jaw lines and musical tastes and self-deprecating humor and slow tempers and high blood pressures and conservative politics and a taste for bourbon and a devotion to the Episcopal Church; who could be expected to stare at her, nonplussed, from a safe distance as though she were an exotic bird of untested temperament and rare, endangered plumage. But more recently, I began to see myself as the misfit, and this child as a mere agent of revelation. I had loved my share of southern girls but married a woman as far from that breed as a woman could be. That did not fit.

I would do anything for parents I had just wounded deeply for reasons less comprehensible to me with each passing day. That also did not fit. I measured my family by a yardstick graduated into the most traditional increments, yet here I was, about to introduce into that family, or suffer its introduction, a component beyond measurement or assessment. I grew up in Charleston, a timeless city which I believed had imbued me with every truth it offered, only to settle in New Hampton, a city of profound enigma. Nothing fit. How did I get here?

Through my passenger window, the huge industrial expanse of the shipyard sprawled out toward the river. I opted for this blue-collar environment during my last year in The Marshall Wythe School of Law at William & Mary, and in recent days had tried to reconstruct the logic that led me from the Old World charms of Charleston to New Hampton. The beginning salary here had been attractive, I remembered. Also, remaining in Virginia maximized my contacts from the University of Virginia, where I sang "the Good Old Song" in the rain at Scott Stadium, arm in drunken arm with many of the same guys I regularly see now at meetings of the bar association. I recall liking the lawyers at Mahoney, Cauthen; recall being flattered by the deference they gave my resume and the lengths to which they went to lure Elizabeth and me to their city. And, I remember acknowledging at the time to Elizabeth during our discussions over coffee, New Hampton exerted an indefinable pull; a pull somehow grounded in ambiance remotely related to pioneering or exploration, although of what,

I could not say. Maybe Charleston was too easy. Maybe the frontier was the place to test myself.

The shipyard defines New Hampton, but the essence of the city continued to elude me. A "beer and hamburger town" was a typical tag. But beyond this obvious and irrefutable trait lurked an obscure soul. The city has a trading post feel about it, as if everyone here expects to be somewhere else this time next year. Yet we had settled here, our sons were born here, and we had made a home and life with good friends. Perhaps it was not the city's soul but my own that was obscure. Did I plan to be somewhere else next year?

At the turn of the century, when the shipyard was a raw-boned pup of an enterprise and three-masted schooners still plied the river, it reared up as promising and pugnacious as any port in the South. From the brawling, fecund tenements of "Hell's Half Acre" came whores and knife fights and shot houses and voodoo, but with them came legends worth retelling.

World War I saw brave troops embark for the death trenches of Flanders in ships built at the yard. Later, those same ships returned the glorious survivors to New Hampton. The Depression tested the town's character, but Pearl Harbor assured a job for any man willing to do a man's work. The yard bought more land, built more ships, and put meat and potatoes on the plates of virtually everyone in New Hampton. During the wars, and for a few boom years following them, the stout heartiness of honest work at common purpose, spiced by dashes of hot, urban tawdriness, produced a rich hunter's gumbo of a city, gamy and pungent and memorable.

But the dramatic expansion of the yard to meet the demands of a postwar defense made what happened next inevitable, and in the 1950s the town lost much of its savor. The original municipality annexed Wainwright County, a bucolic assemblage of Mennonite farms systematically waffled by developers into track subdivisions larded with embellished names like "Oaks" and "Glens" and "Meadows" and "Chases"; names brimming with a romance no longer to be found in New Hampton. With the suburbs came numbing regularity, nerve-testing traffic, and crabgrass. The rugged stew which had once been New Hampton diluted into a bland gruel utterly indistinguishable from a dozen industrial centers. To me, what began as an intriguing alternative to the inevitability of Charleston had come to represent little more than a place to live and work. I had begun to sense the anonymity of the city defining me, and a growing awareness that my magnetic pull toward New Hampton may have been nothing more than an antipolar repulsion from the city of my birth.

I arrived at my office just as the shipyard's 4:00 whistle blew. Two of my partners, exiting the elevator, spoke to me as I entered, but I merely nodded absently, causing them to stare momentarily, as did my secretary as I passed without acknowledgment. My mind was back at the house, on that photograph.

At my desk, I turned my chair toward the window and looked out onto the city. Cars making their daily exodus from the yard jammed Tyler Avenue as hard-hatted workers dodged among them. I had witnessed this tableau a hundred times from above, but today I felt part of it, as though I was locked in the congestion below, leaning impatiently on my horn and cursing the men whose last-second dash in front of me caused me to idle through another stoplight cycle. I wanted to move. I wanted things to fit.

A day or two later, at the midwinter ball, I was privy to a conversation that crystallized something that had been on my mind since our Charleston trip. Ross and I had pushed through the crowd toward the bar, a long, cherry wood affair accommodating four bartenders. Drinks in hand, we returned to Elizabeth and Carol. I knew Elizabeth brought the photo. She carried it everywhere. I got to them too late to see Carol's reaction, but in time to hear, "She's so adorable. Congratulations," which honestly sounded forced to me.

Elizabeth and I separated to circulate, as we often do at these things, but met up to dance later in the evening. That was when I overheard the conversation. Don Mahoney, my senior partner and our host for the evening, stood talking with a plump, balding man whom I recognized as Richard Coughter, a local attorney recently endorsed by the bar association for a judgeship. Mahoney, seeing me in his peripheral vision, beckoned me over. The three of us exchanged handshakes accompanied by "good to see you's."

Don continued speaking to Coughter as though I was not present. He does that sometimes at the office as well, when I sit in on meetings with his clients. Don's an able lawyer. His voice, by its very weight and depth, commands jurors' attention. His reputation as a trial attorney had been made by that voice; an ominous, sepulchral resonance that seemed to emanate from a volcanic oracle, like the slow grinding of faults at the earth's core. The rare jury returning an adverse verdict left the courthouse shadowed by guilt, having defied the wishes of what sounded, for all the world, like a rumbling deity. At five-ten he stood eye level with Coughter, tapping lightly with his free hand the other man's lapel. Coughter's concentration bordered on entrancement, produced not only by the speaker's mesmerizing voice but by the subject matter: Coughter's impending confirmation hearing before the Courts of Justice Committee in the General Assembly, a legislative body wherein Mahoney enjoyed considerable influence both as sage advisor and campaign financial contributor.

"It'll all blow over," Don assured Coughter. "Nobody with any influence on that committee makes decisions based on a newspaper editorial by some snotty-nosed do-gooder. Bill and Ed are both looking out for you in the Committee, and the full House will bring out the rubber stamp. It's not a done deal, but you'll get through. You have my word on it."

Coughter's face, until now cloudy with concern, brightened visibly. "That's mighty good to hear, coming from you." Then doubt again tightened its grip. "It just don't seem fair," he said. "If they disqualified every judge in this state who belongs to a segregated private club, there would be one hell of a lot of empty benches."

With the hand holding his drink, Mahoney gave a dismissive wave, almost spilling his bourbon onto Coughter. "I'm telling you, it's all hot air. You think those good old boys in Richmond give a damn about your membership here? They've got a political problem and you're going to have to sit there at the big long table and nod understandingly and assure them that you are sensitive to all their minority concerns and that you've put us on notice back here in the boondocks that unless we change our membership policies, why, you just might have to consider resigning. Then you'll have to listen to them talk about how it's incumbent on judges in the Commonwealth to be free from discrimination and all the rest of it. It's a game. Just play along."

Coughter took a pull on his drink. "I'll sure be glad when it's over," he said, taking a handkerchief from his pocket and mopping his forehead. "Yes, sir. Mighty glad."

"Well, hell, Richard," scoffed Mahoney in his rich bass. "For what amounts to a lifetime appointment, you can take a few minutes on the hot seat, can't you? The worst that can happen, the absolute worst, is that someone gunning for statewide office next year will demand you resign as a condition of appointment."

"But I like this club. My wife likes it. All our friends are here."

"So Susan keeps her membership and you become her permanent guest. Or do what that fellow in Staunton did last year—resign and rejoin after you're appointed. They can't touch you after you're in. You worry too much."

"Susan tells me the same thing. I guess I do. Still, it means financial security and you can't beat the pension, so I would hate to see something go wrong."

Don turned to me. "What do you think, counselor? Think 'Judge Coughter' has a ring to it?"

"By all means," I answered, raising my glass in an informal toast.

"You're very kind," said Coughter. "I hope you're right. Both of you. Still, I doubt this flap is going to disappear. Wouldn't it be easier on everyone to recruit some minority so we could say we have one?"

Mahoney nodded. "Sure it would. We're working on it. You know Reggie Page, the black dentist?" Coughter narrowed his eyes as if to place Page. "Anyway, he's a good fellow; reserved, soft spoken. He's agreed to apply if we can assure him he'll be admitted and that it won't turn into a newspaper circus."

Coughter gave a short chortle. "Well, I don't know Page but I know most of the membership committee. That's going to be a tough sell." He shook his head doubtfully.

"Maybe," agreed Mahoney. "But we need one. You're a case in point. We'll have to twist some arms, but I think we can get there with a commitment from Reggie Page."

Coughter looked surprised before a slow grin spread his lips. "What kind of commitment. Is he going to agree to turn white?" He guffawed at his cleverness and Mahoney joined in, tilting his head back to laugh.

"Not exactly," Mahoney said. "We want his promise that once he's in he won't put up a bunch of his friends for membership and put us all in a sticky bind."

"Makes sense," said Coughter, still grinning. "Thanks for the reassurance. Oh, and thanks also for your help with the legislators. I'm mighty grateful and I won't forget it." They shook hands and Coughter retreated toward the men's room.

Mahoney turned to me. "How are you and your lovely wife enjoying the party?"

"We've had a great time," I said. "Speaking of my lovely wife, I'd better go find her before she gets a better offer."

"Be sure to make the rounds with the membership committee. They have on small blue ribbons. Hell, you know most of them but it never hurts to kiss a little ass." I knew the significance of the ribbons, but thanked Don anyway.

The next day, Elizabeth paid the price for the wine she drank, blaming it on Sandra Hallet who I find as insufferable as does Elizabeth. I really did not want to have this conversation when she was nursing a hangover, but it couldn't be put off. After the boys and I returned from soccer, I told her about the Mahoney-Coughter conversation.

"Don Mahoney and Richard Coughter were discussing his appointment to the bench." I paused.

"And?"

"And there was a lot of talk about his membership in Riverside; you know, the fact that he'll be a judge and belongs to a segregated club. Hearing them talk strategy firmed up a thought that has been running through my mind since we started this adoption process, but I never put a finger on it until last night."

"I told you they were all a bunch of bigots, your senior partner included." She looked vexed.

"Will you let me finish?"

"Go ahead, I'm listening."

"It's the subtle stuff that you have to worry about; that we'll have to worry about for her. She won't have doors slammed in her face. She won't be told directly, 'No, you can't go here' or 'No, you can't participate in that.' That's illegal, and besides, we're a civilized country. But her life with us would be affected in a thousand ways by the kind of thing I overheard last night; lip service while you hold on to the old days. Poor Reggie Page. I wouldn't be in his shoes for anything."

"Why Reggie Page?"

"You know him?"

"Yes. He's a dentist. Nice guy."

"They're thinking of asking him to join the club if he'll promise not to try to drag any of his friends with him."

"How humiliating. But if Reggie is stupid enough to agree to be their token, he deserves what he gets."

"Exactly. Reggie's lived here all his life. He understands all this. But a young Asian growing up in our family isn't going to understand. When sides are chosen and she isn't picked, she won't know why. When the prom arrives and she's not asked, she won't understand. And if she wins some award, we'll never know whether she earned it or two people like Mahoney and Coughter got together and decided it would be good for appearances."

"So what are you saying?"

"I'm saying I don't want to put a child through that. I think we should call this off."

Tears welled immediately in Elizabeth's eyes. "No. I want this child. You promised."

"That was four years ago. I've thought it through."

She fought for control as I leaned back, my arms folded across my chest, ready for what I knew would be a furious assault. The color drained from her face as she said, "You don't want to put yourself through it. It has nothing to do with the child."

"That's not true. You have a totally unrealistic view of what she will face, and every time I point it out you attack me as a selfish racist."

"You are selfish. You only care about angering your parents and alienating people like Don Mahoney. I know she will face problems. But if we don't adopt her she may face life in an institution, which has to be worse than anything she will confront here. But that will be her problem, won't it? You won't be inconvenienced, your career won't be jeopardized, and that makes all the difference, doesn't it?"

"You're yelling," I said calmly.

"Of course I'm yelling. And I'll tell you what else I'm doing. I'm adopting this child and you better get used to it. I'm calling Open Arms Monday morning to tell them we'll take her and if you don't like it, fuck off and leave."

I'll never know if she would have carried through on her threat to call Open Arms. Early Monday morning, while I was in the shower, Mother called, telling Elizabeth my father had suffered a stroke during the night, and that she needed me in Charleston as soon as I could get there.

I caught a mid-morning flight, arriving just past noon. Mother greeted me somberly at the arrival gate. Yes, Dad had seemed fine the night before. No signs of dizziness or headache. He had left their bed around two. She had stirred, heard him enter the bathroom, heard the faucet turned on and off. The most jarring moment of his collapse came when the glass he was holding smashed against the tiled floor. The EMS response had been twenty minutes.

We drove from the airport to the hospital. Mother, exhaustion evident, refused to enter the ICU, saying she had been there all morning and wasn't up to returning at the moment. Dad lay comatose, an IV running into his left arm and digital readouts surrounding him. I approached the bedside, grasped my father's hand, and squeezed. No response. For the fifteen minutes I stood at the bedside, monitors hummed and winked. Pixilated graphs rose and fell, keeping physiological score with automated indifference.

I drove Mother home, urged her to go to bed, then unpacked for what I sensed might be a stay of some duration. She needed me. The law firm could manage without me for a time. I called home, reporting what I knew.

"And how's your mother?" Elizabeth wanted to know.

"Holding up and holding on. I need to spend some time down here."

"Yes, you do." Then, a pause. "Coleman, you don't think Sarah will blame this on me, do you?"

I hesitated, because that thought loomed. "I think in her heart of hearts she blames us both."

"Then that means me."

"Dad's doctor warned them both last year that his blood pressure was too high."

"I don't want to come down there if she thinks I caused this."

"Let me talk with her over the weekend."

"Okay."

"Elizabeth, promise me you won't call that agency."

"Now's not the time. I see that."

"Good. I'll call you tomorrow. Kiss the boys for me."

In the days that followed, sobering retreats followed faint spikes of optimism, Dad's doctors straddling that vague line between medical art and science and refusing to place bets either way. If they held a long range view, they withheld it in professional reticence. Should we urge my aunt Constance, Dad's sister, to abandon a long planned South American cruise to come to Charleston? No, that "probably isn't necessary," the doctors opined. If he lived, as it appeared likely now that he would, it was doubtful he would regain all of his speech, and he would require speech and physical therapy. Mother could not care for him without so much assistance that a nursing home made economic sense, doctors advised. She balked. He would come home, and that was that.

I spent the next few days shuttling back and forth to the hospital and, between trips, helping Mother acquire the medical equipment and supplies that would make Dad's return home after therapy possible. Still in ICU, he communicated in a rudimentary code by blinking. No, he was not in pain. Yes, the nurses treated him well. Yes, he looked forward to going home.

Returning from the store, I passed the tree Philip Huger and I climbed during one afternoon of prepubescent exploring. It made me smile, despite the broken arm I received when Philip jumped down too soon. I forgive you, Philip, I thought, thinking also about how many times over Philip repaid me in Mexico. At the thought of Mexico, my smile broadened.

Back at the house, I sat in my room, at the old oak desk where I did my homework while in high school. In front of me rested a stack of files I asked the office to ship down. I had been working my way through them for over two hours when Mother knocked at the door.

"He's better," she said brightly. "Some movement in his left hand. Dr. Adams says he's being moved out of ICU."

I rose to meet her as she sagged against me, relief palpable. "He's tougher than he looks," I said. "Let's go check out his new room."

On Sunday, friends and neighbors who had stayed away from the hospital in deference to the uncertain outcome brought food. A party of sorts evolved, subdued at first. Visitors conversed in a respectful hush, raising the covers of chafing dishes silently, as if the sudden clash of silver would precipitate a relapse in the man sleeping five miles away in the Newberger Rehabilitation Center. Gradually, like spring edging winter, the library hush gave way to laughter and boisterous chatter.

I served drinks, thinking as I mixed and poured how, under any other circumstances, Dad would have been first in line. I spent time with the members of his poker club, who gathered in one corner of the sunroom and told stories, little vignettes of brazen bluffs and memorable calls meaningless to just about anyone outside this group of retired card table warriors.

"Your daddy has this tic," explained Horace Wannamaker as he swirled ice in his second gin and tonic. "Every time he draws a really strong hand he gets this twitch in his right eyelid. He knows it, but there isn't one goddamn thing he can do to control it. Am I right, Scotty?"

Scott Lesesne, nursing his first bourbon and ginger, smiled. "Dead on."

"So he got into the habit," continued Wannamaker, "of covering his eye with his hand which, don't you see, is a bigger red flag than the twitch." Wannamaker laughed loudly.

Scott Lesesne clapped a hand on Wannamaker's shoulder. "But he got you good that once."

Wannamaker shook his head. "He did that. Pot must have been twenty-five, thirty dollars. Big money. Whipped that hand up to that right eye and bluffed me out with a pair of fives. Never has let me forget it, either." They all laughed.

Lesesne took up the sportsmen's tale. "Over the years, he's found something on every one of us. Nothing malicious, you understand, just some little quirk or habit he's noticed and ribs us about. Whenever he looks at you with that twinkle in his eyes, you know it's coming."

I circulated, greeting those I had known growing up. As I entered the den I recognized Barron Morris, seated in the leather, overstuffed chair my father preferred. The ample old gentleman, whom I judged to be perhaps seventy-five, wore an impeccably tailored three piece suit of dark blue wool and faint pinstripes. From his suit pocket protruded a burgundy silk scarf matching his tie, and his collar, white on the pale blue background of his shirt, held a gold stick pin. Across his waist, which in the compression of his body in the chair, tilted upward toward the ceiling, he sported a gold fob. As I approached the chair the man held out his hand.

"Hello, son. My circulation isn't what it used to be or I'd stand to shake your hand. Please forgive me. Pull up that ottoman and let's talk if you have the time."

When seated, I said, "Good to see you, Mr. Morris. It's been a while."

"Indeed it has. I don't believe I've laid eyes on you since that reception your parents gave before you were married. I'm so glad your father's doing so much better. He's a good man; a mighty good man."

"Your name came up in a conversation with him just before his stroke."

Morris shifted slightly in his chair. "Is that so? I remember asking him to have you give me a call sometime. I hope you'll do it. Tell me, how are things going up there in Virginia? Your father told me you made partner."

"A few months ago. I guess some luck and the network among UVA and William & Mary grads was enough to fool them."

"Fine schools," acknowledged Morris, "but I suspect you paid your dues. I suppose you know that I've got a little law firm down on Broad Street."

I grinned. "The last time I checked Martindale-Hubble, your little firm had thirty-five lawyers and represented just about everyone in South Carolina worth representing."

Morris nodded his oversized head decidedly, a wisp of ivory hair falling onto his forehead. "We do all right for country boys. We have a few country girls as well. Your practice is litigation if your father told me right."

I nodded.

"Big business, that litigation. The world's got too much of it, in my opinion, but you have to change with the times. I sure miss the old days. Why, no Broad Street lawyer worth his salt would be seen in his office before eleven. By the time you signed a couple of letters or, on a big day, drafted a will, it was time for lunch."

"That doesn't sound much like my schedule."

"Nor mine anymore. Tell me about your practice up there."

I outlined the structure of my firm and its primary areas of expertise. Morris listened with his eyes half closed, nodding occasionally, but his questions showed his mastery of every detail I disclosed.

"Tell you what," Morris said. "I want you to come have lunch with me. Can you do that?"

"I'll be here for a few more days. I'm sure I can."

"Good. How's Wednesday?"

We agreed and shook hands.

On Monday evening, in a call to Elizabeth, I told her to expect me that weekend. "Dad gets a little stronger each day, and Mom likes having me around, but I've got a trial next week, and if I stay any longer I'll have to get it continued."

She hesitated. "I hate to bring this up, but we have to give Open Arms an answer. Soon."

I sighed, and I'm sure she heard it. "The timing couldn't be worse. Besides, I thought we had that discussion."

"I hoped you would reconsider."

"To be honest, I haven't given it the first thought."

"That's understandable, but we need to make a decision. Perhaps I was too emotional the other night. This is not something I want to do alone." Under other circumstances, I would have seized upon her concession. Elizabeth did not normally give ground.

I locked and bolted the front door as Mother watched from a chair in the living room.

"You bolted that door just like your father," she said. "When I do it, which isn't often, I brace it with my knee, nearer the floor. He always pushes against it with his left arm, above the lock, while he turns the key."

"It's late, Mother. Is there anything I can do for you?"

"Yes, you can fix me a drink and sit up with me for a few minutes. Bourbon, two fingers over ice." At the bar, I poured twins. When I returned, she continued. "So many years, son. We lived our lives in phases. I suppose everyone does. Remember, your father and I had only each other for over twelve years. That's longer than you've been married. We'd given up hope of having a child. We figured it was the two of us, for better or worse."

"Stop me if this sounds too personal, but was it better, or worse?"

She looked at me in a way that transformed us into contemporaries, lounging in a fraternity house. The whisky helped. "He was so shy," she explained. "The mystery of our marriage has always been his need to limit the world and my need to expand it. Here, in this house, with just the two of us, he could be himself. I made certain of that. I swore I'd never press him to be other than he was. My gift to him was an appreciation for his vulnerability, and he loves me for it. He was a shy, honest man with a wonderful sense of humor. That was enough for me, or so I thought. Then you came along and my world changed, like it's about to do again. I kept my promise; I never pressed him, but you did. Innocently, of course. You were just being a kid, just being yourself. But in a very strange and painful way–I don't want this to come out wrong–a painful way you reminded him of every well adjusted, athletic, ambitious guy he'd played second fiddle to all his life."

"He resented me?"

"Not for an instant. He worshiped you. He turned the resentment on himself."

I stared, fitting things together. "Did you ever talk about it?"

"Rarely. But I knew him as well or better than he knew himself, so we got by. I've worried more about its affect on you. He was never one to put his feelings into words or to discuss . . . personal things, like his shyness, for example."

Or adoption? I thought, then thought again. "I can't say I've ever really understood him."

Mother's voice dropped. "He loves you."

"I've assumed that."

She leaned away to look at me directly. "You intimidate him."

"But that's crazy. He's been successful."

"In his modest way, yes. He comes from a fine family and he made a good living in accounting, but never the kind of money that attracts attention here. Even in Charleston, your name only gets you so far."

I began to wonder why this conversation, or others like it, had not taken place five years before, or ten. Why wait until invalidism to air such thoughts? My mother, the most outgoing of people, must have been drawn into my father's web of reticence, I reasoned. Was it sheer loyalty? By showing candor of which Dad had been incapable, would she have somehow highlighted her husband's failing, like a woman who would never think of criticizing her mate, yet complains to friends about having no money when her husband produces all the income? Or was it futility? Was there something in my father's illness that freed her?

In the muted distance, church bells tolled the hour. "Tired, Mother? Maybe we should call it a day."

"In a moment." For the first time she swirled the ice in her glass, nervously signaling something. I guessed. "First, tell me what is happening with your plans to adopt this foreign child. You haven't spoken of it."

"That's been intentional. It's obviously a sore subject and neither Elizabeth nor I thought it appropriate to bring up when . . . on this visit."

"Then your plans have not changed." She said it flatly, without emotion. But she glanced at me expectantly from the corner of her eye.

"Our plans aren't certain. Elizabeth and I haven't . . . worked it all out yet."

"I gathered as much. For what it's worth, your father is very set against it. He worried himself sick about it."

"Enough to cause a stroke?"

"I didn't say that."

"Blame me, not Elizabeth."

She took an extended sip from her drink. "How much do you know about his time in the Navy?"

"Only what he's told me, which isn't much. He mentioned long stretches in the Pacific during the invasion of Japan. He made it sound like a desk job on board ship."

"That would be his way. But I have his letters, and even the censors couldn't tone it down but so much. He didn't want me to worry, but he saw some very grim things out there. Like Iwo Jima. Did you know he landed on the beach there?"

"He never mentioned Iwo Jima."

She shifted in her chair. "I pulled it out of him. He never understood the Japanese, the way they wanted to die for their emperor, the way they holed up like rats."

"He wasn't a Marine."

"A beach master. He organized all that equipment our boys needed. Your father saw so much death, and he's never forgiven the Japs."

"I had no idea. He was in real danger."

Mother nodded. "Don't think his reaction to this idea of adoption isn't wrapped up in Iwo Jima."

"But who said anything about Japanese?"

She looked annoyed, thrusting her glass at me. "Oh, Coleman, the Orientals just don't share our values. You must see that. That sneaky attack on Pearl Harbor is the way they live. You can't trust one as far as you can throw him."

"This child isn't Japanese."

"She's foreign—it's all the same. Son, I have a theory on this whole matter if you'd care to hear it. If you would rather my stay out of it, I'll try, but any child you adopt becomes my grandchild."

"What theory?"

"Elizabeth is a charming girl. Your father and I love her and we think highly of her as a wife and mother. But we know so little about her; where she came from; who her people are. We met them at the wedding, of course, and everyone seemed very nice, but that was years ago and she never talks about them. The few times I've raised the subject she's changed it. Are they estranged?"

"Her family isn't close."

"But ours is, or at least I've told myself that all these years. Whatever communication problems you have with your father–and I'm not blind, I see them, you may be sure–never altered his affection. My theory is that she is jealous of your closeness to us, and that in adopting this child, a child she knows we can't accept, she is putting you to a choice between us and her."

"I'll have to give that some thought, Mother. She has her insecurities, but whether she would go this far to test our relationship is a question I can't answer. She has said that she doesn't think you and Dad entirely approved of her."

Sarah scoffed. "It was never a matter of approval. We didn't know her."

"Be honest, Mother. Are you denying your disappointment that I didn't marry a girl from around here?"

She recoiled momentarily at that, as though this thought had been beamed to her by alien intruders. Then, she recovered. "Well, I suppose there was some small amount—"

"That my wife sensed very early."

"It's a cliché, dear, but we only wanted what was best for you."

"Parents do that. We're doing the same. But I'm curious as to why you think Elizabeth would want to make me choose between you and her."

"I'm afraid," she said, suddenly looking quite wise to me, "that the answer to that question lies in your marriage. Women have certain instincts where those things are concerned, but I can't help you there."

"You can't, or you won't?"

"I have theories about why a wife might want to reassure herself by putting her husband to a choice, but they're only theories." She paused to smile in self-deprecation. "Listen to me, with all my theories. You know her far better than I. But even if I did know, I wouldn't say. It's like UFOs; until you see one yourself, you think everyone who claims to have seen one is crazy. I'm tired now. I think I'll turn in."

On Wednesday, I met Barron Morris at the Huguenot Club for lunch. The incestuous aromas of garlic, oregano and basil met me at the door. A thin, prissy waiter escorted me to a private table just off the main dining area, where Barron Morris was already seated, dressed as resplendently as before, but with more color in his tie and a walking cane visible beside his chair. A half-filled Bloody Mary rested on the plate in front of him. He smiled as I approached.

"Circulation's no better than Sunday," he said, extending his hand. As soon as I was seated, Morris gave an almost imperceptible nod of his head. Moments later, a Bloody Mary appeared in front of me.

"You like shrimp?" Morris asked, then gave a glottic chortle. "What kind of question is that to ask a Charleston native?" After the waiter brought us steaming plates of shrimp Creole, Barron Morris offered me a job.

"I beg your pardon?" I said, dumbfounded.

"You shouldn't be so surprised. When a young man begins to get a reputation, people like me take notice. I've checked you out with some of my old friends in the Tidewater. You've got quite a future in this business."

"But I just made partner in Mahoney . . ."

"And you're wondering why you should pull up stakes and start over here in Charleston."

I smiled lamely as Morris buttered a roll, broke it in half, and dipped one end in the Creole sauce swimming near the edge of his plate. Light glinted off his cuff link. "I do love the food here. Before me and five others started this club about a million years ago, you just couldn't find sauce like that without driving thirty minutes. How's your drink?"

"Fine, sir."

"Coleman, I have several reasons for making this offer. We need a good trial lawyer. We've got two, but they're older—fiftyish—and we need a young Turk to take over some of this case load. I can promise you twenty-five percent more money in your first year than you're making at Mahoney, whatever that figure is, plus a complete benefits package, relocation expenses and a full plate of some mighty challenging legal work."

"Holy Pete."

Morris laughed. "Your father uses that expression; Holy Pete. You'd better attack that Creole before it gets cold. Then I'd like to take you to the office to meet my partners. They know you're coming even if you didn't."

It was after 4:00 when I emerged onto Broad Street. My reception at Morris & VanCleve had been nothing short of overwhelming. Either they liked me as much as they seemed to or they liked me as much as Barron Morris wanted them to. And I liked them. Morris had told me to take as much time as I needed to reach a decision. But it had been something else Morris said that accounted for my turning north on Meeting Street toward the Charleston Public Library instead of south, the direction home.

We had been seated in Morris's commodious office at the corner of the building, with its fine view of Broad Street and the "four corners of law." Morris had been sounding me out on my reaction to the individuals I had met over the course of the previous two hours. We had almost concluded when Morris paused, looking past me out the window.

"There's another thing I think you should consider, Coleman. Your roots are here, in Charleston. I've known your people for three generations. As I look about Morris & VanCleve today, I see fewer and fewer of the old names. I don't have but so much time left to practice, but before I retire I'd like to do what I can to insure that fifty, maybe even a hundred years from now, there will still be Carters and Sinklers and Brailsfords and VanCleves and Morrises associated with this firm."

"It's odd you mention that," I said. "For some reason, I feel less a part of New Hampton than I did when I arrived."

Morris chuckled softly as he withdrew a cigar from his top drawer and clipped the end. "That's called 'maturity,' and it has nothing to do with the people in New Hampton. Some of those fine folks came over on the boat; yours came here and theirs landed a little farther north." He lit the cigar, then blew a puff of smoke upward. "If you stay there, I've no doubt that your grandchildren will feel about New Hampton what I feel for Charleston."

"I went there to get away from Charleston. I see that now. Are you sure you want someone like that?"

"Absolutely," said Morris, leaning forward. "I worry about the ones that haven't been around some. Do you know that one of my earliest memories in this business involved your grandfather?"

"Tell me about it."

"I had just finished Carolina. Started to work on a Monday. In those days the firm was Jenkins, Rogers & VanCleve. That Thursday, I went to a meeting of the Democratic Party at the Hibernian Hall. Your grandfather, Warren Carter, wasn't active in city politics but he showed up that night because of the subject under debate, which was the presidential election of 1932.

"Now bear in mind we were in our third year of the Depression, and folks here were hurting like they were everywhere. The party was split because the details of some of F.D.R.'s cures had begun to leak out, and the conservative folks around these parts were none too wild about the idea of these massive programs.

"Your grandfather found himself in the same boat as a lot of others that night; they couldn't bring themselves to even contemplate voting for a Republican, the party of Lincoln, but they didn't think much more of the governor of New York. Tempers flared, and for a time I thought fists were going to fly. In the middle of it, Warren stood up and gave as rip-snorting, fire and brimstone condemnation of F.D.R. as you've ever heard. I remember the shock throughout the room because this was a man as prone to public speaking as donkeys are to ballet.

"Next day, the newspaper story about the meeting carried this big picture of your grandfather, standing up in the crowd giving F.D.R. hell. You should look it up some time. It's part of your history."

I promised that I would, but left Morris with no real intention of doing so. Once on Broad Street, with time on my hands since Mother, I knew, was being taken to dinner by close friends, I changed my mind.

At the public library, I began my research in the microfilmed records of the *Post and Sentinel* and instantly regretted not having obtained from Morris the exact date of the meeting. I called Morris, but the old gentleman had left for the day. Without the date and with no help from the reference librarian, I had no choice but to begin my search at an arbitrary date in 1932. I chose June 1st. After reading a lead political story for June 2, I realized that F.D.R. had yet to be nominated, so I fast-forwarded to July 2, the day after the convention ended. By closing time, I had plied through September 27. I resolved to return, intrigued and challenged to find the elusive article.

At home, Mother met me at the door. "I was beginning to worry," she said. I kissed her on the forehead.

"How was your lunch with the girls?"

"It was so sweet of them to invite me, but there was so much food. How was your meeting with Barron?"

"Interesting. We talked lawyer talk. Then I spent some time in the public library."

"What on earth for?"

"Barron Morris told me a story about grandfather and a political meeting. I thought I'd check it out."

She took on a pensive pose, as if trying to determine the origin of a noise in the next room. "I don't know what he might have been alluding to. It must have been before I entered the picture. But I remember him well. He and your father were so alike."

At the breakfast table the following morning, Saturday, I said, "Mother, I'm flying back tomorrow afternoon. I'm worried about you being here by yourself."

Mother, dressed in her warmest housecoat, showed the listlessness of a fitful night. "I'll be fine. It's been a luxury having you here these past few days, but I need to get on with . . . things."

"Why don't you come spend some time with us in Virginia? A week, a month, as long as you like. Dad's well cared for. You need to look out for yourself, too."

"Thank you, dear. As soon as I feel like I've come to grips with this, I'll do just that. Elizabeth won't mind?"

"She would welcome it, although I can't promise we won't stick you with baby-sitting duty from time to time."

She smiled. "Some time with my grandsons? Throw me in the briar patch."

I drove slowly down Meeting Street toward the library. The streets were deserted. A morning mist from the river lingered at the height of second floor piazzas, giving the wrought-iron railings and trellises the appearance of black ink filigreed into a dream. I mulled Morris's offer. Until now, I had thought only in terms of the rush I received from being courted by Charleston's premier firm.

But as I passed landmarks of my youth, my thoughts moved beyond flattery. I slowed as I passed the house where Marie Donaldson, my first girlfriend, had lived. I idled for a few seconds in front of Cresanto's, where I had ridden my bicycle when Mother sent me to buy the vegetables she had forgotten at the market and where the awning would soon be rolled out to signal that it was, as it had been for fifty years, the first-to-open enterprise south of Broad. I drove past Dr. Seigler's, my pediatrician until I left for college. Why had I left? Why not return?

At just past 11:00, as I scanned the front page for October 22, 1932, I found my article. The text of the story did not mention my grandfather, but the picture Morris had described identified "an irate Warren Carter." I studied it. In the physiognomy of the man standing above the seated crowd with his arm extended toward an unseen dais, his index finger pointed at an invisible enemy, I saw shadows of my father and of myself. The squareness of the shoulders and the cant of the neck upon them were heirlooms of an unmistakable bequest. But the facial features were lamentably blurred, owing to either the sophistication of archaic photography or the microfilm process, I could not be certain which.

I photocopied the article and picture and noticed how the definition in my grandfather's face had deteriorated further with the copy. I approached the reference librarian, hoping to find her better informed than the one who attended me the day before.

"I'm sorry, sir," she said. "The only place I know that keeps the original papers is the *Post and Sentinel.* Collectors might have the edition you need, but it would be hit or miss finding it."

It was noon. I had promised to take Mother to lunch at one. With a vague sense of killing time I drove to the newspaper offices, where I was directed to a third floor office labeled "Archives." A clerk motioned me toward a table and minutes later returned from a door behind the counter.

"Be careful turning pages," she admonished as she placed it in front of me.

I gazed down. As I had hoped, the facial definition in the photograph was a vast improvement over the microfilm. My grandfather's mustache, which appeared as a long smudge above his lip in the microfilm, was clearly identifiable. Now, I saw sideburns where none had existed in the library. The profile of the nose, the Carter nose, was also vivid.

As I stared harder, longer, I felt drawn into the photo. The feel of the crowded, unventilated room became palpable, as if I could reach out and lay my hand on the shoulder of the man sitting in front of my grandfather, turned in his seat with his head inclined toward the speaker now giving F.D.R. hell. I looked up, pushed the paper aside, and rested my chin on my fist, for some reason thinking not of my grandfather but my sons.

Fatherhood was a strange game, I had come to realize as Josh and Steven grew older and the rules grew more complex. It was like soccer, a game I never played—had never even seen played—as a child but was now called upon to coach, to teach as an adult. Each Saturday morning I stood authoritatively on the sidelines, urging my boys forward, blissfully ignorant of "offsides," "indirects," "yellow cards," "dummies," and the remaining argot of this Continental tongue. Gradually I got it, rule by rule, trial by error, the way I hoped to eventually master parenthood.

But my hours on the sidelines also served me as a primer on the fundamental laws of genetics. Above all other similarity, it had been Josh's loping run that had impressed upon me the unbroken thread of heredity. I could still hear Coach Clemmons at Ashley High, screaming at me to spring forward from the balls of my feet; "There is simply not one ounce of bounce in the human heel," he would repeat, proud of his apt little doggerel. But try as I might, I possessed a congenital flat-footedness which withstood all admonishment, rhymed or unrhymed, from coaches, trainers, and teammates. It withstood hours of "toe-lifts" requiring me to balance on a raised surface, heels off the ground, and lift myself on toes and forefeet. It survived Coach Clemmons' last desperate measure to coax more speed from his otherwise potent quarterback: an Olympic training film featuring Bob Hayes, the world record holder in the sprint. When the lights came back on, I protested weakly that I was "no Bob Hayes."

"That's true," said Coach Clemmons. "You run more like Helen Hayes." By my senior year, the coaching staff had accepted the reality that my flat-footed lope was as much ingrained as my height and the green of my eyes.

I accepted it on the day I saw Josh's lope across a soccer field, followed two years later by Steven's. Seeing myself in my sons became a hobby. Little things intrigued me: a distinctive downward glance at being scolded; an early love of music without the faintest accompanying proclivity for carrying a tune; the wry anticipation of a smile when they told their first jokes; an incipient vertical furrow between the eyebrows when puzzled. I noted all of these shared variegations in the fabric of my being, and more.

But having noted them, what was I to make of them as I sat at the table in the company my irate grandfather? I sensed a connection, an intertwining of these ancestral threads. Had my father loped? My grandfather? Were these variegations which so fascinated me mere brush strokes on a larger portrait I had yet to examine? For each dye and tincture visible to casual, even studied observation, how much more lay indelibly below the surface, shading the essence of character and judgment and courage and compassion?

I reached for the paper and held it at eye level. When I backed away from the detail, when I held out the paper so that I took in the whole of my grandfather's scowl, the indignant contortion of facial muscles marshaled against a politician he had never met, and never would, I saw a face I had seen before. I saw my father, sitting in the car, with his hand on the door handle ready to escape from his brief but fiery confrontation over the impending adoption.

And I sensed, for the first time, a reflection of that same look, and the defiance it captured. Had Elizabeth photographed me in our recent deliberations over this Asian child, I knew I would be wearing that look, that identical fear of the unknown, that same vehement denial in the face of inexorable forces, the nature and strength of which I only dimly perceived. I pondered it over dinner with Mother that evening, and on the flight home the next afternoon.

Elizabeth met me at the airport. She had left the boys with a sitter. "They missed you," she told me.

"How about you? Did you miss me?" I asked.

She merely winked, as she did when things were on her mind. For the moment, I omitted any mention of my lunch with Barron Morris.

Elizabeth, turning onto the highway from the airport approach road, said, "Hey, how about taking me to dinner?"

"Deal. What sounds good to you?"

"How about . . . Chinese?"

"You never give up, do you?"

A waitress, who might have been Puerto Rican, possibly Mexican, but clearly not Chinese, took our order. As we sipped tea and spooned hot and sour soup, the discordant plunks and twangs of Far Eastern music fluttered in the background. I waited for a lull in chit-chat about how these places rarely gave out chopsticks anymore.

"Elizabeth, how would you feel about moving to Charleston?"

"As in, permanently?"

"As in, for good."

She dabbed her mouth with the bright red napkin. "What brought that on?"

"A lawyer named Barron Morris." I related my lunch with Morris and subsequent visit to the firm.

"And he offered you a job, just like that?"

"A partnership. And a big sweetener called 'more money.'"

Dinner arrived. Teriyaki vegetables for her and something called General Chan chicken, very spicy, for me. "What does it say about a general's combat record when they name a chicken after him?" I asked, and she laughed.

"I must say I'm surprised," she said as she swirled a broccoli spear in the dark, briny sauce. "I've never heard you express any interest in returning."

"I'm a little surprised myself."

"Speaking of surprises," she said, "and not to change the subject, but we owe Open Arms a decision."

I stopped a forkful of chicken halfway to my mouth. "What does that have to do with surprises?"

"Well . . . I'm confident Open Arms is surprised it hasn't heard from us already."

"Weak. Very weak." But I could not suppress a grin.

"I can't help it. I'm afraid someone else will get her."

"You've bonded to a photograph; you need counseling."

"Don't make fun of me. You can tell a lot from a picture."

"You certainly can," I agreed, with a confidence that seemed to surprise her.

"I just feel she's right for us."

I looked at her evenly. "Perhaps she is."

"Do you mean that?"

"I think so. Hey, don't do that. We're in a restaurant."

"I don't care," she said, grinning and wiping her eyes with the red napkin. "I just don't care. And now, Mr. Carter, please take me home. I intend to be physically exhausted when I call Open Arms tomorrow morning."

11

Hana

I thought back to grammar school; to the day of the shot. At age eight, I lingered near the back of a long line, reluctant to undergo a smallpox vaccination. Ahead, my classmates surrendered themselves one by one to the inevitability of the needle while I unconsciously clapped my right hand over the spot on my upper arm just below my bare shoulder. Friends closest to me shuffled their weight from leg to leg, the way you do when you are nervous. I watched each one as they approached the medic with the needle. Some looked away as they felt the alcohol swab their arm, knowing that seconds later they would feel the stick. Teachers stayed at the rear, making sure no one left the line, as I admit I had thought of doing. There were three in front of me, then two, then only a girl who was shaking as she walked toward the white coat. She cried out in pain when injected, then sobbed as the band aid was applied. When she turned toward me to leave the line I saw such pain in her face that I feared I would start crying before I was hurt. I fought against it, but then it was my turn. I shuffled forward, but evidently not close enough because the medic reached for my arm and pulled me toward him. Then I did something I didn't expect. When he applied the gauze with the alcohol, I looked directly at him, and when he pinched the skin of my slender triceps to form a ridge of sorts, I continued to stare, and when he raised the syringe and brought the needle close, I shifted my attention from him to it. I watched the point of the needle disappear into my skin, do its work, then withdraw. I watched it all, and I didn't cry out or moan or even flinch.

Today, twenty years later, I sat in my tiny office at the home. A metal desk, flush against the wall in my windowless office, permitted the opening and closing of my door virtually without tolerance. Overhead, a florescent light hummed. Eyeing a thick stack of portfolios piled in front of me, I sensed movement toward something harmful, a dread not unlike that produced by the needle; less defined, perhaps not as acute, but identifiably fear. The green portfolios contained "matches," adoptive parents matched to a child on my ward. Faith Stockdale had dropped them off that morning. Soo Yun's portfolio, almost certainly within the stack, threatened the ethical dilemma I had foreseen from my first glimpse of the scars.

Inside the folders, copies of the biographical data on the adoptive family, the home study, and the family's correspondence with Open Arms proclaimed the future for those fortunate enough to match that family's specified criteria. Faith Stockdale had collected these materials, then prepared a summary which she translated into Korean. These she forwarded to me to enable me both to inform the child of the match and to educate the child about the family of which he or she would soon be a member. Obviously, for infants matched, this synopsis served only to enlighten me as to the child's destiny. As often as I reminded myself that every pairing represented a triumph for the home in its mission to place as many children as possible, and thus a vicarious triumph for me, I nevertheless opened each portfolio with bittersweet resignation. A departing child meant more than an empty cot for the days, sometimes hours, needed to fill it. A funny business, this: striving for an inseparable closeness to a child who, in my fondest hope, would soon be taken away.

I picked up each green folder, perused them one by one, until my hand fell to a folder labeled "Soo Yun." I thought back to my meeting with Faith Stockdale on the day of Jong Sim's visit. I had intended to bring Faith into my confidence. The words formed on my lips: "The child has a horrible incision but is in perfect health." But I had been unable to utter those words, then or since.

At home on the night of that meeting, I rationalized my silence. To inform Faith of Soo Yun's biopsy was to transfer to her the very decision I made by remaining mute. Viewed that way, I felt a bit like a martyr. Thanks to my bravado, Soo Yun would receive the unimpeded chance she deserved to be adopted, and I, Hana, would take the consequences. If the biopsy triggered an inquiry, Faith would be shielded by her ignorance.

But as I went about my duties on the ward the following day, my wishful thinking showed itself for what it was. Unless disclosed, the scars were certain to launch an inquiry, meaning loss of credibility for Open Arms, angry recriminations against Faith Stockdale, ignorant or not, and untold consequences for me, including loss of my job or worse. And so, as the day progressed and my hastily constructed, undernourished rationalization of the previous night crumbled, I knew I had to set the facts fully before Faith Stockdale at the first opportunity. But that had been weeks ago. I could no longer say whether fear, or guilt, most accounted for my failure to approach Faith; only that they competed within me, one gaining on the other in a circle of diminishing diameter until they lodged just behind my frontal lobe, causing headaches.

From Faith's summary, the Carters of New Hampton, Virginia appeared to have been ordered from a catalog. Upper income, biological sons, stable marriage. I stared at the photo of them in their den, the boys seated on a sofa with the parents standing behind. I projected Soo Yun onto the sofa as a child of four or five, seated between her brothers, her hair in ribbons and her dress crisply ironed, with puffed sleeves at the shoulders. The terrible scars would have faded, and her health would be good, and neither boy flanking her and neither parent overlooking their three children would have given a thought to those inept invasions in years. Soo Yun would be lucky to call this home. I closed the folder, left my office, and walked toward the cafeteria. My recent headaches had cost me an appetite, but now I had to eat.

In a remote corner of the dining area, I tasted soft noodles from a white ceramic bowl. At least the uninspired concoction was hot. I almost dropped my chopsticks when I saw Faith striding toward me. She knows, I thought, diverting my eyes to the mass of noodles from which steam arose. Faith stood over me.

"Just the person I need to see," she said. "Have you had a chance to look over the matches?"

"Yes. Seven leaving my ward on the March flight."

"That's what I wanted to talk with you about. May I sit down?"

"Of course. Forgive me."

Faith pulled out a chair. "The problem is Open House. They've scheduled the March flight for the same day. I tried to get my people in the States to move it because it will create so much confusion, but they have already made arrangements with the airline and it will cost too much money to reschedule."

"Perhaps the home can move Open House." I breathed again.

"Tried that, too. No way. Too many churches have already made plans to visit. We'll just have to make it work."

"How many children leaving from the home?"

"Twenty-three. Quite a large group. You look worried."

"I have reviewed the matches you left on my desk."

"And?"

"I face a problem with one of my children; one selected for the March flight. I need your guidance."

"I'll help if I can. Is there a problem with the child?"

I hesitated. It was time for me to get that shot. Time to look the medic in the eye. Again, the words formed on my lips. "Yes," I said. "Her mother came to see me. I think she wants the child back. Do you think it is right to send an infant still wanted by her mother?"

"Has the mother applied for custody?"

"No. The woman is poor and uneducated."

A look of mild bewilderment formed on Faith's face. "Then I think we have no choice. We have to honor the match."

"I thought so, too." I paused. "I remembered the form we must sign just before the children depart. We have to certify that we know of no reason the child does not qualify for adoption, and I worried that this knowledge might be such a reason. I feel much better."

"Good," said Faith, watching with curiosity as I stared into my bowl. "But you don't look relieved."

"I am tired. I do not sleep well these nights."

"That's a shame. Try to get more rest. This group of matches leaves in three weeks, and getting twenty-three of them on that plane will take all our energy."

I returned to my ward, turning inward the contempt I felt for my indecision. I entered the nursery and walked to Soo Yun's crib. The child slept, covered to the neck by a blanket with her head turned toward me. The edema of birth had completely subsided, deflating her eyelids, forehead and cheeks to permit her skin, soft and smooth, to adhere faithfully to her delicate facial structure. As a physically plain woman, I knew only too well the components of appeal. I had spent painful periods as a young girl in front of mirrors in a silent prayer that what I saw could be otherwise, that the box of my face would elongate with adolescence, that the cheekbones would assert themselves to assume some dominion over the jowls and that the chin would emerge to take its proper, classic proportion to a mouth which would surely, with any luck at all, widen with age. In Soo Yun, I saw or imagined the beauty I lacked, and as I stared I pictured the child as I had projected her into the photograph, blooming into my unanswered girlhood prayer.

In days that followed, I suffered for my deceit. While not a perfect human being, I had managed to avoid many of the vices plaguing my siblings and friends. During a brief fling in my early twenties, I offered up my virginity to a boy who did not deserve the gift. But I did so honestly, as I hoped I had done all else since. Now, having passed up yet another opportunity to level with Faith Stockdale, I was trapped in an irrefutable deception, and for me to deny it, even to myself—especially to myself—would be to make worse a shame I could relieve only at the price of Soo Yun's continued residence in the home.

To quiet my fears of exposure on restless nights, I pulled a pillow over my head and around my ears to insulate against impending disgrace. I imagined Soo Yun in America, as an educated young woman with a constant stream of glamorous boyfriends all competing against the demands of her career as a journalist, a doctor, a university professor, a clothing designer. When her job and the demands of men grew too great, she would slip home, to parents who loved her as their own and whose pride in her she held like a trophy. At some point during these dawnless nights, I must have slipped over an edge, no longer focused on risks to myself but instead making positive plans for this infant; plans which, with my help, could be realized. Leaving things up to fate was not enough, because the visit from her mother, Jong Sim, told me all I needed to know about her chances. I thought back to that woman's peasant dress, her disorientation in Seoul, her teeth in need of dentistry not available in the countryside. That was Soo Yun's birthright, her past and almost certainly her future. Had Jong Sim not given her up, she would have grown into not just her mother's love but into some variation of her mother's life as well, and her odds of shaping a destiny different from her mother's were at least as great as those she now faced in leaving the home. In altering that destiny, I risked much, for how could I be certain that destiny was not the one for which the child was best suited? Suppose the child's talents and temperament matched instead the very future from which I was now determined to divert her? Did I do such a child any favor by sending her to a foreign land, to be raised in affluence but also with the pressure to bloom into the rose her new family expected? Merely transplanting a weed would make it no less a weed; was that what I was risking my career to do?

Possibly, but there were other things to be considered. First, Jong Sim's decision to give up her daughter. A mother in love with her own fate does not put that fate beyond the path of those who follow her. Jong Sim would have had only the dimmest vision of what lay ahead for Soo Yun following her afternoon in the doorway, but she knew with murderous certainty what future she left behind in their squalid village. Perhaps Jong Sim herself possessed talents and a temperament ill suited to the prison in which she found herself, and had watched such talents, like parched barley, dry up and drift uselessly to earth.

Then, there was the infant. She had seemed to me from our first contact in the police station to be struggling toward something. I could not give a rational explanation for this impression, nor could I totally discard the notion that I myself had ennobled Soo Yun's distemper as some kind of telepathic communication when objective evidence pointed to nothing more than the ranting of a tired, wet soul abandoned in a doorway. Still, the child had calmed immediately in my grasp, as though in approval of this step in the proper direction. At the home, in her crib, she took little interest in her surroundings, even for an infant, and this indifference I took as evidence of her determination to remain in this way station for the minimum time required to recover her health.

I suspected that my embroidered interpretations of habits and disposition projected onto the child ambitions purely of the my own creation. As a test, I challenged myself to answer whether, given the chance to walk into a nursery containing one hundred newborns, I could have singled this one out as possessing qualities lacking in the others. No, I could not, but neither did life play out in such sterile laboratories, stripped of the very scents and tracks which led to my divination. I responded to a call from Jongam for Soo Yun, not some other abandoned baby. I found the named pinned to this infant. The mother of another child could have arrived at the home seeking that child, but it was Soo Yun's mother who actually made that trip. These incidentals and others, so benign in isolation, together formed in my mind a composite image of a child with a destiny calling from beyond the home; indeed, from beyond the borders of her own land. But, as a helpless presence not yet weighing five kilograms, she could answer that calling only by bending those around her to her will. In me, it seemed to be working. Events, not words, came to me as the monosyllabic uttering of a tongue too freshly formed to speak, but directed at me, as though I alone could translate this unspoken but loudly and insistently broadcast infant language.

Well, I thought, you really have slipped over an edge if you have come to believe your time on the ward permits you to hear sounds inaudible to others, or to read invisible signs, or to speak in tongues. You might just as well call yourself a gypsy and purchase tarot cards. You need a vacation.

Yet, upon deeper reflection, I felt less certain there was anything abnormal or paranormal at work. Those who spent all their time with animals, for example, claimed a rapport with them produced by extensive contact. Mi Cha had hinted at such communications with her lost dog, Mojo. Was it not equally possible that my experience on the ward had honed some instinct within me into a finely tuned receptor of sorts? I chose to believe so, and in the days following I held tightly to my new religion.

As the departure of the matched children neared, I carried Soo Yun to Dr. Kim, who again reassured me that the child bore no ill effects from her hospitalization save the ugly scars, all the more savage now in their florid convalescence.

With the dual challenges of Open House and the March flight upon me, I overslept on the last Saturday in March. I had tossed fitfully until almost dawn, falling soundly to sleep only when it was time to get up. I rose, counting on raw adrenaline to carry me through the emotional day ahead. As I washed my face, I noticed the rash on the back of my hands. It began earlier that week, with a splotching around the knuckles that gradually spread. I am certain it is caused by nerves; my decision to withhold from Faith the information on Soo Yun's scars.

I dressed in semi-darkness, fixed hot tea, and bundled myself in my warmest undergarments, sweaters, muffler, and coat. Several inches of snow had fallen during the night, with winds gusting at a single plow attempting to clear the roads. I wondered if the weather might close the airport, delaying the 7:30 P.M. flight which would carry the matches to Hawaii for refueling, then on to New York. At the very least the bitter temperatures foreshadowed a reduced attendance at Open House. I cleared the snow from my doorway and went out into the cold.

I arrived at the home as the children were preparing for visitors. The atmosphere on the ward was different this morning, as I recognized at the moment I stepped from the elevator. The texture of this difference I attributed to the simultaneity of Open House and a departure, a coincidence unprecedented in my time here. Possibly, I reasoned, the distraction of Open House would prove a merciful blessing to those left behind. If so, I was thankful for it—for it and any other ally in steeling myself against both the loss of the seven children from my ward and the reactions of those remaining as well.

As I made my morning rounds, I witnessed sights to which no frequency of departures could accustom me. Something in their nature triggered a denial of sorts by those for whom this would be just another day. Such denials explained why the remaining children gave circumspect glances to the six beds on which suitcases lay open. As they set their Projections on the navy blue and white bedspreads, those old enough to appreciate the significance of the small travel bags outwardly reflected a stoic indifference, the way children can do when sides are chosen and they reckon their team by walking in the opposite direction from the last one selected. On my way to the nursery, I spotted Eun skipping rope near the cot of her best friend. The two girls had been like sisters, arriving at the home within a month of each other three years before. As her friend emptied her few personal articles into the travel bag, Eun chatted excitedly over the "thwapping" of the rope on linoleum. Her friend seemed to have trouble lifting her smocks, her jeans, her underwear from the locker, as though some glutinous force held them. She was matched to a childless couple in their late thirties, and I knew from our talks that the secret of her heart was a melancholy fear of loneliness.

In the nursery, I walked first to the crib of Soo Yun. "Where is she?" I inquired of an aide.

"That woman from the agency, the one with the short hair, came for her a short time ago."

I felt my chest compress. I glanced again at the empty crib and heard myself say, in a voice I did not recognize, "Where did she take her?"

"To the infirmary."

I ran to the stairs, my pulse racing but my legs encased in the concrete of impending doom. At the door to the infirmary I paused to catch my breath, then pushed through.

On a gurney at the far end of the room lay Soo Yun. Dr. Kim stood over her, speaking to Faith Stockdale. Both turned as I approached. Dr. Kim lowered his eyes as those of Faith Stockdale narrowed.

"I was just coming to see you," she said. "It seems our recent discussions have not been detailed enough. In checking the immunization records for our matches, I came across a very disturbing chart." Dr. Kim took a step back as Faith advanced.

"I can explain," I said.

"You weren't honest with me."

"Yes, I was. I told you she had been ill but had recovered. That is true."

"You failed to mention surgery."

"The scars are mere imperfections unrelated to the health of the child. They appear as surgical scars only because the testing was done badly."

Faith Stockdale crossed her arms. "That is for the adopting parents to decide after a review of the records. They are surgical procedures which you know full well must be reported so an Alert can be issued."

"I discussed her health at length with Dr. Kim." I glanced at him for confirmation.

"That is so," he said. "She was most concerned."

"It was my judgment that such a cosmetic flaw did not require a report."

"This child spent a month in the hospital. At the moment her new parents examine her all hell will break lose. I would say your judgment was very poor in this instance. I need to wire the States for instructions. In the meantime, let's get this baby back up to the ward. She's not going anywhere today."

12

Elizabeth

Did Coleman really suggest we move to Charleston? And was I actually considering it? Not that night, the night he agreed to the adoption, but in the days following I found myself contemplating something I never thought I'd even consider. But in fairness, hadn't he agreed to something

I feel certain he didn't see coming? So maybe it balanced out. The offer from Barron Morris promised to put Coleman years ahead of where he stood in New Hampton, even as a new partner. In our married life he had never once suggested moving back, but somewhere in the recesses of my intuition I sensed he wanted to. Sarah would certainly need him now, as none of the reports of his father's condition contemplated a full recovery. So will we relocate from the South to the Deep South? I need to decide in the days ahead. There better be no white wine shortage down there.

Coleman mentioned inviting Sarah to visit, but it didn't occur to me that she would accept until the day she called to let us know she was coming. She arrived in New Hampton in the late afternoon, tired from her nine hours on the byways of the Carolinas and Virginia, because despite the luxury of interstate highways she doesn't like them and will add hours to a trip to avoid them. Josh and Steven saw her from a window and rushed to greet her. Coleman and I followed, instructing the boys on her luggage. There were so many bags I wondered if she was moving to New Hampton just as we were heading to Charleston, a move she knew nothing about and wouldn't until the time felt right. We hadn't even told Josh and Steven because kids at that age think a secret is something you keep if you just whisper the information. She went immediately to her room, to "freshen up." The boys lingered, knowing that she would have gifts for them as always.

The first days of her visit passed pleasantly. While Coleman worked and the boys were in school, we had long conversations about her new life, and there was no doubt, even to her, that is what it was; a life transformed. She told me that when she wasn't at her husband's bedside, she kept busy with garden club, bridge club, Bible study circle, Daughters of the American Revolution. Three afternoons a week she went swimming at the YMCA. She served as hostess for the Society for the Preservation of Charleston. Just listening to her schedule exhausted me, and I was less than half her age. Many women dropped in, she said, alone or in pairs, for coffee or just to chat. Friends invited her to dinner, urging upon her a second glass of wine if she felt like it.

But the stillness of the house loomed undeniably each evening. She resolutely rejected invitations to "stay over; it's so late anyway." She kept lights on, more than before, so the house was never dark when she turned the corner of Church Street and rumbled over the cobblestones to the driveway. She locked her car, walked to the side entrance, and entered the house without fear. A couple of her friends, widows, reported feelings of a presence in their houses, wraiths they thought they sensed—sometimes even saw—which, they insisted, deepened their nostalgia for loved ones who were, at such moments, close enough to touch.

Sarah told me she sensed the opposite. If any apparition inhabited the house on Church Street, it came to her, stole silently in and out of rooms, hovered over her as she slept, as a ghostly absence of anything she recognized as connected to her husband or their life together. This was not to deny the reminders; the leather chair in the den where he had religiously perused the *Post and Sentinel,* his slippers in their closet, his old Navy uniform still suspended in the attic. When she saw these and other countless relics of his existence, she longed for, cried herself to sleep for, a wraith, for any corporeal presence however flimsy or ephemeral, to relieve the unmitigated emptiness of that house.

The fact that her mate of five decades required skilled care in perpetuity became clear. Watchful hours at the bedside made her ready for it to be over, for Coles to rise from his bed, reach for a cane or perhaps a walker, and announce that he was ready to go home, to mix a cocktail in time for the evening news. Instead, he drooled, and while she wanted to believe his efforts at speech intensified while she visited, she couldn't be sure. She knew his mind was still there as he became more proficient at the blinking code that forced her into questions answered yes or no. His left hand became more active, allowing him to return the affectionate squeeze she greeted and left him with. His physical therapist suggested a computer might be feasible, which fostered in Sarah both encouragement for better communications and the pessimism of endless paralysis, a prognosis Dr. Adams refused to rule out. At one visit, she asked if he would mind her visiting Virginia. No, he blinked.

Sarah slept a little later than was her habit, and Coleman had usually left for his office by the time she arose to have coffee with me. She dutifully phoned the nursing home to get a report. She asked the nurse to place the receiver at her husband's ear, into which she reported news of their grandsons, some funny comment Coleman or I had come up with, or perhaps world news filtered through her peculiar lens. If she asked a question, the nurse reported the answer. She ended each call with assurances of her love and her return to him as soon as she wore out her welcome.

Sarah seemed to derive comfort from reminiscence, so I encouraged her recollections. Always fascinated by genealogy, particularly her own, she seemed to relish it all the more, telling stories of her youth surrounded by eccentric aunts, tormenting siblings, and memorable cousins. "Coleman's great grandfather on my side," she reminded me, "was the youngest full professor in the history of the University of South Carolina," while I, washing dishes or attempting to stay ahead of the ironing, would prod her to tell more, and she did.

On the evening of the fifth day, just before Coleman's arrival home, the telephone rang. Sarah knitted at the breakfast table and I had just gone into the basement to see why the washing machine emitted the high-pitched squeal which often signaled an unbalanced load. Sarah answered, a fact I learned only later, and not from her. Sarah hung up as I came upstairs. "Did I hear the phone?" I asked as I entered the kitchen. "You can't hear over the racket in the basement."

"Yes," said Sarah, her eyes downcast at her knitting on the table. "A sales call . . . I told them to try back." She lied.

"You should have told them 'no,'" I said. "That's what I'll tell them."

Sarah gathered up her knitting. "I'm not feeling quite myself this afternoon," she said. "I think I'll lie down for a time."

"I'll check on you for dinner," I offered.

Sarah did not appear at dinner. Later that evening, Coleman and I prepared for bed.

"She just said she wasn't feeling well," I told him.

He dropped one shoe to the floor. "She told me the same thing when I called through the door. It's odd; she has the constitution of a horse."

In my nightgown and robe, I sat at the edge of the bed. "I'm surprised I haven't heard from Open Arms. When we called to tell them, they said we would be getting confirmation in two weeks. It's been three. I think I'll call them tomorrow. And incidentally, have you told your mother what's about to happen?"

Coleman, in shorts and T-shirt, his standard sleeping attire, pulled back the covers. "I was going to ask you the same question?"

"Not in this lifetime. You're going to handle that one." I paused. "Coleman, what are we going to do if this baby arrives while your mother is here? Where will we put her?"

"The baby or mother?"

"I'm being serious. We have one guest room . . ."

"And two guests, potentially."

"I'd hardly call our new daughter a guest. Do you have any ideas?'

"I suppose they could be roommates," he said, climbing into bed.

"Do you have any serious ideas? Has your mother said how long she's staying?"

"Not to me, but I don't think it's fair to put pressure on her. She's been through a lot and I want her to feel like she can stay here for as long as she wants."

"I do, too," I said, setting the dial on the electric blanket. "I'm enjoying her company. I just worry that we'll get a phone call and have two or three days to sort out where everyone will sleep."

"Well, I know where I'm going to sleep," he said, snuggling into his pillow.

I turned off the last lamp by the bed. "Good night. You're hopeless."

"I know it," he said. "I'll break the news tomorrow. Good night."

When I called Open Arms the following day, they put me through to someone named Benita Mallory, who seemed puzzled to hear from me. "I left a message yesterday," she reminded me. "I gave the person who answered the news. About 4:00 in the afternoon. I'm sure of it. I have a line through your name on my call list."

"No," I said, and then it hit me what must have happened. "I want to make sure I have the details right. Can you repeat them for me while I write them down?"

"Of course. Your application for Soo Yun has been approved and she will be arriving on Monday, the thirty-first of this month, at Kennedy Airport in New York. I'll be calling you back later this week with the flight number and the arrival time, but I knew you'd want this news as soon as possible so you could make your plans to meet the plane."

When I told Coleman the news, he said his mother probably forgot. "Forgot?" I said. "No way. When you break the news today, ask her how something like that slipped her mind. Coleman, she said it was a sales call. What would have happened if I hadn't called the agency? We don't have much time as it is."

"Maybe she was just waiting for the right time to give you the message."

My doubts got the better of me. "And maybe the Easter Bunny will stay for dinner."

I wasn't there the next day when his mother confronted him. He swears she told him about the Benita Mallory phone call before he asked, and I'd like to think that is true. He said she made a pitch to call off the adoption; that she got emotional about it. All I know for certain is that when I walked in from shopping on that dreary Saturday afternoon, Sarah had retreated to her room and didn't come out until the next morning, when she went to church. Perhaps she was embarrassed. She should have been. Church must have done what churches do for some, because when she returned she apologized for not telling me Benita had called. I accepted the apology, as it seemed heartfelt.

That made the week that followed less tense, although I held no illusion that she had given up. When she didn't return on time from church the next week, Coleman went looking for her, and sure enough she made a final plea to stop what to us now seemed inevitable. She still had not said how long she intended to stay, and it wasn't until the next week, a mere two days before Soo Yun was to arrive, that we learned her plans.

I spent that morning in the attic, where I found the crib in which Josh and Steven had slept and which would now hold Soo Yun. Dusting it, cleaning it with a strong solvent, and painting it in the green and white I had selected for the nursery filled me with nostalgia for those prior pregnancies. I marveled at the coincidence of emotions and sensations welling up inside me following the confirmation of arrival details by Benita Mallory, like I was actually pregnant again. I could almost feel in my legs the swelling I endured in the final throes of my eighth and ninth months with Josh and Steven, and one night I woke up giggling at an imagined elbow or knee in my pelvis. The crib, we had decided, would be set up in our room until Sarah's room became available.

That afternoon, Coleman changed into work clothes and reported to the attic for lifting duty. Together we carried the components of the crib down the disappearing stairway to our bedroom, where Coleman whacked it together in a matter of minutes as the quirks of its assembly came back to him.

As I smoothed the comforter down, I said, "I wish we could have gotten a direct flight to Kennedy. We'll arrive La Guardia at eleven in the morning and sit."

"We could run into Manhattan."

"Not enough time. Her flight arrives at 5:48 and the Open Arms briefing starts at 4:30. Benita Mallory was emphatic that we make that if possible."

"So that's all we have to do, eh? Show up at a briefing. I wonder if they'll hand out some kind of ticket or chit; you know, 'Present this to the flight attendant to claim your kid.' You don't suppose she'll be in baggage claim, do you?"

As I admired the now-ready crib, I found him admiring me. A good sign, I thought.

13

Coleman

I stayed in touch with Barron Morris. He put no expiration date on his offer, telling me he realized it represented a major decision and urging me to take whatever time was needed. Elizabeth and I discussed pros and cons, but casually, as though the debate was a hypothetical one not truly related to our future. In the meantime, I pressed ahead with billable hours.

A few days before Mother arrived for her visit, I sat at my desk, a stack of depositions piled in front of me and notebooks covering the credenza to my left. Two weeks remained until the McLauren trial, at which I hoped to punish a stingy insurance company for its latest offer, one the company termed "final." Our client, Ted McLauren, had been a passenger in a Volvo broad-sided by an eighteen wheeler in an intersection. The damage to McLauren's right leg was severe and permanent. Experience made all the difference in evaluating such claims, and it was here that I felt I earned my pay, weighing as objectively as I could evidence, depositions, medical reports, legal theories to determine a range of value.

My door opened and Don Mahoney's head appeared. "Stop in when you get a moment," Mahoney said. I knew, as did every other lawyer in the firm, that the outside limit on the "moment" was fifteen minutes, and that failure to report within that time would bring Mahoney back, "wondering what the hell happened to you." I gave it ten minutes, straightened my tie and ambled down the hall to Mahoney's corner office.

"Sit down," Mahoney intoned in his cavernous voice as I entered. "Coffee?"

"Thanks. I've had my quota."

"What are you working on these days? How's the Anspach matter?"

"Can't get to it. McLauren goes to trial in two weeks and I'm getting 'litigator's lament.'"

"A terrible affliction," Mahoney agreed. "I've had it myself many times. What's the offer?"

"Fifty grand."

Mahoney winced. "And we said 'no?' What are the damages?"

"Seventy-five thousand and climbing, but liability is the problem; the old red-light, green-light debate. Our key witness had a very poor vantage point. They know it and we know it. Naturally, our client sees that as a technicality and plans to retire on our efforts."

"Naturally." Mahoney paused. "Changing subjects, I hear you and Elizabeth are expecting. Chinese, did I hear?"

"Korean." I felt pressure in my throat, as though I tightened my tie to excess.

Mahoney nodded but said nothing, turning his gaze toward the blind-covered bank of windows to his right and drumming his fingers lightly on the surface of his desk.

"Is that a problem?" I asked, sensing in Mahoney's silence the air of admonition.

Mahoney grinned, but without humor. "Oh, I don't see why. Besides, it's your business. But it has been the subject of some discussion at the club. A couple of folks on the membership committee have come to me wondering if they risk setting some sort of precedent . . ."

I saw where Mahoney was headed, but decided not to help him get there. "Gee, aren't there already some adopted children among the members?"

"Well, sure there are," said Mahoney with a hint of impatience. "The point is this child is . . . ethnic."

"Ah," I said, feigning a dawning of the light. "The Reggie Page problem."

"No, no. Reggie Page is another matter altogether. You can't equate the blacks with the Orientals."

"No, of course not," I agreed. "I only meant that both involve exceptions to the norm, and I guess any time you make exceptions you have to consider the long-range implications."

"Naturally," agreed Mahoney. "Everyone likes you and Elizabeth and wants you in the club. You've no doubt got your reasons for taking in this child and who are we to second guess. But in that Cynthia and I will be sponsoring your application, I wanted to make sure you understood the sensitivity some of the members are feeling on the minority question."

"Absolutely," I replied, surprised at the edge in my own voice and newly conscious of a latent indignation within. "It's just hard for me to imagine a little orphan being the source of controversy at the club."

"It's not so much the orphan."

"What then?"

"Jesus, Coleman, you're a bright guy, think about it. The last thing Riverside needs now is controversy over a racial question. I know where you stand because I've practiced with you for five years. But I have to tell you that some people are less sure about your wife. Her refusal to join the Junior League still has some folks upset."

I gave Mahoney a respectful scoff. "That was no great statement of principle on Elizabeth's part. She's not the League type and wasn't interested, pure and simple."

Mahoney grew animated, flaring his arms upward as his voice descended to its most imperial, regnant depth. "But joining the League is something you do when you live here and are married to a lawyer in this kind of firm. You should have forced her to join."

I laughed. Maybe having the Charleston offer in my back pocket made me cocky. "I commanded her to sign up. She said, 'No.' That was the end of it."

"And now you see where people get their suspicions."

"So that's it," I said, eyeing him with a steady glare. "My wife is considered some type of rebel and people are nervous."

"'Rebel' is too strong, but I'll be honest and say that some have doubts. Don't be shocked if your invitation to join isn't unanimous."

"Then don't be shocked if we don't apply for membership."

Mahoney waggled his finger. "You've taken this wrong. Your application will sail through. I only wanted to warn you about what some of the more conservative members are thinking."

I stood. "I don't know, Don. It seems to me that we may be putting you and Cynthia on the spot by applying. Naturally, we wouldn't want to embarrass you. Why don't we both take a few days to think it over."

"Good thought," affirmed Mahoney, standing. "We'll talk again. And keep me posted on how the McLauren negotiations are going."

"I sure will," I promised with a smile.

Mother teared up as she confessed to lying to Elizabeth about the phone call. Truth bears the weight of other religious obligations she shoulders, so I knew the guilt must have pained her. Our conversation took place the following day, while Elizabeth shopped and after Josh, Steven, and I endured a thrashing on the soccer field at the hands of the mighty Rowdies, the league's best. A chilly, driving rainstorm late in the game contributed to the coughs and sniffles they brought home. Mother made a fire and fixed soup, apologizing to Josh and Steven as she served it that she had not come to their game. After lunch, when the boys had gone upstairs to play a board game that required them to fight their way through an endless string of ever more potent dragons to rescue some maiden named Penelope, I took a seat near the fire. Mother, seated on the other side of the hearth, read a book. She looked up to find me staring at her.

"Something on your mind, dear?" she asked.

"You," I said. "Just wondering how you've been coping with dad's situation."

"Some days are easier than others. I've stayed active. He won't be coming home. I see that now."

"Have you given any thought to what you'll do? That's a big house for one person."

She closed her book in her lap. "All my memories are in that house. I won't think of selling it until the day comes I can't keep it up. I might take a trip."

"Good," I said. "You've wanted to travel for years."

She sighed. "Your father hates leaving Charleston, as you know. Whenever I've pried him away, he's been no fun at all."

I smiled. "I can imagine. Where would you like to visit?"

"Europe. Italy, Greece. I've never been abroad, so there is plenty to choose from."

"Go for it," I said. "Stay here with us until the boys drive you crazy, then take off. The change would do wonders."

I got up, walked to the fireplace, pulled back the screen, and placed another oak log on the andirons.

"Change is a part of life, I suppose," she said with a sigh. She folded her reading glasses and put them deliberately on the table beside her chair. "I wouldn't be surprised if things were changing here as well."

"Why do you say that?"

Sarah looked into the fire. "I had a feeling that Elizabeth would get her way on this preposterous adoption." I eyed her, my surprise tinged with wariness. "I answered the phone yesterday. Before I could set the caller straight on who was speaking, she started spouting information about the arrival of this child." It was at that point the tears came. "I . . . wasn't honest with Elizabeth when she asked me who called. I couldn't sleep last night knowing I owe her an apology."

"Did you speak to her?"

She sniffled but regained control. "I wanted to talk to you first. I hope you see what's happening here. She's positively determined to force this on you, and on us. I just hope it hasn't gone so far that it can't be stopped."

"Mother, I think you should know that I'm the one who called the agency to accept. She didn't force this on me."

Her eyes widened, and in them I could see not only the reflection of the fire in the fireplace but the glint of her indignation where tears were moments earlier. "But, why on earth would you agree to such a thing? You know it makes no sense."

"No, I don't know that," I said softly.

"Oh, how can you be so naïve? She's a foreigner you've never even laid eyes on. Some of them carry terrible diseases. Then you read these tragic stories of pregnant women on drugs with horrible effects on their children; how do you know she won't have a brain disorder? It's a pig in a poke!"

I looked away. "We're going through a reputable agency. There are risks. We realize that."

"And you'll see just how risky it is when you have to pay thousands of dollars in medical bills for a child who can't even feed herself or learn the alphabet."

"With all due respect, I think you're looking at the dark side of the moon."

"I just knew she would do something like this. She's always resented your heritage, although God knows why."

"Mother, leave Elizabeth out of this. It was her idea, yes. But this child needs a home, and we have a home to offer. Why does it have to be any more complicated than that?"

"Because society is complicated, as you will find out when she has doors slammed in her face. And it wouldn't surprise me if your sons experience the same thing." She tossed her book onto the table. "The whole thing makes me ill. Positively ill. To think you'd do this when your father is in such fragile health. I don't speak to him about it. It will bring on another stroke."

Expecting this line of attack sooner, I had no easy counter. "I've considered that," I said as evenly as I could, and it was true. "The reality is that he may be in this condition for years, Mother. We can't put life on hold. He wouldn't want that."

"He wouldn't want *this,*" she said. "I'll make my apology to Elizabeth, but I won't change my mind about the mistake she is making."

"*We* are making," I corrected, then let it drop, and it more or less stayed there until that Sunday when she didn't come home from church. When she had not returned by 1:30, I grew concerned. Even when Communion coincided with a visit from the Bishop, church ended by 12:30 and the walk home was a mere ten minutes. I zipped up my jacket and started for St. Andrews.

The day was milder, with clear skies and no wind. The chill of the previous day had been replaced by warmth of an imminent spring, and I could almost hear the sap groaning in the desiccated trunks of hibernating hardwoods, see on the tips of branches the embryonic nubs and folds of renewal. A squirrel scampered across my path before retreating in the same direction from which it had come.

I had served on the building committee for the prayer chapel recently added to the main body of the church, and it was in this chapel that I found Mother, the sole occupant of the tiny sanctuary, seated on a middle pew, her head bent and her eyes closed. I entered, bowed my head to the Cross, and slipped in beside her. We sat, wordless, for ten minutes. I broke the silence.

"Mother, it's important to me that you approve of this adoption."

She opened her eyes, but her head remained declined. "I can't do that. I'm sorry. Your father is so against it."

"But he's not here, not really. It's not his decision. How do you feel about it?"

"I've told you."

"No, you told me what you think, not how you feel."

"I feel you should honor his opposition, which he has expressed to me very strongly."

"He expressed it to me once, in a single sentence that came as close to being a personal conversation as I ever had with the man."

"As I said, you intimidated him."

"Well, now he's intimidating me, and he's doing it from the safety of the nursing home, where he runs no risk of the kind of confrontations he dreaded. But I don't have that luxury. I'm here, in the middle between my wife, whom I love and wish to please, and you, whom I also love and wish to please."

"I do understand your dilemma, son. I truly do."

"When Elizabeth and I began discussing this, my objections were the same ones you raised. In fact, it was eerie how similar they were. The more I thought about them, the more I realized how easy it is to be against something strange and unknown. For me, it seems second nature, and as I look at Dad and Grandfather, I think I come by that nature honestly. I intend to, as you phrased it, 'honor his memory,' but I have to do it my own way. Where this child is concerned, I think there is more honor in saying 'yes.' All the dire predictions may come true. We may even be underestimating them. If we are, you and Dad will get the satisfaction of a big, fat 'I told you so.'"

"That would give us no satisfaction at all."

"But whoever she turns out to be, you'll be her grandparents, and it will mean an awful lot to everyone if you can accept her."

Mother shook her head slowly from side to side. "Why does life have to be so complicated?"

I stretched my arm around her shoulder, pulling her to me. "Because death is so simple. And until you, Dad and I arrive there, we have to take risks, and this is one worth taking. Who knows? Maybe she'll turn out to be cute and smart and healthy."

She stared off in the direction of the altar. "This may kill him."

In the days that followed, I helped Elizabeth put together the old crib, freshly painted. We were now less than a week from our appointment at Kennedy Airport. Elizabeth very diplomatically approached Mother about arrangements for the boys on the day we planned to be in New York, reminding her of their return from school at 3:30, the need for snacks and the allowed play time.

"But I won't be here," Mother said casually, as though it were a mere detail she had forgotten. We stared at her. "It is time for me to leave."

In a somewhat guarded voice, I said, "But we assumed you would be here with the boys. We've been counting on it."

"I am sorry," said she. "I guess it's short notice, but I just decided that I'd be in the way during what I'm sure will be a special time for your family. Besides, you need my room."

"I told you, Sarah," said Elizabeth, "that you were welcome for as long as you wanted to be here, and I meant it."

"We both meant it," I echoed.

"That's kind, and I believe you both. But I want to go. And look at the time," she said, checking her watch. "I've got to pack." She stood, carried her plate to the kitchen, and returned to her room.

We remained seated at the table, me with my arms folded across my chest, staring at the pattern in the placemat, and Elizabeth studying my reaction to Sarah's announcement.

"She'll come around," she assured me.

I shook my head. "Maybe, maybe not. I'd hate to think she's leaving for the last time."

Elizabeth telephoned Betsy Miller to explain our dilemma with the children. From the guest room came the muffled but discernible opening and closing of drawers, suitcases and closets.

"Well, that's covered," she reported. "Betsy said she'd be happy to come over tomorrow and stay with the children until we get back from New York. I warned her we expected to be late."

When I made no response, she walked to my side of the table and placed her hand on the back of my neck in a gentle massaging motion.

"Can you think of anything else we can do?" she asked.

"No. Too many changes in too short a time. It can't be helped. I wish I knew how much of this reflects her own feelings and how much of it comes from her new job as my father's keeper."

We heard the distinctive creak of the guest room hinges and then Sarah's footsteps in the hall. She entered the dining room in her traveling clothes and walked to where she had been sitting for lunch, gripping the back of her chair. "Dear," she said, "I just realized that I didn't ask you if I can leave my car here."

"Of course, but how will you get home?"

"I'm not going back to Charleston just yet. Actually, I'm going to London." She gazed down at her hands.

"London?" I asked. "For how long?"

"Two weeks. Doesn't that sound like a nice break?"

"Fabulous," I replied. "Really fabulous. You got a passport?"

"Several years ago, hoping your father would loosen up a bit." She paused. "Before I go, I'd like a word with you both on the subject of this adoption."

"Sure," I said as Elizabeth slipped into the chair beside me.

"I believe you're making a mistake. I've told both of you as much. And Coleman, certainly your father feels strongly that an Oriental orphan should not carry the Carter name. I'm not supposed to tell you this, but a few weeks before his stroke he changed his will. Josh and Steven are in it, of course, and any child you may have that isn't adopted. For him, it's about blood. Not a great amount of money, mind you, but the principle was important to him. Now that he is so . . . incapacitated, I don't know if it can be changed, even if he wanted to.

"But we've had our say, and now I think the time has come to accept what is clearly going to happen. I can't pretend I'm excited, but you are and that's good. I think this young girl, this baby, is very lucky to end up here."

I studied her. Elizabeth said, "That's very gracious of you to say, Sarah. I know it's not easy."

Sarah gave a short smile. "With Coles so sick, you two and my grandsons are all I have, and nothing is worth jeopardizing that. You may find, as I have more times than I can relate, that to make a family work, someone has to give. In the end, it comes down to that. If this child doesn't fulfill your expectations, you'll see soon enough what I mean. Coleman, please give me a hand with my bags."

"Give the Queen my love," Elizabeth told Sarah as she left the house.

I'm delighted she decided to go to England. Her desire for travel has been suppressed long enough. When she announced she was leaving, we all felt it was best. She was stoic on the ride to the airport, but I sensed underlying excitement to be embarking on an adventure I knew she had dreamed about.

"What do they eat?" she asked me as we neared the terminal.

"Who?" I asked.

"Oriental babies. They must have their own diet."

I laughed. "I don't think so, Mother. As far as I know it's just your basic pabulum sprinkled with a little soy sauce." I watched her from the corner of my eye, but she seemed to nod in acceptance of my explanation.

We parked in a short-term metered space and unloaded the bags. Josh and Steven each carried one, flanking her as she walked toward the terminal. In front of the ticket counter, we paused. As I waited for the boys to deliver their farewell hugs, I gazed at her with what I hoped was undisguised affection, wondering if I could summon the same poise in defeat. Perhaps I could; it was, after all, part of my heritage.

"You know, Mother," I said as I leaned down to embrace her, "I just thought of something. You were always a little disappointed I didn't end up with a southern girl, and now I'm finally going to have one."

"Going to have one . . . ," she mumbled as she searched for my meaning.

"She's from South Korea—don't you get it?"

"Yes, of course I get it," she said, still a little dubious. "Well, I'll pick her up a little something in England."

We stayed to watch through the large observation window as her plane taxied down the runway, then ascended. By the time we returned, Elizabeth had completely rearranged the guest room into the nursery she had mentally decorated a dozen times in the preceding months. We were ready.

14

Hana

When Faith ordered Soo Yun back to the ward, I exploded from the infirmary's side door and tramped two blocks through the snow. Walking into the wind, I lowered her head to protect my eyes from the sting of subfreezing gusts. Frosted breath vented from my mouth and nostrils, expelled with great thrust by adrenaline but immediately blunted, then reversed, by the headwind, sweeping over and behind me in tendrils of human vapor. Despite the frigid air, I gradually regained a rhythmic breath. My anger behaved very much like my breath; as hard as I thrust it forward at Faith, it washed back over me. It was bad enough that Faith had caught me bypassing Open Arms policy, but to have that truth revealed in the presence of Dr. Kim added humiliation. At the corner I crossed the street, without looking, to embark upon a third block until I realized I wore only a sweater and risked hypothermia. I turned back, shivering now.

This entire affair, I thought as I walked, had ceased to be about a child and had become only a matter of consequences. Faith wished to issue an Alert so she could shift the decision onto the Carters. She had become a prisoner of that photo of Sohn on her desk. The wind blew faster than I could walk, forcing me to lean back against it. I could no longer feel my ears at all.

This match was still possible if I took all responsibility. It was a simple matter of assuring Faith, Dr. Kim, and anyone else unfortunate enough to place a foot within the circle of blame. If I was wrong, what could they do? I did not see lines of nurses forming at the home to work eighty hours a week for the modest hwan they paid me. I saw only lines of children waiting to leave.

By the time I returned to the nursery, Soo Yun again lay in her crib, at the foot of which rested a plastic traveling bag stocked with diapers. I tried not to look at it as I adjusted the covers around her shoulders. From the clock on the wall I knew that the first visitors for Open House would be arriving soon. I paused, gazing down at the child's head protruding from the blanket. Her eyes were closed but her lips quivered in a suckling motion, either in anticipation of her next feeding or in memory of some past nourishment, recalled now only in dreams.

I knew I must act swiftly. I thought of the family in the photograph, the Carters. If the situation was to be fully and fairly explained to them, they might instruct the home to send her anyway, but I was unwilling to take such a risk. The wrong decision amounted to rejecting a bar of gold over the presence of a scuff mark. I had to overcome Faith to avoid this outcome. I turned from the crib and in a pace closer to a run than a walk I approached the elevator.

The door to Faith Stockdale's office was closed but I entered without knocking. My walk had numbed me to whatever chill had overtaken my relationship with Faith as a result of our earlier confrontation. I determined I would speak as though nothing had happened, but my tone proved only a partial screen for my impatience. Faith, dialing the phone, looked up, startled.

"May I sit down?" I asked, seating myself in front of her desk without waiting for a response. Faith replaced the phone in its cradle.

"Have you been outside? Your ears are crimson."

"Soo Yun must be allowed to leave today. I will take full responsibility when I sign her certification this afternoon."

"If it were that simple," said Faith, leaning forward, "I would let you. But the call will come to me. What explanation can I give? That I was unaware? That would plainly be false."

"Tell them you investigated thoroughly. That you consulted the doctor and the child's nurse. Tell them you relied on my assurance, as you will be for the other matches leaving my ward today."

Faith sighed, a signal of controlled provocation. "But I have a duty to my agency and to the parents who have agreed to take this baby. You are placing us both in a terrible spot. Why?"

"Because I have a duty to the children on my ward . . . even the ones who cannot speak."

"Of course," agreed Faith. "And you've always performed that duty in a professional manner. Which is one reason I'm having so much trouble understanding your judgment where this particular child is concerned."

I leaned forward, resting my hands on the leading edge of her desk. When I remembered the rash, I returned my hands to my lap. Without intending it, I lowered my voice as though at risk of being overheard, although we were quite alone. "That is a question I ask myself. The child came to us in the usual way, abandoned at a police station." I related finding the name pinned to the linen, the mirror, and the subsequent visit from Jong Sim.

Faith nodded in recollection. "You said you thought the mother had changed her mind."

"Perhaps not changed her mind. Perhaps regrets . . ." My voice trailed off as my eyes fell to the surface of Faith's desk. Then, as if remembering my purpose in coming, I resumed. "I do not feel Soo Yun belongs here. She has not done well at the home. Some children adapt better than others. That has been my experience. This child is not content. She needs a mother very much like her own, but one able to care for her always."

"That's true for all of the children here."

"Yes," I acknowledged. "But Soo Yun now has a family ready to take her, at an age so young she will have no recollection of any other life or family. I do not want to see her lose this chance."

"And I don't want to see us lose our reputation, not to mention our jobs."

"As I said, I am prepared to take full responsibility with your agency. I do this now, perhaps more than you recognize."

Faith's face clouded. "What do you mean?"

"Suk Non is one of the seven matches scheduled to leave my ward tonight. His fear of automobiles is extreme. He lost his parents in an accident in which he survived."

"I know that child," said Faith. "That accident is in his history. The adopting family knows of it and should be prepared to deal with his fear, which is very natural for one who went through such an ordeal."

"But they do not know that he feels responsible for their deaths, nor of his fear that any new parents he finds are also likely to die and thus be taken from him. I learn of such fears by talks with the children, but I do not report such things. I learn of so many fears, so many angers, so many distrusts. But I tell no one, as I have told no one for years. If all these things were known, many of these children would be rejected. All parents want perfect children. Soo Yun's scars are only on the surface, and are of far less consequence than others I could relate to you."

Faith gazed away. "When you visited recently, I showed you Sohn's photograph." Faith extended her arm to the frame, turning it to me. "I was not directly responsible for what happened to that child. A doctor made a very human if perhaps careless mistake. Like this one. But I felt responsible, and I have carried the burden of that sadness for seven years now. I don't wallow in it; it has not ruined my life for all time, but the thought of the poor Saunders . . . I feel a little like the taster at a food factory: everything that goes out the door must pass my inspection. A child is not a product, of course, but I owe a duty to those parents. If I advise them of a problem, I have done all I can do. It's their judgment, and my conscience is clear. But not to tell them, to have them blindsided—"

I shook my head. "Sohn was a child who seemed perfect but was flawed. Soo Yun is the opposite. All of the pain her family will feel will be felt at once, like an immunization. When they have her, they will not let her go. I know it. They will learn almost immediately that what at first appeared serious is nothing. It is such a small price to pay."

"Whether small or large, you are taking it upon yourself to impose it. That troubles me."

"It no longer troubles me. The new parents will handle it. If I am mistaken, we are indeed sending her to the wrong family. Besides, those parents are, at this very moment, preparing to receive the child. They must have planned her arrival. They must be traveling to New York. An Alert now can only confuse and mar what will otherwise be an exciting day in their lives. I will dictate a note to accompany her. If you will translate it for me, the parents will be reassured at the same moment they discover the scars."

Faith stared at me in silence, no doubt thinking of how demanding Americans could be in even the smallest deviations where their expectations were concerned. I understood her fear of repercussions. Perhaps her experience with Sohn had left her scarred, as had her divorce. We all have scars eventually. When she brought her hands to her face and rubbed her eyes with the tips of her fingers, I felt sure she would turn me down, but she said, "I'm warning you now," from behind the screen of her hands. "When they come looking for scalps—that's an American expression for big trouble—I'm going to tell them I relied on your judgment and if pressed I'm going to agree with them that your judgment was very bad in not notifying the agency."

"I understand," I said. "Thank you. Now, I need to go back to my ward for the remainder of Open House."

As I predicted, the weather held down attendance. The regulars were present, as always. I saw the Parks shuffling along in their usual pattern, staying a few moments at each cot so as to have sufficient time to visit them all. Conspicuous by absence were the six matches spending their last day at the home. For these children, a special day had been arranged which included a church service at one of the home's principal sponsors followed by a luncheon and movie. They would return after Open House ended, in time to collect the travel bags on their cots and to say their final farewells to the staff and their friends on the ward. Buses would be waiting in the cold to ferry them to the airport.

I surveyed 3E for prospects. I spied an Army Major and his wife. They were older than most Americans who came in search of children, and not all military couples who attended Open House were in the market for adoptions, so I was uncertain of their purpose. I watched them for a time before approaching them, introducing myself and signaling for the interpreter.

A few exchanges established them as visitors, with children of their own and no interest in acquiring more. But they asked many questions, engaging me on a variety of subjects related to my duties. I found them charming, and had fully immersed myself in the conversation when, over the shoulder of the Major's wife, I saw, through the plate glass window separating us from the nursery, a sight that stopped me in mid-sentence. Over Soo Yun's crib stood a woman, her back to me and her features concealed by the bulk of her coat and hat.

The interpreter paused, looking at me expectantly for the completion of my thought. When I said nothing, the interpreter prompted. "You were telling them about the field trips the children take into the countryside."

"Yes," I said absently, my eyes fixed on the woman in the nursery. "Field trips."

I watched as the woman bent over the crib and lifted the child into her arms. She drew back the front fold of her coat as she looked furtively around. It was Jong Sim.

So intently did I now stare at the drama unfolding in the nursery that the collective gaze of the Major, his wife and the interpreter all turned to follow mine. In that instant I grasped the meaning of Jong Sim's movements.

"Excuse me," I said as I brushed by the Major's wife. I charged through the double doors into the nursery. I came up behind the woman, placed my hand firmly on her shoulder, and spun her around. Jong Sim's mouth gaped open in surprise.

"You were going to take her," I rasped, reaching into her coat and pulling Soo Yun to me. The child squawked in protest of rude handling.

"No!" Jong Sim stammered, falling back a step.

"Then why are you concealing her in your coat?"

She looked at Soo Yun, then at me. "I only wanted to feel her against me. My coat is so thick I . . ." She stopped, staring plaintively. "Please, I only meant to be near her." Her head dropped, and through the thickness of her coat I could see her shoulders begin to shake.

Still holding Soo Yun, I placed a softer hand on the younger woman's shoulder, still shaking. "Come with me," I instructed, and Jong Sim, her head still declined, fell into my wake as I pushed through the nursery doors and entered the hallway leading to my office. I beckoned her inside.

"Hold her while I look for something." I sorted through folders on the desk. "I am forbidden to show you this," I said, "but I will do it anyway. You see this picture? This is the American family that has agreed to take her. She leaves tonight."

Jong Sim took her eyes from the infant long enough to stare at the picture, then up at me. "Thank you. Was there a mirror with her at Jongam? It was my mother's and now hers."

"I packed it in her travel bag. I will send a note with her explaining the mirror, as you sent a note to me introducing her. It will comfort her as she grows older."

Jong Sim looked down and managed a smile. The child, fully alert, returned her stare with infant curiosity. She gathered her child to her chest, and I assumed she kissed her, but at that moment I turned away, unable to look.

That day, that hour, with the mother clasping the child and the photo of the Carter family resting face-up on the desk, is unlike any I experienced in my many years at the home. No other mother came back for her child. Not one.

15

Elizabeth

We flew to New York, and if I die tomorrow that day will rank among the most memorable of my life, because you cannot imagine the drama of all those children coming off a plane into new families, a new country, new lives. I get emotional just thinking about it, and that afternoon at Kennedy Airport the combination of nerves, anticipation and wonder threatened to overwhelm me. Coleman was just as anxious, I think, but he hid it better by flirting with the flight attendants and cracking jokes, like asking me if, when she grew older, she might apply to RuCLA for college. I can't believe I actually laughed at that, but stress affects us all differently.

We landed at La Guardia and took a cab to Kennedy, where a representative of Open Arms convened a briefing on do's and dont's. She spoke from a portable dais, an older woman who reminded me of photographs I'd seen of Margaret Mead. "Please do not cry," she instructed, "as Korean culture does not associate tears with happiness, so if you cry the children will think you are disappointed or sad."

Coleman couldn't resist another joke. "Great," he whispered in my ear. "You've been crying since we left New Hampton," which was not literally true, although the excitement of it all did cause me to dab my eyes a few times. I asked him to please shut up so I could listen.

"We want you to stay in touch with the agency as your child grows up," continued the representative. "Send us pictures or notices of special events in your child's life."

I looked around at the faces of those who, like us, were about to be matched with a stranger, a "pig in a poke," as Sarah put it, and I thought about the fact that regardless of who stepped off the plane, the lives of every person present for the briefing, and every orphan currently nearing the airspace over Columbus, Ohio on Northwest Orient Flight 451, would be altered beyond recall in the next two hours, and for a lifetime thereafter. Talk about pressure.

The briefing ended at 5:00, leaving a whole, endless forty-five minutes until arrival. The greeting families gathered in a special reception area set aside by the airline. Clusters of parents, children and grandparents huddled together at the fringes. We mingled in the crowd, finding ourselves at one point standing next to a young couple who gazed about with the uneasiness of two people who wanted to talk but were too shy to introduce themselves. I introduced myself to the man.

"Steve Zarnell," he said. "This is my wife, Betty."

"Oh," I said. "We have a son named Steven. Do you have children?"

"This will be our first," said Betty Zarnell, a plump brunette with dark eyes and a faintly pug nose.

"Boy or girl?" I wanted to know.

"A boy," she said. "Three months old. We can hardly wait."

"A new one, younger than our daughter," Coleman observed. "Have you picked out a name?"

"Steven, Jr.," said Steve.

The Zarnells lived in Pennsylvania, near Scranton. They had married knowing that he was sterile and had been on a number of adoption waiting lists for several years. "We couldn't wait any longer," said Betty Zarnell, her excitement growing visibly as she rocked on the balls of her feet. "And just think—only twenty more minutes."

Coleman excused himself and walked to a nearby monitor displaying arrival updates. Northwest Orient Flight 451 "on time," he reported when he returned.

I saw an older couple with three Korean children, two boys and a girl, talking to the Open Arms representative. All about us families clustered, talking in low voices and repeatedly looking toward the arrival gate. Through the window flanking the gate we saw the jetway, ready to swing out to couple with the aircraft.

Coleman surprised me by a serious question. "Remember when you suggested this? It was what, four years ago?"

"About that."

"Did you ever think you would be standing here, waiting?"

I didn't answer right away, but nodded. "My instincts for things like this are pretty good. I thought it would happen one day, although you put me through some anxious moments in the process."

"I'm sorry for that," he said, and I knew he meant it. "Resolving my doubts was an essential part of the journey for me."

"I realize that now. Are they resolved?"

"Ninety percent. That's close enough."

My attention shifted to a young Asian girl, maybe six or seven, who appeared to be Korean clinging to her mother's dress. Would our child grow to look like that? I knew Coleman wanted a daughter, and when he pictured one he no doubt had envisioned someone who looked more like me than that girl. I wasn't sure I wanted biological competition. Was that caddy?

An excited murmur went through the crowd as people began edging closer to the gate. I looked out the window as a giant 747 maneuvered into position beside the jetway, which swung out to meet it when it came to a stop. I grabbed Coleman's arm and pulled him toward the gate.

A man dressed in a blazer and identified by the Northwest Orient insignia over the breast pocket addressed those pressed around the cordon separating them from the gate. "The regular passengers will deplane first. When they have left the gate area, the children will deplane in order of age, oldest first. This was the procedure requested by the chaperons on board the flight."

An attendant propped open the door leading to the jetway as the first passengers filed out. We waiting families created a thin corridor just wide enough for them to pass. Several of those leaving flight 451 paused at the back fringe of the crowd to watch. "Cute kids," I heard a woman carrying a briefcase say as she elbowed her way through the crowd, which contracted gradually as the plane emptied. Finally, the stream of passengers stopped. The gate area beyond the cordon was deserted. The waiting crowd settled into a collective stillness as all eyes focused on the doorway leading to the plane.

A small, slender boy of perhaps fourteen emerged alone, his eyes widening in bewilderment as he took in the crowd. He was dressed in jeans and a navy coat, on which a name tag identifying him as Roy Malone was affixed. As he approached the cordon, a couple I could only guess to be the Malones reached out from the crowd, which parted to absorb the boy. My view of their greeting was obscured.

Then came a girl, her hair in burettes and dressed in a skirt and sweater. Her name tag read, "Melissa Thompson."

On they came, one by one, each claimed by a family of at least two when they reached the cordon. We moved steadily toward the front of the crowd as all around us adults presented flowers and embraced the new arrivals. Children stared at new brothers or sisters awkwardly before braving the first contact, a practiced phrase or a reticent touch.

Finally, it was just us and the Zarnells who stood gazing at the doorway. All of the children who had deplaned so far, down to a very overwhelmed two-year-old girl whose hand was held by a chaperon, had come off under their own power. The math was simple; Soo Yun would be next.

The chaperon returned to the plane as I brought my hands up to my face, trying to hold it together manually. Coleman put his arm around me. At the door, the chaperon again emerged, carrying a blanketed bundle. When she reached a point halfway to the cordon, I could not stand it another instant. I broke through, taking the bundle in my arms and retracing my steps to where Coleman stood watching. As the chaperon, following me, handed the plastic travel bag to Coleman, I peeled the blanket back from the child's face.

And there she was. Tiny, sleepy, in desperate need of a new diaper and fresh clothes, but there, lying in my arms like she belonged. I bent over her as tears came.

"They said not to cry," Coleman reminded me, but I sensed he was a bit emotional himself. He told me later about seeing the Zarnells receiving their son, but I was too overcome to notice anything but the baby who was now my baby, our baby. When I pulled myself together, I started toward the Zarnells to wish them luck, but they were as focused on their new arrival as I had been, so I settled for a thumbs up which Steve Zarnell acknowledged by one back to us. It was just as well, because at that moment Coleman, glancing at the wall clock, said, "Let's go. We can't miss that flight home."

We hailed a cab and arrived at La Guardia with a modest margin of time. I used it to change Soo Yun. I carried her into the ladies room along with the change of clothes I brought from New Hampton.

"Wait here," I told Coleman at the door. "This child could use some freshening up."

It took longer than I thought. The dress I had selected swallowed her. "I had no idea she'd be this small," I said as we emerged. "Josh and Steven were bigger than this at birth."

Thirty minutes later, as Coleman looked out his window at the jeweled tableau which is Manhattan from the air at night, Soo Yun, awake but hardly alert, contorted restlessly in my lap as the plane gained altitude and the seat belt sign went off. Coleman ordered drinks. When served, he proposed a toast.

"To the future," he said, touching the plastic rim against mine. I sipped my wine as Soo Yun stirred.

"It's going to work out," I said. "I can feel it."

"Promise me that before her fifth birthday you'll let me hold her."

I smiled and said, "You know what amazes me? Your mother. I never thought I'd hear from her what we heard yesterday. I can honestly say I'm not sure I would be capable of that kind of grace."

"She's tougher than she looks," he agreed. "One of these days she and this little one will be great pals, but it won't be overnight."

"They would get closer sooner if we lived in Charleston, don't you think?" I turned my head away as he absorbed my words.

"Are you serious?" he asked.

"Sure. The offer from Barron Morris is almost too good to pass up. Besides, I think you want to go home."

"I never sensed that Charleston held any appeal for you."

"No, but I'm not sure I've given it a fair chance. And it's your heritage —Josh's and Steven's, too."

It was almost 11:00 when the plane touched down in New Hampton. Forty minutes later, we pulled into our driveway. The house was lit up on both floors, and from the cars parked along the street I knew Ross and Carol Vernon had organized a small welcome party. We parked and started up the walk, Coleman walking in front to open the door and I followed with Soo Yun. When he reached the front door, Coleman paused, then erupted in laughter.

"What's so funny?" I asked, looking over his shoulder as he pointed to the door. Hand-printed on a sign were the words, "Aliens use rear entrance."

"I'm going to kill Ross Vernon," I said as we opened the door and entered the living room, where Betsy and husband David, Ross and Carol Vernon, Josh and Steven, and two other couples waited to welcome the new addition to the Carter household. Our boys, extended hours beyond their normal bedtime, were given a quick introduction and sent to bed.

As I displayed the baby, our friends offered congratulations. It was well after midnight when Betsy and David, the last guests, yawned and stood to leave.

I carried Soo Yun to her room. When I reached into the bag that had accompanied her from Seoul, my hand fell on the pearl-backed mirror, around which had been attached, by means of a rubber band, a piece of paper. I unrolled it and spread it on the changer.

> *The two scars under this child's arm are a result of biopsies performed at the Korean Children's Hospital. They are not serious. Her medical records are available for your doctor's review.*
> */s/ Faith Stockdale*
> *P.S. The mirror belongs to the child.*

I removed her dress and inspected the scars. They were indeed large, and alarming. I marveled that I had not seen them at La Guardia. In the morning, I would take her to be examined by a specialist, to have confirmed by American doctors the reassurance contained in the note.

But now it was late. I dressed her in the sleeper set out on the changer. As I laid her in her crib, she seemed to settle in with a sigh of approval, although it was undoubtedly mere fatigue from a trip halfway around the world. I placed the mirror on the night stand, turned out the light, and closed the door gently, to give her peace.

Part 2

RAPIDS

Ever thus the pulse of Time
Ever thus youth sings its song
Ever thus day ends with moaning
Time is fierce, and tides are strong.

ROBERT WOODWARD BARNWELL, SR.
"The Course of Life," *Realities and Imaginations*

16

Elizabeth

Those scars? Of course they worried us, but our doctor reviewed the records from Korea and reassured us so promptly that had it not been for seeing them when we changed or bathed her, I would have forgotten they were there. Of far greater concern, to us and to every adopting couple who lacks knowledge about the biological parents, the child's prenatal care, and genetic predispositions, are signs of impairment, mental or physical. The ones that take some time to manifest themselves. And there is a name for adoptive parents who deny that these were a concern with their particular child. They are called liars.

We named her Allison and called her Allie. The first few mornings revealed something about each of us. The mobile suspended above her crib fascinated her. From the doorway of her bedroom I watched as her eyes went from the monkey to the fish to the giraffe to the squirrel. When she moved, they moved, and this brought the first smiles we saw. I say 'we' because Coleman joined me there on several of these first mornings, and sideways glances told me she was not the only one smiling. Aside from occasional squawks from hunger or irritation, she impressed me as content in her new environment, which naturally justified my "it-was-meant-to-be" optimism.

The most remarkable thing about Allie's early childhood development was how unremarkable it was, as if she had started life over within traditional markers. She ate everything put in front of her (except squash) or left within reach. Her neck, too weak to support her head when she arrived, strengthened. Her legs lengthened until her body took on proportion. Gradually, she thrived, but with developmental differences I noticed and Coleman ticked off to me one day not too long after her first birthday. Josh and Steven had crawled looking up; she kept her head down. The boys, taking their first steps, had fallen backward, on their diapered bottoms; she fell forward. The boys deflected strained vegetables with their right hands; she used her left, and only for squash, which she hated. "Mom" was the first word said by the boys; for her it was "milk." At least that is what I think she said.

We were in Charleston by then, where Coleman's father passed away two months after we arrived. He regained only limited speech, and what little he communicated was spent on subjects well wide of adoption. He died without ever meeting Allie. Sarah composed his obituary, and when I realized she had omitted Allie's name as a surviving grandchild, it was all I could do to attend the funeral and to feel empathy for his widow. Sarah knew I was livid, and I stayed so for weeks afterwards. It was not until that summer, on the beach, when we watched Sarah instruct a toddling Allie on the proper way to build a sandcastle, that I began to sense things would only get better between them. And they did, but it was gradual.

At eighteen months, Coleman took her for her checkup.

"How is our girl?" I asked as he loosened his tie and tossed his coat over the back of a kitchen chair.

"She's still not on the growth chart, but Rick says she's healthy. She didn't like the shot at all. She let the whole clinic know how unhappy she was."

"Good lungs, eh? If she develops a chest I'm going to be very upset."

Coleman laughed. "You're feeling threatened?"

"Asians are supposed to be small breasted. I'm counting on it. She can be as beautiful as she likes, but I refuse to be intimidated by a daughter who won't wear my dresses because they are 'snug.'"

"Maybe you can bind her chest. It works for feet."

On the day President Reagan was shot, Allie tripped on a pull toy in the playroom and struck her mouth on an end table. For a time it looked as if she might lose a tooth that had just emerged on her lower gum. Like Reagan, the tooth survived.

Josh and Steven, adapting to new friends and surroundings, ignored her. They rode their bikes, tested their imaginations against neighbors, adapted to a different school. Occasionally they would use her as a prop in a game, or grow bored enough to torment her by hiding behind doors and jumping out suddenly with a yell. I found a playgroup for her, watchful for any sign of alienation from toddlers her own age, but she mixed well. Parents of other children either hid their curiosity behind a mask of indifference or, at the other extreme, asked so many questions for which I had no answers. "We know very little about her," I would say, and the more I repeated the phrase the more it came to me that it was true.

I shared those doubts with Coleman one evening over drinks. The kids were all in bed and I mentioned Dot Ellis, whose daughter Catherine was in Allie's playgroup. "I guess I was a bit defensive with her," I told him. "She didn't come out with it to my face, but she implied I was nuts to have taken a child with no background check or history. Looking back, maybe it was a little nuts."

"Oh?" he said, and I felt a huge I-told-you-so on the way. "My dear, coming from you that is quite an admission."

But then, just when I thought he would lecture me on how truly rash it was, or at least how rash it seemed to others, he said, "But you went on your instincts. You usually do. And in this instance I think you were right, so to hell with Dot Ellis." I could have kissed him for that. In fact, I did kiss him for it.

Still, we both worried, and although we did not talk about it much, I know we both studied her for signs of trouble, particularly in the early days. How bright was she? Would she grow up awkward and ugly? Had her parents bequeathed lethal, time-delayed drug addictions or lymphomas? Like the survivor of an accident who has no time to appreciate the danger until after it has passed, I nervously studied her for any sign that my great experiment had been, in fact, a fanciful whim destined to disappoint. In time, I came to associate these anxieties with the move to Charleston rather than any objective observations of her. To my eyes and ears, she showed every sign of relentless normality.

For Coleman, the adjustment to having a daughter, this daughter, seemed to me to take an opposite course. Before her arrival, he had echoed the prophecies of skeptics. I knew he was waiting for confirmation of retardation, of family-wrecking mental instability, of mortal infant illness, of deformed growth. In Virginia, he had bathed her, changed her, fed her, and rocked her on nights when I craved sleep and Allie didn't, all the while certain that he held a time bomb of sorts.

But when we reached Charleston he relaxed, and these dreads had been supplanted by feelings I think he was just beginning to understand. When she learned to walk he took her to the Battery, holding her hand as she tottered along the edge of the parapet. She kept her head down, eyes focused directly a step ahead, concentrating. When they reached the end, she turned at once to retrace their path. Sometimes he directed her to the railing, where they could see the harbor and he could teach her words like "wave" and "boat" and "fort" and "ship." The bond they were forming thrilled me, even if he didn't recognize its strength right away.

She liked the games our sons had liked at that age. When Coleman sat in his den chair, crossed his legs and she straddled his foot to ride the bucking bronco, she laughed as hard as they had laughed. At night, she insisted on playing "Superman." Bathed and dressed for bed in feeted pajamas, she spread her arms as he held her aloft by material gathered behind her shoulders. Squeals of pleasure echoed through the house.

By the time she entered preschool, her foreignness had become no more remarkable to Coleman than Josh's cowlick or Steven's slight overbite. When the Soviets shot down a Korean airliner, killing 269, the grim news stories reminded us that we had not given the country of her birth a thought in months. Shortly after that disaster, I planned a picnic. We would travel in separate cars, as I planned to go directly from the park to visit a sick friend. The boys were waiting in my car, and Coleman had just told me he would meet us there when Allie climbed into the front seat beside him. On the way, according to him, she said that her mother must have been poor.

"What makes you think so?" he asked.

"I just think so," she said.

When Barron Morris retired, the law firm fell into rare dissension. Coleman played the role of peacemaker until it became apparent that the competition for control would be bitter and protracted. He met with Harris Deas, a lawyer his age also impatient with the infighting, and together they formed Carter & Deas. The new firm prospered. When Sarah downsized to a small house on Sullivan's Island, we moved into the house on Church Street.

On Allie's fifth birthday, I arranged for a pony. In the back yard, seven other children from her kindergarten class took turns being led. Allie returned to the line after each ride. She giggled with the waiting girls and ignored the two invited boys, who darted among them playing a form of tag that required a slap to the top of the head. But she kept an eye on the pony. By her third or fourth mount, she grew possessive, seeming to resent turns the others took and imagining that the pony responded when she approached, threw her leg over the pommel, gathered the reins, and planted her feet in the stirrups. When it was time for the cake and presents, she reluctantly went inside after I assured her the pony would be there when she finished. That Christmas, a pony topped her wish list. I prepared her for disappointment in a short, elementary lecture that was part economics, part zoning. Later, I reported to Coleman that the child was obsessed.

"She wants pony books, pony videos, pony clothing. Maybe I'll look into lessons. I think I'd like to ride as well."

"That's a great idea," he said, telling me it would be good for both of us.

Mastering Charleston's antiquated rules and conventions would challenge the most determined transplant and God knows I tried, genuflecting to customs, traditions and rules of etiquette centuries in the making, and little changed. Coleman had warned me that folks here believed "nothing should ever be done for the first time," and how true that proved. I gave and attended teas. I took my turn on the garden tour and the open houses. I resisted the urge to crash after-dinner drinks in wood paneled libraries thick with cigar smoke and men. I fussed over debutantes. I kept track of invitations given and received with the precision of the most meticulousness accountant. I volunteered, donated, served, supported, venerated, and praised. I did these things and more for Coleman, for our sons, for the life and family we had resettled in Charleston. They were all part of the informal bargain struck in Virginia. "Lord, I'm mellowing," I told a friend.

To feed my inner rebel I relished tiny acts of defiance, venial as they seemed, which kept something within me alive. I refused to leave calling cards ("fucking absurd," I muttered on more than one occasion). I refused to wear hats or white gloves ("people, it's 1987, and it's 98 degrees out there, for Chrissake"). Behind the walls, I sipped tea and re-read Camus, Virginia Woolf, and Garcia Marquez.

For a time I looked at Allie as both a daughter and an ally. We had both been transplanted, seeking air, light and water in foreign soil. She was my comrade-in-arms, a fellow pilgrim on the humid, azalea-lined road the family had taken. Then, just after her seventh birthday, I came home to find the strains of *Die Fledermaus* blaring loudly from the study. Opening the door, I saw them waltzing on the hardwood floor, Coleman holding Allie with ballroom formality. She wore her soccer uniform. Her feet, clad in athletic socks, rested on the tops of his. "The perfect lead" he called it after they became aware of my presence. And I wondered, not for the first time, just whose ally the child was.

Her "otherness" gradually, and at times painfully, asserted itself. In grammar school, her teacher asked each member of the class to identify their family heritage as part of a geography lesson. She replied "English and German," an accurate answer as far as we were concerned: "A plus." But a boy behind her laughed, and I feel sure the teacher thought she was being tactful when she suggested Korea. The child shook her head and said no, "English and German."

There was the day when I caught her posed in front of a hallway mirror. "Allie?"

Without turning she said, "Yes, mom?"

"What are you doing?"

"I'm . . . different."

"You're beautiful."

"All moms say that."

"No, I mean it."

She returned her full attention to the mirror. Nearing it, her face three inches from the glass, she pulled at the corner of her left eye. "I don't look like the girls at school."

I winced. That which I had forgotten, she was only now discovering. "Here we go," I muttered inaudibly. But she drew back from the mirror, shrugged indifferently, and walked to the kitchen to make a sandwich.

The truth is that, try as I did to empathize with all the assimilation issues I knew she must be wrestling with, I doubt I succeeded, and no amount of adoption literature—and I read it all—bridged certain gaps between the world she was born into and the one we brought her to. Yes, she and I were each in our own way transplants, outliers, but her challenges dwarfed mine and were made greater by the fact that she herself was undoubtedly unaware of many of them. A prepubescent child cannot articulate turmoil the source of which is only vaguely felt. As a parent, you look for clues to understanding what she herself cannot understand. You try to help solve a problem for someone who does not know they have a problem. For example, she never expressed curiosity about her birth family or Korea, nor did she appear to feel any affinity with the handful of Asians at her school. I saw this as a form of denial, a distancing that says to herself and those around her that she is the same as the rest of us. It must be the young mind's defense against a dislocation that demands a more mature mind to cope with. I've read about parents who went to extraordinary lengths to immerse their Asian adoptees in their native culture, but I always believed that was a mistake, an end run around the instinctive defense. I guess time will tell.

How would I have felt, transported to Asia as an infant and surrounded by people that looked like aliens? And we, the caregivers and nurturers, tell ourselves that we have given them a better life by adopting them because we know from reading and experience how harsh conditions are, especially for girls, in foreign countries where the supply of children so greatly exceeds the demand. But *they don't know that.* They have not yet learned that girls are abandoned in landfills, or beside highways, or drowned as if they were a litter of unwanted kittens. They know only what they have until the self-awareness, the kind I witnessed that day when she stood at the mirror, tells them they are different in fundamental ways, which can trigger profound questions like, "Who am I? Where did I come from? Who are my parents?" And most critical, "Why was I abandoned?" For many of these children, those inquires are never answered. Some stop looking for answers. Would Allie be one of those?

Her middle school years challenged all of us. Social cliques rule in those grades. She had friends, but the movers and shakers at Porter-Gaud kept her at arm's length. We heard about sleepovers to which she was not invited, and while she always protested that she didn't care, we did. Bullies are endemic to every middle school, and although she never suffered physical abuse (that I learned of), she endured her share of mean jokes about chopsticks and kung fu and slanted eyes and fried rice. These taunts hurt, to the point of tears. She refused to ever use chopsticks and for a time she even disdained rice, a staple of the southern diet and a starch she had loved as a young girl. Her teachers wrote notes home expressing surprise she wasn't doing better in math and science, when in fact she loved English and struggled with other subjects. This difficult passage was the only time I questioned my decision to avoid immersing her in Asian culture. At one point I suggested we go together to a Korean church newly organized in Charleston, and she responded by using a new phrase popular at her middle school: "no way."

If any boy showed interest in her, we heard about only one. She mentioned Tommy Worth, and the way she said his name told me she was in crush mode, that painful passage girls her age navigate as best they can. At the time, the poor girl had a mouthful of metal from braces plus some complexion issues. During a long walk on the beach, she confided that she thought he was going to kiss her but instead he asked if she had brothers or sisters in Korea. She told him she didn't know. I dreaded the awkward dating years that lay ahead, but as things turned out I wasn't destined to see them and would have given anything to be a witness.

The Seoul Olympics gave us all a chance to see Korea, a land that struck me as vividly colorful, exotic, and intriguing. News coverage included reports of a temporary halt to international adoptions due to potential embarrassment, a loss of face, for the Korean people and their government since both were sensitive to the notion that orphaned children had become a leading export. Allie showed little interest, opting to do her homework during the evening broadcasts and asking me to let her know when the equestrian competition came on.

The year 1989 brought the great hurricane. Like many in the city, we made the initial decision to ride it out at home. Sarah joined us as the barrier islands, vulnerable to even modest storms, evacuated. By the time the storm's ferocity was appreciated, it was too late to leave the peninsula. Highways clogged. A neighbor who panicked at noon returned in the late afternoon, reporting a three hour wait on a single bridge, during which his car moved twenty feet. Allie, age ten, voiced her intent to stand on the sea wall to watch the whitecaps in the harbor. She had never experienced a hurricane, nor did she appreciate how winds that had two weeks before swirled off the African coast could be brought to such a pitched force and concentration as now approached Charleston. After Hugo, the mere word, "hurricane," knotted her stomach. As the storm bore down, Josh laughed and talked on the phone with teenage indifference to danger, while Steven watched the news and repeated to us every precaution broadcast. They should store some water in the tub, he suggested. Fresh batteries for the flashlights would be prudent. A transistor radio. Pets should be brought inside, though we had none.

Tornadoes plague Kansas, but not hurricanes, so I also had never witnessed a real one. By dusk, when the winds strengthened, I went to our room and stood at a window with the lights off. I studied the mammoth live oaks that bordered our property. They must be two hundred years old. Silhouetted by the fading light in the harbor, they spread stately arms over the yard and roof as if to guard the house and us from wind, from sea, from rain, from shelling by the Yankees, from all threats from any source. I found comfort in their presence. Like avuncular sentries they stood stolidly, too massive and too old to move or even to bend more than a few inches. From their muscled limbs hung Spanish moss, and it was the winds stirring this moss that first parted for me the atmospheric curtain hanging over the harbor, to reveal the power of the storm gathering behind it. Gently at first, but with ever increasing whips and lashes, moss blew toward me, the trees themselves hardly moving. But the storm was still a hundred miles offshore.

I joined the family, gathered in front of a television. Coleman and I did our best to conceal nervousness, feeling the weight of our decision to ride it out at home and deriving no comfort from the presence of neighbors, equally regretting their decisions. "It will all blow over," Coleman said breezily. Josh insisted that Bennie McNamara's father had predicted five thousand deaths in the city just before the McNamaras pulled out for Greenville the day before. Steven looked at us for a more optimistic assessment. "Oh, bullshit," I said, with more conviction than I felt. We ate dinner on trays, watching news reports track the storm. For a time, an impetuous northward veer promised to spare the city at the expense of points closer to Myrtle Beach. Just as suddenly, a westward turn fixed the city in the storm's cross-hairs.

I returned to our room. A window inches from my face began to vibrate. Rain pelted the window in sheets. An eerie moan rose and fell from outside. I could not locate its source, as if gusts of wind were being driven by a giant, unseen engine that whirled and whined in a growing mechanized frenzy. Darkness fell. In the house, all was quiet. Behind me, every security I had come to know, to rely upon, remained in place, calmly waiting. But outside, in the artificial light from the street, I saw the oaks begin to grow animated. Between torrents of rain, limbs begin to sway. Spanish moss clung stubbornly to branches that had been as much a home to it as this house was to us, but the wind howled louder, the branches bent, and the moss extended parallel to the ground before losing its grip and flying wildly into the night. The storm's mounting fury took on a tribal arrhythmia. In my imagination, the street lights became fires on an aboriginal plain, with the oaks bending and swaying as I had never seen them do, warriors building up their wills to face some cataclysmic force just now making its way over Charleston's horizon. My trance was interrupted by Allie, who stood in the doorway to ask me to call the stables to check on Libbie, her favorite pony, but by then lines were down. I went back to the window, willing myself to watch until the power went out in the city. When it did, I groped to the stairs, guided downward by the faint glow from an array of candles Coleman lit. We sat in the living room, listening to wind howl at an impossible pitch as a seventeen foot storm surge washed over Ft. Sumter.

In a five hour span, Hugo affected Charleston as the years of Civil War had affected it. The city was not the same on the morning of September 22, yet instead of redefining it the storm added a bold brush stroke to a patina of timelessness, much as the war had done. True, in the dawn hours, that brush stroke resembled one that Jackson Pollock might have inflicted—ancient trees uprooted, homes flooded, power lines strewn in psychotic confusion, roofs transported to neighboring municipalities, chimneys reduced to rubble, boats suddenly and violently drydocked in parking lots. While the loss of life never approached our neighbor's rumored forecast, the storm did kill. Yet the defining landmarks remained. The steeple-graced skyline stood mussed but enduring. Historic homes along the Battery and throughout the city, rather than succumbing to condemnation, renewed themselves on a tide of insurance that flowed through after Hugo's waters receded. In the weeks that followed, roofing nails became the gold standard to which the local currency was pegged.

If I had a philosopher's bone in my body, I would find a way to cast my time in front of the window, watching Hugo approach, as prescience, a harbinger of the news I got months later from my oncologist. I'd been feeling weak and sluggish for weeks, thinking I was perhaps anemic. When doubling up on vitamins and iron didn't help, I blamed my thyroid. My stomach began to ache, and bouts of diarrhea became more frequent.

Coleman asked if I was losing weight, and from the fit of certain outfits I knew I had. But the last thing I suspected, the. very. last. thing, was pancreatic cancer, and it was only following the tests and Dr. Jameson's insistence that both Coleman and I come to his office that I knew something was very wrong. I left that office with a death sentence. Coleman knew it. I knew it. He put his arm around me and we walked to the parking lot in a daze. "Wait," I said, as if remembering I'd left something in the oven, "I'm only thirty-eight. I have children to raise . . ."

But the disease did not wait. It progressed rapidly, an angry, aggressive invader that intended to kill me, and the sooner the better. For the next two years, chemotherapy and radiation made me really sick, to the only point in my life when I considered suicide. I honestly think I would have done it had not the prognosis, "perhaps six months," been so imminent. Toward the end, attended by some wonderful hospice people who deserve laurels in the hereafter, I stayed at home, took morphine as sparingly as possible, and, as they say, put my affairs in order.

As any mother would, I worried most about the children. Although quite nauseous, I attended Josh's high school graduation and helped outfit his room at the University of South Carolina, where he is now a sophomore, essentially a grown man, which comforts me some. Steven, a senior in high school, still relies on me for advice with girls, and he distresses me because he refuses to believe all this is happening. I can't believe it either. If I make it that long, I'll be at his high school graduation if I have to watch it from a gurney.

And then there is Allie. I know to feel guilt is insane, but I do, because I will be the second mother to abandon her. She spends hours in bed with me, holding me and hugging me and asking if she can do anything. No, dear, no one can do anything, Goddamnit.

Coleman leaves for work late and comes home for long lunches, which he usually eats at my bedside. In the evening we watch the news together, although more often than not I drift off before the first commercial. World news doesn't engage me much now, for obvious reasons. The news in my world revolves around graduations and weddings and grandchildren, and I won't be here for any of it.

Toward the very end—I sensed it coming—I gave him a letter I'd written to Allie, with explicit instructions to deliver it on an exceptional occasion; admission to college, engagement, wedding—the choice will of necessity be his. But special, I insisted. He took the letter with tears in his eyes, and we had a good cry over what was and might have been. He kept telling me he can't do it without me, but I know he can. I've always known him better than he knows himself. And now I am tired and need to rest.

Part 3

FLOW

Yet e'en as I rowed I felt the great tide
Relax in its mighty endeavor
'Tis the fate of a restless heart to subside
And to end is the fate of a river.

ROBERT WOODWARD BARNWELL, SR.
"River and Tides," *Realities and Imaginations*

17

Coleman

Power failure. I grope for the desk drawer, open it, and pan for a flashlight front to back but find nothing closer than the hammer I used last week to mount a picture. The room is in total darkness and, once I settle back in my chair, palling silence as well. It will not last, I think with a grin. I'll give her thirty seconds.

Allie is studying in her room on the floor below. She retains her Hugo-induced fear of the dark. We joke about it, but only in daylight. Her chair scrapes against the hardwood below and my grin expands a fraction.

"Dad?" she calls out from the landing on her floor.

"Up here, sweetheart! In my study."

"What do you think caused it?" she asks as her voice draws nearer.

"Beats me. A transformer must have blown. I'll get a candle."

"I'll go with you," she says, a bit too quickly.

We feel our way to the banister and edge downward. At the middle landing off her room our hands overlap on the newel post and we each give a faint start. In the main hall the grandfather clock, a wise old mahogany monarch never a vassal to electricity, ticks reliably and louder as we arrive on the first floor. The windows, virtually floor to ceiling in the dining room we are passing, emit no light. All of Charleston seems entombed, and the moon is new or smothered. We reach the kitchen.

"They're not here," I report, rummaging in the logical places. "I must have used the last match trying to get the grill started."

"Here's a candle," she says from the direction of the pantry.

I shake my head to signal the futility of a candle without a match when I realize the futility of the gesture.

"The camping gear," I say. "The lamp is stored by the tent and the waterproof matches are in the backpacks."

"But that's in the basement."

"So get them. I'll wait."

"Dad . . ."

"Come on, let's go."

Access to the basement is through a door off the laundry room. Its stubborn knob has irritated me for years, but not enough to fix. This basement is one of the few in old Charleston and something of an engineering marvel in that it stays dry, hurricanes excepted. The stairs creak and the ceiling makes a tall man pay for walking erect but then that is the way basements should be. I like the place, spiders and all.

Only I like it lit, and tonight it is an ink spot in a lead-lined coffin. The knob yields, I probe blindly for the first step, and cool, captive air tinged with mildew rises to meet me.

"Hold on to me," I instruct over my shoulder. "I can't see a damn thing."

"No," she says softly. "I'll wait here."

"You're sure?"

"I'm sure," and she sounds it.

So I descend alone. On another night, I would have covered these nine steps in less time than it will take Allie to seat herself, whistling as I went. But now I pause. Is something down there? I listen. She breathes behind me—nothing more. Inwardly, I laugh at my foolishness and feel a flush come to my face, but my grip on the banister seems to be guarding against something more than a fall. "Wimp," I mutter silently. Forty-six is long past the age for ghosts. I take two more steps.

"Is something wrong, Dad?"

"Nope. Thought I heard something, that's all."

I continue down, faster now because she is watching me though she cannot see. I feel the concrete floor and exhale, surprised to find I have been holding my breath. I am thinking of this—my withheld breath and my boa constrictor grip on the railing and the eerie mood of disquiet that has come over me since turning that stubborn knob—my mind is wandering from one strangeness to another when I realize I have strayed into what must be the center of the room. Now I am disoriented, without bearings. A mild but distinct panic seizes me and for the first time I can actually sense another presence in the basement.

"Allie?"

"Yes?"

"I need to find the stairs again. Talk."

"What about?"

"Anything . . . never mind, here they are."

This silliness has gone on long enough. I fumble for the shelf that abuts the wall forming the left side of the staircase and, touching it, make my way hand to hand along the wooden supports spaced every four feet or so. I am aggressive now, impatient with myself but mindful of the small clearance for my head. In seconds I am on the other side of the room, having stumbled only once over some old valances.

The tent is where I remembered and the lamp beside it. A fine veneer of dust coats my fingertips as I probe. Hanging on a peg just beyond is my pack, and this I have felt in the dark often enough for its pockets and compartments to become a familiar Braille. I locate the matches at once.

At the first strike Allie is on the stairs coming down. I raise the lantern's chimney, touch match to wick, and the room brightens as she nears, her elongated shadow gliding down the steps and hulking behind her.

"Much better," she says, relief in her smile. "I wonder if I'll ever get over it."

I thought I had. "You will. It's natural." Beyond her, my noisy apparitions of moments ago linger among stored furniture, invisible and now silent. As I turn to lead, Allie hangs back. Having been reluctant to enter the basement she now seems reluctant to leave.

"Dad, I need to ask you something."

"Here?"

"Somewhere, it doesn't matter. Graduation is only five months away. Have you thought about my present?"

"Who said I'm going to give you a present?" My poker face crumbles and she laughs. In the radiance of the lamp between us I see her crescent eyes dance and a glint of light from the black orbs within. She knows I would give her Saturn and its rings.

"Be serious," she admonishes. "My request is going to surprise you."

"Anything but a wedding," I say.

"I want to go back to Korea."

I suck in a little. "You're right, I'm surprised. You've never mentioned the slightest interest in returning."

Her head drops faintly and the lantern lends her forehead a copper glow. "I know. It's just that lately I've been thinking about it. Not missing it, of course, because I have no memory of it at all."

"Recall is pretty limited at four months."

"But here I am, getting ready to go off to college and I've never been exposed to . . . you know."

"Your people? Your homeland?"

"I feel like a Charlestonian. I'm an American. Still, I wonder about it."

"I would wonder if you didn't."

"So, can we go? You and me. We'll have fun."

"Sweetheart, I don't know the first thing about Korea. I'd be lost over there. Neither of us knows a single word of Korean."

"So? We'll hire an interpreter and a guide."

I shake my head. This plea has caught me totally off guard and, for some reason, troubles me.

She presses. "Mom would have taken me. She told me so lots of times."

"She told me, too. She really wanted to see the place."

"But she's gone, so it's up to you." Her stare penetrates. "What's the matter?"

I sigh. "I guess this is something all adoptive parents have to deal with. It's selfish, frankly. You said a moment ago you feel like a Charlestonian. And I feel like you're my daughter. Maybe it's just the thought that somewhere over there are a man and woman who could claim you, in the biological sense." I hesitate. "You know, I think I'm jealous."

I must also be a bit embarrassed, so I complain about my arm being tired from holding the lamp. She drags over the camp stove, unwilling to leave this plea in the basement unanswered. I rest the lantern, waist high and flickering.

"Now father," she says, looking as firm as her congenitally pleasant features will allow, "surely you don't suspect I'd go searching for people who abandoned me. You're my father, my only father, and that's that. I just want to see the country and now that I'm old enough it seems a shame not to go. Please."

"Let me think about it," I reply, wondering if the gloom of the basement accounts for my dark reaction.

On the following morning, power restored, I sit hunched over my coffee and the morning paper when she breezes through the kitchen, kisses me on top of my head, and flies out the door to school. She targets that same spot each morning because, she says, when I start to lose my hair I'll find comfort in a spot worn bald by kisses.

After Dad's death, Sarah moved to Sullivan's Island, into the beach house that had always been our summer place, giving me the house in town where I grew up and now call home again. I visit her often, and on this morning, the morning after the power failed, I have something on my mind.

My Range Rover eases from the driveway into the path of Jason Collins, a neighbor's son who rides his ten speed to Bishop England High. More alert, the boy swerves neatly around me without upshifting, downshifting or braking, waving to boot. I weave my way through early morning traffic, past the offices of Carter & Deas on Broad Street, and soon cross the Cooper River Bridge.

It is a fine winter morning. The air is crisp and a fresh sun is rising out of the Atlantic undistorted by the humidity which those of us in the South tolerate like a dependent cousin. On my left, far below, the shadow of the bridge shades the bright blue water. Mt. Pleasant comes and goes, and I reach the causeway leading to the island. On either side, winter marsh stretches north and south along the Intracoastal Waterway. A red-tailed hawk circles silently, its wings fully extended but motionless like the brown marsh grass below. Grating of the Ben Sawyer Bridge rumbles beneath as I squint into the sun, framed directly in my path by the superstructure of the bridge. Sunglasses would help, but mine are misplaced. The sign welcoming me to Sullivan's Island could use some fresh paint.

Mother is just returning from her morning walk on the beach. I spot her on the path as I pull into the driveway. She looks up, waves, then renews her downward gaze. Getting older, she is more cautious where she steps.

We arrive inside at the same time, she by the side door and me via the front. In the living room we hug. The scarf in which she has wreathed her head as protection against the cold ocean air brushes against my chin.

"Good morning, dear," she greets. "Such a treat to see you in the middle of the week. Coffee?"

On a hook near the side door she drapes her jacket, then naps her thinning white hair to counter the matting produced by the scarf. She is a sturdy woman in the face of incipient frailty. A tomboy as a child, she retains at age eighty-four an aura of robustness, a vitality only mildly arrested by advancing years. She will no longer climb a tree, as I saw her do when she was in her late fifties, but she wouldn't hesitate to ride her old Raleigh around the island. We gravitate to the kitchen table, where she pours each of us a cup.

"I read in the *Sentinel* that you lost electricity in town," she notes, steam rising as she sips. "Did Church Street go dark?"

"As a tomb," I reply. "It was still off when I went to bed."

"We've become so dependent on electricity," she laments. "Must have been a boring evening."

I pause momentarily, thinking back. "Not at all. Allie and I ended up in the basement having one of our father-daughter chats over the camping lantern."

"In that depressing basement? How unusual. I suppose she is still on cloud nine over her acceptance at Princeton."

"She is, but Princeton didn't come up last night. She wants to visit Korea."

Mother freezes in what I have come to think of as her bad news paralysis, as though she is going through some internal inventory, consulting each element in her psyche to make sure nothing has broken, the way a computer goes through a RAM check. "Oh, my," she says at last. "Oh, dear."

"It shocked me," I admit.

"I hope you told her it's out of the question."

"No, I told her I'd think about it."

"Coleman, you know I don't meddle but everything you hear and read about orphans searching for their parents proves it spells trouble. Allie is happy here."

I replace my cup firmly in the saucer. "The point is she's almost on her own and mature enough to make this call. Besides, she could go see her native land without trying to find her parents. One doesn't have to follow from the other."

"You sound as though you've made up your mind to let her go."

"She wants me to take her. I haven't decided."

She rises and walks to the counter, speaking with her back to me. "For what it's worth, I think it's a bad idea."

"As I say, I haven't decided. Actually, another dilemma with Allie brings me here."

She turns, her face brightening with the prospect of changing subjects. "Oh?"

"Invitations to the St. Simeon go out in a few weeks."

"Yes, it's that time, isn't it. The same week every year for what . . . two hundred something years now?"

"Only this year is different."

She cocks her head to one side, a mannerism while thinking. "How so?"

"This is Allie's senior year, remember?" In her eyes, still clear and bright with none of the rheum I have come to associate with older people, I see dawn, but clouded.

"Surely Allie has no interest in going to the St. Simeon."

"Why not? Most of her friends will be there. It's her year."

"But Coleman, you know adopted children aren't eligible. Allie knows it, too."

I doodle on the tablecloth with the blunt end of my spoon. I have put this confrontation off to the last possible moment. But the St. Simeon and Korea in the same morning may tax even her strength. "Actually, Allie hasn't mentioned it."

She nods decisively. "And she won't. She has great respect for tradition, even when that tradition excludes her."

I maintain my stare at the tablecloth, engraving concentric circles. The kitchen is quite still, silent but for the incessant hum of a fluorescent light above. At length, she sits down in the chair nearest. Her hand encircles my forearm.

"This is about Elizabeth, isn't it?" she says gently. "Elizabeth was always pushing the limits."

I smile weakly in remembrance. "I suppose she was."

"And you feel," she continues, "that she might want you to push this limit for her, in her place so to speak."

"Yeah, I guess that's possible."

"Son, you don't owe her this one. She knew from the day you two adopted that child that there were going to be certain realities no one could change. Why do you think your father and I were so opposed to the whole idea?"

I turn to her, full face. "I always assumed it was just a matter of bringing an Asian into the family."

Her cheeks, still roseate from her walk on the beach, flush as her palms come down squarely on the table. "Well, of course! That was part of it. Plus we didn't think it fair to the child. But Elizabeth was determined—"

"We both adopted her, Mother."

"Yes, but it was Elizabeth's idea. She pushed you into it. Don't deny that."

I shrug. "I admit I was reluctant."

"So accept consequences like the St. Simeon. The oldest, most prestigious social society in the South is not going to change its policy. Why, look at Peter Devereux; so blonde and blue-eyed he could pass for a native Charlestonian and so much like Kate you'd never know he was adopted. Do you think he got an invitation? Even if your father were still president of the thing, the answer would be no. Besides, Allie understands, I can assure you. It won't trouble her for an instant."

"Maybe you're right. It just seems strange. We took Josh and Steven and now Elizabeth's gone and Allie can't go. It makes me . . . sad."

She stands beside me, then reaches out and enfolds my head in her arms, pulling me to her. I don't resist. Perhaps we need this, each of us.

"Oh, son, I know you're still hurting. You don't seem yourself these days. But, 'This too will pass.' Have faith in God and do everything you can to get on with life. That's the formula for success." She releases me, holding me by the shoulders at arms length, and tries to smile. "How is Adelle Roberts? You're still seeing her?"

"Adelle's fine. I took her to Allie's horse show last weekend. She enjoyed it."

"Good. She's such a charming girl."

"Yes, she is." I check my watch. "I have a 10:00 appointment so I'd better go."

She walks me to the front door and waves good-bye. As I clear the driveway and start back toward town, I think back to the weekend we broke the news about Allie's impending arrival. Over the years, Sarah has come around; she is much closer to Allie than she acknowledges. Would Dad have come around? We'll never know.

18

Today, I turn forty-seven. Adelle is on her way over to take me to dinner, having insisted on driving, making reservations, and picking up the tab, all of this being agreeably forced on me in a businesslike call a solid month ago.

Allie will join us later. She has recently begun dating Christopher, Adelle's eighteen-year-old son. Adelle and I find this mildly amusing as Allie and Christopher have gone to school together since third grade—Adelle insists it was second grade; I have to remember to ask the kids—and only now, in their senior year, have they shown the slightest interest in being more than friends. Maybe friendship explains it now, plus a measure of nostalgia at the realization that they're about to go separate paths. Chris is a good kid; off to USC on a tennis scholarship.

For the second time today I shower. The mirror is fogged over, which is why I had intended to shave before showering but I suppose my mind wandered and I forgot. At face level I wipe away enough condensation to apply lather and press the blade first to the base of the left, always the left, sideburn. I shave, dry my face and pause a moment to inspect Dad's mole on my eyelid. I've been noticing my eyebrows lately. An occasional gray one weaves itself among the dark, and their ordered pattern is becoming disrupted by rogue, undisciplined hairs. The creases at the corners of my eyes are deepening a bit; I need to remember to wear a hat on the boat. The Carter forehead is still smooth and my hair is starting to fleck with what everyone assures me is a most becoming gray. Gray always becomes someone else.

The doorbell. Adelle must be early. I exchange my towel for a robe and look around for my slippers. Passing barefoot through my room on my way to the front door, I notice the clock by the bed: Adelle is actually ten minutes late. I reach the foyer, open the door and in she walks.

Adelle is tall, brunette, erect, with an immediate air that often signals a businesswoman or professional, of which she is neither. She must have great peripheral vision because she seems to keep track of things without having to turn directly to them. Her hips roll gently when she walks and she has a way of measuring every step, the way an equestrian calculates strides between jumps. I did not know her growing up, but I reckon her an unadorned teen, a sparrow of a young woman who, upon finding herself in the same woods with cardinal beauties like Elizabeth, became a consummate preener.

She is, for example, compulsively fashionable, to a degree that even her most casual weekend attire is no doubt an ensemble among the pages of some catalog's glossy spread featuring New York models in outdoor chic; snug jeans complementing tartan plaid shirts against backdrops of russet Vermont maples, covered bridges, and blinkered draft horses.

Her knowledge of makeup is encyclopedic. Shopping with her for Christmas last month, I circled a department store in a holding pattern while she selected eyeliner with the studied precision of a pro franchise naming its top draft choice. Nor is her hair neglected. Weekly appointments with Justin, accent on the last syllable, are sacrosanct.

I kiss her lightly on the cheek, suggest she fix herself a drink, and take the stairs two-at-a-time back to my room. Ten minutes later I am back, in gray slacks, a navy double-breasted blazer, a white sea-island cotton shirt and the tie Allie gave me for Christmas. The tie is a montage of blacks, reds, silvers, and whites; a little bold for my taste but it will please Allie to see me wear it. And what the hell, I'm forty-seven.

"What a gorgeous tie," says Adelle as I enter. I fix a Scotch and we catch up on our respective weeks.

"Where are you taking me?" I ask from the passenger seat as she drives down Tradd Street toward East Bay.

"I thought the Cooper Club might be nice," she says, her eyes fixed on the road.

I nod, but find her choice puzzling; we eat there often and so familiarity deprives it of the select ambiance I anticipated.

The parking lot is jammed. A smooth, saline breeze off the river tousles my hair as I open my door. Skipjacks and catamarans, tied up in slips, clink and jangle in the wind as rigging strikes metal masts and booms; the music of the marina. My own boat, a Hinkley, thirty-one feet, is down there, rocking gently on the ebb tide. I must have drifted with thoughts of sailing because Adelle has come to my side of the car and is looking at me expectantly.

"Coleman? Shall we go in?" We join arms and stroll toward the brightly lit portico of the Cooper Club.

Ronald, the maître d' at the Club for as long as anyone remembers, greets us warmly and signals for help with our coats. The dining room is virtually deserted; odd, given the crush of cars in the lot. As we navigate among sparsely occupied tables in the cavernous room, I am seized by the certainty that I am about to be "surprised."

"Surprise!" shouts a hoard of perhaps a hundred people as Adelle leads me into the private dining room. I have just enough time to shoot her a quick you-sneaky-devil look before being engulfed in a flood of well-wishers. My law partners, their wives, my mother, neighbors on Church Street, two college classmates, my tennis doubles partner, even an ex-girlfriend now happily married to a dentist in Columbia. Amid the hand-wringing and back-slapping someone puts a drink in my hand and I am swept along toward a dais at the far end of the room. Already seated there, but standing as Adelle and I approach, are Josh and his date, Steven, Allie, and Christopher. I hug my children, shake Christopher's hand and turn to face the throng of friends now clapping and cheering.

The room is high-ceiling, and from two prominent chandeliers are festooned crepe paper streamers of blue and white. On each table, fresh arrangements of camellias, blush reds mingled among pale pinks, radiate against the starched white tablecloths.

"All right, heathens," intones Rev. Kent from St. Philip's Episcopal into the microphone mounted on one of those Rotary Club podiums. Ignored, he taps his water glass with a fork and the crowd gradually falls silent.

"Lord God," begins Frank Kent, "we gather together within Your sight to honor our friend Coleman. You have seen meet to keep him amongst us forty-seven years today, and we thank You for that. Keep him and all of us for many more, we ask in Your name, Amen."

Harris Deas, my partner and co-founder of the firm of Carter & Deas, approaches the mic. "First we'll eat, then we'll talk," he announces to cheers of approval. Waiters stream in from all sides, trays high over their heads among the tightly packed tables and chairs. As ginger salad is placed before me, I turn to Adelle.

"Confession time, Roberts. Who are your co-conspirators?"

She places her palm, fingertips splayed, against her modest chest and assumes a look of profound hurt. "Are you accusing ME of a hand in this affair?" She grins and bats her eyes, fluttering that carefully selected eyeliner.

"I was thinking of pledging eternal servitude to whoever would go to this much trouble."

"In that case," she replies, "I take full responsibility." She turns and casts a gravid look my way. "Is servitude the same as marriage?" I feel my eyes widening against all effort to remain composed and she gives a short laugh. "A little humor," she says hastily. "Really, I was kidding."

Recovering, I ask about Mr. Quan, the caterer now giving silent hand signals to the six Asian waiters bustling around the room. Vietnamese caterers are the rage, and in Charleston, Mr. Quan is the best. He is a slight man, short, with limbs and waist of rice-diet slimness that fifteen years in Charleston have not altered. I gauge him to be in his early fifties, but it is impossible to be certain.

"Do you like that touch?" asks Adelle, and I sense it is important to her that I do.

"Terrific. I love their food. What did Allie say when she found out?" My daughter has never been particularly comfortable around other Asians.

"She was all for it. Have you seen the waiters staring at her?"

Mother is seated among her town friends whom she sees less frequently now. Adelle is on my left and to her left, Allie. I lean back to make eye contact behind Adelle's back. "Psst! I suspect you as well."

She smiles. "Dad, you're wearing my tie. I was afraid you didn't like it."

"I'm crazy about it, and I've never seen you at a loss to change the subject."

"A lady's privilege is a man's delight."

"Who said that?" I ask.

"I did."

"Not bad," I allow.

Steven is talking to Christopher. They have known each other for years, having played soccer together for Porter-Gaud. Steven, a senior at The Citadel, is in uniform, his dress grays, and watching him fills me with pride. Elizabeth would swoon at the handsome sons she produced.

The next course arrives. Over crab soup I make a point of identifying every person seated before me, satisfied that I have matched each name and face.

Adelle's voice intrudes. "Margarite doesn't look herself tonight. Have you noticed?"

Margarite Huger is something of a grande dame and I have known her all my life. I spent almost as much time in her house as I did my own. Her blood is blue, tinged with the royal purple she can trace to Thirteenth Century England. She married well, has lived well, and takes it all in stride with a couple of jiggers of Old Granddad each night. Hers is the endearing ability to value what and who she is without being absorbed by it. Though a stalwart of St. Philip's, annually giving much of her support anonymously so as not to belittle the offerings of her fellow vestrymen, I have often wondered if she is not a closet Hindu. The trappings of her current world engage her fully enough, but there is always a hint of psychic distance, perceivable in her genteel chuckle at those same trappings, as though her innermost fascination is the dramatic difference between this life and the one she just left or will soon enter. She is one of my favorite people. Her son, Philip, my best friend growing up, died in Vietnam.

"I've rarely seen her so dejected," I say.

Adelle's peripheral vision serves her well. She can appraise Margarite without discernibly breaking eye contact. "Nor have I. Look, she's leaving."

I glance toward the rear just in time to see Margarite slip through the double doors, her sense of urgency obvious. I rise, excuse myself, and hasten to catch up, taking with me in my half-walk, half-run the stares of many of my guests. I overtake her at the coat check. She does not see me approach. I lean over and whisper, "How wonderful of you to come."

"Coleman," she says turning, her eyes brightening for a moment as she reaches for my hands. "I hope you'll forgive me. It was so sweet of Allie and Adelle to include me."

"They didn't think about the caterer. Honest."

"Oh, of course they didn't. I'm just being a silly old woman who'll spoil your evening if I'm not careful. Allie and the boys look wonderful, and so do you. Happy Birthday. I'm not sure what came over me in there. So many years have passed now, but every now and again I find myself in this awful funk."

"You miss Philip. So do I."

"I still see you boys as children. There you are, sitting in your sandbox playing with your trucks and I turn my back for two minutes and you grow to be forty-seven. How did this happen?"

"Beats me, Margarite. I just get up each morning, put both feet on the floor, and do it all over again."

"Well, your family is lovely and Adelle is stunning in that outfit."

"Yes," I acknowledge with a token glance back at the room. "Margarite, I have a problem and you're the perfect person to advise me."

"By all means," she answers, and sensing a change of subjects she brightens.

"There's no time to go into it fully tonight, but be thinking over how I can get Allie invited to the St. Simeon." I study her reaction.

Her eyes hold mine for an instant before darting upward in a sort of regal contemplation, as if she is debating whether to invade the Netherlands. Looking back again, she says, "You do know that I'm the president this year." I feign surprise and we laugh simultaneously before she turns very serious.

"This matter of Allie has already come up in the Board. I'm embarrassed to say I'm not optimistic. Adelle missed the meeting at which it was discussed or else I'm sure she would have told you."

"You think it's hopeless?"

"I think it's . . . remote, and damn closed-minded if you want my judgment. Does she wish to go?"

"She hasn't said. I'm looking into it on my own."

"You'll have to hurry; invitations go out soon."

"I know. Any ideas?"

Margarite purses her lips thoughtfully. "One. Why not make a formal request for an exception? We meet next Thursday. You'll have to do it then. I can put you on the agenda if you'd like."

"Have exceptions been requested?"

"Twice in my twenty years on the Board. Neither granted, I'm forced to tell you."

I bob my head to assure her I understand what we're dealing with. "I'll let you know," I say, kissing her cheek. The toasts, or roasts, are about to begin and I must return to mount the sacrificial altar.

The room drones with a score of conversations as I re-enter, sobered by the remembrance of Philip. I will not dwell on him now. Adelle is engaged in chatter with Allie and all seems upbeat.

I stop along my way, greeting those whom I missed in the press of the reception.

Mr. Quan's entre is beef swimming in a sauce deliciously French. In 1954, when the Vietnamese raised one hand to wave farewell to their unwanted guests, they had the good sense to clutch tightly in the other the recipes they have since perfected. Adelle is right, I think as the meal progresses and I mop up the remaining sauce with a crust of bread; the waiters are buzzing around the room with one collective eye on my daughter, who seems oblivious but is not.

If you cored the 322 years-old tree which is Charleston, Spanish moss languishing from its limbs, the crowd assembled tonight would comprise a fair cross section. Who you were still matters here almost as much as who you are. I have traveled some and in newer communities the social register tends to be somewhat analogous to a suburban Forbes Four Hundred, with fewer zeroes. There, financial statements dictate access; to clubs, societies, and neighborhoods. Every year a few are added to the list, a few suffer precipitous nose dives and fall off, a few move out, some move in, and over time I suppose a continuity of sorts emerges. In California, I once heard a businessman remark that his friend so-and-so was reliable and had been an anchor in the town "for years," which, according to this same so-and-so with whom I dealt several days later, was precisely three.

Charleston is not the same closed city of the last century, and newcomers are welcomed with what we still like to think of as exceptional hospitality. You won't fall off "the list" here when your stock portfolio takes a tumble. Losing your job doesn't mean losing your club, your friends and those things which matter most at the time you need them most. Money counts, but not overly much. And, there is something intangible here that is beyond the reach of even the wealthiest wannabes.

As much as I value that intangible, others don't. Take Adelle's ex-husband, for example. Legare Roberts wore his family's crest like an old T-shirt, tossed into a corner after a two day bender. He roared through money like he roared through liquor and women. He found Charleston, in a word, "preposterous," and he now lives with a ski bunny somewhere in Colorado. Legare could devise a cure for cancer and all the royalties off the patent couldn't get him back into the clubs he snickered at.

On the dais I am greeted by knowing smirks that signal fun at my expense. Harris beckons a waiter to refill my wine glass and the rub begins. My mother delivers a piquant little tale of a seven-year-old me, the doctor, caught in *flagrante medico* with a Victoria Pettit, the patient. Laughter. More wine.

Josh is next. Looking a bit nervous and gesturing liberally, he relates an instance in his early teens when Elizabeth commanded me to discipline him for some egregious offense and I responded by sneaking him out of the house for ice cream. More laughter. More wine.

Next comes Harris. We've been partners for years. A massive guy, he works too hard, eats too much, and hunts ducks with a passion which surpasses comprehension. His hands are the meatiest I have ever seen on a human, yet when he raises his fingers, bulging like cooked franks, to adjust the glasses on the bridge of his nose, he does so with dexterity unmatched by most eye surgeons. He brings that same quality to litigation. Lawyers intimidated by his bulk brace against being run over while he subtly goes around to pick their pockets, figuratively speaking. As he regales them with anecdotes, then exaggerates my virtues as a partner, my mind inexplicably returns to Philip Huger. My friend Philip, dead now for twenty-eight years. "And do you know what?" I ask myself in one of those wine-induced reveries in which the mind seems focused with laser-like precision on the great truths even as the eyes are struggling to distinguish a neighbor from a lamp post, "Philip's going to be dead a long time. He's going to be dead forever and nobody is going to say nice things about him on his forty-seventh birthday because he isn't going to have one." A melancholy comes over me that I attribute mostly to the wine, and I re-double my concentration on Harris at the podium least my guests perceive my mood.

"But seriously, folks," Harris is saying, "Coleman is known in legal circles as the Great Conciliator. Nobody has his ability to go into a room with two snarling adversaries and come out with everyone smiling and shaking hands. Show me a man who has practiced law in one place for any length of time and has so few enemies and I'll show you a special man indeed. Coleman, we love you, boy. Happy Birthday."

I rise, embrace Harris in the manly, ursine hug we both enjoy, and am about to disengage when he half-whispers, half-yells, "See me after—great news!" As I flash a quick thumbs-up, I turn to find the crowd on its feet, clapping and shouting echoes of Harris's praise. I am quite moved. I thank them for coming, thank Adelle and Allie and Mother and Harris and Mr. Quan and everyone who had a hand in planning it. With a wave of farewell, it is over.

Standing down now, in front of the rostrum, I mingle informally with those who come forward to press the flesh. There is gaiety in their manner, heartfelt good will in the clasps of hands, thumps of shoulders, Platonic kisses and it comes to me what has given this celebration its added zest: the last time we—all of us here tonight—congregated was at Elizabeth's funeral. Then, we groped for words because words are demanded even when they are useless. They are relieved; yes, that is the essence of it, as I am relieved, that we gather in the sunshine of food and jokes and reunion and that the long, dark shadow of that magnolia tree in St. Philip's churchyard is part of our past.

Harris and Carolyn, his wife, are among the last to leave. He has that glassy-eyed wobble that tells me she will be driving home, not that I myself have any plans to get behind a wheel. I grin sophomorically at them and Carolyn, a petite blonde toy of a woman, sighs with her boys-will-be-boys patience.

"Ok, Deas," I say, "what have you done?"

"What have we done, ma' boy. The Performing Arts Center?"

"Yeah?" I reply, anticipating what is coming.

"Met with Middleton late this afternoon, and unless he's lying through his dentures we've got the votes."

"Good work, son," I commend him. "Should make for a banner year around Carter & Deas." City council is preparing to contract out the legal work on the new Arts Center. Because of our expertise in municipal bonds and condemnation, we are one of only two firms in the city that can handle it. Harris has been working over councilmen, counting votes.

I am unconscious of the time these farewells consume. Adelle is in the kitchen squaring up with the club and the staff. Josh and Steven shook my hand some time back and Allie bolted, hand in hand with Christopher. The last guest is waiting at the coat check when Adelle joins me. I give her a look that I hope conveys the appreciation I feel and together we go in search of our coats. As we exit, a freshet of chilly air cuts through the fog of the last few hours and my lungs drink it in. I pull Adelle closer as we walk to the car.

She starts the engine, shivering as the various warning lights and signals run their course.

"Great party," I say, giving her a gentle chuck on the shoulder. "Thanks."

"Coleman," she says abruptly, as if she hasn't heard me, "you'll never guess what I saw tonight."

"You're right, I can't guess."

"You'll be more serious when you hear," she says.

"Then tell me. I can take it." I have no clue as to what is coming.

"I came out to the car to get my checkbook—I left it in my other handbag—and I passed by Christopher's car."

"And?"

"The windows were a bit fogged but I could clearly see them kissing, and I don't mean a peck on the cheek."

"Allie and Chris?"

"Your daughter, my son."

"Does that shock you? They are dating."

Adelle winces in a controlled fret. "Yes, but they've always been such buddies. Just good friends for so long."

I shrug philosophically. "Look at us. We were friends for years before Elizabeth died and Legare left. We've done more than kiss. Things change."

"Yes, but we're adults; they're just children."

"Adelle, ease up. They're kissing, not screwing, and they're both mature kids in an age when kids grow up mighty damn fast."

She attempts a confessional grin. "I guess I'm being overly protective."

I lean over, put my arm around her shoulders, and bring my lips to her ear. "If I were you, I'd stop worrying about your son's virtue and worry a little more about your own. You're in danger here, if you haven't noticed." I nibble on her lobe to underscore the obvious. She giggles and yields simultaneously.

She says, "At the risk of a cliché, your place or mine?"

"I feel particularly wicked tonight. How about a hotel?"

"Oh, Coleman," she says, turning impatient, "you don't feel wicked. You just don't want to risk Allie finding us in bed."

I release her and turn toward my window. "You're right. I'm sorry. I just need to work this out so I'll be comfortable."

Now she leans to me, as far as the bucket seat will permit. "You seem tense no matter where we are. Look, it's late and we've both had long days. Why don't I drop you at home and we can talk it over tomorrow."

"Yeah," I say sheepishly, "that's a good idea."

At the curb back on Church Street I lean in, kiss Adelle, and thank her again for the party. By the time I reach the door, her tail lights are out of sight. The kids are not at home, and I am tired but not yet sleepy. At the bar I pour a short brandy and step out onto the piazza, flopping into a wicker chair that takes a minute to settle itself. The air is cold and thin and so still that I could easily converse with Brad across the street without raising my voice.

I think back over the evening and blush anew at my bungled come-on to Adelle. Sex; what a pain in the shorts. By the time you weigh the ethics, the moralities, the logistics, the public fronts and private realities, the explanations given or denied, the contraceptives, the lab reports, and all the rest it's hardly worth it. Still, my relationship with Adelle is something I need to address. I keep reminding myself not to press, that sorting things out after Elizabeth will take some time.

Of course, some time has passed.

"Forty-seven," I murmur. On balance, good years. I was blessed with parents who loved each other. After an expensive education, I married a lovely woman with whom I had a good, but far from perfect, relationship, and whom I miss terribly. Three fine kids, a good career, great friends. Lots of laughs and some tears dropped in for seasoning. That's what life is, right? I've made it. I won my race.

"So explain to me," I instruct myself between sips of brandy, "this nagging malaise of recent weeks. Tell me why a concentration as reliable as dawn has suddenly scattered like its first rays over the Atlantic. Why, when friends engage me earnestly, do I find myself contemplating their noses, or their ears, or neglected dental work? Why do I yawn at receptions, turn off football games in the fourth quarter when the score is tied, or sit in church and dream of sailing but while sailing think of the cocktail waitress at the country club who pressed against me serving drinks?"

Two weeks ago, I left the house as Allie left for school. An appointment with a client scheduled for 9:00 dictated a brisk walk around the block;

twenty minutes max. Instead, in sweat clothes I ambled along the sea wall we call the Battery. There, in one of those absent-minded reveries that seem to transport me regularly these days, I mentally unspiked the massive mortars and calculated the trajectory necessary to hit Ft. Sumter. Around me, hundreds of soldiers and civilians in antebellum dress shouted angry defiance at the harbor, fists raised to underscore their outrage. "Yeah," I yelled with them, "goddamn Yankees." The ground shook beneath us with each successive salvo and an acrid mist mingled among us. Suddenly, a roar erupted and the soldier next to me pointed to the fort and I saw through the smoke the first distant tongues of flame scar the air above.

I stood there a long time, until half past nine, when I jogged back home and called the office. My client wasn't pleased but then too often clients aren't. I dressed leisurely and drove unhurriedly to work.

I see headlights turn onto Church Street and think Allie is returning but the car drives past. It is the Smathers' Buick. Moments later I hear their gate opening and soon all is quiet again. That morning on the Battery—what does it mean when you stand up a client to daydream over a long lost battle? For the first time in memory I feel myself shadowed, but by a person or event or mood I cannot say. In the basement the other night, looking for the lamp, I almost touched it so palpable was its presence. Whatever its nature or substance, it is brooding, insistent, and, I sense with a quick shudder that could be just a chill, disturbing.

19

A steady drumming in my temples rouses me the following morning. Bathrobe on inside out, my slippers still missing, I descend to the kitchen. Two aspirin and sixteen ounces of industrial strength coffee prepare me to charge into my forty-eighth year, more or less. I am reading the *Post and Sentinel* in the den when Allie enters in jodhpurs, her feet in socks.

"Morning, Dad," she says sweetly as she passes on her way to the kitchen. "How is the old bod feeling?"

I lift my eyes from an editorial on the soaring cost of medical care in time to see her disappear through the swinging door. After some kitchen noise, she emerges with orange juice and a banana, sits in an overstuffed chair opposite me and pulls her feet up under her.

"So, what are your plans today?" she wants to know.

"Idleness followed by some relaxation hard on the heels of some serious lying around. My day is packed."

"I guess at your age you need time to recover from staying out so late." She grins around a bite of banana.

"Speaking of late hours . . ."

"I was home by two; if you don't believe me ask Chris."

"Did he enjoy himself last night?" My question seems innocent enough.

"You mean at your party or after?"

My mind flashes to Adelle's account of the fog-filled car. "The party, of course. What happened after is none of my business, is it?"

"Only if you care about your daughter's reputation."

I deposit the paper into my lap and stare. "Oh?" I am not at all sure I want to hear what's coming. Allie has always been too candid about these things.

"Yeah, we must have broken a record for sucking face last night. My lips are chapped."

"I see."

"Want to hear the rest?"

"No. It usually only gets messier."

"Not much," she says casually, as if she doubts it will rain. "I let him get by with a cheap thrill but when he started maneuvering for a big thrill I had to fall back on my elbow-in-the-ribs defense. He took it well. I like that about Chris. I'll bet his ribs are sore this morning."

"Sweetheart, how do you expect me to act casually around Chris when you tell me this stuff?"

"Relax, Dad, nothing happened. He was just giving it his best shot. We've been out four times now. He has expectations."

Why is God forcing me to listen to this? Most of my contemporaries can't get a word out of their teenagers and when they do, black lies follow white ones. Just my fate to have acquired "Miss Open Book of the Orient." I had fair warning she would be this way a few weeks after Elizabeth died. Allie came to me and said, "Dad, it seems like a rubber-based thing like a condom would irritate a woman's sensitive skin. Does it?" At that instant I was ready to trade places with Elizabeth. Allie says she is still a virgin; that she plans to wait until college.

I should be grateful, I am grateful, for her candor, a tool of indispensable utility to a generation confronting AIDs, violence, and drug abuse on a scale worthy of Richter. To the crowd that matriculated with "Just say no" and is graduating with Beavis and Butt-head, her habit of calling a spade by its name is a serum against the ruthless modern epidemic. Whether she inherited it or has adapted to the demands of her era, she is the high priestess of blunt disclosure.

It comes with a price, however; the same one paid by my parents and theirs as each generation drives a few splinters under the social fingernails of its predecessors. For Sarah and her contemporaries, it was bathing suits. Beach wear in her day left everything to the imagination, and she still clucks her disapproval on the beach at Sullivan's at the promenade of virtual nudity. For me it is language, the double edge on Allie's frankness. I have not easily accustomed myself to the female use of the word "fuck," despite Elizabeth's facile repetition. My abhorrence is part chauvinism, part southern, and part recollection of the stigma acquired by the few members of the sisterhood who, in my college years, dared experiment with purple prose. Now, as she reminds me, it has acquired the acceptance of damn or hell, and for me to take issue relegates me, she warns, to sitting on the dunes with Mother, lamenting the demise of western civilization. I have overheard her on the phone or with friends often enough to absorb its use as a benign banality, but after a futile effort to discourage it I gave up. "Dad, I say it, I don't do it. Would you rather have it reversed?"

I want this subject to suffer a merciful death of silence so I resume reading the paper. She sips her juice. In time she asks if I would like to accompany her to the stables.

Frost is uncommon in Charleston and what little remained from last night is gone by the time the car leaves the city limits headed south toward Edisto. She is driving, in high spirits as she talks about a new mare that Kenny, her trainer, has brought over from Aiken. Allie's slender strength is perfect for horses.

We ease up to the barn and park. She immediately goes for the tack room while I take my time.

"Kenny, you old horse thief," I call to him from across some rail fencing.

"Shhhh!" he says, looking around. "When you find out what I paid for this here mare you're gonna think you ain't far wrong."

Kenny is about fifty and "good ole boy" from hat to boot. And he knows his nags. He also knows riders, and has told me often that she, Allie, is the best he's ever trained. His facial features ebb and flow, rise and fall like the tidal creeks he was raised on; open, honest features that you need to win over open, honest creatures like horses. But once in awhile, when he tries to communicate something he needs very much for you to hear and understand, like a significant blood line or aberrant scores from judges, he turns gravely serious by freezing his face in a calcified countenance so that you feel as though you're looking at Abraham Lincoln sitting in his memorial.

"Coleman," he'll say, not moving a muscle in his jaw and barely moving his lips, "the girl has no fear. None. Gimme ten thousand riders and I'll give you one outta the whole lot's got no fear of a thousand pound animal. That girl's the one. Damnedest thing I ever seen."

"Me too," I could tell him, but I don't. Like a photo in your wallet, it's a private memory stored close, the memory of the first time I saw her ride. Not long after the birthday with the pony, we were enjoying a long weekend in the Blue Ridge Mountains. At a weathered sign for "Trail Rides," we stopped. The owner, a dour woman who looked as though she had been sucking on a persimmon for the hour before we arrived, refused to rent us a horse for Allie. "No experience, too young, ain't gonna happen." But Harris doesn't call me Great Conciliator for nothing, so after urging Elizabeth and the boys to start, I went to work on the persimmon ("Nice place you've got here. So well maintained. I can't imagine trying to manage something like this . . ." etc.). I never convinced her to let Allie on the trail, but she finally agreed to let me lead a horse along the corral railing and after planting Allie firmly in the saddle, I trooped up and down, reins in hand, to give her a feel for the horse's movement. Looking over my shoulder, I saw an expression of cautious pleasure mixed with a childish awe that she could be so far off the ground on something that moved. After ten minutes, I heard, "Faster." I cast around for the persimmon, then broke into a slow trot which forced the horse to do the same. Almost instantly there came a high-pitched giggle and, glancing back, I saw the difference between pleasure and glee. With each pass, her entire face animated in the purest joy. "Faster," she said. Back and forth I went, heedless of the persimmon, running the horse into a trot so brisk it approached a canter, and she could not get enough. At last, panting wildly and exhausted, I stopped, nearly collapsing beside the rail. Elizabeth and the boys returned, and I paid the tab. I have wondered in the intervening years if perhaps the persimmon witnessed the whole thing from a secluded spot without the heart to intervene. If not, she surely must have pondered how a horse walking a rail came to be lathered.

Today, I lean on the fence as she warms up the new mare. Kenny, in the center of the ring, calls instructions. "More leg," and she makes what to me but not to Kenny is some invisible adjustment. "Shorten the reins and give her some inside pressure." For an hour they work and if, as Allie and Kenny agree at the end, there has been progress I do not see it. As she dismounts, patting the mare respectfully, Kenny joins me at the fence.

"Green as new corn but she'll be a good 'un," he says. "Got some big shows comin' up this spring." He takes a plain sheet of dog-eared paper from his shirt pocket. "Camden on March 14th, Greenville the weekend after."

"What about April 17th?" I ask.

He consults the paper. "Yep. Big 'un. State fair in Columbia. Why, she gonna have a problem?"

"Possibly," I say. "The St. Simeon is that weekend, but I don't know if she'll be going."

"The Saint who?"

"Simeon. It's a big dance."

"Sheet," drawls Kenny. "You can't tell me she's gonna pass up a show for a dance."

"Things change, Kenny. She's growing up."

"Lemme tell you something," and here his face assumes its frozen stillness, his country intellectual mood. "There's a couple things women never outgrow, and one's horses."

"Yeah?" I say. "What's the other?"

He looks away, but a trace of a grin is on his lips. "The need to be held," he says softly.

I smile and raise my eyebrows. "I rest my case."

In the car returning to Charleston, she asks if I have given more thought to her graduation present. "I read in the paper," she says, "that United is advertising some deals to Seoul. So, are we going?"

"We have a more immediate concern. The St. Simeon is around the corner."

She downshifts as we approach the main highway. "There's not much to talk about, is there? The rules say I can't go so that's that."

"Let's forget the rules for a moment. Do you want to go?"

"Well, sure. The biologicals went, even though Steven took that slut Ashley Porter. You went when you were young. Granddaddy went. My best friends from school are going and the guy I'm dating will be there so why wouldn't I want to go?"

"Suppose I could get the Society to grant an exception. How would you feel?"

"Do you mean, 'Will I feel like a second class citizen?' Yeah, I guess I might." There is a pause as we both stare ahead. After several reflective moments, she says, "On second thought, Dad, it's only a dance and it could cause trouble."

"How so?"

"Charleston is still so conservative. Even if you get the exception a lot of people will resent my being there. Let's just leave it alone."

There is resignation in her voice, an intonation that says, "Move on to something else." It is unlike her not to confront things directly, but then she has always resisted attention or overtures spawned by her uniqueness. As a child, she drew the usual ooh's and ah's accorded young girls, but inevitably mixed in were stares, compliments and fuss made by those for whom she was a novelty, and who approached her as they would an exotic pet. Elizabeth and I came to sense her discomfort, and in the more overt encounters we shared it. I found myself walking a thin line between showering her with the natural affection due an only daughter and withholding that affection for fear of appearing, in her increasingly sensitized eyes, overindulgent. The last thing, the very last thing, she has sought or accepted has been deference to her Asianicity. An exemption to the St. Simeon will spotlight it.

"The other night in the basement," I remind her, "you said you feel like a Charlestonian, as well you should. You have as much claim to the heritage of this city as anyone I know. The St. Simeon is hardly just a dance. And I hate to think of you denied the right to something you've earned."

"But that's just it. You can't earn it. You're born into it or you're not. Well, I guess you can marry in but that seems pretty radical."

"Indeed," I acknowledge, "although I know of marriages where I'm sure it's been a factor. At any rate, I don't want to do anything that will make you uncomfortable. Will you let me know?"

She nods thoughtfully but says no more. We leave it there, and there it stays until Monday night, when I pause at the door of her room.

"Any more thoughts on the St. Simeon?"

She looks over from the book spread before her. "Yes." There is a finality in her inflection. I walk in and sit on the edge of her bed. "I've decided that you're right. It's part of my heritage, or should be."

"Good," I say. "I'll call Margarite Huger in the morning."

"But suppose the Board says no."

"There are no guarantees, but between the Great Conciliator and a Princeton girl we should be able to work it out." I rise and stray to her dressing table nearby. On it rests the mirror which arrived with her on the afternoon she came to us. It is small, round, with a lattice design on the handle. Its most prominent feature, however, is the back; a time-worn mother-of-pearl. As it was the sole article that accompanied her, other than the kimono she wore on the flight, she values it highly. As with her, the mirror arrived without much explanation.

"I don't know," she says. "I have a feeling it's going to be harder than you think."

"Leave it to me. I know these people."

20

Margarite, gratified by the prospect of my intrusion on an agenda that follows the rote routine of bus stops, instructed me to arrive at 7:00. On Thursday evening, I turn down Water Street, then onto Meeting for the short hop to the Hall. I could have walked.

The St. Simeon Society is one of a diminishing number of anachronisms deliciously southern. Founded in 1766, it was modeled after a musical society in Edinburgh, Scotland, of the same name. The by-laws empowered the Society's managers to fix the dates and times for concerts, ". . . the Anniversary only excepted." That concert, "the Grande Ball," was to be held on St. Simeon's Day, the third Saturday in April. My great-great-great-great-great grandfather, Alston Carter, was one of eighty-two founding members.

I know little of the Society's history during its fledgling decades. There must have once been minutes of its gatherings, records of its dues, and the other usual stitches in the social fabric. Certainly I know of no distinction conferred by membership; other equally quaint associations predated the St. Simeon. But none, it seems, survived it, and in 1795 an event occurred which changed it in the eyes of its members and, not long afterwards, enhanced its esteem among average Charlestonians.

In June of that year, fire broke out in Lodge Alley and spread to Queen Street, destroying every house between Church Street and the Cooper River. Arson was strongly suspected, with the focus of inquiry on some newly arrived French "Negroes" from Santo Domingo, where the 1791 slave rebellion produced accounts of murder, rape, and bedlam on a scale that frightened Charlestonians to their core. The distant strains of the Civil War prelude could be heard in the events of the day, and among more attentive listeners a dark suspicion arose that Charleston slaves had abetted this arson.

The owners of slaves perceived, with perfect insight, the most extreme danger to themselves, their families and property in the event of a general rebellion. Founders of the St. Simeon were, almost to the man (for it was then all-male), slave owners, and as an additional precaution against an uprising targeting the landed gentry, a member suggested that the membership roll be destroyed and that henceforth all business be conducted in secret. A diary left by my ancestor Alston records the night, August 15, 1795, the oath of secrecy was taken:

> At half-past five we dined and upon adjournment instructed Theo to dismiss the servants and absent himself from the premises. Brandy and cigars went round. After a modicum of discussion, accompanied I must say by no idle amount of good-natured derision aimed at its more vociferous proponents, the measure was approved by a near unanimous chorus of "ayes!", with the "nays" of a few token recalcitrants drown

down in a boisterous demand for more brandy. Thus, by decree of seventy-one gentlemen, five opposed, this entry could well serve as my last recorded memoir of our blessed St. Simeon Society.

And it was. He lived for twelve more years and there is not a single additional reference to be found.

In hindsight, their rationale seems tenuous if not absurd. The landed gentry comprising the membership were well known, particularly to slaves. A fire in St. Philip's at 11:30 A.M. on a Sunday would have netted virtually the entire membership plus dozens more. Slaves were illiterate; did these gentlemen fear the roster falling into the hands of rebels who could not read it? The perspective of two centuries seems to me to dictate the conclusion that this pledge was an aberrational reaction of panic by a few at a loss to take meaningful steps to quell their fear. Reading Alston Carter's report of "derision aimed at its more vociferous proponents," I am persuaded that most voting in the affirmative did so tongue-in-cheek and brandy-in-hand, fraternal spirits like those found on any college campus. Whatever the cause, the effect of the pledge was to entrench reticence.

In 1805, a man named Andrew Ramsey was elected president. A Scotsman, he descended from Stuart Ramsey, the Society's second president. Andrew had only one child, a daughter, foreshadowing the end of the Ramsey line under the rule of male-only descent. In an age emphatically chauvinistic and more than a century removed from the female franchise, Ramsey prevailed upon the Board to alter the rule, so that thereafter any legitimate blood issue of a member qualified. Consistent with its inviolate secrecy, there is no official record of the Board's action but the story is well known and the admission of Martha Ramsey as the first female member is described in letters that survived her death in 1839. She reported her margin of victory as four to three.

It is easy to make too much of the 1805 Board's enlightenment. As a musical society, the St. Simeon sponsored concerts regularly attended by women, as of course was the Grande Ball. Thus, while actual membership and the management were strictly male from the founding until Ramsey's motion passed, women had always been welcomed as indispensable participants.

The early nineteenth century brought decline to the popularity of musical societies in general; they withered like unpicked cotton. All save one: the St. Simeon. Its roll, unpublished anywhere but increasingly etched into the consciousness of both members and non-members, swelled, and the less said about it the greater its prestige and the more ardent the fervor of those seeking to establish their bloodlines for admission. The rosy patina of exclusivity highlighted with a rouge of hushed intrigue created a goddess of social desire, dark and mysterious and maddeningly elusive. Over decades, through the Civil War, the goddess grew more lovely, more seductive.

Entitlement remained unchanged for the next 170 years. In 1975, rising divorce rates forced a reassessment. Until that time, divorce automatically terminated membership, for both the couple and their descendants, and this rule held more than a few tortured relationships together, so highly is membership prized. I have been told (the rules are unwritten) that a divorced man or woman may now maintain affiliation if: the marriage was of at least ten years duration and produced a child, a potential St. Simeon. It is this change which allowed Adelle to remain a member after her divorce from Legare.

Until Elizabeth's death, I had attended every Grande Ball since returning to the city to practice law. The Ball is held in the Society's headquarters on Meeting Street. The gag rule prevents me from disclosing details, but I will offer two that have enjoyed wide circulation.

The front door of the headquarters is opened only once a year; the Anniversary. Access at all other times is a rear door which opens into an enclosed, high-walled parking lot. On the afternoon of the Ball, a long, opaque, custom-made canopy, teal in color, is erected from the curb of Meeting Street to the front door. This allows guests to come and go without being identified from the street. Secondly, the orchestra is shielded from guests by a curtain drawn full length across a stage. This barrier serves the same purpose as the canopy. White-tie and tails for men, formal floor-length gowns for women, all swaying to the muffled strains of an invisible orchestra. For an evening each April, the Old South lives in all its splendor. The social goddess summons her children to suckle the honey of privileged birth.

The man on the street, I must admit, views the Ball as a wealthy dalliance, and the paranoia over secrecy as proof of the members' arrested development, whoever they are. Such contempt is, of course, the point, and those of us who relish the Ball relish equally the disdain of those who have never been, and never will. It is our way of having fun in an age when all this self-righteous egalitarianism has gotten completely out of hand. And before the average Charlestonian gets too smug in his condemnation, he should honestly appraise his own attitudes. The vein of snobbery running through old Charleston does not stop at Broad Street but runs west to the Pacific Ocean. I know bowling leagues that consider themselves as exclusive as the St. Simeon.

On the other hand, bowling leagues do not dominate the city, its politics and its wealth, and it is here that the rubber meets the road, for the members of St. Simeon, in a word, control Charleston. It is not the Ball people aspire to but access to those in attendance. Long ago the Society abandoned its music motif to become what it is: the one organization dedicated to keeping the city in the hands of those who founded it, and anyone who tells you otherwise lives in Cleveland. The Ball is the annual reminder of that trust.

The debut remains a rite of passage for young women returning from their first semester in college. Although less common now, the practice still has its devotees in many areas of the country and in Charleston, where Assemblies and Cotillions launch these girls into formal society. But once again, the St. Simeon takes the road less trod. No young adult is eligible to attend before his or her senior year in high school, so that the appearance of the child at that spring Ball is an announcement to all in attendance, the social and political power structure of the city, that this kid has arrived. On that night they become trustees for the next generation, and to miss the Ball, or to be excluded, is a serious matter indeed.

I turn off Meeting Street into the venerable parking lot behind the Hall. Five or six late model cars dot the area. Adelle's car is parked against the far wall.

Constructed in 1840 and paid for (in cash) by the members, the Hall is a monument to the permanency of the Society itself. It looms over Meeting Street with the ethereal quality of a pyramid. Six Ionic columns rise from its wide portico in support of a Greek revival roof. Even Hugo, the 1989 hurricane, cowed before it, merely displacing a few slate tiles from the roof, perhaps as a concession that Nature too knows limits. Its massive oak door, salvaged from a cathedral in Spain, requires eight hinges. I park in the rear and ring the bell at the back.

The light behind the peep-hole changes. I am being surveyed before being admitted, but accustomed to this I smile at my anonymous voyeur. The door opens and I step into a small foyer, greeted by Margarite herself.

"Coleman, how nice to see you. Right on time." She smiles genially, overly so, as if to reassure, but there is the faintest tension around her mouth and jaw that signals all is not perfect within. "We're running a bit behind; would you mind terribly if we took a few more minutes before calling you in?"

"Not at all. I'll wait right here."

A chair, Queen Anne sturdy and uncomfortable, rests nearby. I paw the coffee table for this week's *Time* and sit down as Margarite returns to the library, where business meetings are held. The floor is marble, and the click-click of Margarite's retreating heels echoes. The library door opens, then closes, leaving me alone with *Time.*

Ten minutes elapse, then ten more. What are they doing in there? At last, the library door opens and Margarite calls my name. She swings the door wide and holds it as I enter.

The library is grandly auspicious. The ceiling is twelve feet high, adorned by a chandelier of Waterford crystal. Scaled-down Doric columns frame tall bookcases spaced evenly along the walls except at the far end, where a marble mantel predominates. Above the mantel hangs a Gilbert Stuart portrait of Arthur Ross, the Society's first president. The mahogany conference table, once an elegant dining room appointment in a local plantation, dates from the founding. The grandeur of the room dwarfs its present occupants, the Board, now seated around the table.

I give a self-conscious wave as I walk toward them. I know them all, of course—have known them all for years, so am surprised by the nervousness I feel as I approach. I manage a twitchy little grin at Adelle as Margarite joins me at the head of the table.

"You all know Coleman, I'm sure," she says rather formally. "As we briefly discussed before I asked him to join us, I have taken the prerogative of the chair in allowing him to come before us personally. His family's contributions to St. Simeon over the years are well known, not the least of which was his father's excellent stewardship as president in 1947, the year I began my active affiliation." She turns to me as she lays a comforting hand on my forearm. "We're all friends here, so Coleman, why don't you tell the Board what we can do for you."

I clear my throat in one of those lawyerly mannerisms that portend erudition. Why I am not more at ease baffles me as I face the seven members.

There is Adelle, of course, so I count one vote my way at the outset. Clarkson Mills is a client, a bridge partner on occasion, and a very nice man. I saved his furniture business a few years ago with a Houdini-like loan from some banking associates and I believe he will do anything within reason for me. Clarkson is short, compact, with a birthmark on one temple that faintly resembles Ohio. Vote number two.

With Margarite in my corner, I need one more supporter, but a survey of those facing me reveals this will not be easy.

To Adelle's left, my right, at the far end sits old Dr. Francis, a retired orthopedist with a long tradition of bow ties, stale breath and, during his practicing years, a bedside manner unrivaled in Charleston until World War II, when newsreels of Nazi generals at the heads of invading armies gave his patients a sense of déjà vu. Your bones better heal, and on schedule, or you got a snoot-full from Doc Francis. He is one of the few men I know who still wears a vest with watch and fob. Unfortunately, he had himself nominated for president of the Society in the very year my father was elected. He has never forgiven the Carters, and although my personal relationship with him has always been satisfactory, I am not optimistic about his vote tonight.

That leaves three members, all women. Jeanette Wilson is a well-proportioned, kudzu-like social climbing vine that, once rooted, wraps itself around everything that will help it grow and which thereafter cannot be stamped out or controlled. She seems to like me, has in fact come on to me a few times when she's been drunk. Her vote will be cast with index finger raised, tip moistened, to see which way the social wind is blowing.

Sandy Charles is the youngest member of the committee and the newest, serving her first term. Cute, bubbly, in her late thirties, she is married to Edgar Charles, a very fine architect from a distinguished family. I like Sandra, and would be more confident of her support were it not for her lamentable habit of following Charlotte Hines's lead.

If Margarite is the grand dame of our city, Charlotte Hines, her Royal Ampleness, is the dragon. She is eyeing me now through bifocals perched on the bridge of her nose, and my gut feeling is that the request I am about to put to the Board will shake her to her ample foundation. On the surface she has much in common with Margarite; wealthy, cultured with a heritage that includes two former governors, as she will let you know at the drop of an ice cube into a julep. But she lacks Margarite's grace and exhibits an insecurity which I attribute to intellectual deficiency. She is one of those people who will take a position on almost everything, but when probed fall back on clarifying what is already clear, as if by appearing adamant she appears wise, or she will muddy the argument beyond recognition with non sequiturs piled upon irrationalities. She is Professor Emeritus of a school I call the "often wrong, never in doubts."

"Curbside garbage collection," she told me during a time when city council was debating it, "will ruin Charleston. We might as well close Broad Street and all move out to the Isle of Palms." When I countered with the tax savings to the city, she fixed me in one of her condescending smirks and said, "Ugly, green things on wheels. It's unthinkable!" Somehow, when you disagree with them, people like Charlotte manage to impugn your motives, I suppose because impugning your logic would put them in the center of the very storm they wish to skirt. She will likely be a formidable opponent tonight, and her sway over Sandy Charles means an uphill fight ahead.

"Thank you, Margarite," I say as she takes her place at the table with the others. "Let me begin by telling you all how much I appreciate your accommodating what I know is an unusual request." With the exception of Doc Francis, they return imperceptible smiles with a collective nod that says, "Yes, we're very busy and yes, this is not our normal procedure but we're all nice people." Doc Francis stares at me, stone-faced.

"I think you all know or have met my daughter Allie. She is in her senior year of high school, off to Princeton in the fall. Obviously, she is adopted." The room is in total silence. The absence of windows insulates us from whatever street noise may be generated outside.

"Allie came to us when she was four months old. We know very little about her background, other than that she was placed in a Korean orphanage before being brought to the States." I glance toward Adelle for support. I am determined to keep this request on a plane above paternal sentimentality.

"Allie's record is an outstanding one. She is salutatorian of her class, a cheerleader, an excellent soccer and basketball player, and a gifted equestrian who has won many honors throughout the state." Margarite nods emphatically.

"Beyond her accomplishments, she is very much a child of this community. She has lived here most of her life and knows no other. We instilled in her what we believe to be the best values reflected by our city, and she has learned those lessons well. She considers herself a Charlestonian and we, or I, consider her one too." Doc Francis has turned his head toward a bookcase, lost in thought and still unsmiling.

"Of course, I know the rules. Margarite alluded to my family's involvement in the Society and we like to think we have contributed to what it is today. I would not want to do, nor ask you to do, anything that undermined what St. Simeon stands for. As we all know, the Ball is a rite of passage. For most of us, it marked our entry into the social fellowship we value so much. It is badge of belonging, and I think, as Elizabeth thought while she was with us, that this child belongs as much as anyone who has attended the Ball. For that reason, I am asking you to grant her an exemption from the usual requirement and extend her an invitation."

My eyes sweep over their faces, searching for clues. Adelle flashes a "well-done" grin that gives me heart. Sandy Charles has been following every word with rapt attention, and I think I detect in her the subtle communion of spirits. She seems with me.

Charlotte, on the other hand, is firmly opposed if her pursed lips and general scowl mean anything, and I think they mean all. She has not opened her mind a fraction of an inch, and the opinion she walked in with is the one she'll rain upon them when I leave.

Clarkson Mills, my client, gives me a manly wink of encouragement with the eye closest to Ohio. Doc Francis maintains an inscrutable sullenness, his head now inclined toward the table. Jeanette Wilson seems as intent on the others as I am, her eyes darting furtively around to gauge reactions. She is a pretty woman, but with a refined sleaze I cannot read.

Margarite stands and resumes her place beside me, turning toward her committee. "Are there any questions of Coleman before we let him go?" No one moves. Stillness merges with the silence to produce an uncomfortable hiatus that Margarite adroitly hastens to fill. "Fine," she says, again facing me, "then we'll leave it at that. Let us talk this over and I'll call you in the morning."

I leave with a curious indecisiveness. No rookie at counting noses, I know this is probably going to be four-to-three, one way or the other. I usually win when it's close; perhaps some kind of favorable mathematical probability follows the ability to negotiate well. But in the parking lot, I remind myself of the very real possibility that it will go the other way.

I return home. Allie is in her room studying.

"How'd it go?" she asks as I enter and flop down on the bed.

"Just fine," I say. "I left so they could talk but I think we'll come out on top." She smiles and waits, expectantly. "Of course, it could go against us," I continue. "And sweetheart, if it does, I don't want you to take it personally."

"I won't," she says, then quickly turns back to her work on the desk.

"Margarite said she would let me know tomorrow, but I have a sneaky hunch Adelle will call tonight. It never hurts to have a spy in the enemy camp."

"I guess not," she says indifferently, not looking up.

At eleven the phone rings. I have just turned out the downstairs lights and locked the doors. I answer in the kitchen, expecting to hear Adelle's voice. But it is Margarite.

"Coleman, I'm ever so sorry for calling you at this hour. I hope you weren't in bed."

"Getting ready to go. You aren't just getting out of your meeting?"

"Actually, I just got home, but I'm very upset and thought it best to call tonight." A pause.

"Then I take it the Board voted no."

"I'm so sorry, embarrassed, and mad all at once. I hoped we could prevail. You made a splendid appeal. I wish I had a recording of it."

"But obviously not strong enough."

"It's a tough bunch," she says.

"I figured it would be close; one vote either way."

"One reason the meeting lasted so long was because there is little protocol for handling a request like this. We had to discuss ground rules, voting procedures, all those things, and then the merits, of course."

"What can you tell me?"

After an audible hitch in her voice, she says, "Hardly anything. As you can imagine, this whole thing is quite sensitive. Everyone likes you and admires Allie so no one wanted to step on any toes. You can understand."

"Sure," I say, trying to sound philosophical.

"We voted by secret ballot and agreed to keep the deliberations confidential."

"I guess that explains why Adelle hasn't called."

"She's in a difficult spot."

"She needn't worry," I say. "I'll respect the confidence."

"I knew you would. Oh, I just feel terrible about this whole thing. I've half a mind to resign from the Society in protest."

"Don't be rash, Margarite. And thanks for everything. I know you did your best."

Allie is asleep. I'll tell her in the morning. I go to bed, but not to sleep until past 2 A.M., when a vision of the Board floats in with Philip, still alive, still youthful, inexplicably seated among them. Doc Francis sits defiantly, arms crossed. Charlotte Hines shakes her head with fat, imperial firmness, an arrogant twist to her lips. The image wakes me. Not one vote from among the four possibilities; so much for my golden tongue. As little as I prepared Allie for rejection, I prepared myself even less and here, in the hush of the bedroom, my disappointment takes hold.

Things always look bleak in the dark, I remind myself. In months during Elizabeth's illness and following her death, I spent literally hundreds of hours staring at this ceiling in the quietest times of the night, when the city sounded the same with the windows opened or closed. I grieved. I worried, first for her, and then mostly for the kids. I've lived long enough to know that the world is not necessarily a fair place to all people at all times, and that if in the global, overarching sense some rough justice is at work, it is very rough indeed. My anger at Elizabeth's fate has been tempered by statistics. A certain number of women suffer severe illness every year. Of those, a predictable if growing number recover, fully or partially, and an equally predictable number with the most egregious diseases do not. Who am I, who was she, to insist that such math work only to our advantage? Even my tempered anger lacked focus. Precisely who was I to blame? But tonight has been different. This vote wasn't a disease and it wasn't death, and no matter how bleak things look in the dark my rejection by the Board is but a library fine when compared to Elizabeth's ordeal.

Still, I feel anger beginning to build, perhaps because this result, unlike hers, was entirely preventable. Maybe that explains it. Cancer is such an anonymous, impersonal enemy, while here sat at least four people I know. I drift off just before daylight, with one thought that I suspect will be with me when I awake: my daughter is going to that Ball.

21

Charleston has been the New World incubator of Carters from the day the boat landed in 1670. My mental movie of that landing has been spliced together frame by frame from genealogies, family lore and later, in the second half of the nineteenth century, grainy photographs depicting an unblinking succession of grim-jawed, mustachioed men flanked by cautious women and children in sailor suits. Early in that imagined film, Thomas Carter, the original émigré, walks to the head of the gangway after seven months at sea, surveys the April splendor sprawled before him and his ninety-two fellow passengers, then, turning to Captain Brayne, asks if the brandy that has been under lock and key for the last six weeks can now be liberated.

I forgive Thomas's initial indifference to the uncut gem which was to become Charleston, set exquisitely in its raw state between the tines of the soon-to-be-named Ashley and Cooper Rivers. Evidently, such indifference had evaporated shortly after his boots bogged in the marshes of shrimp-stuffed Old Town Creek, where the party came ashore. Thomas became a successful merchant, grim-jawed and mustachioed, and never left, as few who followed him have left. And, his atavistic love of brandy has endured to the current year, 1996.

From earliest memory, Charleston has beckoned me like a porch light, friendly and nurturing and visible from anywhere. Returning from summer camp in western North Carolina after two weeks that seemed like two years in the rock-kicking amble of prepubescent time, I scanned the tops of loblolly pines for a first reassuring glimpse of the Cooper River Bridge, its silver spans arching down like a pair of maternal arms poised to scoop me up. From the bridge looking left I saw the steeples of St. Michael's and St. Philip's, to the right the main turret of The Citadel, and like the baseball cards and 45 rpm records in my room, they were right where I had left them.

At the University of Virginia I pledged Sigma Nu, and for weeks at a time I could deceive myself that I no longer lived in Charleston, that I had a new life and a new home and a fresh family of fraternity brothers. But even from Charlottesville I'd see the porch light, the aureole of the Holy City. During the years in New Hampton the light dimmed, flickered, but never died, and when I returned it brightened in its welcoming arc, within which I could be certain of my place, my history.

But in the week following the Board vote, I feel for the first time the slightest distancing from people and things once as close to me and as comfortable as an old bathrobe. The city looks the same; the palmettoes along Broad Street still exude an air of stately serenity, the church bells toll the hour more or less on schedule, the black women make and sell their sweetgrass baskets in the same spot near the courthouse. But at my office, in shops or around the neighborhood, I meet people I have known for years with a reserve more characteristic of a visitor.

I must be imagining this estrangement. Lifelong relationships are not altered by a handful of people taking a vote on what, in the great scheme of things, can be counted a trivial matter by most. Even at the St. Simeon, a Ball is merely a ball. And yet, as I greet innocent old friends, untainted employees at Carter & Deas, and even waiters in restaurants who have never heard of the Society, I sense alienation, as though the Board's decision embodied an ecumenical verdict by the city as a whole that I have failed a fundamental fidelity. By loyally asserting Allie's claim to go, I have breached a living code of consideration owed to members of my circle: I put them on the spot. The case Sarah mentioned, that of adopted Peter Devereux, who looked so much like Kate, presented the Devereuxs with the same dilemma. In deciding not to request exemption, they surrendered to the communal abhorrence, strong in these genteel parts, against forcing embarrassing confrontations. As a devout St. Simeon, I am expected to know the rules of eligibility, and to challenge them, as I have done, is to spread across several dutiful backs the load I should, in their view, shoulder alone. No one has said that to me, but it echoes with a crystal chime of certainty.

Over the weekend following the vote I bump, literally, into Sandy Charles in the drugstore, the only Board member I have seen since my rejection. Predictably awkward, Sandy makes overly gracious gestures, yielding more awkwardness as I try to shuttle between a pale nonchalance I do not feel and nods of polite understanding, summoned hurriedly to avert a confrontation beside foot hygiene aids.

"We all realize," she says as I idly finger a talc, "how much this meant to Elizabeth."

That comment offers insight into the social contract in this city. Having declined to take one for the team by foisting upon the Board members a decision they do not wish to make, I must now be inoculated against my own (forgivable) rashness by a face-saving attribution to Elizabeth, whom neither Sandy Charles nor any other member fears confronting in the pharmacy, at the theater, on the cocktail circuit, or at any of two dozen other flash points.

And, contradicting Sandy will be difficult. Allie's attending the St. Simeon did mean a lot to Elizabeth. She viewed the Society as one of a handful, a generous handful, of Charleston heirlooms. The Nathaniel Russell House, Rainbow Row, and the old market were others. Not being a native of the city, she brought with her an outsider's detached appreciation for that which makes Charleston unique. For her, indignation evoked by Allie's exclusion from the St. Simeon would have been no less, but no more profound, had she been barred at the threshold of a venerable residence on the candlelight tour of historic homes. Her bench mark reckoning, that of, "My daughter will go *anywhere,*" sighted along an arcing emotional azimuth bent by maternal zeal, and that zeal overran and subsumed the identity of the particular barricade. It is fortunate for Sandy Charles that it is not Elizabeth to whom she makes her stuttering explanations in the drug store.

Which sounds, I must confess, as though I am less outraged than I should be. Why hasn't the incipient anger felt in my bedroom on the night of the vote erupted into wrath? Why haven't I heaved a can of Pedisooth at Sandy?

The answer is grounded in my nature. I am decidedly non-confrontational, odd for a lawyer but true for me. Had Sandy blown up my mailbox and arrogantly mailed me the debris, I would not go to war in the drugstore.

Also, I am only so surprised by the answer I got from the Board. The point Sarah made is not without validity; we knew the rules seventeen years before when we adopted. To some members of the Society, my situation is analogous to another with which we are all familiar. A club to which a number of us belong has a long-standing rule requiring gentlemen to wear jackets and ties after 6:00 P.M. in the main dining room. The penchant for golfers to arrive for dinner in their casual knits and spiked shoes after several soggy hours at the nineteenth hole brought about this rule many years before. A friend of mine, Lawrence Hess, brought as a frequent guest a cousin from France who, being quite European, habitually wore a turtleneck under his coat to dinner. The management politely explained the rule, which seemed to affront Lawrence on behalf of his cousin. He became indignant, causing a scene one evening at the reservations desk by insisting that Cousin Marcel wore imported cashmere turtlenecks, that they were quite acceptable among the bishops and barons with whom he mingled on the Continent, and that the club's insistence on a tie was "provincial," all of which the manager acknowledged while apologetically pointing out that the rule required a tie. I remember a conversation with Hess shortly thereafter in which I hinted with impatience that Hess was undermining the standards of the club. For all her empathy, I sense the same impatience in Sandy Charles.

At Carter & Deas, Harris comes into my office and flops down on the couch. Although himself a St. Simeon, Harris is unaware of the Board's action. He has no court appearances today, so pinstripes are replaced by dark wool slacks, a gray herringbone jacket, and a tie resplendent with maroon ducks. In all our years together, he has maintained the unflappable amiability that makes him so easy to be around. He crosses his legs and looks at me soberly.

"Counselor," he says, "I have just come from lunch with the city attorney, your friend and mine, Carlton Middleton III."

"How was the food?" I ask dryly, knowing that despite his normally healthy appetite, Harris's mind is on business.

"The city has revised its estimate of the legal fees it will have to fork out on the Performing Arts Center."

"Oh, no," I say.

"Upward." An impish grin flashes. "It just makes me sick to think of all those tax dollars, yours and mine, flooding into the account of Carter & Deas once we're awarded this contract."

"What's the revised figure?"

He raises his swollen fingers, adjusting his glasses leisurely for dramatic pause. "Three mil, up from two point five."

"Why the increase?"

"Balking landowners with visions of retirement. The condemnation work is going to require some quick-takes that will keep us in court for months."

"Did Carlton have a time frame?"

"He checked with the mayor's office this morning. It's on Council's agenda for the February meeting."

"Great. The votes are still there?"

"You betcha," he says, nodding. "Only, Cathcart has not given up. He's been wining and dining councilmen almost as much as I have."

"With three million on the table, I can't say I blame him. Plus, with only two firms in the running, he figures the odds are no worse than fifty-fifty."

"Oh, but they are," Harris assures. "We have something they don't have."

"Of course. We have a two vote margin on council and the backing of the city attorney from the moment he realized this project would swamp his staff."

"Aside from those," he says with a smirk, "we have me."

I clear my throat. "Indeed we do."

Harris rises with an energetic start, as though suddenly remembering an appointment. "Back to work. Getting rich is a full time job." He lumbers out toward his corner office at the other end of the hall.

I spend the balance of the afternoon examining and reviewing a lawsuit to be filed for a wealthy apartment owner I have represented for years. The draft, prepared by one of our young associates, contains all the legal essentials but lacks a few "real world" touches which years of experience tell me might give us an advantage in settlement discussions. The work is tedious, and though I am well-paid for what I do, I have come to question the value added. Although the public hasn't fully grasped this, lawsuits are essentially a waste of time and money. They polarize people who should be talking to each other, not to us. Much of my work is a vain exercise in pointing out to people who should know better where their real interests lie. To fill that role, I need some knowledge of the law and a lot more of human nature. Human nature is incomparably more interesting, which I guess explains why I'm still at it. This cynicism has led me to formulate Carter's first and last rule of litigation: among people of goodwill and honest intent, civil courts are rarely needed, and among others they are seldom worth the cost to all concerned.

It is after 6:00 when I finish. Dottie, my secretary, has shut down her PC and gone. At my desk, packing my briefcase, I look up in time to see a woman I do not know pause in the corridor, then turn toward Harris's end of the building. As she walks away, my eyes go to a shapely derriere snugly bound in her tight skirt. I gawk admiringly as she peeks in Harris's door, turns, then starts toward me. I fumble folders in my briefcase. Seconds later I am conscious of her standing just outside my door.

"I'm looking for Coleman Carter," she says. She looks mid-thirties, quite pretty, with an ethnic darkness, possibly Italian, but her speech is northeastern, not far from Long Island in intonation. To a southerner, it is not a pleasing voice.

"I'm Coleman," I offer. "Come in."

She strides forward, proffers her hand, and shakes mine with a decided firmness. "Natalie Berman," she says. "I'm with the ACLU. May I sit down?" She turns toward a client chair before I can respond.

"Please," I say, indicating the chair she is now seated in, adjusting her finely tapered legs. I take the chair opposite. "How can I help you, Ms. Berman?"

"I'm here to talk about a lawsuit," she says.

Her tone surpasses businesslike to a level of formality which strikes me as stilted. I mentally review my current stable of clients in an attempt to pinpoint which one would likely have run afoul of the ACLU. "I'm not aware of your suit," I admit. "Who is my offending client?"

"There is no suit," she says. "Not yet. I came to talk to you about filing one. For your daughter."

"I beg your pardon."

"My organization is doing a lot of work in the area of private discrimination. I understand your daughter has been denied access to an annual affair given by something called the St. Simeon Society, a social club. We'd like to persuade her, and you as her father, to fight an indefensible prejudice against adopted Asians."

She is intently earnest, leaning forward slightly with her hands folded in her lap. Her eyes flash and her nostrils flare faintly as she speaks. Her sincerity is so severe I have to stifle a laugh.

"Ms. Berman," I say gently, fingering the arm of my chair in order to avoid her painfully riveting eye contact, "may I ask where you got your information?"

"That's privileged."

"I see," I reply, still suppressing the bubble of laughter that has formed in my throat.

"You're familiar with the ACLU, of course," she wants to know and I nod condescendingly, not quite convinced she has asked that question. She appears not to notice. Her eyes are brown, but not the warm brown I associate with feminine softness. These eyes are hard, as though galvanized with a metallic veneer reflecting light. Her mouth is finely formed, her lips thin and set.

"Have you heard any good jokes lately, Ms. Berman?"

"What has that got to do with anything?" she demands.

"Oh, I don't know," I reply, exaggerating my native drawl. "It just seems to me we've hardly met and already we've jumped into this very serious discussion about my daughter's constitutional rights and I don't know the first thing about you except what I'd find on a business card."

For the first time, a semblance of a smile encroaches upon her lips, which part enough to reveal desert-white teeth perfectly aligned. "I forget I'm in the South," she admits in a tone as close to apologetic as I can imagine her mustering. "Sometimes I come on a bit strong."

"Really?" I ask. Sarcasm is my visceral response to irritation, and her presence, broaching this subject, is beginning to wear on me.

"Let's back up," she says. "My name is Natalie Berman. I finished Columbia Law magna cum laude. I moved to Charleston two months ago from New York as a coordinator for the ACLU. Most of my time is spent identifying cases I think will have the most dramatic impact on civil rights. On Monday I got a call about your daughter and I came here to talk to you about it. If you agree to become a plaintiff, I'll either represent you or, if you prefer, find another local attorney to handle the litigation."

"That's all very interesting, Ms. Berman, but I don't believe there is going to be any litigation. You see, my ancestor was a charter member of the St. Simeon, my father was its president, I've been in it all my life and my friends belong almost without exception."

"But you've said nothing about your daughter."

This takes me momentarily off my pace. "I don't want to be short with you, nor appear ungrateful for the interest you've shown, but my daughter and any other element of my family's business are private. If we feel the need to call the ACLU, we'll call." This conversation is straying perilously close to the confrontations I dislike.

Her eyes resume their flashing. "Mr. Carter, you don't like my organization, do you?"

I shrug, knowing before I reply that baiting her is going to prove irresistible. "What's not to like? Someone needs to fight to keep kids from praying in school. Somebody's got to take action when prison wardens cut off cable TV to throat-slitting criminals, assuming, of course, those throat-slitters don't walk out the courtroom free men because one of your lawyers has convinced the judge that the arresting officer failed to recite the Declaration of Independence in the squad car. Gosh, where would we be without you folks?"

She returns my gelid stare as we sit appraising each other, two icicles point to point. "Typical," she says evenly.

"Ah, yes," I say, flourishing my hands upward as though my prayers for rain have been answered, "here is confirmation of the southern archetype, the pone-eating, cracker-barreled, scorched-necked bigot you anticipated in the car on the way over. You know, with some advanced notice I could have scheduled a lynching."

Her face flushes, but she holds her ground. "What I meant was, your reaction is a typical one among those not fully acquainted with our work."

"That's what you meant, and it may be what you said, but what you were thinking is that you've strayed into the office of a southern sheriff."

"I really don't understand your attitude, Mr. Carter. I came here because I thought we might help you solve a problem."

"But your very first sentence contained the word 'lawsuit.'"

"Is that significant?"

"It is indicative," I reply.

"Of . . . ?"

"Of a mindset that thinks every problem ought to be litigated. Do you really think I'd sue my friends over this?"

"If you're talking about some kind of compromise or negotiation, it simply doesn't work. The people excluding your daughter aren't going to be fazed by logic or fairness."

"You seem to know them pretty well after . . . what, two months in Charleston?"

She turns toward the window, her dark hair shifting on her shoulders and her profile sculpturesque against a far wall. "I've spent several days sightseeing. This is a lovely city."

"Thank you," I say, softening against my will. Compliments to Charleston affect me like a sorbet, cleansing the palate of lingering aftertastes.

She rises, crosses the room to an end table, and picks up a framed photo of Allie. "This must be your daughter."

"Yes."

"What a beautiful young woman. Her age?"

"Seventeen; still needing her father's consent to file a lawsuit, if that's what you're thinking."

"Or her mother's," Natalie Berman counters.

"That's going to be tough to get. She's dead."

"I'm truly sorry."

As she replaces the picture I sneak a look at my watch. It is past 6:30 and I am feeling the gravity of a ten hour day pulling me downward. "If you're parked outside, I'll walk you to your car."

"No need," she says pleasantly.

In the elevator, she hands me her card. "If you change your mind, call me," she urges. "Perhaps there is something short of suing that will help."

"Maybe," I say to be polite. "Enjoy your evening."

From the car I call Adelle. She has not eaten either and I agree to pick her up in thirty minutes.

Mr. Quan's restaurant is the Red Dragon. Its decor is stark, consisting of aluminum and Formica tables like those found in most kitchens in the 50s and 60s. The lighting is dim, to save utility costs. The walls, bare but for a few scattered Chinese characters, display brass plates, hung randomly and representing, I suppose, yin or yang or happiness or who knows what. There is piped-in music, the Asian equivalent of elevator junk featuring those high-pitched discordant strings. I don't appreciate this music; to my western ear it all sounds like a recording of a cat being tortured. I eat here often for one compelling reason: the food is great and not expensive. Adelle and I are shown to my usual table near the back.

Mr. Quan emerges from the kitchen, spots us, and hustles over with two menus. I have never been here when he was not, and I can only guess that the number of hours he works each week exceeds eighty.

"Good evening," he says in his competent English, smiling broadly. Although I am a perdurable customer and generous tipper, anyone off the street gets the same congenial greeting. He bows faintly from the waist to Adelle. "So nice to see you, Mrs. Roberts." To me he says, "And may I say how wise you look these days."

I regard him suspiciously. "Wise sounds like a euphemism for old." I see his brow knit and guess he is struggling with the language. "Euphemism; it means a less offensive way of saying what you really mean."

"Ah," the owner says, mischief in his eyes, "then allow me to say how exceedingly wise you appear this evening." Adelle laughs with him as I glare at both.

"Adelle, is there still time to stop payment on the check for my party?"

I insist that Mr. Quan join us. The room is in its familiar rhythm, with a steady drone of dinner crowd conversation muffling the cat torture. In the kitchen, the clang of dueling woks can be heard each time the double doors swing wide. Pert aromas of ginger and garlic and soy-based oils seduce us, an irresistible foreplay to the meal itself. Adelle compliments him on the food at the party as I nod agreement.

"I am most pleased with the catering," he says. "When I began, I thought it would be a small part of my enterprise, but it grows stronger each year." He likes to refer to his business as an "enterprise" for the connotation of something grand and sprawling. When I helped renegotiate his lease three years before, his accountant provided his financial statements. From those, I concluded that not only was enterprise a fair characterization but that he could buy most people I represent.

Mr. Quan has accumulated all he has since his arrival in 1977. One gold nugget, he swears, is all that remained after his grueling exodus from Vietnam. The boat on which he escaped was direly overloaded, and in addition to a constant threat of capsize it faced pirates, who boarded in three separate raids before the boat reached Malaysia. He will not say where he hid the nugget; only that he started with many and that, after the first raid, he secreted his last one in a "place not easily searched." Upon arrival in Charleston, he borrowed $10,000 from a network of Vietnamese émigrés already settled here. He repaid it in six months. He lives over the Red Dragon, with no family and no close friends as far as I can tell. He refuses to discuss his life in Vietnam prior to becoming a boat-person, and I know little of his politics with the exception that at the mention of the word "communist," his face contorts in a grimace of disdain, and watching him I sense the leap to hatred would be very short.

He motions for a waitress and we order. The waitress is American, but all the cooks and waiters are Vietnamese. He inquires about Christopher, and at Adelle's mention of sore ribs I can only smile inwardly.

"And how is Allie?" he asks. "After your party there was much discussion of her among my boys." He cants his head toward the back, indicating the kitchen.

"She's fine," I reply. "She mentioned the other day that she might apply here for a job this summer."

Adelle's face grows quizzical. "Oh? I thought she had a job all lined up with a camp in New England."

"You mean the riding camp in Vermont she worked at last summer. They've invited her back but she isn't sure she'll go."

Mr. Quan says, "She is most welcome here. I would consider it a privilege to employ her."

"Great," I say. "I'll let her know. By the way, what do you hear about travel to the Far East these days?"

He shifts in his chair before answering. "Two of my employees have been to Vietnam recently. They say things are opening up and that U.S. dollars go very far. They lived like royal princes for ten days."

"In Ho Chi Minh City?" I ask, thoughtlessly flaunting political correctness.

"In Saigon," Mr. Quan counters. "It will always be Saigon." After an awkward pause, during which we momentarily avoid eye contact, he says, "Why do you ask?"

"Allie wants me to take her to Korea. For graduation."

"And will you?"

"Haven't decided. We don't know the language, Seoul, anything really."

"Yes, those are concerns," he acknowledges, then as an afterthought says, "I have a brother there."

I whistle softly. "I had no idea."

"My only brother. He left Vietnam before me. In the refugee camp in Malaysia, he had a chance to go to Seoul. I waited for America. He also owns an enterprise."

"When did you last see him?"

"He visited me. Almost ten years ago."

Adelle, until then a passive listener, suddenly becomes animated. "I know," she says, looking at me, "Mr. Quan should go with you."

I say, "That's an idea."

He smiles wanly. "It is most thoughtful of you to suggest, but I am afraid that would be impossible. I have my enterprise, all these employees depending upon me."

"But everyone takes a vacation," Adelle says.

He bobs his head in seeming agreement but all his facial features are at odds with her suggestion. "No, Mrs. Roberts, for me a return to Asia could not be a vacation. I will never go back. And now, if you can excuse me, I will see what is holding up your dinners."

We watch him retreat through the swinging doors.

"He certainly closed that discussion," she says.

"Politely but firmly."

"I wonder what it was like for him there," she muses.

"Who knows? With the war, the U.S. withdrawal, the communists taking over, it must have been ugly for unrepentant South Vietnamese, and Mr. Quan is clearly one of those."

Our soup arrives, followed by entrees. My sesame chicken in curry is delectable and Adelle reports her pork the same. I mention my visit from Natalie Berman.

"But how did she know of the vote? We all swore secrecy. That's why I haven't been able to discuss it with you, and it's so frustrating because I want to and I know you're curious."

"Someone called her, she wouldn't say who."

"Male or female?"

"She didn't say."

"I can't imagine," Adelle says, perplexed. "If you could have been a fly on the wall of that room; if you could have heard people who masquerade as your friends. It made me sick, that's all I can say. I can just imagine that group of old fogies turning thumbs down on Christopher; I'd strangle them, particularly Jeanette Wilson, the bitch. Well, what now?"

I look past her. "I wish I knew."

22

Sarah, for all her geriatric vivacity, needs help with the yard. At least twice a year we dedicate a Saturday to her place on Sullivan's. This morning, Allie and I stop at the college, pick up Steven, and the three of us, dressed in the oldest clothes we could find, are on the causeway headed east. We have not seen Steven since the weekend of my party so there is catching up to do.

"Physics is going to kill me, that's all there is to it," he is saying from the passenger seat and I flash a look in the rear view mirror to warn Allie against gloating over her grades in science.

"Boy, you and me both," she says heavily. This is worse, I think disapprovingly. Condescension; how unseemly. "I panicked toward the end of last semester." She lets us ponder this anomaly in silence before adding, "Yep, toward the end I was afraid I would have to buy a textbook." Steven, stone-faced, fishes into the glove box, grabs a map, and flings it over his shoulder as she ducks, laughing gleefully.

Watching these two spar is like watching heredity and environment go fifteen rounds for the title. Steven and Josh are both their father's sons, a fact simultaneously pleasing and terrifying. When Josh was three, running around the yard chasing the neighbor's dog, I noticed he ran on his heels. Instantly, I knew that run, and I accurately predicted he would be straining, as I did, for middling speed as an athlete, struggling to break twelve seconds in a hundred yard dash on his best day in sports. To a confirmed jock, the run of his teammates is as distinctive as a photograph, and on a football team with seventy guys dressed out but without numerals on their jerseys, I could have named all of them from fifty yards away by watching them run a few strides. Put Josh in my old uniform, slap No. 50 on his back, and you couldn't get odds from my teammates that it wasn't me lumbering along under those shoulder pads. The Carter forehead, the curl of his hair in humidity, the square chin, the green eyes all attest to a biological unity.

But physical likeness pales in fascination on the day you notice a biological child's character flaw. Like the caveman who bends over the lake for the first glimpse of his own image, you are stunned to see reflected back flaws, unseen until that moment. "Don't procrastinate," you instruct as you inventory the projects lying fallow on your own to-do list. "And don't be a hypocrite."

But a clear picture of a fuzzy image is fuzzy, and the melding of two genomes is a fuzzy matter indeed, a reality Elizabeth and I remarked upon many times as she also saw herself in them, as though the caveman had glanced down at the precise moment a jet ski roiled the water below. As with most, our boys are identifiable blends of their impassioned architects. So what to make of Allie?

An orphan adopted at birth is not so much a mirror as a prism. Look at her directly and you will not, cannot, see yourself looking back. Instead, you will see refracted in facets cut by her unknown jewelers the pale inks and dyes of your behavior, culture, and station melded among and into the iridescent hues of her genetic weave. Trace the rainbow to its source and behold nothing more varied than a sanctified shaft of light, God's random sunshine beamed at another's cradle but diverted by grace to yours.

Now, put a mirror and a prism together and the result is a light show, and I have enjoyed the fireworks between these two for years.

Mother is bedding azaleas along the front when we arrive, taking advantage of weekend temperatures forecast to remain mild until midweek. At sight of us she steadies on the weatherboard siding and raises to full height, waving gaily as she shuffles toward our car with a rheumatic limp, stiff-legged from the time on her knees among the plants. Although we see her often, she embraces us as prodigals.

Today, a load of topsoil delivered during the week must be distributed among patches of ground worn barren by winter winds off the Atlantic. We four encircle the mound, assessing our task. On the perimeter, two long-handle shovels are embedded like giant candles in a mud pie. Nearby, the old wheelbarrow awaits. I walk to it, grab the handles, and maneuver it into position. Allie and Steven begin shoveling.

The wheelbarrow is heavier than I remember as I cross the yard with the first load. Its service as a beast of burden is less heroic than a legacy of improvised amusement. When the kids were small, a heartier, more virile me would load them in this wheelbarrow and push them all over this same yard. Each clamored for "my turn," and once seated would begin laughing and squealing in anticipation. The bulbous balloon tire and the physics of momentum combined with my by-gone strength to produce a passable version of a theme park ride.

At the start I kept the angle acute, lending a magic carpet effect as we passed over the lawn. But as we gathered speed I raised the handles and made a point of steering toward every bump and irregularity presented by the landscape, thereby increasing my passenger's happy anxiety over the probability of being bounced unceremoniously onto the ground. A microscopic examination of the sides today would probably show their fingerprints embedded into the metal, so fiercely did they cling.

The climax came as we traversed the apron of the yard where tended ground bleeds into crystalline dunes, beyond which lies the ocean. At the highest speed attainable, I stopped suddenly and simultaneously jerked the handles to ninety degrees, thereby propelling my passenger into the forgiving sand of the dune. After three or four individual rotations, they would insist on one tour together and by this point, near collapse, one tour was all I was good for. The ejection at the finish was worth it.

Elizabeth tolerated this juvenile delectation with amber ambivalence, torn between the risk of dissolving into a wet blanket and her sound, primal judgment where the safety of her children was at stake. She sometimes called out what I think of as her "yes-no." This was a "no" for the record, leaving her free to mount, however subtly, the high ground of "I warned you" should a broken arm or concussion ensue. She relied on me to ignore or override a yes-no. This, never discussed between us, was nonetheless an ingrained modus operandi in dealing with the children, and even between us when, at bedtime, a no-yes made an occasional appearance.

The work today is therapeutic. My muscles unlimber with the first loads and a cleansing sweat breaks out on my chest and forehead. Sarah is humming softly in my wake, spading the imported earth to her specifications and content to have us around her. Over the dunes, sea gulls screech their glottic gossip before gliding seaward. Steven alternates with

Allie and me on first, the shovel, then the wheelbarrow, and the work goes quickly.

Near noon, Sarah disappears into the house to prepare lunch. No manual labor goes unrewarded here. She summons us to a feast: oyster bisque, shrimp salad, soft shell crabs, red rice, asparagus, and chocolate cake. An hour later I am immobile. Except for the rice, Allie has eaten as much as I have and feels the need for exercise.

"Let's go, Dad," Allie says, grabbing my hand and pulling me out of my chair. "Take your favorite daughter for a walk on the beach."

As we are leaving I hear Sarah defining for Steven her incessant torment at the hands of a particularly dexterous raccoon. All efforts to secure her garbage against this intruder have failed.

I love this beach and so does Allie. The tide is ebbing. We roll our pants to knee level and shed our shoes at the dunes. At surf's edge, cold water washes over our feet and runs up our ankles. She will let me hold her hand out here, away from possible sight by friends, the way she did as a young girl.

"I had dinner at the Red Dragon the other night," I offer. "Mr. Quan says a job for this summer is yours for the asking."

"That's really nice of him. I'll pay him a visit. I have to work to stash away some bucks."

"Clothes shopping for college?"

"That, plus I'll probably blow all my savings in Korea—we are going to Korea—so I'll have nothing left for my surgery."

I stop. "For a moment I thought you said surgery."

She grins and pulls at my hand. "C'mon, walk. Eye surgery. Nothing to it, but since it's cosmetic I feel I should pay for it myself. You have enough on you with Princeton."

"Hold it," I command, stopping again and digging in. "What eye surgery? What are you talking about?"

"Dad, haven't you noticed my eyes?"

"Of course. Almost every day for seventeen years. They're beautiful. So what?"

"You're prejudiced. They have a flaw that Asians notice. Here," she says, closing her eyes in front of me. "See it?"

"No."

"My lids are smooth. It's not attractive. It's too . . . Asian." She opens them again. "There is a simple, safe procedure to put a tuck in the lids. It's called upper blepharoplasty. It adds depth."

"How much depth?"

She grins. "About $2500 worth of depth."

"Impossible. I absolutely forbid it. No, no, a thousand times no."

"Dad," she says in her plaintive voice, "how will I ever get to look like Madonna?"

"A million times no."

We turn at the far end of the beach and retrace our steps, the breeze now in our faces and the sun warming our backs. There is no further talk of surgery, or of Korea. It is a quiet, reflective stroll.

At the house, neither Sarah nor Steven answers our announced return. Some noise in the side yard draws me around the house. Steven is hammering some wire mesh over the garbage bins. At my approach, Sarah beams.

"Your son, my clever grandson, is setting a trap for the raccoon."

"Why not put a brick on the lid of the can?"

Sarah scoffs. "It doesn't slow him down for a minute. I suppose five or six would keep him out, but I can't take off and lift up a half dozen bricks every time I deposit garbage. I know this critter," she adds, glancing toward the adjoining lot, still wooded and one of the few undeveloped parcels left on the island. She raises her finger and points. "He lives over there and comes here for food at night."

"What will you do when you catch him?" I ask as Allie comes up behind me.

"Call the dog catcher. They'll put it down."

"Ohhh . . . ," says Allie, her sympathies with the raccoon.

"You wouldn't say that if you lived next to one," says Sarah, turning her attention back to Steven. "They play havoc with the sea turtle eggs and they carry rabies. They're cute to look at but a nuisance."

Allie winks at me mischievously. "I guess I'll stop worrying. With Steven building the trap there's not much chance of catching one."

"I heard that," Steven says, not looking up. "And you'll eat those words one day soon. Grandmother, do you have a recipe for coon stew that will make my sister's humiliation a little tastier?"

Sarah looks down thoughtfully. Sarcasm is to her a foreign tongue, as decipherable as Shawnee smoke signals, and I can see her going over her recipes in search of coon stew.

"I think Steven was joking, Mother," I say gently, then ask him to explain his device.

The enclosure for the garbage cans is set off to the side of the house. It resembles a small fenced yard, with one side all gate. Wooden pickets five feet high border a square concrete slab on which the cans rest, hiding them from public view. Steven holds the head of the hammer and points with the handle. "She always keeps the gate closed but of course the coon climbs over. By covering the top with wire, the coon will have no way out once he springs the gate closed."

"How are you going to spring it?" I ask.

"Watch," he instructs. He opens the gate wide, attaches a wire to an eye-hook he has embedded in the gate's wooden frame, and runs the wire through several pickets to the lid of the can. He attaches this end to the raised handle of the lid itself, which he has rigged with a weight from an old barbell set he found in the garage. He places the lid on the can. "Go ahead," he says to me. "Play coon and go for the can."

I hunch slightly to duck under the wire mesh on top and lift the lid. As I push it aside, the weight brings it down hard, tensing the wire and pulling the gate shut with a decisive clang of the latch. Without doubt, I am imprisoned. "Very clever," I say as Sarah applauds. "Rube Goldberg is smiling in the hereafter." The pickets are set too close together to permit my hand access to the latch, so Steven must spring me. Free again, I lead us back into the house. He stays to apply the finishing touches and clean up.

I flop on the couch with the current issue of *Southern Living.* In the kitchen, a jangle of pans tells me Sarah is preparing to bake. She and Allie are chatting about Princeton, about Dad, about things. I hear Christopher's name, then Adelle's, and join them just in time to hear Sarah remark that she remembers when Chris was born and that he seems like a fine young man. To be called "a fine young man" by Sarah is to have the royal seal pressed into hot wax on your forehead.

"Yeah," agrees Allie, "he's pretty cool."

"Will he come visit you at college?" Sarah wants to know as she extracts a flour sifter from a cupboard.

"Hard to say. That's still a long way off. I'd like to come to USC for a weekend; maybe see him play a tennis match."

"Oh, yes," says Sarah, "he's a star at tennis, isn't he?"

As they talk, I say a small prayer of thanks for Christopher. He is her first real boyfriend, a frosting on her high school cake. She has had a few dates and lots of friends, male and female, but nothing like this. At first, I attributed it to intellectual intimidation. Drawing on my own experience, I remember how girls with straight A's made me nervous. Allie's smart, but hardly brilliant. She works hard; it's that simple. But gradually, from listening and observing her at school functions and around her friends, I realized that intimidation of another sort was at the root of her romantic isolation. It was her different appearance, and although that seems quite obvious looking back, it was unclear at the time because she was so familiar to us, so normal, so ingrained into the fiber of our family that we ceased to notice. By the time I mentally rejoin their conversation, they have moved on. Allie has said how much she enjoys yard work.

"Perhaps your people were farmers, dear," Sarah suggests. "Mine were, back in the plantation era. They came from Virginia."

Allie and I exchange imperceptible glances, wondering if Sarah has been inspired to launch one of her genealogical salvos. She pauses, walks to the sink decisively, and rinses the flour from her hands. Without a word she disappears. Drawers open and close in the living room followed by a triumphant, "Here it is." She returns with "the book," which she places on the table in front of Allie.

"When you were younger," says Sarah, "you spent hours with this, remember?"

Allie nods and grins in recognition. The Carter genealogy, published by the University of South Carolina Press twenty years ago, is dog-eared among the pages covering our branch of the family. Mother is correct; Allie seemed fascinated by it and would spend literally hours looking at the photographs and reading the biographical sketches. Now, she opens it and thumbs pages with the same reminiscent smile which she will one day direct at her high school yearbooks.

Sarah, hardly a student of irony, cannot miss it in Allie's prepubescent absorption with generations of white, Anglo-Saxon Protestants. Finding a genetic link between us may require stepping back to Lucy some three billion years ago, but Allie's interest in all things Carter helped build a bridge between her and Sarah that strengthens each year. Another plank in that bridge was Sarah's VHS copy of *Gone With The Wind.* Years before, Sarah had seized upon a rainy afternoon at the beach to suggest she had a film Allie might enjoy. Mother rarely missed a chance to proselytize for the South, and I've often wondered what might have been her reaction had Allie found *GWTW* to be silly, sappy, and inaccurate. But she loved it, watching it over and over while Sarah beamed, sometimes from the kitchen and at other times seated beside Allie with popcorn. By loving what Mother loved, Allie endeared herself in ways none of us could have envisioned, and the sight of them huddled on the couch, eating popcorn and waiting for God to witness Scarlet's promise she would never go hungry again, brought Elizabeth to tears.

Steven returns as the cookies are placed in the oven. Thirty minutes later we are all doing our best to insure that stale cookies are not among Mother's problems in the week to come. I suggest to her that she spend the night with us in town and attend St. Philip's in the morning, returning her to the island Sunday afternoon. She is packed and poised in ten minutes.

In my reflexive offer to host Mother for the evening I have forgotten that I have a date with Adelle, that Allie has a date with Christopher, and that Steven has plans as well. I have inadvertently invited her to spend the evening alone.

"I've spent many an evening here by myself," she reminds me. "I'll be fine." She is fixing coffee when I go upstairs to shower and dress.

I am standing in front of my bureau, brushing my hair, when Allie appears in the doorway, dressed for her evening.

"How do I look?"

"Much too good," I say somberly. "Go back and try it again. Find something old and out of style with a high neckline and for God's sake do something with your hair. It's perfect."

"Just what I wanted to hear," she says, smiling and lingering.

The doorbell rings and Chris's baritone can be distinguished from Steven's.

"Sorry, Dad," she says. "No time to change. I'll have to go like this."

"All right," I say. "Just be home by 9:30."

"Right. We could come back here and sing hymns with grandmother."

"An excellent idea."

"Where will you be?" she asks skeptically.

"Out, but I'm an adult."

"I'm almost one," she says. "As Natalie reminded me."

I stop brushing and turn to face her as she innocently holds my gaze. "Natalie Berman?" She nods. "Where did you run into her?"

"In the school parking lot. I got out of my car yesterday morning and there she was."

"How did she know who you were?" I ask, prickling at this intrusion.

She laughs. "Dad, when someone shows up at my school looking for a Korean the choices are pretty limited. She says she knows you."

"Oh, yes," I say, turning back to the mirror and resuming my brushing with aggressive strokes and already rehearsing the phone call to my pal Natalie. "We're old chums."

"Then you don't like her."

"I hardly know her. Once I get to know her I predict I'll detest her."

"Yeah, she said you were pretty hostile."

"Hostile!" I say, my face flushing at the jowls. "She strolls into my office uninvited, trolling for plaintiffs in a lawsuit she wants me to file against my friends, and she calls me hostile. She should be on a leash."

She whistles softly. "Wow, you are hostile."

"What else did she say?" I demand.

"Some other stuff. There's no time to get into it now. Chris is waiting."

"Well, I'll be waiting, too; for a full account of every word she uttered. She hasn't seen hostile."

I turn to find her staring a bit nonplussed. "I don't think I've ever seen you like this," she says slowly.

"Enjoy your evening," I say, regaining whatever it was I lost. "I'll be right down."

The kids are in the den moments later when I enter. Chris is seated, a USC baseball cap pulled low over his eyes, his leg dangling over one arm of the chair, and a beer in his hand. He and Steven are talking sports.

"Make yourself at home, Chris," I say as I walk between them. He grins and rises to shake my hand, his grip welding my fingers together.

"Mom says to tell you she's running late and to give her an extra half hour."

"Hey, Dad," Steven says. "What's the scoop with Allie and the St. Simeon? Chris says she can't go."

I clear my throat. "Well, you know how conservative the rules are. We were turned down for an exemption, but that isn't necessarily the last word."

"Oh," says Steven. "Is there like an appeal or something?"

"Not exactly. I'm not sure yet what can be done. I'm going to see Margarite Huger about it next week."

"She's cool," acknowledges Steven. "Think she can help?"

"She's chairman of the Board," injects Chris.

"Chairwoman of the Board," corrects Allie.

"Whatever," says Chris. "I guess it would be too obvious if my mom pushed it, huh Mr. Carter?"

"I'm afraid so, Chris." We are all four seated now. No one seems in a hurry to leave. "Technically, your mother probably ought to disqualify herself. She's done us a favor by hanging in there. She could get some flack for it."

"Boy, it's lucky for them Mom's gone," says Steven with a droll lifting of his eyebrows. "Can you imagine her reaction? She'd have put the heads of those Board people on spikes in the front yard."

"Yes," I acknowledge, recalling Elizabeth's temper on those rare occasions when something personal, close to the core, was at stake, "but getting yourself augured into the ceiling isn't always the solution."

"Then what is the solution?" Steven asks. His question is benign, without reproach, but I feel their stares and I am less comfortable than when I sat down. They are watching me in this instant as children younger than they are, through eyes that still sanction the Rambo solutions to adult dilemmas. Elizabeth's approach—spike their heads as a warning to others—has great appeal. When both sides to a confrontation take that approach, the result is called war. Compromise, negotiation, mediation; all these pusillanimous practices on which I have built my reputation carry a certain stigma of indecisiveness, the shades-of-gray shadowing that the Rambos of the world disdain. They will, I remind myself, mature into my point of view as college and early work experiences anneal them against the glamour of warfare, of take-no-prisoners mentality. Yes, I think as I return their collective stare, feeling better, I am a man of the world, mature and seasoned and possessed of the even judgment demanded by modern existence. The bull in the china shop is an entertaining image until the day you own the shop. Soon enough these three, each in his own way now questioning my resolve in the face of the St. Simeon's recalcitrant directors, will own the shop.

The kids scatter and Mother again assures me of her enthusiasm for spending a quiet evening amidst the rooms and relics of her former residence, the treasured architectural remains of her happier period.

Adelle is lovely this evening, her hair piled on top of her head and pinned for a more sophisticated look. We attend a rather dispirited performance of King Lear at the Dock Street Theater, followed by dinner at Pretlow's, a seafood restaurant near the market.

Halfway through the meal Adelle is radiant. She has on a pale cashmere sweater, high at the neck, which lends bulk to her breasts. One fleeting thought of cleavage and I feel the stirring of desire. The "s" matter will be an issue before dessert is over and I am not about to suggest another hotel.

"That was delicious," she says, dabbing her mouth daintily with her napkin, having left just enough cheesecake on her plate. My pecan pie is gone and I am ready for, to be blunt, her. She seems of like disposition.

"Is our evening over or would you like to come back to the house?" she asks pointedly.

"I'd invite you to mine but my mother's staying overnight."

She smiles seductively. "Somehow I think your mother would be in the way this evening."

Frankly, it's been awhile and being a man with normal hormonal callings I am quite excited by this prospect, so much so that I must perform a dexterous shielding with my napkin as I rise, least an anticipatory tumescence embarrass me. I feel like a matador with something to hide from the bull.

"You're not getting nervous again, are you?" she asks. "Are you thinking about a hotel?"

"Don't be silly," I say, thinking about a hotel. I tell myself to relax. In the car I kiss her, a kiss that turns passionate as soon as I can put the other arm around her and pull her to me. In no time we are twisting and turning ourselves in mating manipulations that will hurt someone if we aren't careful.

"Let's go," she says in a breathy voice, disengaging.

Her house is dark with only her car parked in front. We mount the front steps and step inside, shedding our coats.

"I'll fix us a nightcap," she says, heading off toward the kitchen. "Why don't you put something on the stereo."

Adelle's den is at the rear of the house. The clock on the wall says it's just after eleven and a large, leather couch looks inviting. Were we married, I'm sure we would dispense with this step and proceed directly to bed. But though we have made love a few times, neither of us seems to have attained the requisite degree of informality required to eliminate this rite. Proceeding from the front door directly to the bedroom is somehow too mechanical, too foregone, too married. I kindle the wood set in the fireplace just as Adelle returns with brandy. In addition to fixing drinks, she has used the time away to fix herself and her makeup is fresh and her hair is down.

"How cozy," she says, an unmistakable gleam visible as she approaches the couch. I have selected an Eric Clapton album for its rhythms suitable to more than dance. She slumps against me and we take a few moments to peer at the fire before turning to each other.

Adelle is a wonderful kisser, with lips soft and supple and expressive. We are soon locked in an extended kiss. As our breathing becomes heavier, she takes my hand from her shoulder and slides it to her chest. Soon I am cupping the downy cashmere over her breast as she purrs beneath me. Her hand falls to my lap and she gropes. An audible moan escapes from me in a reedy, high-pitched plea. I am thinking that this is quite a sufficient salute to foreplay when she says, "Help me out of this sweater." I grasp the bottom edge, pull the sweater over her head, and toss it to the floor. She unsnaps her bra, drops it over the edge of the couch, and pulls me to her. "Suck me," she orders, and I am hungrily obliging her right nipple when the front door opens.

"Mom!" yells Chris.

"Shit!" cries Adelle over the music. "My sweater!" I reach for it but she does also and she is trying to put it on even as I hand it to her.

"In here, dear," she yells in a voice of comically forced casualness. "In the den." Her sweater is on and she pats her hair in place as we assume our best pose; two asexual adults discussing the Clinton administration's Middle East policy over brandy.

Adelle's couch is set off to the right as you enter the room. It more or less faces the door and divides the den. Beyond the couch are some bookcases on either side of an upright piano. As Chris and Allie walk in, hand in hand, I remember the bra.

"How was the movie?" I ask cheerfully.

"Boring," Allie says. "How was the play?"

"Boring, but dinner was good," I say, glancing at Adelle as if to draw her into my assessment but covertly studying the lines around her eyes to glean her awareness of the rogue bra. Her gaze is riveted on the kids, I assume in prayerful anticipation that they will sit down in front of us rather than stroll behind the couch.

"Sit down," she says forcefully. "The movie must have had at least some redeeming scene."

"Not really," says Allie, seating herself in a side chair between us and the fire. "The obligatory sex stuff, but it was pretty crass. The guy is choking her while they get it on."

"That's not the way they did it in Casablanca," I agree. Should I risk standing? I could walk around and kick it under something.

Adelle asks, rising, "Can I fix you kids something to eat?"

"We ate burgers," says Chris.

"Oh, you're always hungry," says Adelle. "I'll just fix us a snack." Moments later she returns with chips and dip, which she places on the coffee table. After setting them down, she casually circles the couch to a position behind me, then puts her hands on my shoulders as though we are sitting for some formal portrait. I can feel her leg against the back of the couch, her foot fishing for the bra in a circling motion.

Chris reaches for the TV remote. "Will this bother you guys?"

Allie looks at him reproachfully. "Chris, they probably want to be alone."

"Oh, yeah," he says, standing. "Okay, well, I'm going to run Allie home. I've got a doubles match at eight in the morning. See you in a few."

Allie looks at me on her way out the door. "Now, don't be too late."

"Don't worry," I say. "I'm right behind you."

Allie is in the kitchen when I arrive home minutes after she does. Adelle and I have said the briefest, blushing good-byes with vows to try again. As I take a carton of milk from the fridge, Allie looks at me sympathetically.

"Dad, I'm so sorry we busted in on you two like that. I told Chris we shouldn't go in but he seemed to think you would be sitting around playing cards or something. I can't believe how naive he can be."

"Well, maybe we were playing cards."

"Right. We busted in at a terrible time; a few minutes more and it would have been really embarrassing."

"What are you talking about?" I demand.

"Dad, get real. Does Adelle always wear her sweater with the label on the outside? Don't worry, Chris didn't notice."

I am certain that my blush would have put a pomegranate seed to shame. I am still blushing the next morning at St. Philip's and into the afternoon, when I carry Sarah back to Sullivan's. As I tote her bag to the house, yelping sounds come from the direction of the garbage bins. I drop the bag and walk over, Sarah slightly ahead.

"It's Ralph," Sarah says, stooping. Ralph is the Irish Setter from down the block. He is sitting on his haunches inside Steven's trap, looking forlorn and whimpering. The top to the can is off and some garbage litters the concrete.

"Well," says Sarah brightly as she opens the latch, "at least we proved it works." She has a way of putting the best possible face on calamity.

23

On Monday morning, while dressing, I fixate on a one-item agenda: verbal dissection of Natalie Berman. Her covert solicitation of Allie, her effrontery in the school parking lot, her eel-like stealth in slithering behind my back have me in the blackest of moods.

In the parlance of modern psycho-babble, I am among the anger disadvantaged. Coping tools available to others—flailing, screaming, fuming, ranting, raving, throwing, breaking, stomping, cursing, spitting, snorting, biting—I employ only by means of imitation since, as with any handicap, I have developed certain compensations. Acting out a missing reflex is not easy, no easier than suppressing a functioning one, such as sitting behind home plate and not blinking when a foul ball hits the screen directly in front. I suppose this malfunction should itself make me furious, but . . . ?

It is with nervous envy that I observe others throw tantrums, instinctively reverting to the pacific calm which is my nature, retreating into something akin to a temporary hibernation in which my body temperature drops, my breathing shallows, and my pulse slows. It drove Elizabeth, whose anger reflex remained a well-oiled, finely tuned precision instrument, crazy.

But when angered myself, either by a pricking of my pride, a calculated slight, or a direct insult, rare as those are, I feel acid in the stomach, the muscular stirring of rebellion, a taunting of nerve endings so that I am positive I possess the gene for anger, but this gene is unschooled in what comes next. It flounders, sending out its neural messages in a signing my brain does not read.

I suppose this all adds up to some variety of psychological deficiency in that everyone seems to feel that anger is healthy. Certainly there is no shortage of anger in America today so we should be healthier than we have ever been. Places like Detroit and Miami, New York and L.A., should be downright rapturous.

So though I know I am angry at Natalie Berman, that a logical, finite, and well-placed reason exists for that ire, and although I can feel within me the rising flood and surge of emotions I recognize as anger, I am very unsure of what I will do about it. The tongue lashing I am rehearsing as I abuse my necktie will not be delivered. That, my experience makes clear. In private, I can feign prickly, vitriolic, even animated, but in confrontation, sarcasm remains the outer reach of my left jab or right hook. Words snarled into my mirror this morning guarantee only that Natalie Berman will not hear them later.

As soon as I arrive at the office I dial the number on her business card. Her address is listed as King Street, far to the north of Calhoun Street, an area in transition; what some might and do call slum. On the second ring a female answers.

"ACLU."

"Natalie Berman, please."

"Ms. Berman is at the courthouse this morning. Is there something I can help you with?"

"This is Coleman Carter. Are you her secretary?"

"A paralegal. She doesn't have a secretary. I'm Susan Shiflet."

"Susan, I'm an attorney here in town and I need to speak with Ms. Berman. Which court is she in?"

"She's not in court per se. She went to watch the Swilling trial."

Roland Swilling is a black drug dealer who claims two white policemen maimed him in a holding cell after an arrest. He is suing for damages in a trial that will receive lots of attention in the press. Jury selection is scheduled to begin this morning in the courthouse near my office.

I am determined to see her today so I don the trench coat I have just taken off and start out. A cold, misty rain is falling, slanted toward me by a brisk headwind. I point my umbrella forward, thrusting my free hand deep into a side pocket. Fronds atop the palmettoes along Broad whip and sway while their trunks give the illusion of leaning with me toward the courthouse. Iron gray sky, unbroken to the horizon, promises a daylong drizzle. Though dreary, the weather is not nearly harsh enough to drive the flower ladies off their corner and I see them bundled up against the wrought iron fence, adverse possession forever in bloom.

The U.S. Courthouse, on the southwest corner of Broad and Meeting, dates from the turn of this century. To its Renaissance Revival architecture has been appended a quite modern glass and steel wing in today's ubiquitous style that makes a building in Portland indistinguishable from one in Plymouth. The elevator lifts me two floors, to the courtroom of Judge Lydia Tyler, whose duty it will be to give that drug dealing, glue sniffing, Mercedes driving Roland Swilling a fair and impartial trial on his claim of police brutality. Personally, I'm pulling for the cops.

Prospective jurors are already seated, so the courtroom is crowded. Up front, on my side of the railing separating the attorneys from spectators, I see what I am certain is the back of Natalie Berman's well-formed head. There is space next to her and I walk forward, nodding imperceptibly to Lydia as I slide into Natalie's row. The judge and I go back a ways.

Natalie cuts her eyes at me but shows no emotion as I settle in next to her. After a moment, she leans my way.

"Pardon me," she says, "but this is the bride's side. Aren't you here for the groom's, or should I say goons?"

This unexpected japery takes me off guard. Serious, crusading Natalie plays the Improv. I grin involuntarily, not wishing her to be the least bit personable or witty. At this moment I would prefer her a two-hundred-seventy pound lesbian with a harelip and an ill fitting toupee to the shapely, tightly harnessed, and attractive young woman beside me. To the overweight ogre I might, with divine intervention, deliver something passably close to the diatribe to which I treated my mirror this morning. To a convivial Natalie, all bets are off.

"I should have guessed you'd be here," I say through the side of my mouth. "Did the Bat-signal for a possible constitutional rights violation appear in your sky this morning?"

She turns her head, whispering aggressively. "Possible? These two Black Shirts beat this man to a pulp."

"For which the mayor should give them both medals and promotions. Look, we need to talk outside. Lydia's going to hold us both in contempt."

She shakes her head. "I can't miss the voir dire. Besides, I know what you're going to say."

"I'll bet you do," I mutter. "When?"

"She announced a lunch break at noon."

"The café in the basement?"

"See you there," she says.

I am waiting when she arrives, having trudged back to the office in time to bill an hour and a half and then back to the courthouse in rain falling harder. My dripping coat hangs on the chair beside me, puddling the floor beneath. Several colleagues stop to chat, ribbing me gently about being out of my element.

When she approaches I must decide whether to stand. My visceral southernness is pulling me up, but I resist and stay seated, thinking that this gesture of defiance, if anything, should signal just how sober this meeting will be. She appears not to notice and extends her hand as she sits opposite.

"I know why you're here and I know you're upset," she says bluntly. "I had a choice to make in seeing your daughter or not. She is a few months from eighteen."

"And I am her father. Why didn't you tell me when you came to see me that you planned to visit her?"

A waitress approaches. Natalie orders a toasted tuna fish sandwich on whole wheat and mineral water. I order the soup and sandwich special and more coffee.

"I hadn't decided then," she says. "It was an inspiration that came to me after you and I met."

"How did you know where she goes to school?"

"Easy. I followed her." She stares blankly, as if relating the barometric pressure.

"Hold it. You staked out my house?"

"For about twenty minutes. I drove past the day before and saw her car—her name is on the license plate—and guessed she would leave for school between 7:30 and 8:30."

I am a bit dumbfounded. "Don't I have some constitutional protection against that?"

Natalie smiles, drawing me again to her even, snowy teeth. "You might. I'll have Susan research it."

"You seem mighty casual about something I consider very serious."

"What escapes me, Mr. Carter," and here, her smile has vanished, "is why you are not taking her exclusion more seriously. I'm only trying to help."

"I'm doing what can reasonably be done."

"Which is?"

Which is none of your business. Her tone and demeanor today are non-threatening. To fall back upon my privilege of privacy is to appear defensive. "I have a meeting scheduled with the president of the Society. I intend to let her know that the Board's decision is not acceptable."

"Really?" Natalie seems mildly surprised, and interested.

"Absolutely," I say with conviction.

"So what kind of ultimatum will you give her?"

"I've known this woman all my life. I don't think ultimatums will get me very far with Margarite Huger."

Natalie shakes her head as though clearing it. "Let me understand. You intend to let her know that the Board's decision is unacceptable—"

"Positively."

"Yet there are no consequences for its failure to change its mind?"

"Not exactly," I say, scrambling. "The consequences are understood. People dig in their heels at ultimatums."

"That's true," she acknowledges. "What are the consequences that are understood, therefore can go unmentioned?"

"Margarite will know."

She nods, but it is a skeptical nod so full of doubt and hesitation that she could have as easily laughed.

"Look, Ms. Berman," I say, guilty of the very defensiveness I wish to avoid, "this is a very delicate situation. It is delicate for the Society and for us, my family. Everyone is taking steps to insure that no lasting scars are inflicted. It's called civility."

"Call it what you will, Mr. Carter, I predict that your friends will not change their minds and that your daughter will not be granted an exemption from their stupid rule. If you accept that judgment and go peacefully, then you will minimize the lasting scars to one: your daughter. If that's acceptable—"

"I told you it wasn't."

Our food arrives, and for a few minutes we turn to it as a device for turning away from each other. Jury selection is going as expected, she reports, with Swilling's attorneys trying to impanel a black jury and the city's attorneys seeking whites.

"I don't know," I muse. "This Swilling is such a slimeball that it wouldn't shock me to see the blacks string him up. His customers are their kids."

She cants her head to one side, squinting as though concentrating. "On the drug charges themselves, perhaps. But this is a civil claim against the police. They'll have more empathy."

"What would you do?" I ask. "If you were me, what would you say to Margarite tomorrow afternoon?"

"Honestly? I'd tell her that unless my daughter got an invitation, I'd sue not only her sacred society but her personally along with every other member of that Board, that I'd seek punitive damages under the Civil Rights Act, that I'd demand attorneys fees, and that I would spend every cent I had, and all I could borrow, to make sure that unless my daughter attended the ball there wouldn't be any more."

I stare at her. "That's what I thought. Your opening bid would be scorched earth, kind of like our mutually assured destruction policy with the Ruskies a few years back."

"It worked. They never attacked."

"Yes, but JFK and Khrushchev didn't live next door to each other and borrow sugar over the back fence."

"You have to be prepared to give that up," she says. "I know from personal experience."

"Oh, did you nuke someone?"

She laughs, but with a hint of sadness and irony. "In a way, yes. When I was young, my parents filed suit against a country club that didn't admit Jews."

I sense she is about to elaborate when Scott Edwards, the court reporter from the *Sentinel,* approaches our table. Scott is a good reporter, but frustrated. He came here from Ohio in his mid-twenties expecting to be in Charleston only long enough to establish himself as a thoroughbred, to be wooed into the stables of a major daily with a fat contract for serious money. Ten years later he is still prowling the halls of the courts, waiting for his summons to the big time. He is tall, lanky, affable, with radish hair and the kind of cynical grin that rides well on the lips of reporters, who, with their questions, always seem to be mentally checking your answers against some invisible collateral source, even when they have only asked for the time.

"Hi, Natalie," he says. "Coleman," he acknowledges. I suggest he join us and he pirates a chair from the next table.

"Saw you upstairs," he says to her. "What do you think?"

"By the script so far," she says and he nods. The waitress approaches but he waves her off.

"Where's your story?" she asks.

He shrugs laconically, his arms distending from the sleeves of his old tweed sport coat. "You read the background pieces we ran last week. Not too much sex appeal to jury selection. We'll probably focus on the healthy percentage of whites who raised their hands when the judge asked if anyone had formed an opinion about the case from the news accounts."

"Think they're just dodging jury duty?" Natalie wants to know.

He nods. "Some of them, for sure. I got a couple to talk to me after they were excused. Swilling sure doesn't want them on his jury anytime soon."

Scott does not seem himself; more reticent than usual, occasionally looking at me with a cryptic glance that is somehow accusatorial and makes me nervous. He is pleasant enough, but his mind is not on the Swilling matter in spite of the discussion he and Natalie are holding. Perhaps it is merely professional boredom. He excuses himself with the need to phone in for messages.

"Nice man," I say as he walks off. "You were about to tell me of a suit your parents brought." I want to engage her on something other than my problem with the St. Simeon.

"I was twelve," she says. "My father was teaching at the local university and a colleague there, a well-intentioned but obviously unaware Gentile, invited him to join the country club not realizing that there was an unwritten rule against Jews. He was blackballed in the membership committee so he sued."

"What happened?"

"The club was very embarrassed, or said as much publicly. There were a number of prominent members, including some politicians and judges. None wanted the discrimination highlighted in the media, so a reasonably quick, quiet settlement was put together. The club admitted us and paid my father's legal fees in exchange for his agreement not to publicize the terms of the deal."

"A victory for scorched earth," I say. She wears a distant look, remembering this episode, and her gaze is not altogether one of triumph and vindication. "Was the club nice?" I ask. "You're going to tell me you lead the swim team to victory that summer."

"I only went once," she admits. "Our reception was not what you would call warm."

"Did your parents go often?"

"My father went once also. My mother never set foot in the place. The point is, when you're right, you have to push regardless of the consequences. My parents believed that very strongly and instilled it in me."

I am softening, in dismay. My awkward, unmarshaled, and directionless anger at her is dissolving into an image of a swimming pool in which pink-skinned Christians disported playfully while a darker, slender young girl—a girl perhaps not unlike Allie—stood away from the crowd, immured in her isolation by her crusading parents as much as by the narrow-minded parents of those in the pool. No doubt I am dramatizing under the spell of the moment; after all, I have no idea if she ever went near the pool, or if they had a pool, but I swear I can see something not so far removed in Natalie's melancholy. If her family's admission was for her parents a moment of triumph, it was for her a vicarious loss as much as a win, and for the first time I intuit that the tough righter-of-wrongs sitting before me, finishing the last of her tuna fish sandwich, is underneath a very lonely person. It is only a theory, but has in me the heft and tactile feel of truth.

"May I call you Natalie?" I ask.

"Sure," she says.

"Call me Coleman. In spite of my opinion of your tactics and your attempt to recruit my daughter, I do appreciate your interest in her."

"Thank you. I can see I haven't persuaded you, but I'll be interested in the outcome of your meeting with the Huger woman. Will you let me know what happens?"

"Sure," I say.

We each pay our checks and shake hands. She returns to the courtroom for the afternoon session and I walk back to my office thinking that my radar of first impressions, normally unerring, failed me where Natalie Berman was concerned. This nascent warmth is to last all of three-and-a-half hours, until the phone rings and my secretary puts through a call from Scott Edwards.

"Hi, Scott, what's new since lunch?"

"Nothing on Swilling. I'm calling about the St. Simeon. We're getting ready to run a story about your daughter's exclusion and I wanted your comments."

"Scott, you're not serious," I say, knowing full well from his tone that he is and thinking back to his peculiar demeanor at lunch, when he seemed to study me like a lab specimen.

"Yeah, there's a lot of human interest in it; the lily-white St. Simeon, your family's heritage, the Board's refusal to grant a waiver. Good stuff."

"Good, personal stuff," I say. "I hope Julian will reconsider. It's a bit awkward and my daughter doesn't want to be spotlighted, nor do I want it for her."

"She hasn't done anything wrong. Julian brought it up in the editorial meeting last week and the people here think it's news. Naturally, we don't want to upset you—"

"But news is news."

"Pretty much."

"How did you learn of the vote?" I want to know.

"Sources," Scott says.

"Sources I know you're anxious to name."

"Sources I am ready, willing and able to disclose were it not against the policy of my employer, as you well know."

"Yeah," I confess, seeing the brick wall form in front of him as we speak. "But Scott, I'm confused. Your beat is the courts."

"True. That's where it gets touchy. Frankly, the purpose of this call is twofold. First, I wanted to let you know we were running the article tomorrow morning . . ."

"I appreciate that."

". . . And secondly, to get your comments on a rumor that you're about to file suit against the St. Simeon."

"What! Who told you that?" I demand, forgetting we have just waltzed this box step moments before.

"As I said—"

"I know, I know."

"I need a comment. Can you confirm?"

I take a breath. "I can deny, and if you print otherwise I'll sue the *Sentinel.*" I am startled at my own assertiveness, marveling that my indignation has managed, of it's own accord and with no conscious consultation in the council of my reason, to find its voice.

Scott seems startled as well, lost for words. After gravid silence, he says, "You're denying you talked about the possibility of a suit?"

Natalie Berman. The forlorn image by the country club pool returns, but now she is demonic, fire in her eyes as she points and laughs.

"Scott, that's like the old, 'Are you still beating your wife?' question; either answer is damning. Yes, I have discussed it but not in the context of actually doing it."

"So the answer is yes."

"No, I mean the answer is that I have no present intent to sue the Society."

"So you're not ruling it out," he says significantly.

"Scott, listen to me. I'm not suing the Society. That's all I have to say."

"Fair enough. We'll print it."

"You do that," I say, kicking myself as we hang up because I let him goad me into fluster. I immediately dial Natalie.

"She's with a client, Mr. Carter."

"I don't give a damn who she's with," I hear myself saying. Maybe I'm getting the anger thing down after all. "Put me through. It's an emergency." After a minute on hold, Natalie's voice wants to know what's wrong.

"Don't play coy," I order. "Scott Edwards is running a story tomorrow and I have a strong suspicion where he got the material."

"You're wrong," she says, firmly and controlled. "He called to ask if we had discussed a lawsuit and I was honest. I told him yes, we had discussed it but that you had not engaged me to file a suit on either your behalf or your daughter's. That's true, isn't it?"

"You aren't the source of his information about the Board's vote?"

"Absolutely not," she says, still in control.

"Then where . . . ?"

"I got the impression he'd been sitting on the exclusion story for a while. Maybe when he saw us having lunch together he made certain assumptions."

I concede plausibility of this, but it brings me no comfort. I don't trust Natalie. She's lying to cover a treachery born of her single-minded determination to inject herself into this battle.

"Maybe," I say, hanging up abruptly and thinking ahead to morning, when the Carter family's rebuff will be spread on doorsteps and breakfast tables all over Charleston.

24

Margarite's house is among the finest in Charleston. Sited on South Battery, grandly fronting the panorama of harbor beyond the seawall, its two large piazzas run east to west the length of the house, so wide and deep that the shuttered windows opening onto them are in shadow most of the day. I picture them always as I saw them first.

My parents took me to a party at the Hugers' in midsummer. This was before Philip and I became friends, so I must have been eight or nine, walking between them with the trepidation common to children at adult affairs. As we approached, the sounds of a string quartet lilted among the throng of brightly clad guests on both upper and lower piazzas, and a benevolent evening breeze off the water fluttered the women's skirts like multicolored flags. Black waiters with silver trays, held shoulder level, circulated with champagne. Men in white dinner jackets clustered here and there, smoke from cigarettes blown straight up in skyward exhale before the breeze took it the way of the skirts. The women seemed as fragile as hummingbirds, with pallid summer silks and chiffon glorious against pecan tans. Even now, in the dank dreariness of February, I think of this house as a monument to gaiety, and as I ring the front doorbell on the lower deserted piazza, I can still feel festive ghosts brushing past on their way to greet new arrivals or for one more pass at the shrimp. Of course, not all the ghosts are festive. Philip's lurks here as well. On days when I came over here to hang out with him, which was almost every day, I used the back door, never knocking.

Daniel, a black man of seventy years and heroic bearing, answers the bell. He has run Margarite's household staff for almost forty years. He beams when he sees who has come to call. We shake hands, both hands, but my urge to hug him is restrained by the formality he insisted on, even when I was a boy. He is dark, with a closely trimmed wreath of silver hair and, as I notice when he takes my coat and turns to lead me in, an ebony carapace of smooth, unspoiled pate.

"So glad to see you, Mister Coleman. Miz Huger upstairs, in the Haiti room," he says in his resonant Gullah. As I pass the formal living room, I eye Philip's portrait above the mantel.

I mount the wide stairway. At the first landing is a Thomas Elfe table, in burnished mahogany and intricately fretted, on top of which is set an enormous Ming vase holding the largest poinsettias I have ever seen outside Mexico. Such appointments, so dramatic in appeal, are characteristic of Margarite's elegant but unadorned style. Rather than packing her house with antiques, so cluttered that a single misstep occasions a call to her insurance carrier, she has selected over the years only the crown jewels, but these she displays in royal, spacious settings, allowing the elegance of each piece a throne to which homage can be properly paid.

The Haiti room remains the lone exception to this rule of restraint, and it is also her favorite. Years ago she and John purchased a villa in Port-au-Prince, and from frequent visits she has assembled a Caribbean oasis on the second floor. As I reach the top of the stairs she calls out to me.

She is seated on a divan in the French sleigh-bed style, surrounded by cumulus pillows. Dressed casually in jeans and a flannel shirt, she reaches up to clasp my hand. I take a wicker chair and the tropical ambiance of the room infects me at once. Every space is filled with an artifact or memento of what she calls, with proprietary pride, "My island." Between us is a cocktail table of cedar, not actually a table but a box painted on five sides with animals lurking in dense flora. A glass top protects the oils, and on this rests *Gingerbread Houses, Haiti's Endangered Species.* Two of the intricate original line drawings, featured in the book and done by the famous Anghelen, hang framed on the wall behind her.

To my right along another wall is a long sideboard, on which stands out from the collective clutter an iron sculpture by Brierre, "The Expulsion from Eden," and three progressively smaller antique olive jars, originally used as storage vessels aboard ships bound from Europe. There is a photograph of Margarite and John, smiling and relaxed, toasting each other in the bar of the Oloffson Hotel.

The art, spaced around the walls, is eclectic and costly: a Christening scene by Benoit, a self portrait of Philome Obin, seated in his studio, and a jungle menagerie by Philippe-Auguste, haunting wide-eyed leopards peering from behind green, orbicular leaves.

This room encapsulates my image of Margarite. In virtually every aspect of her life she is the house I entered; civic-minded, philanthropic, cultured, solid. Yet in one corner of her being I sense a room like this one wherein pants a spirit of the untamed, an imbiber of the exotic, an outlander on a castaway beach. If she is a closet Hindu, this is her ashram.

"I cannot tell you how upset I am about this article," she says, holding up the front page that I have all but memorized by this time. "When John comes home from Europe I going to insist he sell our stock in the newspaper. It's an outrage, and I let that Scott Edwards know it. Then I called Julian directly and gave him a piece of my mind."

"What was his response?"

"He hid behind the skirts of the *Chicago Tribune,* insisting that now that they own the *Sentinel* they have had to kowtow to powers that be in Chicago. How absurd!"

"What did you tell Edwards?"

"Why, not a thing. I wouldn't confirm, I wouldn't deny. That's why the article doesn't quote me. I contented myself with one comment that I told him was strictly off the record, and that was to the effect that if we have reached a point in this city where the comings and goings of the

St. Simeon are open to public scrutiny, then Charleston has ceased to be Charleston and his newspaper is to blame. Oh, I don't remember when I've been so irate. And as if it wasn't humiliating enough to find our soiled linen aired in public, this horrible business about you suing us is just too much."

"I hope you don't think—"

"Of course not. I see their game. Divide and conquer, but it won't work. Who do you suppose gave them their information?"

I sigh, locking my hands behind my head. "My guess is the same person who called Natalie Berman."

Margarite's face clouds. "Who is Natalie Berman?"

"The ACLU lawyer I'm supposed to have consulted about suing you, I mean suing us—it's my organization too."

"I don't know her."

"You wouldn't. She's new in town, freshly hatched from some liberal nest."

"She sounds dreadful. I hate it when I have to agree with them. They're so . . . intolerant."

"I'm not sure what to make of her," I say. "She says she wants to help, but she comes out swinging a mall hammer."

"What was Allie's reaction to the story? I see they quoted her as saying she was disappointed, but not discouraged with the decision. What can that mean?"

I shift uneasily in my chair. "It means she still has hopes of attending. We're hoping the Board will reconsider."

Margarite looks away, pursing her lips. "Hmmmm."

"I asked to see you before I knew the paper was getting involved. I was looking for some crack in the rules through which we might slip just this once."

"What you lawyers like to call a loophole?"

"Exactly," I confirm. "You know the Society better than anyone. I was counting on you to help me formulate some strategy that would change the Board's mind."

Margarite glances down at her hands, twisting the multiple rings on either side of her wedding band. "Don't overlook the membership, Coleman. Remember, a number of my voting colleagues think their duty is to represent the majority will of the organization."

"Perhaps. But there is nothing I or anyone else can do about the general membership. We'll have to rely on the Board doing what's right."

"As I told you when this matter first arose, my sympathies are with you and Allie. I'll do anything I can to help. I'm not aware of a loophole, but I'll be glad to look. Surely, somewhere the rules have been stretched."

"Great," I say, relieved. "We need to move quickly."

"By all means," she agrees. Then she pauses, studying me. "Coleman, what will happen if we can find no loophole?"

"As the expression goes, Margarite, we'll have to jump off that bridge when we get to it. I don't have an answer. I'm certainly not inclined to go to court. It's heresy for a lawyer to say, but I'm not at all sure I believe in litigation. And to sue my friends, the St. Simeon . . . it's unthinkable. Still, I have an obligation to Allie, and one person should not be allowed to deprive her of what she's earned."

A curious perplexity comes over her. "Why do you say one person?"

"Because I think I know that group, and I'd bet the farm that the vote was four to three, meaning one convert turns it around."

"I see," she says, in such a way as to throw into foreclosure the farm I have just bet.

"Margarite, why am I getting the nasty impression that one vote did not decide this?"

"Coleman, I'm in such a quandary. I've given my word to the Board."

"I understand. Believe me, I'm not pressing you."

"I want so much to help."

"You have helped. I'm grateful." There is an awkward silence, during which I hang my head, staring down at the sisal rug overlaying the hardwood floor. "You know, if I ever doubted the power of the press, I had my blinders ripped off with this article."

"Why do you say that?"

"At ten this morning my mother called, asking how in good conscience I could entertain suing a society that my father presided over? This, despite the fact that I denied such a suit and the paper printed my denial."

Margarite nods knowingly. "Yes, but it also reported the rumor of a suit, and hence people read into the article what they assume the paper cannot tell. I've done the same thing myself many times, I'm sorry to say. Plus, there was Edwards' observation that you refused to rule out a suit in the future, leaving people to draw their own conclusions."

"Edwards knew what I meant. He took semantic license." I rise and walk toward the windows opening onto the piazza. Tiny whitecaps dot the river, and Fort Sumter looks like a desolate massing of the gray waters flowing around it. Between these tall windows is displayed one of Margarite's treasures, the white marble, half-nude sculpture of Pauline Leclerc, sister of Napoleon, sprawled provocatively on a chaise lounge. According to Margarite, when Habitation Leclerc closed its doors to its jet-set clientele, she and John bought the piece at auction. Above it hangs a sequined voodoo flag of Saint Jacques, who seems to be leering downward at Pauline's exposed breasts.

"Any pointed questions from the Board today?" I ask over my shoulder.

She hesitates. "I was afraid you'd ask that. Yes, three or four have called to see what I know. Two of them, who shall go nameless, hinted that you may have set up the request with a lawsuit in mind. I politely told them I thought they had taken total leave of their faculties; that it was I who suggested you seek the exemption in the first place."

I shake my head ruefully. "You wonder sometimes. Right after my mother called, Harris walked into my office. He commiserated with me right down the line but it was almost like he was doing it because he had to, and that somewhere in the back of his mind he too is wondering whether I intend to go to court." Standing before the window, staring out at the cold harbor, I finger Charlotte Hines and Jeanette Wilson as the sources of the "set-up" theory.

Margarite rises behind me and comes forward, placing a comforting hand on my shoulder. "I'm going to make some calls of my own," she says. "I'm going to tell everyone who'll listen that you've been here, we've talked it over, and that you have the Society's interests at heart, as always."

I turn. "Thanks. That should help, coming from you. In the meantime, I'll do some digging on a loophole. I owe it to Allie."

"We all do," says Margarite. "Would you like some coffee? I put some on in the den just before you arrived."

We cross the hallway into the den, memorable to me because when Philip and I talked some girls into playing spin-the-bottle here, I experienced my first kiss. Family photos populate the bookshelves, where Philip stares out from one taken three months before he left for Vietnam. His dress blues mantle him in the iron dignity of a seasoned soldier, but he does not need a uniform to appear manly to me and I remind myself he was only twenty-two. I smile at the portrait; a fitting greeting to an old buddy after such an extended absence. Margarite hands me coffee as the last trace of my grin fades.

"I spoke with your mother at your party," she says. "We had some time together before you arrived at the Cooper Club. She looks as though life at Sullivan's still agrees with her."

"She's amazing," I acknowledge. "I'd kill for half of her energy." I instantly regret the choice of the word "kill" but she seems to be unfazed.

She picks up the photo of Philip. "Such a waste," she says. "You read today of U.S. businesses looking for investments over there. One minute we're bombing them and next we'll be hiring them. Such a senseless, horrible waste."

"He was determined to go."

"Don't I know it. He could have found a dozen ways out if he had wanted to." She looks at me with a sadness I haven't seen in years.

"He was the best man I ever knew," I say.

She reaches for my arm. "If we're going to talk about Philip, I'll need some fortification. I've got some Kahlua in the sideboard. Would you like a spot in your coffee?"

"That would be great," I say.

She leaves and moments later returns with the brown bottle. "Coleman," she says as she motions me to a leather armchair, "there are many hardships in the death of a son. There is the overwhelming sense of loss, of course, and there is anger and bitterness and remorse and a dozen more. But as time passes, a new hardship comes on that I never knew existed. It is a fear."

"A fear of what?"

"Your child being forgotten. Take the scholarship at the school in his name. After it happened, your family and dozens of others contributed and everyone on the committee to select the recipient knew Philip and had vivid memories of him and some big or little story to tell about the way he touched their lives. The afternoon of your party—it was a Friday—I went to the school for the annual meeting of the committee and as we reviewed resumes and analyzed needs it dawned on me that not a single other person in the room had ever known or met my son. I can't say why I just now realized it; it's been true for a decade or more. Isn't that strange? Here was this wonderful boy with his fabulous talents who meant the world to his father and me and it's as though he never lived."

I breathe deeply, the cause and effect of her sudden exit from my party now fully formed. "And hard on the heels of your committee meeting you came to a birthday party for me and found a room full of Vietnamese waiters. What awful timing."

She replenishes her Kahlua and mine, dispensing with more coffee. "I thought so too, at first. 'Margarite,' I said to myself, 'it's just too much in one day.' But after I got home, a curious thing happened; I felt much better than I have in a long time. I went up to his room and looked at his things and sat on his bed and had myself a good cry but it wasn't the sad kind of cry I'm used to but a better kind, like a happy reminder that I really did have a son that gave me almost twenty-three perfect years."

She is smiling now, and I am taking a rather ironic satisfaction at being the catalyst for her bracing re-visitation when she asks, casually, "When was the last time you were in his room?"

"Me?" I ask stupidly.

"It would have been after college, of course. That summer he went into the army?"

"Probably."

"Would you like to see it?"

"His room? Sure," I say, not wanting to.

She collars the Kahlua and leads me to the third floor. Over her shoulder she says, "Now please don't think this is some kind of shrine. I have a sewing table in there so it's hardly just as he left it."

We walk in. I look about, thinking no, it is not exactly as he left it but it is mighty damn close. Her sewing table is near the rear window, the one we crawled out dozens of times to drop onto the roof over the breakfast room, not because of any need for stealth but simply because we liked to climb out windows. She seats herself on the bed as I walk to the dresser. On it rests a small Bible that was certainly not there when Philip was, but there is also an ashtray from the Grand Canyon, the same one he kept his loose change in. And there is the picture of Julie Alexander, his "main squeeze" from college. I have no idea what happened to her, but I am tempted to bend down, open the third drawer, and feel under the sweaters to see if Philip's condoms are still where they used to be. I wink at Julie, still twenty-one, still lovely.

"Well, does this bring back memories?" she asks.

"No doubt about it," I acknowledge. There is a chair near the dresser and I sit facing Margarite.

"Tell me a memory you have of him," she says. "I'll bet you have stories I've never heard. Tell me one."

"I don't know . . ." I say doubtfully. "I'm sure you've heard most of the ones that are suitable to tell."

A droll skepticism steals into her stare. "You mean, all but the really good ones that no one tells their mother."

I laugh, relieved. "Yeah, I guess so."

"But what can it hurt?" she asks. "Tell me one even if he might not have wanted me to know it. He was a boy, a man, not a saint. I know he raised his share of hell. Tell me about Mexico. I never heard much about your trip. For years he kept an old Corona bottle in his closet, but that and the picture of you two in those blankets is all I remember him bringing back."

I hesitate. Philip's memory is in this room, no doubt, but he is not here and despite the mementoes of his existence all around me I have no tactile sense of his presence. Quite the opposite; he seems a hundred years gone. But Mexico! That is something quite different, and the mere mention of the name evokes Philip's supercilious grin over our first shared bottle of Tequila on the train headed south.

"You were running out of money in Dallas," she prompts, rising to pour me more Kahlua. "That much I remember. How did you end up in Mexico?"

"An idle comment in the train station," I recall. "We had come to purchase our tickets back to Charleston. Neither of us was ready to come home but we were afraid of being stranded in Texas with no money. Standing in line, Philip struck up a conversation with this guy. When we told him how broke we were he laughed and said it was a shame we weren't in Mexico because we could live for six months on that much money. Philip got this gleam in his eye that I had seen too often. We were headed for Mexico on the next train."

"Where did you cross the border?" she asks. Already I can see the pleasure she is deriving in anticipation of new details of his life, even something as mundane as Laredo, Texas in the mid-sixties. We had come to Dallas after graduating from high school, drawn by a morbid fascination with Dealey Plaza, the site of Kennedy's assassination three years earlier. But everything cost more than we had and we were just hitting a stride, just beginning to savor the subtle leavening of being on our own in a new city so far removed from Charleston when we were forced to "feed the bulldog," as Philip termed coming to grips with economic reality.

"What was the train ride like?" she wants to know and I want to tell her. I lean back in my chair, take a pull on my Kahlua, and feel again the austral wind rushing through the window of the old train as we pulled out of Laredo and lumbered across the Rio Grande.

"It was hotter than Charleston on the hottest day in history. There weren't five other people in the car, and they slept. Philip and I each had a window on opposite sides of the aisle and he would cross often to take in my view, not much different from his but he was too excited to stay in his seat and he kept saying how unbelievable it was we were really in Mexico."

Margarite smiles. "He loved adventures, even as a small boy. When other moms got calls from homesick sons at camp, I never worried." She pauses thoughtfully. "Where were you headed?"

"Mexico City, to see the bull fights."

"But you never made it. Why?"

I cross my legs and pick at a tiny tick of leather protruding from the sole of my shoe. "Tequila," I say with a wry grin, not looking up. "We changed our money into pesos at Laredo. The train stopped outside Monterrey and these Mexicans got on selling everything you could want. We each bought a sombrero, a serape—those blankets in the photograph, some tamales and our first bottle of Tequila and neither of us knew a word of Spanish so I stuck out a bunch of pesos and the Mexicans made change out of my hand and after thirty or forty minutes they got off and the train started moving again.

"We ate the tamales and watched the sunset out my window and you've never seen anything more beautiful. Philip said it looked like a giant gold coin had been heated to a liquid and balanced on the edge of a mountain. We broke open our Tequila and didn't really know how to drink the stuff and we didn't have anything to mix with it so we drank it straight out of the bottle. When the sun went down it got cool so we put on our new serapes and with the Tequila going to our heads we felt like real Mexicans even though we'd only been in the country a few hours."

I study her reaction. She has an ethereal calm about her, a dreamy peace like she's on the train with us, seated in the back so as not to be part of action but able to observe every word and act of her son. I am pulling her with us toward Mexico City. I remember a few details of that night's long ride south. The car rocked along in the dark with Philip and me facing each other and nipping from the bottles. We were high in practically no time. I stared at him in the dark as we talked and I can still, almost thirty years later, recall the exhilaration of being eighteen and cocky and free and a little drunk miles from home in a strange land. Damn, we had a time.

"We passed out sometime that night and I awoke with my head splitting like some Mexican had stolen onto the train and wrapped it in steel cable and Philip didn't feel any better. We were stopped at a small station and we got off and I walked a few yards into what looked like the beginning of a desert and threw up behind a bush that had some wicked thorns all over it. Philip felt so bad himself that he couldn't even make fun of me. We decided there was no way we were getting back on that train; I'd have died. A sign on the station told us we were in San Miguel, wherever that was.

"Philip went back into the car for our stuff and we walked into town. Between puking my guts out and the walk I felt better, which is not to say good. I squinted so hard to filter the daylight that it was tough to see where we were going. We walked up a long, gradual hill and after a while we were on cobblestones, which added a homelike touch to the place because I was so used to the cobblestones on Church Street. We came to the town square and through the trees I saw on the other side the spire of a huge gothic cathedral. We were standing in front of what looked like a hotel, and Philip told me to stay there with the stuff while he checked it out and he left me standing there beside a couple of burros. One carried some broken sticks and the other some metal cans that I later learned contained milk.

"Philip was smiling when he came out. He had us a room for the equivalent of $2.50 a day. We grabbed the stuff, walked inside and across a brightly lit courtyard and up a flight of stairs. He pulled out a key that looked large enough to have belonged to some medieval castle and we stumbled into this spacious room, sparsely furnished but all I cared about was the bed. I fell on mine, he on his, and the next thing I knew it was evening. Philip was still snoring. I got up, splashed water on my face from an ancient tile sink, and opened the doors to a balcony."

I pause, forgetting for a moment that Margarite is with me. So far in the past, and I am just realizing how very long it has been since I have dwelled on Mexico, relived it.

"Margarite, have you ever felt so awful that bouncing back to normal is euphoric?"

"I certainly have," she says. "I got a flu bug one winter that did that."

"Then you'll understand how I felt at that balcony. The coolest breeze surrounded me as I leaned on the wrought iron railing. Our room overlooked the square, what the Mexicans call the *jardín.* A small group of mariachis played somewhere under the trees. I couldn't see them but the music floated up along with the smell of tortillas being cooked by a street vendor just below the balcony. I yelled for Philip to get up and he must have been awaken by the new air in the room because he joined me a minute or two later and I could tell that balcony had the same effect on him.

"Philip looked down to see where the smell of food was coming from, then asked how much money I thought it would take to buy the vendor out and haul that cart up to our room. We were both ravenous and we hit that tortilla stand like a couple of locusts."

Margarite pours herself more Kahlua, holding the bottle out for me, but I decline. "Philip had an odd appetite," she says, staring into her cup. "He could go for days without eating anything substantial but then gobble up everything in sight for a meal or two. But milk? He never lost his passion for milk."

"You don't drink milk in Mexico, or water. Only beer."

"Oh, my," she says. "It's a wonder you two didn't turn into alcoholics. I'm beginning to see why Philip never told us the details."

No, Margarite, I think as she sips from her cup, our drinking was not the reason Philip refrained from stories of Mexico. There was something else.

"There was a girl, wasn't there?" she asks as if reading my thoughts. "I seem to remember something about you falling in love. Philip said only that she was Mexican and very beautiful."

"Yes," I acknowledge, "there was a girl."

"I hope you boys didn't fight over her."

I know what you mean, Margarite. You imply a rivalry between friends for the affections of one girl. No, in that sense we did not fight over Adriana.

"Tell me about her," she urges. "That is, unless it's private."

"Not at all," I say in the kind of clever half-truth we lawyers master early. "The following morning, the roosters were going nuts while it was still dark and the bells of the cathedral sounded like they were in the next room so Philip got up at dawn to go exploring."

"Of course. He would want to get his bearings right away," she confirms decisively.

"I stayed in bed, lazy but feeling great. Just as I started to get up, I heard the key in the door. It opened, and into the room came a girl about my age. She walked straight to the bed, looked down at me, and said in broken but understandable English that she was there to make up the room."

"And this was her, the girl?"

"This was Adriana. I don't think I had ever seen a Mexican girl up close. What I remember most is her skin. The only thing I can compare it to is a peach with a suntan. She had a trace of rouge on her cheeks which I thought was unusual for a chambermaid, but then I learned that her family owned the hotel. When she looked down at me her black hair fell to either side of this perfect face and the darkest, most inviting eyes I had ever seen. She wore a white dress that was immaculate against that skin and I had trouble breathing for a moment, thinking an angel had come to make up my bed. 'I will back come,' she said. She had an endearing way of mixing the order of her words in English but I always understood and since I knew no Spanish I shouldn't have laughed but I did. She figured I was making fun of her and she turned abruptly and walked out and closed the door rather forcefully."

"How romantic," says Margarite. "You made it up to her?"

"That morning. I found an old woman selling flowers, bought an armload, and tracked her down in the back of the hotel supervising maids who were washing bed sheets by hand. She seemed embarrassed but the flowers pleased her and she agreed to let me take her for a walk. I said I needed to get to know the town and she said she would show me only to practice her English because the nun at her school spoke it only during the lesson and her skills were 'dusty,' by which she meant rusty. So we concealed our instant attraction in logic and spent the day together."

"And where was Philip?"

"He joined us that afternoon. The three of us walked everywhere. The sidewalks are stone and so narrow you must go single file at times. We would pass a decrepit door set into a pock-marked wall and I remember thinking that behind the wall lay squalor worse than any I had seen even in the dreariest slums of Charleston. But a couple of those doors opened as we passed and inside were formal gardens with tile fountains and bougainvillea in explosive reds and purples and pinks. That was my first clue that Mexico is nothing like the facade it presents to the world. Lining the tops of these walls were glass shards embedded in the mortar to discourage encroachers, and if that wasn't enough fierce dogs who live their entire lives on the roof would bark as we approached below. Much later, Adriana led us to a promontory overlooking the town. We watched the lights flicker on as the sun went down. This sunset was even more spectacular than the one I'd seen on the train and I decided then that Mexico had found the secret for perfect sunsets."

"It sounds like your enthusiasm for the view might have been influenced by your companion." Margarite winks at me knowingly. "But did Philip have no interest in this lovely girl?"

"Oh, he did at first. He was as smitten with her as I was. But for some reason she took to me. Philip saw that. He bitched about it but then seemed to accept it and treated her like a sister. They had a great relationship; just friends."

"But yours was more."

"I fell in love and there isn't any other way to describe it. Head over heels, whole hog crazy about her."

"And she reciprocated."

"As best she could."

"What do you mean, or is this getting too personal?" she wants to know. "I don't mean to pry."

"It's okay," I assure, flipping a hand as if to waive whatever privilege I might enjoy. "Adriana was the only daughter among the six Martinez children. Her parents were fanatical Catholics in the way only Catholics can be fanatic. Suddenly, their daughter was cutting her workdays short to spend time with a gringo heretic. Their worry turned to panic as we grew more obsessed. One night we stayed out until almost dawn and her father was waiting in the courtyard. He was furious, yelling loud enough to wake every guest in the place. He ordered her to stop seeing me and told me to clear out of the hotel. It was very ugly."

"But that didn't stop you," Margarite surmises.

"It brought us closer, although not in distance because of course Philip and I had no choice but to move out. Once we did, we were totally out of sight of her parents, which actually made things better or worse depending on where you stood."

"Did they try to break it up?"

"Yes, but it was the way they went about it that created the trouble. At some point they informed Rodrigo, the oldest brother, that the mortal souls of the family hung in the balance if anything came between Adriana and her education, then her marriage to a suitable Mexican. Rodrigo cornered her and, from what she told me, gave her the pitch as though he were Christ Himself."

"What did she do?"

"Turned on him like she turned on me that first morning in my room. She had a mind all her own, and her plans to attend the university in Mexico City had been thrown in doubt. She even mentioned moving to Charleston."

"That must have put her family in a real panic."

"Frenzy might be closer."

"And you were encouraging her to abandon school?"

"I didn't think so at the time. All I knew was that I had to be with her whatever it took. She told me she wanted to please her parents but not at the cost of giving me up. We continued to see each other. I think they knew but they couldn't keep her under house arrest. In Mexico, family is everything and it took courage for Adriana to defy them."

"What happened?"

What happened, Margarite? That is what I cannot tell you. Not even the ample amount of Kahlua we have shared can loosen my tongue to that degree. I cannot relate the story of the night Adriana's fate was decided, of Rodrigo's rashness, of Philip's role in what followed. I should tell you; you of all people have a right to know. But I cannot. It is my failing, one that is with me still, I suspect. No, I will tell you what did not happen. I will do what I do best; cast myself in a light most favorable to those who stand near enough to judge. A few lies after all these years cannot hurt, can they?

"What happened, you asked?" and she nods. "With my encouragement she confronted her parents with her decision not to enter the university. There was a furious reaction, as she expected. She described it between sobs that evening. Well, the longer it went on the more troubled I became about taking this girl away from her family. And what were our choices? I mean, I was headed off to UVA in September, and while I was in love with her I couldn't take her with me, couldn't promise her anything."

"That's true," she agrees. "You kept your senses."

"I had to," I continue in my most self-congratulatory tone. "What right did I have to blow into this small town and change this girl's destiny if I was unable to offer her an alternative?"

"So true, so true," mutters Margarite, the Kahlua beginning to impact her speech.

"So Philip and I talked it over and he convinced me that the best for all concerned was for us to leave town before I got in any deeper."

"Philip wasn't involved so he could see clearly about changing this young girl's life."

"Exactly," I affirm and I can see this pleases her. Good, Margarite. I will try to lie as best I can so that all your images of your son are intact. Forgive my need, my compulsive need, to preserve the mirage of the living.

"It must have been difficult breaking the news to Adriana."

"God, it was awful," I lie. "She cried and pleaded and I almost gave in. I think I would have if Philip hadn't been there to keep my feet on the ground."

"You would have done the same for him, Coleman."

No, Margarite, I would not have done for Philip what he did for me. Not in a dozen lifetimes. "Oh, sure," I agree. "Philip and I had that kind of friendship."

"And so you left?"

I should simply nod and leave it at that, but I see no real harm in weaving into my fiction a few more details. "Philip and I packed the morning we pulled out. Adriana walked us to the train station. The train was late, of course. We sat talking and I think she had cried it out by then and when we finally got up to go she kissed us. She kissed us both. We climbed in and that was that."

"Oh, Coleman, I think I'm going to cry. The thought of you two boys standing beside that train kissing that beautiful girl; it's too romantic."

That's exactly what it is, Margarite: too romantic, not that the truth lacks romance. "She took our addresses but I never heard from her. I don't guess Philip did either. He never mentioned it."

"No," she says, "I don't ever recall him getting a letter from Mexico. I wonder what happened to her?"

"I've wondered that many times. Some lucky Mexican man married a beautiful wife, I suppose."

We stand and she steadies herself discreetly. "You have no idea how much I appreciate your coming here. It makes me happy to think you boys had each other."

"Philip was a big part of my life. As long as I'm around, you don't have to worry about him being forgotten."

"I know that. In a few years or maybe sooner—we never know—I'll be seeing him again. That's my faith and it keeps me going. But now I'll have something else to talk to him about when I get there, and to think about while I'm here. Mexico."

We walk down stairs and she sees me to the front door, smiling again at the pleasure I have given her. I tell myself that I have done well by Philip today. To ease his mother's burden I would do almost anything. Anything, that is, short of accounting for myself in Mexico. Same old Coleman.

Later that evening, with Adelle at the Cooper Club, I relate conversation with Margarite and share my guess at the set-up culprits.

"Charlotte Hines for sure," she agrees. "Jeanette . . . ? I'd be more inclined toward Sandy Charles."

"Because of Charlotte's influence?"

Adelle nods. "It's like the pied piper." I am listening intently without appearing to be straining. This is as close as Adelle has come to discussing the fateful vote. I am too much a gentleman to ask her to boldly violate a confidence, and to her credit she has lived by the code of silence. But the calls to Margarite offer a fresh opportunity for discussion, and every gentleman knows that the back door is more revealing than the front. By assaying her thoughts on reactions to the news article, I may deduce much she is too discreet to share.

"Naturally, Margarite was reticent," I prompt. "She merely said two people, so we can't rule out the men."

Adelle sips her bourbon and ginger, nodding agreement but offering nothing further. The club is busy tonight, and I am certain that my imagination is a freshly coated flypaper for every furtive look behind my back, every askance I think I see from those passing near the table. The news article has left me feeling like a visitor being appraised from the deep reaches of leather tufted booths, by eyes operating like two way mirrors. I am uncomfortable where I have experienced only comfort and security before.

I tell Adelle of Margarite's commitment to the search for a loophole. "The fact that no one has seen the rules since the 1700s may cut both ways," I note. "On the one hand we're fighting a phantom and on the other hand they'll have a tough time pointing to the provision that keeps her out." I stab the remaining olive in my martini. "I just wish I knew how many votes I actually need. I've been assuming it's one but now I'm not sure." This is blatant baiting, a shameless circling to the front door.

"Actually, I'm surprised you need any votes at all," she says meaningfully.

"What?"

"Coleman, we pledged confidentiality on the discussion because of its sensitivity, but perhaps you ought to know that no one other than Margarite knows the outcome. She counted the ballots. I couldn't tell you what the margin was because she didn't tell us. She merely announced that the exemption was denied."

"You're kidding."

"Charlotte Hines was going to object if a different decision was announced because Margarite seemed, on the surface, to be with you."

On the surface? Suddenly, I am blindsided by the fear that more lurks in the jungles of Haiti than wide-eyed leopards. Margarite? Impossible.

Adelle continues. "I see now that I should have made the same demand Charlotte was planning, because I was sure you had four votes."

"The discussion persuaded you," I say, charging through the front door after demolishing the screen.

"I am honor bound not to divulge the discussion. But I hope you know me well enough to believe that if I knew the vote count I'd find some way to tell you even if it meant one blink for yes and two for no. Perhaps that's why Margarite kept it to herself."

I sit back in utter disbelief.

She leans forward conspiratorially over her drink, her eyes casting about as though spies linger. "You cannot breathe a word of what I've told you. I can't prove it. I just hate to see you put your hopes in someone that could let you down. If she's against you, Allie's chances are nil."

I nod, resigned. So true. My basis for optimism has all along consisted of Margarite and Adelle. So that's why Margarite hinted at the larger margin for the nays; she wants to discourage any hope I might harbor that turning one person around will clinch victory. She wants me to perceive such an uphill struggle that I give up and go home. While I sit in her Haiti room disclaiming all manner of legal action, she is secretly breathing a huge sigh of relief. Unbelievable!

Adelle's voice pulls me back. "Coleman, I've said too much. You've got to promise me, your most solemn oath, that you will never let on that I told you. If you do, Margarite will know the source at once and so will the other members. Promise me."

Her pleas are genuine. I have to work at holding my composure. All too strange that Margarite would stoop to treachery over such a matter. Does her self-image as a conscience-compelled egalitarian mean so much? If Adelle's implications about the debate are true, my gut feel of a narrow win, so strong with me the night I addressed them at the Hall, was on target after all. Once more I find myself a victim of my inability to attribute bad motives to good people.

I have been told that among the qualities contributing to my reputation as the Great Conciliator is the respect I habitually accord the opinions and desires of warring factions. Those generous souls assume this trait to be, in me, the perfection of a practice fundamental to my art, like putting to golf. They imagine me sitting in protracted negotiations reigning in my prejudices with the strength and skill of a consummate teamster, whose arms have been flexed and muscled by the repeated weight of raising his judgments above his biases. "Of course Coleman knows who's right," these admirers tell themselves. "He's just allowing the other side to have its say."

Yes and no. Certainly a mediator who wears his bias on his lapel will shortly be looking for other work. Undeniably, an aura of impartiality is oxygen to the beast. But such an aura need not be the product of a rigid discipline nor iron practice; it can, as with me, be sincere. This much I have learned: a bad person is sometimes right on the facts. I grudgingly acknowledge this truth, and when I happen upon such instances, either professionally or in private life, I remind myself that some higher justice, if it exists, will sort it out later.

In a good person is found, whether right or wrong on the facts but at all times, a pulse of compassion and the willingness to be ruled by it, though his or her worldly interests lie elsewhere. My asset is my most glaring liability: I assume all people to be good. It is as primal in me as a salmon swimming to spawn. It is not a judgment; to persist in demonstrable illusion is the rankest naivety. But instinctively, in negotiations or my personal affairs, I feel for the pulse, at times probing beyond prudence in the expectation of its beat and often, particularly with someone close, willing to ascribe its absence to my own feeble powers of detection. What others credit to equanimity can be my stubborn refusal to give up on the corpse.

Elizabeth, on the other hand, was sprinkled with the salt of cynicism. In her, a latent mistrust lingered, predisposing her to guard her valuables and lock her doors against those untested souls she knew only casually. She was right more often than not, and when wrong took it less to heart, so that when someone she had initially been leery of proved worthy, she accepted it as gift, a pelf of unexpected pleasure. I miss the balance she brought to our collective assessments. Had she been in my place the night of the vote, she would have viewed that Board through her peculiar telescope, one hand firmly on her purse.

Margarite is a good person. I have known her too long and too well to believe otherwise. It will be a struggle against my nature to find in her character the infidelity suggested by Adelle, brought to view by a motive so impelled as to arrest the pulse I have felt often. I also lack Elizabeth's charity when proved wrong. I am devastated.

25

Today has been one of those marathons, beginning at 7:00 A.M. with a breakfast meeting at the Marriott. Some doctors are putting together a limited partnership to construct a medical complex in Mt. Pleasant and have hired me to build the paper fortress assuring them maximum return, minimum risk, and tax liability $1.00 above the IRS's profile triggering audits.

Doctors are a strange breed where money is concerned. They have it, of course, despite in many of them business judgment so erratic that were the same discretion to color their practices they would kill more people a year than lightning, floods, and drunk drivers combined. Several of the younger ones are "struggling" on three hundred grand a year. Over orange juice, one confides that his malpractice premium fell due last month, causing him to miss the payment on his Porsche. "Actually, my wife's Porsche; the payment on mine is current."

After the docs break up I rush to a meeting of Junior Executives, an organization doing some good work among the minority youths of our city. Some business acquaintances got me involved two years ago. The kids organize and run their own businesses as tyro capitalism, while my senior friends and I look over their shoulders. I do this as part of my pro bono work. I like it. One of our kids, Anthell, started a T-shirt operation two years ago and it will be a close call as to whether he will be able to afford college—not the tuition, he already has that banked, but whether he can afford the opportunity cost college for him represents.

I break away from the Juniors early to make a 10:30 meeting at the office. Russell Evans, a long time client, is three months in arrears on his mortgage and about to lose his home. We review his finances, I make some calls and we buy another month, during which he will attempt to accelerate or borrow against an expected tax refund. At 12:00, Russell departs and so do I, for a Rotary meeting I would joyfully skip were I not today's program. My twenty minute talk on the strengths of the Junior Executives program is received well. My afternoon is no lighter, with appointments beginning at 1:00 and ending at 4:30.

With a cup of coffee and my feet propped on my desk, I at last have a moment to read the morning paper. The Soviet Union continues its plummet, sheering off states as it falls. The Swilling jury has been impaneled; four blacks and two whites. His lawyers have called him, the perjuring little pervert, as their first witness. Scott Edwards reports that his lies are expected to take two days to relate. The Chicago Bulls are still flying high in the NBA, leading their division by a mile. I am about to turn to the classifieds when Harris's voice comes over the intercom.

"Coleman, we have a problem. Can you come to my office . . . now."

Harris's office is decorated in early Audubon. There are stuffed ducks mounted on the walls, numbered prints of geese in flight purchased, I should say ransomed, at inebriated Ducks Unlimited auctions, decoys of mallards, widgeons, and woods, photographs of hunting trips in which he and his fellow assassins display their limits, enough ducks to denude Nebraska. The only paper weight on his desk is a lead crystal swan.

As I enter, Harris is sitting behind his desk in a serious frame of mind. Because his client chairs are high-backed, I am not immediately conscious of another presence. His eyes dart to the chair before him and I now see Carlton Middleton, the city attorney, seated with his frail legs crossed effeminately and his delicate hands folded in his lap.

"Hi, Carlton, don't get up," I say, bending slightly to shake his hand. He greets me only with a smile that is too broad. I take the companion client chair beside him.

Harris, nodding toward him, says "Carlton has come here as a friend. Tell him, Carlton."

"Council meets tomorrow night," he says in his sibilant lisp. "You may have seen the agenda in the paper."

"I read it not fifteen minutes ago," I reply.

"Then you know that they were scheduled to approve you fellows on the Arts Center legal work."

"Were?" I say, catching a whiff of the ill wind Harris has been inhaling.

"In their work session last week I detected some wobble in a couple of councilmen who have been solidly with us. I did some checking and because I'm no longer confident we would win a showdown vote I thought it best to delay. I recommended to the mayor that they table it. I told him my office needed more time."

"Harris told me that Cathcart hasn't given up lobbying on this. Do you think he got to them?"

There is an awkward stillness as he and Harris exchange glances. Harris drops his gaze, fidgeting with the edge of his desk blotter.

"I don't think Cathcart has made headway," says Carlton softly.

"Then what?" I ask. Harris isn't looking at me.

"Let's put it this way," Carlton continues. "There is some concern in City Hall that you may be contemplating litigation against the city."

"I am?"

"Coleman, are you aware of the fact that the city chartered the St. Simeon Society? Granted, it was in 1766, but it happened."

"I was not aware of that," I admit.

Carlton steeples his fingertips near his chin, his elbows resting on the padded arms of his chair. "Nor was I," he says. "But it's my job to be on the lookout for things that could involve the city in court and after I read Scott Edwards's column about your troubles with the Society, I checked it out. Sure enough . . ."

"I'm sorry, Carlton," I say. "I'm at the tail end of a very long day and none of this is fitting together."

"Very simple," says Harris, suddenly glancing up. "The city chartered the Society. Any suit against the St. Simeon will inevitably bring the city in as an additional defendant. The city is reluctant to have as its attorneys on the Arts Center project a law firm, one of whose senior partners is suing it." He looks to Carlton. "Does that pretty well sum it up?"

Carlton nods, and now both his and Harris's eyes are riveted on me.

"Ridiculous," I say. "I denied any intent to sue anyone and Edwards printed it."

"But you left the door open, or he did."

"He did," I say flatly.

"Also," says Carlton, "you've been seen around the courthouse with that ACLU woman. That hasn't done much to reassure anyone."

"The most expensive lunch I've ever eaten," I say weakly. "So what do you want me to do?"

Harris speaks. "Why not call Scott Edwards, tell him that as a result of his article there seems to be some lingering confusion as to your position, and that you categorically deny any intent to sue the St. Simeon now or at any time in the future. Tell him you'll sign an affidavit. Hell, make it as strong as you can."

"That would do it," says Carlton. "That would dispel the rumors, which I don't mind saying are rampant."

"Are you sure this isn't some smoke being blown by Cathcart in hopes of starting a fire?" I ask.

"Well," says Harris, "if it is, it's working. By tomorrow night we would have had the contract and now we won't."

Carlton interjects. "Cathcart has been beating it like a drum, I'll admit. To be totally upfront with you, it was he who suggested I research the relationship between the Society and the city. He wants this contract in the worst way."

"So do we," says Harris. "And too much work has gone into it to let it slip through our fingers now. Right, Coleman?"

I nod but remain silent.

"Any chance of council awarding this tomorrow night?" Harris wants to know. Carlton shakes his head, a quick flutter. "Then we have some time. We'll get right on it."

We rise and shake hands. Harris walks Carlton to his door, his meaty arm slung around Carlton's slender shoulder, stressing how appreciative Carter & Deas is for the continued support of the city attorney's office. As Carlton retreats down the hall, Harris closes the door and turns to me.

"Well, counselor, why don't we get Scott Edwards on the phone right now?" Harris is not a procrastinator.

"Let me think about it," I say.

"What's to think about? We've got to clear this up."

"I've got to clear it up," I correct, "and I need to think when I'm not so tired." A half truth. Although fatigued, I am thinking fine. I am also thinking delay.

"Old buddy," he says, "you can stew on this next week, next month and next year but it isn't going to change the outcome. Let's call Edwards."

"No," I say firmly.

"Now Coleman, listen to reason, for Chrissake. I've wined and dined those councilmen until I've committed damn near every menu in Charleston to memory. The firm's future is on the line here."

"What about Allie's future?"

He looks at me, stunned, like I've just changed the shape of my nose in his presence. "It's a fucking dance!" he exclaims.

"You're going," I say, my voice diminishing as his rises.

"Yes, I'm going," he rasps.

"Carolyn's going?"

"Of course."

"I'm going, Steven's going, Adelle, Christopher—they're going."

Harris shakes his head, exasperated. "It's still a dance against a multi-million dollar contract. I'll give her my invitation."

"You're only saying that because you can go."

"Maybe so," he says. "Look, I'm sorry for losing my temper. Take it home, sleep on it. We'll figure something out."

"Yeah," I say meekly, "I'll sleep on it."

"In the meantime I'm going to find out for myself what's going on in City Hall." Harris sets his jaw in a way I recognize. He will stalk those councilmen like he stalks ducks; patiently, and early in the morning.

I drift back to my office, my weariness unrelieved and my spirits lower than they have been since the night of the vote. On my desk rests a folder labeled "St. Simeon Loophole," a puny folio indeed. Recent nights and a complete Saturday devoted to research have yielded scant information. When great-ancestor Alston and his cohorts decided to take it underground, they buried it.

My probe began at the offices of the *Sentinel,* in its archives room. The room is not the same one I visited, many years ago now, to find the photograph of my irate grandfather giving F.D.R. hell. I examined microfiche until the room spun around me. As in most cities, Charleston's daily paper has survived a forced march through rugged terrain littered with the corporate corpses of its predecessors. In the journalism thicket of the 1800s, competing publications waged a war of attrition where survival demanded, as with the *Sentinel* in 1896, one straggler to climb upon the back of another.

The records dating from that merger are complete, but virtually silent as to the Society. Indexed references to "St. Simeon Society, The" revealed decade-long gaps during which, if indexed accurately, there was no mention at all. The sole exception to this remarkable lacunae were posthumous acknowledgments of membership, as predictable as a mortality table, found in the obituaries of Charleston's elite. So faithful were these recitations that I soon developed, during frivolous moments of flagging concentration, a mental image of these dead members greeting one another in the great beyond, escorting newcomers from the Pearly Gates through a divergent canopy, hunter green in color, to the waterfront corner of heaven restricted to St. Simeons.

But the *Sentinel* search was not wholly fruitless. In 1923, the paper's endorsed candidate for mayor was attacked by his opponent as an aristocrat out of touch with the people. Exhibit A in the opponent's indictment? The mayor-elect's alleged membership in St. Simeon. In 1934, a fire broke out in the kitchen when the caterer for the Ball placed a cardboard crate too near a flaming gas jet on the stove. Two fire trucks reported, one fireman quickly subdued the blaze, and the guests, who had crowded into the parking lot, returned to the building without missing, as the tongue-in-cheek report stated, "two foxtrots and a tango." In keeping with the treasured conspiracy of silence, the paper divulged no names of attendees.

The years prior to 1896 were tough sledding. No indexes exist for fallen standards like the Charleston *Mercury*, the *American*, or the *City Gazette*. Where old copies survive, there is no alternative to reading them cover to cover, an impossible task given my time. No book or treatise on the Society has been published, so I cannot go to school on the labors of some historian. The St. Simeon is like a giant luxury liner, regal and imposing and drawing volumes of water in displacement, but wake-less minutes after passing, so that no one not on her decks can prove she exists.

The library of the Historical Society abounds with genealogies, the kind which fascinated Allie as a girl. Their authors, driven from the first recorded sentence toward the foregone conclusion that they indeed hail from a long and storied line, are eager to recount any brushing their ancestors had with the St. Simeon. I examined eight or ten of these during an inclement Saturday but found nothing to aid my quest for a loophole. In the Lesesne tome, I learned of a claim for the record in consecutive attendance: fifty-four years by one Dr. Rawlston Lesesne between 1871 and 1924, but in that no attendance records are kept I would not be surprised to find the same boast in several others had I the time to read them. I left the library tired, discouraged, and with my nose firmly pressed to the marmoreal surface of an impenetrable wall.

Today, the day following Carlton's visit, has been less frenetic. I have had time to read the paper and eat lunch. It is mid-afternoon when I return to the office. Dottie hands me a message to call Leslie McKeller, who reports on City Hall for the *Sentinel.*

"That's got to be about the council meeting tonight," I say, handing the message back. "Harris is handling it."

"That's what I told her," says Dottie. "She insisted she needed to talk with you."

"Is Harris in?"

"I saw him twenty minutes ago."

I walk the hall to Harris's end. He is just completing a call from an insurance adjuster, politely declining another low-ball offer to settle a serious personal injury. They'll end up giving Harris his demand. He knows it, they know it, and I know it. His approach is simplicity itself: set a reasonable figure and don't budge. I once saw him turn down a $50,000 offer because it was a thousand short of the minimum he told them he had to have. That case was twelve years ago and sent a strong message to the insurers, underlined and capitalized when the jury brought in a verdict for $178,000. I stop in front of his desk, feeling the stare of every waterfowl in the room.

"What do you make of this?" I ask, dropping the message on his desk.

He rubs his chin as he thinks. "I better return this one."

"That was my reaction, but Dottie says she asked specifically for me."

He reaches for the phone, jabbing the numbers with his meaty fingers. "Leslie McKeller, please . . . Leslie? Harris Deas. You all ready for the council meeting tonight? . . . Yeah, I'll be there. Listen, I've just been handed a message for Coleman to call you and I was wondering if there is anything I can do to help. I'm our point man on the Arts Center; I'm assuming it has something to do with that."

Harris nods several times as he listens, rolling his eyes as Leslie evidently runs through preliminaries. Then he stops. His head is quite still and his eyes are animated. "I see now," he says, "why it was important for you to speak with him. Can I get back to you? . . . Half hour? . . . Thanks."

"Bad news?" I ask.

He covers his face with his hands and mutters, "The worst. Leslie's been doing her job, dammit. The word is out on the reason for tabling the contract at tonight's hearing. She and Scott Edwards are working on this together now and she's trying to reach you for comment."

"What a bite," I say.

"What an opportunity," he counters. "Now's a great time to clear the air. Call her back and tell her it's all a big misunderstanding. If you'd rather, I'll call and say it for you."

"I'm still not prepared to do that," I say.

"Well, perhaps you need to get prepared," he says. "Coleman, they're running another story tomorrow, this time reporting the fear in City Hall that you're coming after them. This entire thing is getting ridiculous."

I pick up the lead crystal swan paperweight from the desk, palming it from one hand to the other and avoiding eye contact. He rises, walks briskly around his desk and shuts the door to his outer office. "Sit down, partner," he commands.

"You know," he says, seating himself opposite me and waxing into a tone relaxed on its surface but undergirded with impatience, "you haven't been yourself for some time now. Are you aware of that?"

"Yeah," I acknowledge, still holding the swan.

"What is it, some mid-life thing?"

"I'm stumped," I admit. "Can't put my finger on it."

"Have you thought about some counseling?"

"Let's just say I haven't done anything about it."

Harris folds his arms across his chest. "You seemed okay after Elizabeth died. Sad, grief-stricken naturally, but okay. You know what I mean?"

I nod absently, looking at the swan.

"If you don't want to talk about it I understand but—"

I hold up my hand, palm out. "It's not that. I appreciate your concern."

"I'm not the only one who's noticed," he says. "You need some time off?"

"That might help," I agree. "The workload here saved me in the months after Elizabeth, but it doesn't seem to be working anymore. I'm not sleeping, and when I'm here I have an awful time concentrating."

"You've got a lot on you right now—"

"I don't think that's it. If anything, it might be not having enough on me." Harris looks confused, and with cause since I, the one talking, have no real idea of where this is going either. "I don't really need the money," I say. "The clients irritate me, frankly. It's as though the end of the world is coming and they all want to get theirs before they go. No one wants to get sued but they think nothing of suing others. The divorces get me down; I stopped doing them because I got sick and tired of listening to people who, with a straight face and at two hundred dollars an hour, lay all the ills of mankind at the feet of their mates."

Harris whistles softly. "You do need some time away."

But I am off and running now, still thrashing around in the woods but moving, putting some distance between where I am and where I was. I charge on. "Josh is grown and off, Steven's away, and Allie won't be far behind. Then what? Prop my feet up on Church Street and wait for death?"

Harris gazes with indulgent sobriety. Yet, in this instant, I cannot help wishing he was someone other than who he is. Our relationship is such that I can say to him, without fear of reproach, anything that comes to mind, no matter how disjointed. If my need is for a sympathetic ear, his is unfailingly reliable. But his dutiful attention stems from innate appreciation for the value of being a good listener rather than an intensity for what is being said. He is not a man who easily assimilates feelings or experiences beyond his own.

After a pause, he says, "Maybe you just need to get laid."

Harris often prescribes this remedy for a variety of ills, but I know he has said it only to lighten the air. He is a model of marital fidelity. I think of Adelle's bra coiled behind the couch, poised to strike, and a fresh blush kindles. It is odd that when I think of her, even Adelle naked, this blush now overrides every emotion which should compete with it. I tell myself that desire, longing, passion, hunger should rule my idle images of Adelle in bed, Adelle aggressive, Adelle in heat. Yet I resist. There is something missing. The bedroom of our relationship is new but the furniture is somehow worn and familiar. I have just realized, while talking with Harris, that the errant bra is the most exciting stimulus I have discovered with Adelle, and that cannot be normal.

Harris leans forward in his chair and places a meaty, comradely hand on my knee. His impatience is gone, replaced by a businessman's determination to close the sale. "Coleman, we've got sixteen lawyers here depending on us. Losing this contract with the city wouldn't be the end of Carter & Deas but getting it would mean a lot to what you and I have built here, not to mention what it will mean personally to the other partners and associates who count on us. You know damn good and well you're not going to sue the St. Simeon. You'd be the last person in this city to sue your friends. We both know that as sure as we're sitting here. Don't we?"

"Yeah, I guess we do."

"Then let's call Leslie McKeller and tell her that. She'll print it, the flap in City Hall will go away, and we'll get the contract that all but has our name on it now. What do you say?"

"You're right. Do you have her number?"

"Right here," he says, withdrawing the message from his shirt pocket.

I stand, walk to his phone and dial. Leslie comes on the line and I tell her that I have "absolutely" no intention, "now or in the future," of suing the St. Simeon.

"In other words, Mr. Carter, you are categorically ruling out legal action."

"Correct," I say.

"Very well. I'll quote you."

As I hang up, Harris beams his approval. "Spoken by a true statesman," he says. "I'm sure the newspaper is crestfallen that it won't get to stir this pot any longer, but you couldn't have made it any plainer."

Later that evening, I watch the evening news. The lead is the continuing crisis in the Soviet Union, followed by the Swilling trial. Roland Swilling is on direct examination by his attorneys and there is speculation the trial will last longer than the two weeks originally projected. Then, the council meeting. A camera pans the chamber and I get a fleeting glimpse of Harris seated in the second row. A rail-thin male reporter in a tailored suit and a L.A. haircut speculates on council's decision to delay voting on the Arts Center contract.

"The city attorney recommended tabling the matter until his office could assess a potential claim against the city by a local attorney whose daughter has been denied membership in the prestigious St. Simeon Society," he reports. He does not use my name or Allie's, perhaps on advice from the network's attorneys. Clearly, Leslie has not shared my disclaimer with her rivals in the media.

Oh well, I console myself. Tomorrow, the paper will quash this canard and the Carter family will step from the spotlight it never sought in the first place.

26

Leslie McKeller's story is brief, accurate and buried on page six, befitting disavowals that puncture inflated stories trying to achieve altitude. With alarm, I find myself packing the paper in my briefcase, as if to remove it from Allie's view.

I study her at breakfast for signs that she is disappointed in me, as disappointed as I am with my token resistance to Harris's blandishments. Perhaps he was right; no amount of time or thought would have produced a different result. Allie seems distant, occupied, so it is with some relief that I accept her invitation to accompany her to the Red Dragon for a summer job interview.

By the time we reach the restaurant, she is her old self again. Mr. Quan insists on feeding us, as he always does, then suggests we adjourn upstairs where we can talk privately. We climb the stairs behind the kitchen, its clangor of woks and dishes incessant.

He unlocks the door and steps aside, ushering us in with a wave of his arm. We enter a living room singularly free of whatever mysticism I may have anticipated. A vinyl-covered couch is against the far wall. At each end of the couch are end tables of motel quality and on these rest large ceramic lamps with fading shades. There is a coffee table, some old issues of *Newsweek* mixed among magazines in Vietnamese. Against the left wall, facing the street, is an entertainment center with wooden nooks for a wide-screen TV, a large and obviously expensive sound system, racks of videos and CD's and tapes, many of them classical. Two chairs of the recliner variety, cumbersome and covered with imitation leather, angle simultaneously toward the couch and TV. The rug is a short-pile shag in a 70's earth tone. On the wall to our right are two bookcases separated by a doorway leading to the rest of the unit. Mr. Quan motions Allie to a recliner and I take the other as he seats himself on the couch.

"Your father," he says, looking at her, "tells me you have interest in working with my enterprise for the summer."

"Yes, sir," acknowledges Allie formally. "I plan to live at home to save everything I can for college. If you can use me I would be thrilled to get the job."

He turns briefly and throws me a look of playful skepticism. "And are you quite sure you would be here to work or is it possible you have your eyes on the young men I employ."

Allie laughs with him. "I'm a hard worker. You can ask my dad." She glances at me for support.

"The boys hold no attraction for you?" he asks. "They will be veddy disappointed." Mr. Quan's English is almost flawless, but the word "very" he insists on mispronouncing the way Churchill insisted on torturing, to the satisfaction of millions, the word "Nazi." Perhaps he does it as a subconscious reminder that English is his second tongue, but for whatever reason "very" one of only a few words and phrases marring his virtual mastery of our language.

"I have a boyfriend," she says with the trace of modesty.

"Ah! The young man you were with on the night of your father's party. A handsome boy."

"Thank you. Christopher's very nice."

"And veddy lucky to have attracted such a young woman as yourself. Now, when are you able to begin work?"

Allie looks at me pointedly. "It depends on whether Dad gives me the graduation present I want. I finish school on the seventh of June. I could start right away unless . . ."

"Unless your father takes you to Korea," Mr. Quan says. "He mentioned the possibility of such a trip." He turns to me. "Any decision yet? It will be most difficult to deny a request from such an outstanding daughter."

"Tell me about it," I say, stifling a grin. "No, no decision yet. I've had so many distractions lately I've had very little time to think about June."

Mr. Quan lifts his eyebrows. "The newspaper? Yes, I have read of your troubles with our city and with this society." He takes a cigarette from the pack in his pocket and lights up, holding it palm-inward in the European style so that I picture him in a French cafe. "It is a reminder to me that as good as Charleston has been to me, it is not home." Turning to Allie, he says, "My suggestion. Do not let this get you down, young lady. Our people, yours and mine, would do the same. Were your father there, rather than we here, they would exclude him also."

"But this is America," she says. "We're not content with many attitudes prevalent in Asia."

"You are correct," he acknowledges. "Especially where women are concerned." Turning back to me, he says, "Did you know that I catered the St. Simeon last year?"

"Adelle mentioned that," I say. "I haven't attended for a while."

"They have contacted me again but in light of their position on your daughter I must decline."

"That's very loyal of you," I say. "But I'd hate to see you hurt your business over something you can't control."

"My humble protest," he says, blowing a curl of smoke upward. "My enterprise will do well without it. I read in the paper that your enterprise is affected as well."

"I think the worst is over," I say.

"Do not be discouraged by governments. They are of no consequence."

"Really?" I say, unable to contain my surprise that a man still a refugee from his native country would make such a statement. "They can make life hell if they aren't stable. But I don't guess I need to tell you that."

He watches me strangely, as though newly aware of my presence. "You refer to Vietnam?"

"Of course," I say, suddenly uncomfortable in that he never discusses it.

"Life is hell no matter who is in charge," he says. "The government in Saigon was corrupt, only slightly better than the group of cutthroats in Hanoi, and neither could change the nature of existence. There was suffering before, there is suffering now."

I cannot let this pass without protest. "But here in the United States, in Charleston, there is a freely elected government, and fundamental rights. Those make a difference."

"You remind me veddy tactfully that I have been free to build my enterprise here, without the oppression I encountered there."

"I don't know what you encountered there," I say, pausing to let him tell me. He stares at me blankly and says nothing. "But the quality of your life here has to beat anything you experienced in all that turmoil."

"Only in one respect," he says, "and perhaps not the one you mean. Here I have money, I have security in my enterprise, but these are minor benefits."

"Minor?"

"You are surprised, and I must sound to you ungrateful for this country. I am not. It has given me what I need most; the freedom to live correctly, to speak and act and think correctly. That is all that is important in life. It is why I must protest your daughter's exclusion from this society. In my country, my other country, it is called the way."

I am on the verge of asking him, "The way to what?" when there is a sharp rap on the door we entered earlier. Pham, Mr. Quan's manager, pokes his head inside. They exchange rapid Vietnamese, after which Mr. Quan rises.

"I asked to be notified if a particular supplier arrived. He is downstairs and I must see him. I will be only a few minutes." He walks unhurriedly to the door and closes it softly behind him.

"The conversation turned a little strange," Allie suggests and I agree.

"Don't forget," I say, "to discuss money with him. He hasn't said what he'll pay you."

"I'll mention it when he comes back," she says, leaving her chair and walking around the room restlessly. She inspects the music and observes that his taste is certainly varied. The videos are American classics, musicals and comedies mostly, plus a few Vietnamese videos of indecipherable subject matter. Next, she approaches the bookshelves and as she browses I pick up a dated issue of *Newsweek* and scan it casually.

"Dad, come in here," she says. She has gone through the doorway between the shelves and is calling from the adjoining room. "Look," she says as I enter.

She is pointing to an altar, layered with white linen and adorned with thin candles in a multiplicity of sizes. It is quite large and takes up half the wall. In its center is a jade Buddha statue approximately eight inches high, raised above the level of the table on a small wooden stand. Directly below hangs a scroll on which is depicted a spoke wheel. Small bowls, ceramic and charred on the bottoms, possibly for incense, flank the scroll. Spread among the candles are several delicate flowers made of glass. My eyes are drawn to a low table, off to one side of the altar and also decorated with candles. On it are fifteen or twenty framed photographs of Vietnamese of all ages. Some are posed, others are casual shots of groups at a picnic or at a shore, a few are the individual snapshots school children bring home. The quality of photographs vary, so that it appears this collection has been accumulated over a span of years. Near the center of the arrangement is an eight-by-ten of a wedding couple. As I study it in the dim light of the room—there are no lights on and no candles are lit—the groom in the picture looks out at me. Allie, drawn by my intensity, studies it also.

"It's him," she says. "It's Mr. Quan."

"He can't have been much older than you."

"Do you suppose this is his family?" she asks.

"I've never heard him mention one. Only a brother, who lives in Seoul, by the way. I've been meaning to mention that."

"His wife is very beautiful," she observes.

I am looking over the remaining photographs when I hear footsteps on the stairs. Turning to leave, I stop involuntarily. On the back wall hangs an enormous Vietnamese flag, three red stripes against a yellow background, the standard of the now extinct Republic of South Vietnam. We return to the living room and seat ourselves as Mr. Quan enters.

"Suppliers can be difficult," he says. Then winking, adds, "Owners can likewise be stubborn."

As he and Allie renew discussion of her summer employment I debate whether to ask him about what I've seen in the other room. I am curious as to why, having just told me that one government is as good as another, he so brazenly and defiantly displays the old flag. I want to ask about those photographs and his bride, where they were married, if any of those pictured are his children. Most of all, what happened to them? But we strayed into that room without invitation, and my sense of decorum bests my curiosity. After he and Allie agree that she will start "as soon as possible" after graduation for minimum wage plus tips, we depart.

"My suggestion. Take her to the land of her birth," he urges me by way of farewell. "I could call my brother. He knows the city now. And the language. He would be veddy kind to my customers."

"Yes, Dad, the land of my birth," she echoes as we wave good-bye and walk out onto the sidewalk.

Daylight is failing among the buildings as the sun begins its descent. Headlights are coming on among the few cars plying King Street and the neon signs of merchants are humming in the twilight calm, the sidewalks strangely deserted and the street lamps softening encroaching shadows.

"Can we stop by Mom's grave?" she asks as if seized by a sudden inspiration, and before I can respond she turns.

"We'll have to hurry," I say, picking up my pace to catch her.

We walk north on King Street, turn east at Queen, then north again on Church to the cemetery across from St. Philip's. They will lock the gates soon. We hustle past the tomb and monument to John C. Calhoun toward the back wall and the Carter family plot. The carpet of brown grass shows no sign of spring. We are the only visitors.

Elizabeth's headstone is modest, engraved with her name and the dates of her birth and death as she instructed. Nearing, we slow our pace. I am comfortable here now, although in the weeks following the funeral I left church by a side door in order to avoid looking at the mournful magnolia tree that stands near the wall. When I visit with the children, we seldom say much, each preferring the solitude of thoughts commingled with the reinforcing presence of each other. But this afternoon, Allie is talkative.

"The job looks like it will work out," she says. "My leaving for Princeton on the fifteenth will leave him a little short for a couple of weeks but I guess that's a slow period anyway."

The cemetery is well groomed, but several brown magnolia leaves have fallen onto the plot and I stoop to collect them.

"I've got an idea," I say, stretching for a leaf near the headstone. "For graduation, how about a trip to San Francisco? You've told me how much you want to see it."

"That would be nice," she concedes, "but it's not my first choice."

Allie is standing at the foot of the plot, her arms folded and her head inclined toward the marker. From the corner of my eye I see her staring at the engraved name, but whether her thoughts are of me, of Elizabeth, or of herself, I cannot tell. Nearby, a sapling stands naked of a single leaf, its stark branches adorned only by a sparrow perched forlornly near the top. The church bells toll a reminder that the caretaker will soon come to lock the gates. The sparrow flees.

"Dad, if I died could I be buried here, in St. Philip's?"

"Of course," I say, not positive but unaware of anything that would prevent it. "What an odd question."

"Not really," she says. "Think about it." The morning's distance has returned, and she seems unconcerned whether I think about it or not.

"Sweetheart, the St. Simeon isn't directing this at you personally. The fact that it never makes exceptions shows that this has nothing to do with who you are and everything to do with clinging to who they are."

"I don't think," she says, her eyes still focused on the name, "Mom would want us to take this lying down."

"Is that what we're doing?" I ask, my voice betraying my own doubts.

"Aren't we?" The royal "we," but the message unmistakable.

"No. I'm still looking for an answer. Margarite is looking as well. Something may turn up."

I cannot bring myself to discuss Margarite. From the moment of Allie's arrival, she has gone out of her way to indulge her in the unique displays of affection usually bestowed by adoring aunts. At her Christening, she gave a sterling silver cross Allie still wears. When Allie had the measles, Margarite came by daily with ice cream and to read stories. Allie played T-ball, and Margarite rarely missed a single chaotic inning. After her confirmation at St. Philip's, Margarite threw an elaborate reception for all the communicants, but in that she had never previously given one, and has not since, I feel certain that it was a gesture of generosity directed exclusively at my daughter. No, I must preserve Margarite's image as a beneficent godmother; anything less would hurt Allie beyond measure.

"I've been thinking a lot about Natalie Berman," she says. "The paper says you've given up the idea of suing, although I know you never thought seriously about it anyway."

It occurs to me in the diminishing twilight that all day she has been choosing her time and her words; that this trip to Elizabeth's grave is not spontaneous but meant to dramatize, in a macabre but effective way, the contrast between our approaches to the St. Simeon. I circle my wagons, relating the story of Natalie's parents and the country club. "So her victory," I say, "if you want to call it that, was hollow, like a lot of litigation ends up being. She won admittance to a club that didn't want her, where she wasn't accepted and couldn't comfortably go. So what did she win? Is that what you want? Once the well is poisoned, you can't drink from it."

"There was obviously a principle at stake," she says. "She won that."

"I wonder," I respond. In the deep dusk between us now I cannot make out her face but only the contour of her body, standing very still with her head yet inclined toward the marker. "I have a theory that she's a very lonely woman. Besides, at the risk of playing the devil's advocate, there is a principle at stake for the St. Simeons too."

"What is that?" she wants to know.

"Sweetheart, everywhere you look there is change. It frightens people. It always has, but now it seems to be accelerating. At a time when the entire country is losing its culture, these people want to celebrate something that is nailed down, something they can count on being like it was last year and forever before that. They have to adapt to so much that is out of their control that they value even more highly those few things that remain permanent. The St. Simeon is one of those things."

"You sound as though you agree with them." Her voice is even.

"No, but I understand them. After all, I'm one of them."

"I can understand how change frightens people," she says. Then, as if changing the subject, she says, "Dad, the Arts Center project?"

"Yes?"

"Your firm is working pretty hard to get that contract."

"We've put a lot into it, that's true."

"But won't they have to tear down a lot of old homes to make room for it?" In the dimness she turns her head to me. "But I guess that's different." She turns and walks briskly toward the gate, leaving me as alone as I have ever been.

I discard the leaves and follow, but she quickens her stride to maintain the gap between us. I break into a trot, but keys and change jangle in my pocket and she can monitor my approach without looking back. She accelerates, jogging now. I speed up and look for shortcuts to intercept her. There are none, and her conditioning begins to tell as we near the house. I am reluctant to call out, advertising this unseemly chase, but near the house I yell her name and, panting heavily, ask her to stop. She breaks into a full sprint, reaching the door and slamming it behind. As I slump into the foyer, her door upstairs closes with a telltale snap of the lock.

I bend over, hands on my knees, my breath coming in gulps and gasps and my pulse racing beyond any rate achieved by tennis, even strenuous singles. Slowly, the wind returns and I grow calm.

An hour later, I tap timidly on her door. Silence. I knock again, harder. More silence. I press my ear to the panel and hear no sound within.

"Allie, open up. I have more to say."

"Leave me alone."

"Please, sweetheart."

"I've heard it. Go away, I'm tired."

The St. Simeon, I now realize, has become for her a mere skirmish in a wider war, having far less to do with Charleston's stubbornness than my own. Her allusion to "taking it lying down" is a lethally directed indictment of my failure to force the issue, to assault in her name and stead the consanguineous fortress. Elizabeth would have done it, and her ghost hovers over this battle ground like a skirted Napoleon. I knock again, impatiently.

"I'm not leaving here until we talk," I say. "If it takes all night."

There is only silence, but then something in the room stirs and moments later the lock retracts. The door swings wide, exposing her back as she strides to her bed, flopping down without a glance in my direction. She wears her flannel pajamas and a robe.

"That was quite a pace you set," I say. "Have you considered your guilt if I drop dead of a heart attack tonight?" She does not smile. A long silence ensues, lengthening painfully as I search for an approach. In the vacuum, I resolve on the method she most prefers: direct.

"You're disappointed in me," I say.

"I'm confused. I thought you'd be on my side." She is visibly upset, but her eyes are dry and her gaze at the wall hard.

"Does that mean I have to come out swinging?"

"We're getting punched, or at least I am."

"We, and yes it seems that way."

"You should have warned me. If you had come to me and said, 'Look, this is something that I can't control and that's the way it is so get over it,' I'd have probably forgotten about it by now."

"I gave you false encouragement. I regret that."

"And now it's in the papers, a public humiliation and my own father saying he won't lift a finger."

"I didn't say that. I said I wouldn't sue."

"What else is there, wring your hands?"

"I deserve your sarcasm but it hurts."

"Well, join the crowd." She has picked up a throw pillow and kneads it aggressively.

I commandeer the chair from her study desk, bring it over by the bed, and straddle it in reverse, my arms folded atop the back. "I don't blame you for being upset. But regardless of what you're thinking, I have a stake in this too."

"Not any more. That Arts Center deal is in the bag from what I've read."

"Sweetheart, I don't give hoot or holler about the Arts Center. My stake in this is much more personal. Of course I'm on your side, and of course I want to see you go. But I want it done in a way that allows us both to feel like we've won a point, not forced one."

"I don't get what you mean."

"I'm not sure I can explain it because I don't fully understand it myself. I've had a lot of . . . turmoil lately. Within. I'm not asking for your sympathy, only your awareness." She pulls her knees up, sets the pillow on them and rests her chin as she stares at me blankly. "The Society represents tradition; one that I value and enjoy, or at least have up until now. There are all kinds of clubs and organizations I'm not eligible for: foreign war veterans, skydivers, survivors of disasters, alumni of colleges, left handers, IQ gifted—the list goes on. They each represent a niche of some kind, many exceedingly narrow. The St. Simeon's niche happens to be blood or marital descent from the original members. Call it retarded, call it regressive, but that's its niche. You with me?"

She nods faintly, her mouth flattening in an exaggerated boredom.

"Now, things change, and perhaps it's time for this tradition to pass the way of many others. Someone could make a good case for that and I, were I on the Board, might be persuaded. But until then, we're left with the rules we have, and those rules appear on the surface to exclude adopted children."

"But that's so—"

"Let me finish, and what I'm about to say has everything to do with me and little directly to do with you. Suppose this issue involved someone else's daughter. In all fairness, I should support an exemption for him or her if I'm prepared to argue for yours, as I've done. Shouldn't I?"

"I suppose so. You don't want to look like a hypocrite."

"I don't want to be a hypocrite. It all comes down to power."

"Power?"

"Yes, more of my world spilling over into yours. Every day I see things done by people because they have the power, not necessarily the right. In my business, for example, big people run over little people because they can afford the fees at Carter & Deas. They don't give a damn if they're right or wrong; if they hire the smartest and meanest lawyers available they win, which is all they care about. Or the punk in the streets. He doesn't resort to high-priced legal talent, he takes his with a gun. A part of me is jaded enough not to want to play that power game."

"In other words, you don't want to get me in just because you can."

"I want to win, want you to win, by the rules because it's the only way to have anything worth winning when the dust settles."

Her nod is rote, and if I have made a dent in her disillusion it is a small one. She yawns.

In the days following, we speak as always, but it is the perfunctory language of living within the same walls. Without so much as a scintilla of disrespect, she has put an unbridgeable distance between us. She is courteous, but not overly so; businesslike without being gloomy; responsive, but only so far as necessary. She goes about her day with her usual efficiency, seldom idle and with no wasted motions like her kiss on the top of my head as she leaves for school. She is disengaging from me at the most precious level, subtracting out her true self from my formula for existence, and it is unbearable.

On Sunday, I go to church alone. I sit in the family pew removed from the service and those around me. To the sermon I bring the same concentration I have brought to my work these past few days, and as Rev. Frank Kent puts a final emphatic flourish on his message, I am unable to recall a word he has said. The view out of the stained glass windows seems every bit my view of the world; fractured, distorted, turbid. In the center of my ancestral Mecca, where I was baptized, where my parents were married, where such spirituality as I harbor has been nourished and redeemed, where I greet those who enter with a warmth that embraces all this means to me, I am alone. The service ends with a Lenten dirge, sad and funereal. As the crucifix passes, I nod mechanically. The choir's lament seems directed at me, and I stand with no book open, none of its woeful tune on my lips but every note and chord a ballast threatening to take me deeper. Rev. Kent booms out his benediction. The congregation around me rises. I remain motionless, unable to face them or make conversation. Waiting for the church to clear, I feel a bangled hand on my shoulder from behind. Margarite leans over and whispers, "Come see me, dear. I have news."

27

Monday's mail brings engraved invitations addressed to Josh, Steven and me.

ST. SIMEON SOCIETY

THE HONOR OF YOUR COMPANY IS REQUESTED AT THE

SOCIETY HALL . . .

Date and time follow; the nature of the function does not. No one eligible has to ask. The kitchen trash can receives all three.

Margarite refused elaboration in church, pleading a social engagement in Beaufort, to which she was already running late. "Come see me tomorrow night," she instructed. She must have sensed my hesitation because she added quickly, looking down where I remained seated, half turned to her, "It's not an answer but it may lead to one." She rushed off before I could utter the skepticism lodged in my throat.

At the office today replays of her overture, all of thirty seconds in duration, shredded my already tattered concentration as I tried to regain a sense of the moment, studying her in flashback for signs she knows I know. Perhaps some sixth sense has triggered in her a need for damage control. If so, she will need every potion and spell available in her Haiti habitat and beyond. But I will listen.

Daniel answers my ring as before, this evening steering me to the library. I enter through double oak doors, highly finished. The room is empty. A roaring fire blazes beneath a shoulder-high mantel of grained white Italian marble. Near it, I sink into the cloud-like comfort of an overstuffed wing chair covered in oxblood leather. Daniel announces Margarite's imminent appearance and brings coffee.

Margarite enters, dressed as casually as before, now in a navy blue running suit trimmed in pink, and sneakers. If she feels the least uneasiness about confronting me, it does not show. She extends both hands, greeting me warmly.

"I'm excited," she says, approaching the fire. "It's like working on a murder mystery."

Daniel brings a clear glass of amber liquid, her Old Granddad, which she sets neatly on the mantel near an ancient clock displaying both time and phases of the moon. Above her hangs a portrait of General William Rhett Barnwell, her ancestor from the Revolutionary era. "Blushing Billy," Margarite calls him. The source of his name is local legend.

In the months preceding the Declaration of Independence, British Admirals Parker and Clinton arrived off the coast with a substantial force of regulars assumed to have orders to occupy the restless city. General Barnwell, then a captain serving under Major General Charles Lee, the American commander, was delegated by General Lee the odious task of razing some buildings along the Cooper so as to widen the effective angle of fire for new cannons mounted to resist the British. Ironically, among the buildings ordered sacrificed was the home of Captain Barnwell's aunt, Annie.

Aunt Annie was a high-strung spinster whose loyalties were entirely with her royal ancestors. She held British occupation a singular honor. "After all, His Majesty's forces don't occupy just anywhere." For the entire war Aunt Annie fumed over her lost home, holding her nephew responsible not only for the desecration but for Tory demise as well. Several days after news of the British defeat at Yorktown reached Charleston, Barnwell, recently promoted to general, toured the site of the demolished buildings accompanied by a ranking delegation surveying war reparations. Aunt Annie, forced by public sentiment to muzzle her support for her gallant men in red for the entire duration of the war, boiled over. Hearing of the tour, she carried from her substitute residence a rocking chair, which she placed squarely amidst the ruins of her former residence. She knitted and rocked, surrounded by rubble, as the perplexed delegation approached. When they reached what had once been her door, she rose, hailed her mortified nephew gaily, introduced herself to each member as "General Barnwell's favorite aunt," and invited them in for tea and "a cake I just this minute took out of the oven." Blushing Billy's explanations to his entourage have not survived.

"Nothing in this world," Margarite says, "is completely consistent, not even the St. Simeon as it turns out. The trouble is that the legacy of secrets leaves very little to go on."

"It's quite frustrating," I agree. My tone is businesslike and removed, appropriate to what is already a strange encounter. Why she has brought me here, having done all she can to undermine me, is the real mystery. I am anticipating revelation of some trivial detail that will allow her to play the role of supporting friend, but get Allie no closer. It is too much, and I am going to call her hand, tonight.

The glass comes down for a healthy swig of her bourbon. "It's like those oral histories you hear so much about these days; families who don't write things down but pass the details of their heritage along from one generation to the next by spoken word."

I will bide my time, I whisper internally. When her "news" confirms my hunch, I will put to her the questions no one in her position will look forward to answering, questions like why she has waited until invitations have gone out to share this news and why, among a committee sworn to secrecy, no one will discuss with me the results of the vote but at least one member has been willing to share its outcome with the press. Margarite squirming is not an easy image to conjure up, but I try. If it weren't so devastating to have her, of all people, revealed as the culprit, the unveiling might be entertaining. She is earnest and relaxed in front of me, and I will play the foil as adroitly. I relate my research efforts at the paper and the library.

"So you found nothing?" she says.

"Bits and pieces that don't point anywhere. Clearly you've had better luck."

"That's exactly how I would categorize it," she says. "Pure, random luck. Do you know Alger Hart?"

"No."

"Alger is an old friend, in his eighties now. He served as the librarian at the College of Charleston years ago. I think the term 'walking encyclopedia' must have been coined with him in mind."

I am disgusted to find myself wondering if Alger Hart exists, or if he exists whether he has ever been more intimately associated with the library at the college than a patron paying a fine for an overdue book. My cynicism grows malignant, where cancerous disbelief in everything she is saying has attacked healthy faith in a matter of days. My eyes stray up to the imposing portrait above her. Was there really was a Blushing Billy? "And what did Alger allow?" I ask, willing my doubt into remission until the right moment.

"He didn't claim to know much at all about the Society," she says. "But he's read countless biographies, certainly more than anyone else I know. He said he had a vague recollection of something read years before, decades probably, in which a biographer recounted his subject's unexpected invitation to the St. Simeon Ball."

"Who was it?" I ask.

Margarite sips her drink, then grins mischievously. She is relishing whatever sop she is about to spin out, her cat-with-the-canary look heightened by her eyes alive with intrigue. I grudgingly award her full credit for style points.

"Guess," she says.

"No idea," I admit, shrugging.

"I'll give you a clue. He's foreign."

"Is or was?"

"Was."

"I give up."

"Well," Margarite says, lifting her head and feigning the haughtiness to which her ancestry entitles her but of which she seems capable only, as now, by design. "I didn't give up. Whomever it was had to be important enough to be the subject of a biography that would have come to Alger's notice. Also, dead long enough to have been written about years ago."

I nod, unable to fault her logic and, against my wishes, being drawn into the suspense of the anonymous invitee.

"I spent a lot of time," she continues, "focusing on Civil War personalities."

"Why them?"

She purses her lips primly. "In hindsight, I'm not certain. I suppose because many of the outstanding leaders came from backgrounds that would not have permitted them legitimate access to St. Simeon. In the rush of war fervor, a war hero could have been invited as a demonstration of esteem and gratitude."

"Beauregard. He was an aristocrat but not from Charleston."

She smiles. "My first guess precisely, but wrong. I read his biography cover to cover and did find a reference that will interest you. Beauregard, the savior of Charleston, was very pointedly not invited to the ball, a slight which angered him according to his biographer."

"A blind alley," I note. If she indeed read such a work, she has gone to a lot of trouble in perpetuation of this ruse. I decide to test her. "Didn't Beauregard go to Harvard?" I ask, my quizzical expression forced.

"Lord, no. West Point. His family had some history at Harvard but he was trained as a soldier from the outset."

The right answer. Either she read the book, knew West Point from another source, or guessed.

"I returned to Alger," she continues. "I showed him the passage and asked if this could be what he had remembered, obviously inaccurately. He nodded and said that yes, he had read Beauregard's biography, that he had forgotten about the St. Simeon slight, but that he was reasonably sure the man he was thinking about had been invited, not excluded. That was what made it memorable. So I went back to work."

Gradually, word by word, gesture by gesture, Margarite's hoax is being revealed as something genuine, although whether goodwill lies behind the honest effort I cannot yet say. I am like a cynic who comes to a play, a tragedy, fully braced for the dramatic artifices by which an accomplished actress will draw me into her fictional predicament, only to discover, or be convinced, that her distress is real, but unwilling to depart from my role as skeptic for fear of being made the fool. The truth is on the stage, the lie among the audience. Or is it?

"But," she continues, "Beauregard, being from New Orleans and therefore a foreigner as far as Charlestonians were concerned, inspired me to consider other prominent visitors, and that is where I struck gold." She leaves the hearth and walks to a shelf, from which she takes an old book, handing it to me with an expression of triumph.

I open it to the title page: *The Life and Times of the Marquis de Lafayette.* The author is French, and the translation is by one Maurice Poultet.

"Go to the bookmark," she instructs.

On page 341, there appears the following:

Nowhere along his grand farewell tour of America did Lafayette encounter more raw, raucous congeniality than in Charleston, the port

> city in the state of South Carolina. Lavishly praised, wondrously feted, Lafayette was touched beyond words according to Mr. Timothy Ford, one of his many hosts during his stay in the city its natives call 'Holy.' Parades preceded receptions followed by dinners, more speeches, honorary titles and gifts of the finest silver and china available anywhere, inundating the aging Frenchman with riches to the point of embarrassment. If, as he had heard, Charleston's Tory sympathies at the outset of the war were stronger than those held in Richmond or Philadelphia, they had, by 1824, dissipated beyond recognition, supplanted by a nationalism unrivalled during the old man's tour.
>
> In that his stay coincided with an annual gala held by the Society of St. Simeon, he was accorded an invitation delivered personally with great fanfare by Mr. Joseph Keenan, president. Lafayette attended the ball, reporting to his hosts at that time a 'glorious evening of formal dancing, lovely ladies and memorable spirits,' although, as he later learned, his invitation was attended by no small amount of internal dissension within the Society and harsh words among some members owing to an exclusivity rigidly enforced.

"Holy Pete," I say, looking up to find her waiting expectantly.

"Fascinating, isn't it? When I read the part about internal dissension and harsh words I almost fell out of my chair. Nothing has changed since 1824."

"Except they issued him the invitation," I remind her. "Wouldn't you love to have been a fly on the wall of that meeting?"

"In a way, I became one."

"How?" I am increasingly impressed by her diligence.

"Another book, this one an autobiography of Randolph Manigault. I found it among all those dusty tomes in the Historical Society library. Since I now knew the year, my search was narrowed to men active in St. Simeon at that time. He turned out to be one of the few who published his memoirs."

I close the book, resting it in my lap. "Are you about to tell me he was present during the harsh words?"

Margarite beams. "I am. If you'll put another log on our fire I'll get Daniel to fix me another drink. Would you like one?"

"Maybe later." I have finished my chore before she returns with her glass.

"Where was I?" she asks.

"About to give me Manigault's account of the meeting."

"Oh, yes. It must have been fierce, this meeting. Invitations had gone out weeks before, of course, long before Lafayette's arrival. A few members voiced opposition to issuing a late invitation as socially unacceptable, but this appears from Manigault's account to have been a minor flap. The majority—there were nine people there for the debate although he doesn't identify the others—felt that because no one knew Lafayette's schedule with any certainty before his arrival, the hasty invitation was excusable."

"So that was the easy part," I say.

"Compared to what followed, a virtual walk in the park. Apparently, the lines were drawn early, with each side represented by a powerful man whom, as I said, Manigault does not name. The majority cited Lafayette's service to America, the toll the war took on his personal fortune, and one other very practical fact: On the night of the ball, everyone who was anyone in Charleston, including Lafayette's hosts, would be attending, leaving an unexplained void in his schedule. The spokesman for the majority pointed up the risk of Lafayette finding out where everyone was and taking offense at being excluded, for which you could hardly blame him. This observation seems to have carried a lot of weight."

"I can guess where the cons were coming from," I say dryly.

"Their leader—I'm determined to find out who he was—made every argument I heard when Allie's request was being considered. He talked about heritage of blood, about homogeneous societies, about the privileges that are reserved for those who bear the responsibilities of leadership, a slant on noblesse oblige."

"I can hear him now," I say, and I can. "All to no avail."

"He won a small victory," she corrects, "important to Allie's cause. He insisted after the vote that because Lafayette was about to become the first exception in the Society's history, a rule be passed embracing it. He therefore proposed what Manigault calls the Lafayette exemption and," she says after a meaningful pause, "it passed."

"I'll be damned," I say. "Does Manigault record the exemption?"

She does not answer but instead reaches into the zippered pocket of her running suit, extracting a folded piece of paper. "I knew you'd need this so I copied it verbatim. It says, 'Special invitations to the annual gala may be extended from time to time by a majority vote to foreigners of royal descent or distinguished birth.'"

"That seems like odd phrasing," I say.

"Not if you read Manigault's account. I tried to check the book out, incidentally, but you know the library's policy on reserves. The leader of the cons, whomever he was, feared that a single exemption, adopted for a celebrated individual without criteria or guidelines, would inevitably lead to exemptions, first for lesser notables than Lafayette, and then for people who were merely friends of committee members, notable for little else."

"Without a policy the floodgates would open. I can see that."

"A better choice, they decided, and this seems to have been almost unanimous, would be a policy that would appear to encompass others besides Lafayette but in fact would not, absent the most unusual circumstances."

"Incredible," I say, taking the paper from her and turning toward the light. "I wonder if anyone has come within this exception since Lafayette?"

"That," she says smiling, "I'll leave you to research. Now, given what we've learned, I need to ask a question. How much do you know about Allie's birth?"

"Less than 'the biologicals', as Allie calls them," I deadpan. One response seems as good as another to a question plumbing an imponderable, not that I haven't plumbed it over the years. Life's disasters have a way of rushing at you, nailing you violently against a high wall with your feet flailing helplessly and your senses crazed. But the miracles steal upon you softly with padded steps, opening before you like a flower. I look again at the wording of the Lafayette exemption as Margarite sits patiently by. "We know little," I confess. "Remarkably little."

She calmly accepts this. "I assumed as much, in that I had never heard it mentioned. Do you suppose there is any way to find out?"

"I doubt it. So much time, records probably destroyed—it would be almost impossible. We had such scant information when we got her."

"Maybe they knew more than they shared."

"It's possible," I admit.

"The important thing is that a documented precedent exists. It seems better than nothing, although perhaps that's simply wishful thinking on my part."

I stare at her, the actor in the audience baffled. All thoughts of calling her hand have fled, yet doubt lingers. Her research has been arduous and fruitful, miles beyond the sop I anticipated. That the uncovered loophole is tiny, an eyelet where an adit is demanded, cannot be charged to Margarite. Still, the very scantiness of the hole confirms the stoutness of the dike; in two-hundred-plus years a single exception has been documented, and that in favor of a universally acclaimed war hero and not without controversy. If anything, the odds have shown themselves lengthened.

"Margarite, I've got to hand it to you. What you've come up with may not be enough but it beats what I was able to do. Thanks."

"Don't thank me. My guilt over this entire thing was motivation enough. And I don't intend to stop here. I'm going to pull out every stop I can between now and the Ball, so don't give up hope. Those shall we say 'less foresighted' members of my Board will hear more from me."

Driving home, I am more perplexed than ever, vacillating evenly between tracking down Alger Hart to verify her account and welcoming her back into the void inside me since sniffing betrayal. I am both heartened and discouraged, buoyed and deflated. But whatever my outlook, the inescapable reality looms just weeks ahead: Allie will be excluded unless I act.

I pull the car to the curb of South Battery and turn off the engine. The night is fair and mild and the breeze at the top of the seawall clears my head. A quarter moon is rising over the ocean, slivering the top of whitecaps like shards of china. Perhaps, I think, I am making too much of this Ball business. Sarah said it best when she reminded me that from Allie's first day with us, even before she arrived, we knew she would face limits. In fact, she has faced damn few, and this the biggest. But why fight it? Is one evening of her life going to alter the path of success she has so nimbly trod? Is there a single sinew in her well-toned body that will snap at this rejection? Not a chance, I reassure. I'll tell her so in just those words. And Natalie Berman too.

Natalie. What is it about her that simultaneously repels and attracts? This is her business only to the extent she has made it so, yet something in me seeks to justify itself in her eyes. I owe her nothing, less than nothing in light of the trouble she has made, but how much better I would feel if she acquiesced in the wisdom of surrender to the inevitable. She won't, I tell myself leaning over the railing, feeling the chill of the metal penetrate my shirt and forearms. Her type never sees a controversy they wouldn't be better off in the center of. So why worry about her?

I think back to Allie's retreat from Elizabeth's grave, my banging on her door, and the chill between us since. Suppose she refuses to accept this limit like she has disdained so many others? I have long suspected she holds Elizabeth's penchant for war more dear than mine for peace. I know, as surely as I stand here gazing toward the coast of North Africa, that I cannot risk her further disappointment in me. Natalie Berman may curse me to her content, but Allie must love and respect me as she always has and kiss me on the head when she leaves.

I turn, leap from the seawall to the pavement, and rush back to my car. At home, I look for the file from Open Arms. I haven't seen it in years, but locate it among some old financial records. From the Open Arms letterhead, I get the number for its headquarters in Minneapolis. I don't expect anyone to answer at this time of night, but I can at least leave a message. Someone does answer, mistaking me for a telemarketer until I explain. I've reached the Gunderson residence and no, they've never heard of the agency. I call information. No listing. Open Arms has apparently closed its doors. Then, I remember Mr. Quan's brother, the only contact I can think of in Seoul. There is but one alternative to Natalie Berman and her scorched earth, and that is the slender reed just held out by Margarite. It may collapse of its own weight, but I will lean on it until it does. At least it is something. I drive off.

Mr. Quan is seated at his usual place near the back when I enter. He hails me over, but appears to sense in my stride or the stiffness of my greeting a business purpose to this visit. In his apartment, I relate Margarite's research and my failure to contact a working number for Open Arms. I explain the need to find the Korean Children's Home.

"There's no address in the file."

He takes out a pen, jots down the name, and says, "I will call my brother. He will find it. You require only an address?"

"I'd love to know if they have files going as far back as 1978."

"I will tell him my best customer and a future employee must know. He will understand a need like that."

I thank him and return home. It is not much, but it is something, I tell myself as I climb the stairs to render to Allie a report of my evening.

28

The Camden Cup, a steeplechase held annually in spring, serves in its rambunctious way as an outdoor compliment to the St. Simeon Ball. You see many of the same people at both and each has accumulated a legacy worthy of the appellation "command performance." Some have observed that, given the massive crowds, the incessant drinking, and the shoehorned socializing, the chances of seeing a horse at the Cup are not much better than at the Ball.

Criteria for entry is the humble price of admission, yet tradition and heritage are as much on display as festive spring wardrobes and late model cars. There is nothing quite so chic as eating fried chicken and gulping bourbon from the trunk of a new Mercedes, and South Carolinians soak up the sun and the dust in equal measure to be seen at this sacred rite of spring.

We often go, but today the sixth race, for the Cup, brings us here. Allie is riding. Female jockeys in this event are still uncommon but hardly unprecedented; she herself rode last year in an early race and finished fourth. My car is bloated as we drive west on I-26, with Adelle and Sarah in the front with me and Allie, Christopher and Steven in the back. In the boot I have stored enough food to feed Mosby's Rangers. Allie arose early to trailer her horse and stow her tack; both should be there when we arrive.

Adelle and Sarah indulge in Bloody Marys, bushy stalks of celery protruding like miniature palm trees from their glasses. Traffic hums along, every car's occupants inspecting every other's like they do when Carolina plays Clemson and fans of both clog the state's major arteries. Clemson/Carolina and the Camden Cup commandeer the road system as effectively as martial law, and not a mile passes without one of us waving to some pilgrim we know.

As we near the grounds we slow to an idling creep. The first race will not be run for two hours and already acres of tailgaters are parked and set up. Steven cracks his first beer of the day and inquires of Sarah how his trap is doing.

"I'm so glad you reminded me," she says, turning toward the back seat. "That raccoon is the slipperiest creature you can imagine. He keeps getting into the garbage but he's never there in the morning."

"The trap isn't working," Steven says, disappointed.

"You know, I have a theory that the noise of the top falling startles him and he bolts through the door before it can close on him."

Steven is doubtful. "Then how does the garbage get out of the can?"

She cocks her head, considering this carefully. "Well, I just don't know."

"Must be a small hole in the fence somewhere," he says. "I'll come check it out for you."

Sarah again faces forward as we inch along, the windows raised to seal out dust for a little longer. "I wish you would," she says. "Poor Ralph got himself trapped again the other day. I heard him yelping early in the morning and let him out. I'm afraid that one of these days I'll be away and he'll starve in there, or die of thirst."

Christopher claps Allie affectionately on the shoulder. "Do good today," he says. "I bet a bunch on the sixth race so bring home the bacon." In the rear view mirror I see her flash a smile I recognize as controlled nervousness. Her mind is on the race and will be until it's over.

Adelle stirs her drink with the celery and asks Allie which horse she'll be riding. "Carbon Copy," Allie says. "A man named Jamison asked me to ride him. He trains in Aiken. I rode him a few times this fall."

"How good is he?" Adelle asks.

"Great by himself over fences and hedges but skittish around other horses. If I don't ride him strong he'll take a bath."

"I may join him," says Adelle with a chuckle. "When it's hot and dusty at this thing I can't think of much else by the last race."

We arrive at the gate where I tender my money. A rotund teen in a loud T-shirt—"Toad the Wet Sprocket," whatever that is—waves us on. A lengthy, serpentine route threads us through until we park, climb gratefully out, and stretch out car cramps. The race course is not visible from this spot due to the revetment of people parked along the rail, not that they are anymore interested in the actual races than those parked away. Proximity measures arrival time rather than devotion to sport, and those closest toasted dawn with Bloody Mary's and champagne cocktails. Whether they are standing when the last trumpet beckons horses to the starting gate is often a matter of degree.

Protocol at the Cup requires first, a drink if, like me, you have borne the responsibility of driving. Next, tailgates lower, trunks open, or card tables unfold before linen tablecloths cover them. Wicker baskets and coolers abound, but so do chaffing dishes and ice buckets.

Setting your spread here is not unlike maintaining your yard at home; properly done it makes a statement. I aim for a panache I once heard described as elegantly shabby. Achieving it is not easy in a $50,000 Range Rover. It demands beat-up flasks, but leather and venerable, with each scuff and scar earned in battle inside some crowded football stadium. Wicker is out, but Tupperware is okay for the food as long as drinks are served in glasses of good quality displaying logos from a sun or ski resort. No one striving for elegantly shabby would be caught dead using ice tongs.

Adelle and I set our spread as the kids drift off to scope the crowd. Sarah has brought her favorite lawn chair and will let the crowd come to her. Adelle, unwrapping chicken salad sandwiches, asks if I've had any luck contacting the orphanage.

"Not yet."

"Time's getting short," she observes. "Allie tells me she's going to work for Mr. Quan this summer."

"That's true," I say, gumming a deviled egg.

"Does that surprise you?" She is busy with the spread and means to sound flip but her tone has an underpinning of seriousness.

"Not really. It could be her last summer at home."

"You don't think it's just to be near Chris?"

I smile at her. "That could have been one factor in her decision." She smiles back, but tension renders it flat. "Adelle, are you in your 'they're getting too serious' mode again? If so, stop worrying. They're level-headed kids."

"I realize that. It's just that they're together all the time and hormones play strange tricks."

This is not her first reference to an animal attraction between these two. "What makes you so sure it's hormones?" I ask, not without my own edge. "What if they simply like each other's company? Is that so hard to imagine?"

"You know what I mean."

"No, I don't. Whenever you talk about them I come away with a picture of two lustful degenerates who have trouble keeping their clothes on."

"Oh, Coleman, you're exaggerating."

"You seem to believe their relationship is entirely physical instead of just a couple of sweet kids in love."

"They're not in love. Don't be absurd."

"How do you know? And why is that absurd?"

"I'm sorry. Absurd is too strong. It's unlikely."

Before I can respond, Jessie Tolbert, an old friend from Orangeburg, approaches and calls me a rat fucker. One difference between the Cup and the Ball is that at the latter I run a very low risk of being called a rat fucker, at least to my face. But Jessie is a lovable redneck who would plow your field, bale your hay, and paint your barn if you needed it done, and his unlikely term of endearment is lavished on forty or fifty of his closest friends. We hug and I offer him the drink I know he'll take. Jessie greets Adelle and Sarah with more reserve, hitching up low-slung jeans and waving a calloused hand while asking, "How y'all doin'?" I breathe easier. Sarah, whose tolerance level is substantial, draws the line at being called a rat fucker, and were Jessie to do so she would revert to that puzzled look she gets when something sails by her, ask him to repeat it, then turn a shade darker than the Bloody Mary she is holding.

Cars continue to pour through the several gates sprinkled around the perimeter. Old friends hail each other, careful not to spill drinks in their rush to embrace. The college men tend toward war cries for salutations while the women squeal a lot. There is much whooping and squealing near our car.

I check the sky. Some low clouds scud across from the west but they look benign and the sun will be out by the first race, still over an hour away. A good time to work the crowd. Adelle and Sarah are talking with three of Adelle's friends so I pop a beer and strike off on my own. I have not gone thirty yards when I bump into Dick and Karen Lambert, old friends who left Charleston for Greenville several years ago when Dick's company transferred him. They sent flowers to Elizabeth's funeral but a sick child kept them from the service. We establish three years as the last time we've been together. Forty-five minutes later, we agree to meet for the last race. Allie's first babysitting job was for the Lamberts and they want to see her ride.

Ten yards further I meet another old friend. It is nearing the start of the first race and I am still within sight of my car. Adelle and Mother are engaged with new company so I continue around, shaking hands, slapping backs, kissing women old and young. At one point I spot the kids and wave. I am absorbed in the meeting-and-greeting demanded here when, over the shoulder of a woman who used to be my secretary, I see Natalie Berman.

She is alone, walking casually toward me, a red insulated cup in one hand. I turn away, still speaking with my former secretary, when Natalie walks by. She is wearing jeans, tight and new, as are her boots. Her blouse is ruffled, covered by a lightweight jacket the same color as the cup she is holding. I would bet she has not seen me.

A trumpet sounds signaling the start of the first race. Natalie pauses, changes direction, then walks toward the course. I break away from my friend and follow from a safe distance behind. At the rail she eases in among the crowd and from fifteen yards I see her head turn as the horses thunder past. When the race ends those around disburse, leaving her leaning on the rail. I approach and lean beside her.

"Hello, counselor," I say, wondering how I'll be received.

"Hello," she returns. "It's nice to see a familiar face. Are you a regular?"

"Pretty much. I've missed a few."

"I've missed them all," she says. "My first one. Quite a spectacle."

"Just wait," I suggest. "It's sedate now compared to what you'll see this afternoon."

"So I've heard. Didn't I see your daughter listed as one of the riders?"

"Sixth race. The Cup."

"Does she have a chance?"

"Outside," I say, shrugging. "It's a tough field and she and this horse don't have a terribly long history together."

Natalie smiles, warmly. "I'll put some money on her. I like long shots."

"Did you come by yourself?"

"I did," she says. "I couldn't pass up a chance to work on becoming a 'good ole girl.' Does everyone here know everyone else? I've never seen such a reunion."

I nod. "It's what keeps us coming back."

We stare ahead at the course being readied for the next race. Crossbars have been dislodged from three jumps and must be replaced. After this momentary lull, Natalie inquires about the St. Simeon. I relate my evening with Margarite and the discovered exemption. I realize I am elaborating to lend bulk to an effort lamentably thin, posturing to appear forceful and decisive before someone whose aggressiveness I have condemned. I watch her closely for signs of reproach, but see nothing beyond sincere interest in what I am telling her.

"I hope it works," she says. "For your sake and for hers."

"Care to put money on that one?" I ask, facetiously but nonetheless interested in her answer.

"I like long shots," she repeats, "but there's a limit. How about the city? Where's the Arts Center contract?"

"Harris handles that. Last I heard it was back on track. Council meets in two weeks."

A fatal lull, one of those junctures at which a conversation is going to die unless resuscitated. She pleasantly waits, a half-smile on her lips, possibly thinking herself of some conversational prescription.

"Would you like some food?" I ask. "I brought a ton and it won't keep. Come with me to my car and I'll freshen your drink."

"Thank you. I'd like that." A fresh spike in the EKG.

The second race is run behind us as we walk, talking between the inevitable run-ins with people I haven't seen. I introduce Natalie and she seems to be enjoying herself, asking questions of those we encounter and bantering about her first impressions of southern ritual. Mostly, she seems happy to be engaged, delivered from the isolation in which I found her. By the time we come within sight of my car, she is teetering on the brink of carefree and as relaxed as rainwater.

"You should run for governor," she says as we approach Adelle and Sarah. "You've spoken to enough people to get elected."

I make introductions and replenish her drink, a gin and tonic "light on the gin," an instruction I ignore. Within minutes she and Sarah are in animated exchange.

"Where did you find her?" Adelle whispers discreetly.

"In the mob. She was by herself and I felt sorry for her."

"You're a big person, Coleman Carter, after all she's done."

"She tried to help. I have no proof she fed the press."

"But it seems obvious," Adelle says, carefully modulating her voice.

"Perhaps. Anyway, what's done is done."

"I wonder," says Adelle, appraising her with peripheral vision. Natalie is younger than Adelle, and prettier. If it wasn't so laughable, I'd attribute the narrowness in Adelle's gaze to jealousy. Women can be strange that way.

To my surprise, the kids stray back, having been too social to eat. Steven and Christopher lay waste to much of our spread as my fears of leftovers evaporate, but Allie picks, unwilling to trust food on top of nerves. The third and fourth races run while we eat, drink, and continue chatting among ourselves and with newcomers.

Allie announces she must leave to prepare for the Cup, still about an hour and a half away. She and Natalie have, until now, exchanged an awkward greeting and little else, but Natalie asks if she can accompany Allie to the paddock. They leave together as I ponder whether this is something that should concern me.

The crowd is growing restive as always happens in early afternoon. We are treated to our first glimpse of the sloppy drunks, often obnoxious, always sad, but occasionally amusing as well. Today we get all three. A college crowd from Wofford started the day with a Purple Jesus party, judging by the color of rings around their mouths as they stumble past. These drinks are lethal blends of straight alcohol and grape juice tasting like Cool-Aide but delivering a punch I can liken only to laying your head on the bell-ring at the state fair when the mall hammer falls. One minute the imbiber is frolicking freely among his chums and the next he is a corpse, less toe tag, paralyzed from the hairline down in pickled petrification.

Abuse at this event is not limited to young people. As the fifth race is announced, I see two men older than myself approach each other some ten yards apart. Both are clutching cups of something strong and staggering in pronounced imbalance. On spotting each other, they stop cold. The first squints at the second and screams, "Well, I'll be Goddddd damn!" The second, his head jerking unstably, his eyes bloodshot, flashes a sickly grin and responds, "Well, shitttt fire!" They stand there, faced off and wobbling, for what seems minutes, studying each other. At last, perceiving through the haze that whatever similarity they thought they recognized is misplaced and that neither knows the other from Adam's Aunt Millie, they plod on their way without another word.

Natalie returns. I am unsure why I assumed she would but I am mildly surprised to find I have been scanning the crowd for her. She has shed her coat in deference to mounting temperatures, carrying it under one arm. The Lamberts, true to their intent, join us as our group marshals for the walk to the rail, arriving just as the fifth race ends. They will be off and running for the Cup in half an hour. Butterflies swarm in my stomach and no amount of beer poured into it will drown them. We line the rail in no particular order. I anchor one end of our contingent, Steven the other. My binoculars are powerful and I raise them to focus. Natalie, on my immediate right, is pressed against me by the throng beginning to gather for the premiere race of the day. To Natalie's right stands Adelle, serene and removed from the conversations on either side.

As I bring the binoculars into precise focus I am rudely jostled on my left by one of the two drunks who squared off during the fifth race against the man he thought he recognized. He has found a real friend, as impaired as he, and together they have barged to the front, loudly announcing heavy wagers on the Cup. I would move but there is nowhere to go this close to the start. I will endure.

"Born Lucky!" he yells. "C'mon Born Lucky!"

Born Lucky is, in fact, the favorite, a splendid horse as I note through my field glasses. Allie has come into view, the gold trim of her navy blue silks glinting in the sunlight. She sits swan-like astride Carbon Copy, her seat perfect and the curve of her neck graceful as she canters him beyond the starting gate. I may burst with pride.

Ed, the drunk beside me whose name I have involuntarily learned through repetitions by Sam, the other drunk, reaches over and snatches the glasses from me, simultaneously asking, in his own fashion, if he can borrow them. He is in no shape to notice that they are held by a strap draped around my neck. As we clumsily execute this push-pull, he sloshes his drink, narrowly missing me but hitting Natalie squarely in the chest. As I turn to her, the liquid bleeds through her blouse, matting it to her breast, encased in one of those half-cups the French prefer. As I sputter apologies for Ed, oblivious to his crime, I am jolted by the sap rising within me, pulling the ground with it. Natalie's breast, translucently exposed, sends a current of desire through me, intensely sensual. I gaze, too long, then recover. The starter's bell cuts off explanations.

"C'mon Born Lucky!" whelps Ed, pounding the fence with his open palm as the horses break from the gate. Allie is on the outside rail; terrible placement for competition but best for our view as she comes around for the first of two passes she will make in front of us. She gets a fast start and takes the first hurdle, a hedge four feet high, cleanly. Our angle is poor for the second jump, but Carbon Copy leaps first so he must be leading. He tucks his forefeet tightly as he sails over. I hold my breath each time she launches him. This sport, particularly this race, is dangerous to both horse and rider.

Eleven horses fly past us; forty-four hooves pounding the turf toward the next hazard. The ground beneath rumbles as they come abreast, Allie and Carbon Copy leading by a head. Born Lucky appears boxed near the inside rail. "Pass 'em, pass 'em!" screams Ed. At the next jump a horse in green and white silks near the middle of the pack refuses, sending its rider tumbling over its head. Horses to either side are thrown off stride but clear the hurdle, losing only precious time. Two race officials rush to the aid of the fallen jockey as a young groom tries to approach the frightened animal. The field has cleared two more jumps on the far side by the time the stunned rider is able to walk off under his own power.

At the last jump on the first lap disaster strikes. One of the horses set back by the refusal we just witnessed has tried to make up time too quickly. He misses his spot badly and jumps early, his hind legs crashing into the crossbars, bringing them down on horse and rider. The horse gets up quickly but is limping badly. The rider does not move as the medics approach.

The nine riders still in the race are coming our way for their final pass before the stretch. Allie's head is laid near Carbon Copy's neck, her seat off the saddle and her legs like pistons in the stirrups as they draw near. Born Lucky has regained his position and is moving up on the inside rail, his rider flailing his crop unsparingly. Allie is keeping Carbon Copy wide to avoid the havoc plaguing the middle of the pack, and as they near I have a full view of her grimly determined features.

"Son of a bitch," yells Ed as they gallop by. "Look at that gook ride." Ed, drunk or sober, could not know she is my daughter and I suppose I should deck him but at this instant I can only echo his praise. "Yeah," I mutter through clenched teeth, "look at that girl ride."

She takes the last jump as she has taken the others, strong and tight and all-out. I raise the field glasses to watch the finish. Born Lucky has pulled even and shows no fatigue. It is between them now, Carbon Copy on the outside and Born Lucky at the inside rail. Down the stretch, neck and neck, they thunder toward the finish. Ed is screaming and we are screaming and all eyes are on the last ten yards. With a final surge Born Lucky takes the flag with Carbon Copy a fraction behind.

"Su-wee!" Ed yells in jubilation. He must reserve his pig call for truly special events. He and Sam go into some kind of jig as we stifle our disappointment. "I'm buyin' licker, licker for the whole goddamn crowd!" Ed crows.

I tap him on the shoulder. "Congratulations, Ed, but that's not a gook, that's a girl and she nearly won."

He eyes me wildly in his sotted euphoria. "Whatcha mean? I's there . . . Nam. Semper Fi, mac. I guess I'd know a gook when I saw one." He turns from me. Then, over his shoulder, he says, "Besides, close only counts in horseshoes and hand grenades." With a sweeping arm thrown around Sam's neck, they set out to find more licker.

In the paddock, Allie discounts her loss, rubbing Carbon Copy's withers as she praises him. "He gave me all I asked until the end. All he had." Streaks of dust and dirt line her face, outlining the border of her goggles. "Steve Shaw may have a broken leg," she reports. Shaw took the tragic spill over his limping horse, which the vets are trying to determine whether to put down.

Jamison, Carbon Copy's owner, a big cigar planted firmly in the corner of his mouth, recounts the race to anyone who will listen. Having never fielded an entry finishing higher than sixth, he is ebullient. Kenny, Allie's trainer, is likewise basking in her light. "Twelve to one we went out and we gave 'em all they could handle. Another inch and they'd have been talking about this upset for years."

Natalie approaches Allie and whispers. Allie smiles and says, "Thank you." Christopher hugs her as does Steven, after which Adelle and Sarah offer their praises. We leave while Allie stows her gear.

"I've had fun," says Natalie, indicating her car. She extends her hand. "Thanks for sharing your day, and your food." We hold our clasp a second longer than necessary, a gesture seemingly unnoticed, although from the corner of my eye I see Adelle turn away, perhaps weary from the excitement of the race.

29

The Swilling jury is about to make him the richest ninth grade dropout in the state. His attorney simultaneously harbors the hope of becoming the richest lawyer, and his contingent fee on the demanded five million dollars in compensatory damages and another fifty million in punitive would do it. Expert witnesses for Swilling have agreed that he will require "extensive vocational rehabilitation;" words chosen by Dr. Peter Spain, MD, one of his experts paid $4000 for his impartial report and testimony.

Scott Edwards reports that summations will begin this afternoon with the case expected to go to the jury by the end of today. I marvel at the nature of Swilling's rehab. Has his beating at the hands of the police deprived him of his memory so that now, absent this gilded treatment, he will have to look up the pager numbers of his runners before dialing his car phone? Has his brutalization left him so befuddled that he might actually declare on a tax return a portion of his income, estimated by police to have been in excess of three million dollars last year, most of it diverted or extorted lunch money from the schools? Is he sexually impaired, raising the tragic specter of abandonment by his bevy of cocaine-breathing beauties who nightly, in twos and threes, trick him into exhaustion? It's enough to make a man, and a jury, weep.

Allie moves with brittle deliberateness this morning, the fluid flex of her arms and legs poured out onto the track in Camden. Her spirits show more resilience. She hums softly as she prepares breakfast and gathers her books for school.

I lower the newspaper. "You're moving slowly this morning."

"I'd kill for a Jacuzzi," she says.

I clear my throat. "I saw you and Natalie spending some time together."

"Yeah, she's pretty neat. She used to ride so we talked horses."

"Just horses?"

"Just horses. You spent some time with her yourself. What did you guys talk about?"

"Stuff," I say, raising the paper.

"Right."

"Well, I felt badly that she was wandering around without any friends."

"You took care of that, not that I'm complaining. She told me I rode with courage."

"That was very thoughtful, and very justified."

"Thanks. It was scary but fun. Next time I'll win. Gotta go or I'll be late." She disappears, stiff-legged.

The outing in Camden seems to have softened her. Possibly, my chance encounter with Natalie, our chumminess at the Cup, eased her back toward my corner, if only psychologically. Her restraint is still detectable in the way she shortens dialogue, cuts her thoughts in half when she might otherwise expound on some experience or feeling. For instance, when we returned home after the Cup, a postmortem on the race was dictated by familial pattern. This would have been the time for her to reveal her butterflies while waiting in the starting gate, Carbon Copy's demeanor during warm-ups, incidents concerning her rival jockeys or horses, near-fouls or worse out on the course. She relishes these details, as she relishes describing them to me. But it did not happen. She stowed her gear, ate some yogurt and went to bed, showing no sulk or pique, only fatigue, as though lack of energy was the sole cause of her withholding. But I know better.

Approaching the courthouse after lunch I notice an abnormal number of lawyers flocking inside. Swilling's summation is bringing them out like Aztecs to a sacrifice. The courtroom is SRO, or so it seems as I enter. Scanning, I see Natalie wedged among blue suits in the second row. The bailiff barks, Judge Tyler swoops in from a door behind the bench and gavels the room to order.

Swilling, as plaintiff, has the first and last word with the three men and three women who have patiently listened to three weeks of testimony during which their private lives have been put on pause. His principal lawyer, a dapperly dressed black man named Morrison who has been commuting on weekends to Charleston from Washington, D.C. by chartered plane, begins the laborious but crucial task of recapitulating the evidence in his client's favor. He is dignified, his voice modulated, his approach clinical and precise.

Within minutes of rising to his feet Morrison shows himself a spin master worthy of the advanced billing, leading the rapt jurors through the night of the arrest and Swilling's protestations of innocence. He wisely omits his client's exact words, testified to by the arresting officers and reported in the newspaper, tastefully edited: "Hey, muthafuckas, whatchoo hasslin' me fo; I been playin' basketball; I don't know nothin' 'bout no drugs."

Morrison leads them through Swilling's account of his detainment in the bullpen and his subsequent "torture" by the defendant police officers. He weaves a chilling tale of spiked white fury, black vulnerability, and patent, gloating indifference by white supervisors to the pounding being administered in the holding cell. In this civil trial, he does not need the unanimity demanded of criminal verdicts, giving him greater latitude in playing the race card to trump the outnumbered whites. If black experience holds black jurors together, he'll break the bank and he knows it.

I am behind and to one side of Natalie, having found a spot at the wall to back into. As Morrison parades his sad horribles before the jury like crippled, sack clothed mourners in a funeral cortege, I picture her nudging and prodding him on with her body English, restrained only with discipline and by the press of those flanking her, exhorting him to grip the city's jugular and not be shaken free.

In rebuttal, the city's lawyer, Meg Brandon, offers its review of the evidence, as close to Swilling's as the Cooper River is to the Nile. Swilling, the city contends, was beaten unconscious by a man named Gaston Halleck, arrested hours earlier and the only other occupant of the bullpen when Swilling was placed inside. To prove its claim, the city produced Halleck, its star witness during the trial, who swore he had first delivered a fierce blow to Swilling's temple, knocking him out, and proceeded to do the balance of his damage as Swilling lay helpless on the floor. "That's why," testified Halleck, "the po-lice didn't hear nothin'. I stayed real quiet so I could work him over good."

Halleck's motivation in assaulting Swilling stemmed from a drug deal. One of Swilling's runners had inflicted a recent wound to Halleck's attrited pride by selling him some Sweet 'n Low at a price substantially higher than market, and that night at the jail Halleck dealt with the rip-off according to the law of the streets. During Halleck's testimony, Morrison fought to suppress any reference to "a drug deal" as prejudicial to his client's cause and the judge agreed. Halleck had been allowed to say only that he and Swilling had had "an argument."

"I thought 'bout chokin' him to death," Halleck forthrightly admitted on the witness stand, "but I been knowin' him a while. We has some good times in the old days."

The key question was why Halleck would come forward with such an admission, and the answer lay in the twenty-to-life sentence he had just drawn from a jury for armed robbery. Halleck had little to lose by coming forward. Swilling lacked the contacts in the penitentiary system to have Halleck killed and Halleck, a two-time loser, had plenty of protective friends waiting for him at the big house.

As if his confession were not enough to seal Swilling's fate, Halleck had a parting gift for his old friend. Weeks after the beating, as Halleck and Swilling awaited their respective trials, Halleck on the armed robbery and Swilling, once released from the hospital, on the drug charges that constituted the basis for his original arrest, they had a conversation through intermediaries in the jail. Swilling told Halleck that he planned to get a hot-shot lawyer to sue the city for negligence in failing to protect him from Halleck in the bullpen. Halleck then, according to Halleck, told Swilling such a case lacked sex appeal and that if he really wanted to stick it to somebody he should claim the police did it.

"I was kind of jokin' with the dude," Halleck testified for the city. "How's I to know he'd do it?"

As Meg Brandon rests the city's case, Morrison jumps up for his final run at the jury. Gone is his judicious reserve, the "come, let us reason together" demeanor that characterized his earlier appeal. His eyes flash, his arms wave and he moves toward the jury box like a jaguar famished for meat.

"Why," he demands, "did Gaston Halleck come before you with such bald-faced outlandish lies? He said it was because he has nothing to lose by telling you the truth. I'm here to tell you that a man like Halleck, a liar with a record as long as your sleeve, wouldn't know the truth if he found it in his pocket. That truth is that the city can still make life better for Gaston Halleck in two ways; first, it can recommend he be placed in an alternative to maximum security where he will enjoy conjugal leave privileges. For any of you who don't know that term, it means the chance to be alone with his wife or lover at certain intervals. And secondly, it can recommend that he receive favorable consideration on the day, mercifully far into the future, when he comes up for parole. That is why he has agreed to perjure himself for the city."

It has been a clash worth the time of every professional here, and as the jury files out and Judge Tyler announces a recess until a verdict is delivered, predictions fly across the courtroom like Frisbees.

"Get ready for a tax hike," says Boyd Rollins, a CPA standing next to me. "The city's self-insured and we're going to take it on the chin."

"No way," counters Walter Ford from the other side. "I was here for Halleck's testimony and let me tell you he had that jury by the short hairs. When he told about suggesting the whole thing to Swilling they looked over at that black bastard like he'd spit on the Pope. He's got no chance."

Ford is not a lawyer. No one who is would deny the first law of juries: when they're out, anything can happen. The crowd begins to thin, expecting no rapid decision. Scott Edwards is up front, pad in hand, interviewing both sides. Summations and jury instructions have consumed the afternoon and I have no appointments. I edge forward, counter to the flow of those leaving, to where Natalie is engaged in debate with one of the blue suits. He departs as I approach.

"I didn't expect to see you again so soon," she says pleasantly. "What did you think?"

"Morrison's good," I say. "Real good."

"Good enough?"

I shrug. Not having attended the trial as it progressed I am in no position to judge critical factors like credibility of witnesses. Conversely, Natalie has been here every day.

"What's your guess?" I ask.

"Verdict for the city. Just a hunch."

"Want to stake a lunch on it?"

"You're betting on Swilling?"

"On the system. Slimeballs like him have a karma when it comes to taking advantage, especially when they can afford legal talent like Morrison."

"Well," she says, folding her arms and grinning, "isn't this a role reversal for the books?"

"I'm not ready to fill out a membership application for the ACLU, I'm just calling it like I see it."

"And I'm not ready to join . . . what is it I'm not ready to join?"

"United Daughters of the Confederacy?"

"Yes, that," she says, laughing. "That man I was talking with a minute ago was trying to entice me into the pool they have going. Pick the verdict and come closest to the time the jury's out and win a hundred bucks."

"How are the bets running?"

"The money's on a decision for Swilling; nobody thinks it will come quickly."

"Then we have time for me to buy you a drink," I am surprised to hear myself say.

"I'd like that," she says, "but are you sure you should be seen with me? Last time it caused you problems."

"There's an Irish pub down the block. I could follow you from a safe distance."

Together we stroll down Broad Street. A day that began as a harsh afterthought of winter has ripened into a redolent prelude to spring. The outrunners of nature's marshaling bounty are borne on the wind from the sea. Delicate brines lift across awakening marshes, whisked ashore to rustle among jasmines, pears and redbuds in a sibilant reminder that it is once again time to stir, to lend their fragile incense to the perfume of renewal.

At the pub I suggest we continue on and she agrees. We turn on State Street, lined by ever-vigilant palmettoes and late-sleeping crape myrtles. At Queen we turn east to the river, drawn toward Waterfront Park by the scents of spring like two hungry children following a spiced aroma to a cooling apple pie.

From the river's edge we watch the patient migration of freighters in the channel, outlined by running lights and moving with ghostly caution in the accumulating dusk. Up river, the twin spans of the Cooper River Bridge loom in the twilight, giant superstructures festooned between land masses beginning to twinkle with lights. In the park to our right some young boys are playing with a football so dark it seems invisible, lending a surreal touch to their efforts to throw and catch it.

We are standing before bronze topographical displays of Charleston's four centuries, each emblazoned with history.

"Look," says Natalie, pointing to the nearest bronze relief, "the major events are in braille as well."

"Of course," I say. "We were afraid that without that you might sue us on behalf of Charleston's blind." She turns slowly toward me, her expression unreadable in the dimness. "That's a joke," I add, uncertainly.

"You still think I'm unreasonable," she says.

"Don't you still believe I'm a wimp?"

"A nice wimp," she says. "I had fun on Saturday. How about that drink you promised?"

Magnolia's is nearby and compensates for swarms of tourists by serving excellent food. In its bar we sip cocktails, a vodka martini for me and a Manhattan for her.

"Adelle seems nice," she observes from the blue.

I nod. "We laugh over the irony of our children dating after all these years."

"I read Chris is quite the tennis star," she says.

"The kid's got a hundred mile an hour serve that will blow the gut off your racquet if you stick it out there. Allie won't play with him."

"Oh, why not?"

"She's too competitive and he cuts her no slack."

"Are they . . . serious?"

"I doubt it," I say, popping a beer nut into my mouth. "He's her first serious love interest but what she's really serious about is college and beyond. It'll pass."

She is a long way from the jeans and boots of this past weekend. I am struck by her sophistication in the pallid light of this bar. Sitting across the small table, one hand languishing in her lap and the other demurely holding the stem of her glass, she assumes an aloofness I associate with trendy east side haunts in New York or the international milieu of Georgetown. There is an other-worldliness to her here, something vaguely European, as if at any moment she could crook her finger to beckon a tuxedoed sommelier and order, with equal ease, a scarce Bordeaux, the czar's preferred vodka or the Pope's reserved Chianti. Under her placid reserve, on the surface not the least threatening, I sense a certain ruthlessness, a near cousin to the efficacious lawyer who entered my office that first day, with a duality like a feline that purrs in social settings such as this but is fierce and lashing when provoked, able to puncture with a glance any nascent stirring of sentimentality as unaffordable in her bottom-line world. "Get to the point," such women seem to say, "or get lost." I see Natalie in that arena, giving as good as she gets and demanding the check as she leaves.

"Why Charleston?" I ask.

"Why not Boston or Chicago?"

"Yeah. Why come here?"

"You won't like my answer," she says, looking away momentarily.

"In that case, I can guess. You came here because this is a greenhouse for civil rights violations, a veritable cornucopia for ACLU wrongrighters."

"Something like that. I warned you wouldn't like it. It was between here and some dreadful two-step town in Texas."

"Poor, pitiable Texas." I raise my glass in a toasting motion.

"But I'm starting to like it here," she hastens to add.

"Why? Having to step over sprawling constitutional iniquities on the way to the bus stop must wear you down."

"You realize," she says, "that I'm tolerating your sarcasm only because you were nice to me at the Cup."

"Payback is hell." My vodka, so cold in descent, has metabolized into a charged mass, fissioning forth waves of cheer. I am enjoying myself, but wary enough to realize that poking fun at her is a risky zero-sum game.

"You went to Columbia?" I ask, unwilling to push her further.

"For law. NYU undergrad."

"How was it, NYU?"

"Good education. I spent all my time studying. The GPA's required by law schools like Columbia are so high."

"So, no sorority life at NYU, eh?"

"No social life worth mentioning. I think I had one date my freshman year."

"And your parents lived . . . where?"

"When I entered college, in Illinois. By the time I left my dad lived in Ithaca and my mother had moved to White Plains."

"Divorce?"

"A classic meltdown. I think my dad became involved with a coed but I'm not sure. Nor was Mother, but that didn't stop her from alleging it."

"So then you split your visits between two cities."

"Actually, I saw more of New York. Whenever I went to see either of them it was one recrimination after another so I stopped going."

"And holidays?"

"Went to shows, toured the art galleries, museums, libraries. You have to try to become bored in New York. Have you spent any time there?"

"One summer," I reply, summoning our passing waiter for some mineral water. "I interned on Wall Street the summer before I graduated from law school; a small firm in the Irving Trust Building. I don't see how those people stand it."

"The city or the practice?"

"The city I liked. I shared an apartment on the upper east side with some guys from college. I learned the subway system in a day and after a week I had learned to fold the Wall Street Journal just right, so I could hang on one of those metal grips and read on the trip downtown."

Natalie laughs, my description evoking apparent recognition of this tribe of business warriors for whom the Journal, held in crisply folded squares and read in the stroboscopic flicker of tunneling trains, stood as a totem during my time in New York. Serious young men, thin and neatly dressed and commonly wearing wire-rimmed glasses, boarded crammed cars and by this singular shibboleth identified those with whom they might ultimately, with the timing critical to bulls and bears, rub elbows in the same clubby confines of some mid-town smoking room, its members fraternally wealthy and still glued to the Journal.

"I can't imagine that kind of law practice," I tell her. "You come in when you're in your mid-twenties and they assign you to some antitrust case that began when Christ was a corporal and you work on it for dozens of hours a week and the next thing you know you're pushing forty and the case is still rolling along, unresolved. I'm exaggerating but there's an element of truth in it. It's not unlike Charleston on a grand scale; negotiations turn serious when, and only when, both sides finally start running out of money."

Natalie looks at me from over the rim of her Manhattan. "You sound jaded."

I lower my eyes to the candle between us. "I guess I am. What about you? Wall Street is full of Columbia grads. Were you tempted?"

She shakes her head. "That antitrust case you spoke of sounds like a death sentence. I wanted to represent real people. My politics are pretty liberal, so during Reagan's second term I found my sensibilities continually outraged by his disregard for the have not's. He pushed me toward the ACLU."

"Ron's pretty popular around here," I note with a chuckle. A group of Floridians, unmistakable in their florid shirts and premature shorts, descend on the table next to us. They shout out drink orders, drowning out normal conversation.

"Do you think the jury might be back?" she asks.

"Not a chance," I say, sounding dangerously close to authoritarian and mildly chagrined that she is steering us back to business.

"Oh?" she says, grinning. "I'll bet you dinner they're back. If I win, you buy and I choose." She hesitates, suddenly vulnerable as her sophistication slips. "I don't necessarily mean tonight," she explains. "You must have plans."

"Fair enough," I say, "but from all reports you ACLUers don't make much money. I promise I'll select something that won't threaten your Visa limit."

"Well," she says rising, "I'm taking no prisoners. I told you I like long shots and when they come in I collect. Be forewarned."

We retrace our route toward the courthouse. She asks to hear my theory of why Swilling will prevail.

"He got off on the criminal charges," I say.

"Perhaps he's innocent," she says, not looking at me.

"Right. He's been to four juries on felony drug charges and he's only nineteen. Expensive lawyers, intimidation of witnesses, and matchless luck are the only things separating him from long-term care in the penitentiary. If this jury knew how much of this city's drug problem he's personally responsible for they'd string him up. But, of course, they aren't allowed to hear that. To them, he looks like a clean-cut kid after his lawyers burn his pimp outfits and drag him through Brooks Brothers."

"We'll know soon," she says as we round the corner of State and head west on Broad.

The courthouse is dark but for the usual security lights. In the reserved parking spaces abutting the building I see a large, balding man about to duck into his car. "Willie!" I call out. He pauses and stares. "It's me, Coleman. Did Lydia send them home for the night?"

"Hey, Coleman," he answers, one leg inside the car and the door half closed. "She sent them home for good. Verdict for the city."

Natalie's elbow is in my side before I can utter, "You're not serious."

"City Hall is ecstatic," he calls. "The joke is they're taking the 'for sale' sign off the building."

I drift toward him in shock, Natalie following. "You're serious."

He swings his stored leg from the car and sits facing me. "Serious as a little ole' heart attack. Brandon interviewed the jury foreman before she left. Two of the black women are heavy duty Baptists and Swilling calling those officers mf'ers nailed him. They didn't believe a word he said. Excuse me, but I gotta go. I'm late for dinner."

"Go figure," I say, turning back to Natalie as Willie cranks his car.

"French," she says. "Some ambiance, a fabulous wine list. The kind of place where listing entre prices is considered gauche."

"I can't believe it."

"Did I mention Paris?" she is saying. "Our bet said nothing about being restricted to Charleston."

"Arliene's is French," I say lamely. "Three blocks down."

"Perfect," she says. "Did I tell you I've been in treatment for a rare bulimia involving a compulsive hunger for truffles?"

"Are you enjoying this?"

"I'm about to. You're sure tonight suits?"

"Let's eat."

30

Arliene's, hole-in-the-wall gourmet, features twelve tables precisely set with starched white tablecloths, linen napkins, and heavy cutlery. By artful subterfuge of plants, columns, and lighting, it is easy to lull into the illusion that one table, your table, is the sun of this cozy universe, around which planetary waiters, busboys, and chefs hover in measured orbit. Muted strains of Puccini or Verdi, played so softly as to be virtually unheard until a tenor or soprano climbs the upper registers, accompany escargot and pate as fine as I've tasted anywhere.

Within minutes of being seated, my sting of defeat begins to wane. Between us, a single fresh-cut Cherokee Rose blooms in its unadorned vase, its yellow stamens encircled by petals of resurrection white so that in color it compliments the lone candle, in which the same yellow fires the wick and rises into an aureole of white flame, the flower the perfect living embodiment of the candle.

We begin this fete with Russian caviar and a champagne toast to my sure-footed instincts about juries. She accepts my sword with the grace of a kindly conqueror wise enough to leave the vanquished a mule and some land. By the time the waiter uncorks a St Martin Merlot, I have begun to relish losing.

As we await entrees, the fragmentary silica of Natalie's mosaic come together in a pattern of benevolent neglect at the hands of parents well-meaning but insensitive. At fourteen they sent her to boarding school, a female academy in Connecticut magnetic in its attraction of girls with learning and eating disorders. She hated it. After a year and a half, they let her come home, although not to the one she left but a new university town where her father taught on sabbatical. I learn that her reference to bulimia was uttered out of the reservoir of confidence that beating it had replenished. While her mother had urged "fresh air and sunshine" as a prescription for her internal convulsion, she put herself in therapy. A year later she emerged, behind in school but more or less intact emotionally. She modestly described the effort required to make up lost credits, the school at which she spent her senior year being her fourth in four years. She saw its principal "two or three times" prior to the afternoon he awarded her diploma.

"A couple of years after the divorce," she says, tossing her hair with a turn of her head, "Mother confided that they had stayed together for me. It was my sad duty to tell her I didn't believe it, that staying married for the sake of a child implied affection for the child and I had felt very little from either of them. She blamed my dad, of course, and in a way she was right. He's a theoretician, one of those academics compelled to logic even when the results are absurd. He has a fine mind—so does my mother—but he never grasped the difference between thought and feeling."

"And your mother?"

"Warmer than dad but even more demanding where I was concerned. If I shined it was expected, if I screwed up it was the beginning of the end. Dad's aloofness drove her crazy and she was always shouting that he had no appreciation for her needs, which was true, but instead of accepting him as the cold, brainy fish he is she was determined to bring him around. A tragic match. If they stayed together for me it was to argue about who knew best and not out of fear of damaging me. How did we get into all this?"

"I asked," I remind her. "What about men? Any better luck?"

"Late in my last year at Columbia I moved in with the editor of the law review."

"Lucky guy," I say.

"Thank you. I thought so. I stayed with him for six months, although with both of us studying for the bar and working unconscious hours I probably saw him the equivalent of three weeks."

She pauses, treading the edge of an additional thought, a half-smile coming to her lips as she debates.

"Spit it out," I say.

"I find it hard to believe I'm sharing all this, and harder to believe you're interested. Anyway, one day I brought home a puppy. He was most upset. I pointed out that I was there, alone, more often than he was and that I would be completely responsible for it. The following day he presented me with sixteen reasons—I am not exaggerating—sixteen written reasons why a puppy was not practical in Manhattan."

"So you broke up with him."

"So I recognized my father. Isn't that strange? All those years trying to rationalize the distance my father held me at and I go for a man exactly like him."

"Happens a lot," I add.

"I suppose. Anyway, I left that afternoon and never went back. And that's the end of my story. Thanks for being an expert listener."

Her crab meat au gratin, my steak in a delicate peppercorn dressing arrive. The conversation turns to the presidential primaries, to the inevitability of Bill Clinton's reelection.

"So Jimmy Carter didn't sour you on southern governors?" I want to know as my knife slices through my tenderloin like a scalpel through custard.

"Carter is a better man than he was a president," she says. "Clinton is probably the reverse, but Dole? Tell me about meeting your wife, unless she's someone you'd rather not discuss."

"It's okay," I assure. I tell her of the freshman blind date, the long night guarding the campus. "You would have loved it. Couldn't swing a dead cat without hitting a radical." She smiles often, asking questions occasionally and enjoying her dinner. Around us, voices intimate and subdued mingle among the wind-chime murmuring of silver against china, mostly unseen from our secluded spot.

"Can I be honest with you about something personal?" she asks.

"Fire away."

"You don't seem like the kind of man who would adopt an Asian orphan."

"You mean I obviously lack the warmth, the sensitivity, the compassion to reach out the way you liberals do for trees and snail-darters and spotted owls."

"I didn't mean that."

"Sure you did."

"No," she says earnestly. "I meant only that you seem . . . traditional, and it strikes me as a non-traditional act."

I bring my napkin to my mouth before responding. "Regrettably, you are right for the second time in an hour."

"At least this time it won't cost you," she says.

"You never know. It means you've figured me out. The adoption was Elizabeth's idea. She planned it, she pushed it, she made it happen."

"But you agreed to it."

"I didn't object may be a more accurate way of putting it. At first I thought it was just a sudden inspiration that would pass. She could be like that. Later, when I saw how determined she was, I was against it because I knew the friction it would cause in my family."

"Did it?"

"My father stopped speaking to me. Mother called me spineless for not standing up to Elizabeth. I tried to call it off, to convince Elizabeth that it wasn't worth the pain it was going to inflict. She insisted they'd get over it. So there I was, caught in the crossfire of those I loved and all the exits blocked."

Natalie reaches for her butter knife and with it makes a swirl on the bread she is coating. "I watched you as she rode in the Cup; whatever misgivings you may have had died out a long time ago."

"You're batting a thousand," I concede. "But it took her arrival to dispel them. Right up until they put her in Elizabeth's arms I was sure it was a mistake."

"She came by air, of course."

I nod, smiling involuntarily in remembrance. I relate Allie's arrival.

"What a fabulous day," she says. "Aren't you glad you trusted Elizabeth's instincts?"

"Very glad."

"Perhaps you should trust mine when it comes to the St. Simeon."

"I've listened. You want me to sue my friends, foul my own nest and Allie's too."

She stares at me a moment, then lowers her eyes and says softly, "No, I don't."

"But from the day you walked into my office—"

"I've changed my mind."

"What! I didn't think they let you do that in the ACLU. Couldn't this jeopardize your pension?"

"Very funny, and I'm trying to be serious. For the record, there is no pension."

"I'm sorry," I say. "Humor is my defense to shock. What made you reconsider?"

"A combination of things. Mostly, it was watching you among all those people at the Cup. I can't picture you without lots of friends and the litigation I recommended isn't going to make you any."

"True, but keeping my friends doesn't solve Allie's problem with the St. Simeon."

"Also true. I haven't changed my mind on her prospects. This Lafayette exemption strikes me as an impossibly narrow loophole."

"I've never viewed it as anything else," I say. "Only slightly ahead of hopeless."

"But we need to improve the odds. Have you thought of seeing the Board one on one? You're good at that. Collectively, they all ban together for the good of the organization as they see it. Individually, they may be more forthcoming. I'm not predicting that, you understand. I don't know them. At least you'll learn where you stand."

"It's a good idea for the reason you mention, plus one more. If, by some miracle, the phone call to Korea produces something I can work with, I'll still have to go back to this same group. By laying the groundwork with them separately, I'll improve my chances when it comes to a vote. Hey, I like it. Think it will work?"

"No. But I think you'll feel better about what you're doing for Allie. And, there's the outside chance—"

"I'll start tomorrow morning. Time is short and if I don't hear something soon from Korea I'm at a blank wall."

We order dessert and cordials, during which I try to assimilate her new religion, her spurning of her cherished scorched earth. I want to claim credit for this conversion, possibly as an egotistical redemption of my tarnished pride. But it smacks of vanity to take personally a smart lawyer's adoption of a more flexible strategy. Yet, I find something compellingly personal in what she has said and I cannot escape the feeling she is looking out for me. I want to lean across the table and kiss her. The image of her breast, stuck to her soaked blouse, returns. I am falling toward her in a way I never thought possible. The lonely, skinny girl by the pool returns.

I pay the check and suffer my last good-natured jabs at losing the Swilling bet.

"My car is near the courthouse," she says.

"Mine's around the corner. I'll drive you."

We are idled, waiting for the engine to warm. She is staring straight ahead, her hands folded in her lap as I pretend to adjust the radio, stalling for time as I hold a frantic debate within.

"Natalie, I've had a fabulous time this evening. I can't remember enjoying myself more. And if I haven't thanked you, really thanked you, for your interest in my daughter and me, I'm doing it now."

She turns her head, lovely in the glow of indirect light filtering through the windshield. "I know you appreciate it," she says. "You were just frightened."

"I was? Of what?"

"Me."

"Now why—"

"Not so much of me personally but of what I represent. I'm a choice, a nasty, ugly alternative you don't want to face. You know you should for Allie, but you can't."

She is right, of course, decoding in ten seconds a mystery that has been puzzling me for weeks, the looming disquiet I have felt in her presence and the compulsive need to justify myself to someone I thought unreasonable. Her edge is hard, but her instincts unerring and her lips soft, I discover, as I lean over to kiss her. She does not react immediately, as though stunned. Then, I feel her lips part slightly and a hand come up to the back of my head. In that kiss, I confirm an intuition of my own. I want to grab her, pull her close, devour her, but I hold back. Am I still afraid of her? We disengage, each looking down in an awkward recognition that something unanticipated has sprung to life of its own volition.

"I should follow you home," I say. "Charleston isn't all safe at this hour."

She nods, then directs me to her car, alone on the curb. She steers to an apartment complex in North Charleston, thoroughly ordinary and dotted with parking stickers from the navy and air force bases, pulling into a spot marked "414A." I want to make sure she gets safely inside but as I idle nearby another car enters the lot, forcing me into a slot marked "Visitors." She does not start for her door, but instead comes to the window on my side. I power it down and she leans in.

"It's been a great evening," she says. "The best." She kisses me and my mind is racing with images and possibilities and an unbearable need to be closer than this car permits. She breaks it off, then walks quickly toward her door, extracting her key as she nears it. She is turning it in the lock when I call her name.

"Wait," I say, breathing heavily as I leave my car. As I approach she studies me but not with curiosity and, I think, with no surprise. Her perception is spooky.

"I need to tell you something. You were right about me being frightened. It's a hard thing to admit but I admit it."

She is gazing up at me, her eyes wide and head tilted enchantingly to one side. The strength of my breathing grows until it seems the entire complex should be awakened. I enfold her in my arms and she responds.

We press against each other in electric urgency. I lean away to ask, "Want to hear my theory?"

"Your theory of what?" she murmurs, pulling me back and kissing me below the ear.

"Of you."

She raises her eyes to mine. "Go ahead."

"I don't think you came south to right wrongs. I think you came looking for something soft and forgiving." The balance of my theory is smothered in her sublime embrace and kisses.

"You realize the irony here," she says.

"Tell me," I whisper.

"Had I gotten my wish, and you had agreed to become my client, we couldn't be doing this."

31

I cannot be taller on the morning after my evening with Natalie, yet I feel so, alert and alive in ways I haven't felt in what seems like forever. Her scent lingers in my facial stubble. I am brewing coffee when Allie enters the kitchen.

"Did I hear whistling?" she wants to know.

"I don't know, did you?"

"I thought I did," she says, placing her books on the counter. "You're up early . . ."

"Some paperwork backed up at the office. Thought I'd get in before the phone starts ringing."

"For coming in so late." She is eyeing me expectantly.

"I . . . got tied up."

"That's a good one," she says skeptically. "I'll remember that one—I got tied up. Want to tell mamma Allie about it?"

"I do not wish to tell mamma Allie."

"That's okay, Adelle will tell me."

"No! You'll . . . embarrass her. Don't say anything to Adelle."

"So, it's Natalie. Geez Dad, is she old enough?"

"Will you get out of here? Go to school." Miss Open Book of the Orient also reads palms.

"But I have half an hour," she reminds me. "You're the one leaving early."

"Yeah, I know." I grab my coat from the back of my chair and start for the door. Her back is to me as she stands at the counter slicing a banana as a topping for yogurt. I return, and kiss her on top of her head. "I love you, sweetheart." I stride for the door.

"Dad," she calls, still facing away. "It's fine by me if it's Natalie. Just so you know."

I stop, my hand on the door knob. "Some things are private."

"It *is* Natalie. Cool. Maybe I should invite her over. Popcorn, videos . . . maybe a sleep-over."

This is the reason I never play poker.

I leave before she can quiz me on exactly what Natalie and I did last night. With keys jangling I approach the car. For the second time in this young day, a fragrance distracts me. This time, wisteria. I will walk. The city is drawing back the curtain to unveil its spring line, and though the fashions here never change fundamentally, the nuances are worth savoring on foot. Azaleas are still a week or two away from peak but the dogwoods are in bloom and Bignonia abound. A pollen-laden mist coats cars and mailboxes, as if the neighborhood is being dusted for fingerprints. Allie's razing on my way out is a good sign, well worth my temporary discomfort. It signals another tentative step back toward our old closeness, absent now long enough, I hope, to exact a price from her. Suddenly, I am glad to have said nothing to disabuse her of the notion I was with her ally Natalie. Then, just as suddenly, I wonder if last night could be linked to the St. Simeon. Have I, unwittingly, used Natalie as a bridge to Allie? No, I conclude instantly, and it feels right.

A note from Harris sits atop my messages. He is in trial this morning but needs to see me about the Arts Center "at your convenience." Dictation consumes me until ten, when I place a call to Natalie, who is out. More dictation, an interview with a prospective summer intern, and a late-morning conference call keep me buried. Not until after lunch do I have a moment to reflect upon the strategy formulated over dinner the night before. I take a legal pad from the drawer and list the Board members.

Though much has happened since that night in February when I went before the board to request the exemption, my estimate of the situation remains unaltered. I need two votes from among five people. Adelle is a given because of our relationship, one admittedly complicated by the swift turn of events last night and a subject I will have to address. But the crucial vote occurred before I ever laid eyes on Natalie and Adelle has been in my corner from the start.

Margarite is another matter. Unable to confirm or disprove Adelle's suspicions about her faithful reporting of the vote, I have done what I always do: assume the best. In truth, I cannot logically or profitably do otherwise. If her treachery reaches to the depths sounded by Adelle, then all is lost. Her research into loopholes was a shill, a sleight of hand, and the Lafayette exemption merely a straw man to cover petty crime while saving face. As president of the Society, her power extends to any reconsideration of the denial. She will strike again, murdering then what she wounded before. No, it makes no sense to condemn Margarite. Better to discount Adelle's suspicions, freely admitted by Adelle to be no more than that.

In pondering this matter of the vote I have rationalized the behavior Adelle mistook for betrayal. If the results were five to two against, Margarite's announcement of the vote would have exposed the nays as surely as an open show of hands. Those around the table knew that Margarite and Adelle were with me; they would clearly constitute the two ayes, leaving all others in one camp. Sensing this, Margarite chose to conceal the results. Such a surmise absolves her, important to me not only because of her venerable devotion to Allie but also as a litmus of my powers to sort blarney from bullion. Try as I have to banish the optimistic cherubs on my shoulders, there they sit, as convinced as I that Margarite, Philip's mother, did not and could not sabotage me.

But cold analysis along these lines leads also to a less pleasant deduction. If Margarite remains unscarred, Clarkson Mills, my long-time client, is, a priori, among the lepers. Clarkson's desertion would not carry the soul-searing sting inflicted by Margarite's, but it is nevertheless distressing. I saved his business, his house, his future, and to be repaid in so many pieces of silver is beyond galling. His name will be high on my target list.

Sandy Charles is promising. Away from Charlotte Hines, she seems the personification of good will, a cheerful, fun-loving embodiment of everyone's favorite attributes. I know of but one tie between Sandy and Charlotte beyond those which connect all of us "South of Broad's": Charlotte is a heavy patron of the arts and Sandy is an aspiring painter, often submitting her work to juries in shows underwritten in whole or part by Charlotte. If I can spin Sandy free of Charlotte's gravitational pull, I may capture her.

Jeanette Wilson, forever in my thought entwined in kudzu, cannot pronounce the time of day without consulting five of her friends. Blatant and unabashed in her circumspection, she will commit to nothing one-on-one with the possible exception of sex on her dining room table. The experiment we call Jeanette should establish conclusively whether it is possible to sleep one's way to the top in this town. Odds are against it. I will see her in a public place.

Charlotte Hines. Should I bother? Are there words in the lexicon capable of bringing her over? It is not so much humbling myself before Her Royal Ampleness that deters me. If I could count on her to simply expose her queenly behind long enough for me to grovel forward worm-like and plant the abject kiss of a miserable supplicant, I would not hesitate. But with Charlotte I will have to endure the lecture along with the refusal. She will unleash on me the furious brunt of her convoluted mind, pitching non sequiturs one upon another with the force of truth until I retreat out the door, my hands protectively shielding my head from pummel by the last hurled absurdity. On the other hand, Charlotte talks a lot, freely and often without discretion. Perhaps I will learn something that will help with another member.

Finally, old Doc Francis. Authentic grudges tend to be buried with the people who cling to them. By his St. Simeon vote, he visits the sins of the father on the son, but I have too often been the beneficiary of my father's good name and reputation to resent this credit on a debit-studded ledger. I will not call on Doc Francis.

Leaning back in my chair, I examine my notes. I have four visits to make and not much time to make them. Surprise is a tactic well suited to my purpose. I will hit quickly before word circulates. Starting now. I review the list.

Jeanette Wilson works each afternoon in an upscale gift shop near the market. Within ten minutes of my leaving she will have spoken to any Board member who answers his phone. I will save her for last. Clarkson

Mills is also at work. I need to see him this evening. Charlotte Hines I am not up to today, leaving Sandy Charles.

I find her in her studio behind the Charles residence on Stoll's Alley, a short walk from the office and not far from my home. Her husband Edgar, the architect, designed and had built this outbuilding to encourage her fledgling interest in art. That was five years ago, and she has since turned a hobby into a passion. She spots me from her window as I walk the flagstones leading from the house.

"Coleman! Up here," she calls through the open window.

I mount the steps and she meets me at the landing. I greet her as I would at one of the many cocktail parties we all attend during the season.

"You'll have to forgive the way this place looks; I keep the messiest studio this side of the Mississippi."

"I would worry about an artist with a clean studio," I say. Sandy loves being referred to as an artist, but the studio is clean by any standard.

She wipes her hands on her smock. Some drawings have been left on a chair and these must constitute the mess to which she refers. She moves them as she bids me to sit.

"I've been sitting all day. It feels good to stand."

"Suit yourself," she says, bubbling. "Soft drink? Coffee?"

"Not a thing." I walk to the wall where several of her watercolors are displayed, examining them casually. I recognize Colonial Lake, and nanny-led children with balloons. "These are great," I tell her, and I mean it within my paltry, some would say nonexistent judgment where art is the issue.

"My early period," she says. "I'm in oils now. How about this one?" she says, pointing to her easel. "A work in progress but you get the idea."

I do?

"Sure, its got . . . texture." I must have hit a happy nerve because she appears pleased. Sandy is an unlikely artist in my qualified experience. They should be tormented and rangy, with ill-sized jeans and no makeup and leonine hair unbrushed for days except as they run paint-smudged hands with smoke-stained fingertips through it. Sandy is short, curvaceous, well-coifed, and manicured. The internal angst driving her seems on the surface confined to the selection of one European country in which to vacation this summer from among the dizzying number of candidates.

"Sandy, I'll be right up front with you. I came here to talk about the St. Simeon. Before you say anything, let me assure you I will not ask you to violate the confidentiality agreement reached by the group. I'm interested in what might happen at the next meeting, not what happened at the last."

Intrigue collects on her features and her hands undergo a rare relaxation. "Will there be another?"

"There could be." I inform her of the Lafayette exemption and my efforts to pry information out of the orphanage in Korea. "Depending on what comes back, we may ask for a reconsideration."

"And I for one hope you get it," she says emphatically. "Do you know I didn't sleep for days after that vote? I listened very carefully to the arguments on both sides—I can't tell you what they were but you can guess—and I kept asking myself, 'What is the right and fair thing to do?' Allie is as sweet as any girl in this city and more talented than most. Was it fair to exclude her? I asked myself. Of course, as Board members we represent the entire Society. We have obligations that go beyond personalities. I . . . I was so torn I didn't know what to do."

"I'm not asking for a commitment, Sandy, but if I can demonstrate that at least one exception has been made and that Allie satisfies the rule, would you be inclined to support us?"

"Of course I would. It would only be fair, wouldn't it? She's no different from Lafayette as far as I'm concerned. And there's no question of her foreign birth so she's halfway there. Coleman, I haven't laid eyes on Allie since that vote. Is she just ready to throw us all in the river? I wouldn't blame her."

"She understands the spot the Board's on. Naturally, she's disappointed."

"Sometimes I wonder if it isn't time to let go of the St. Simeon. I mean, this is the nineties."

"Sandy, somebody probably made that same statement in the 1890's, and for all we know in the 1790's, but it's still with us."

"Charlotte and I have argued about this. Charlotte does not support changes."

"Really?"

"I love her dearly but sometimes she can be a tad narrow-minded. Between you and me, and if you tell her I said it I'll never speak to you again, I don't think Charlotte would support an exception, whether it was Lafayette or Jesus Christ. She's just that way."

"But you would? You'd agree if it were fair."

"Certainly I would. Do you doubt it?"

Yes, Sandy, I think while walking back to the office, I doubt it, but don't take it personally. Generic uncertainty beclouds your entire group. Reading you is difficult. I think you voted nay last time, but with conscience. Philosophical disagreement with Charlotte Hines, on the other hand, is cause for optimism. Perhaps you have more backbone than I suspect.

Harris enters the office within minutes of my return. He reports on a meeting with Carlton Middleton, our patron saint in the city attorney's office.

"Cathcart refuses to die," he says, puffing his cheeks in a gesture that signals something between bewilderment and disbelief. On the few occasions I have accompanied him on duck hunts, a missed shot caused the same reaction. "He lowered his fees; partners, associates, paralegals—they're all willing to work for ten percent less. The city figures it can save between $150,000 and $200,000."

"Can we match it?"

"Camilla's running a spread sheet now. Let me see if it's ready." He springs up and out the door.

I like Joe Cathcart, along with most of the people in his firm. But I can't shake the idea that the council's deferral of the vote transfused hope into their expiring chances for the contract. Harris returns with a computer printout. For the next forty-five minutes, we sit together perusing numbers and assumptions. We can match Cathcart's reduction, and Harris is on the phone to Middleton as I leave to visit Clarkson Mills.

He lives in a spacious house on Lenwood Boulevard, the house I saved. His wife Rosemary, a timid, apologetic woman despite a sturdy frame, answers the door. She leads me through the house, appointed top to bottom with stock in trade from Mills Brothers Furniture. His brother committed suicide years ago. Clarkson spies us as we step onto the patio.

"Come in the house!" he says when he sees me. This makes no sense in that we have just left the house and he is himself outside but the greeting is habitual. We shake hands as Rosemary excuses herself to "attend to supper."

"You're just in time, Lawyer Carter. See those wasp nests?" He points to the eaves under the second floor some twelve feet off the ground. "We barbecue out here in the summer and they pester us to death. I'm just about to send them up to that great barbecue in the sky."

He is dressed in work clothes topped with an Atlanta Braves cap. At his feet, a plastic container of gasoline rests beside an aluminum extension pole for a paint roller. As I look on he attaches an old rag to the end of the pole by means of fine wire, a jury-rigged torch long enough to reach the nests.

"Should I alert to fire department?" I ask.

"Nope, but you can hold that pole steady while I pour the gas." As I hold, he douses generous quantities from the two gallon container. Fumes engulf us. He fishes in his pocket for a lighter as I consider the odds of abetting the destruction of the house I once fought to preserve. He fires the rag and takes the pole from my hands, trusting it upward. "You allergic to bee stings?" he asks.

"I'm not fond of them," I reply, backing away as homeless wasps angrily circle their charred domains.

Rosemary serves iced tea ten minutes later as we sit at the patio table. There is small talk of interest rates and the presidential race. I am about to broach my reason for coming when Clarkson says, "I feel mighty damn bad about your daughter. That's a tough bunch. I wish I could have done more to help. I haven't forgotten what you did for Rosemary and me during that awful time."

I ask him whether he has heard of the Lafayette exemption. When he shakes his head I repeat the litany I went through with Sandy. He listens impassively.

"I couldn't have told you about Lafayette," he says, "but it stands to reason that there have been exceptions made. You know as sure as we're sitting here that before the St. Simeon got to be such a hotsy-totsy big deal they must have let scores of non-members into the Ball. It's just common sense. In fact, I made that very argument to the Board that night. I had no proof, but I felt I owed it to you to come up with something."

I sip my tea, appraising him across the table. So he went to bat for me that night; a good news, bad news revelation. Loyalty still counts, and that is good. But my five-to-two theory is thrown into doubt. With his vote, I had three and Adelle's hunch of wider support gains weight. Suspicions of

Margarite resurface before I banish them to concentrate on what Clarkson is saying.

"I spoke with a couple of the real hard-liners after the meeting broke up. I guess you heard we were there until after eleven. Anyway, these women refused to concede there had ever been exceptions made so I'm glad you've come up with the proof."

"Do you think such proof could cause them to reevaluate their positions if it came up again?" I couple my question with an explanation of the letter to Korea.

He leans back with his hands clasped behind his head. "Hard to say. With a couple of them you're flogging a dead horse. The others . . . ?"

Adelle's theory takes a hit or Clarkson is being too casual with his plurals. If "a couple" is two, as it always is, and if by "others" he truly means more than one, then at least four people opposed me and Margarite's report of the results stands unblemished. The line-up had to be: Margarite, Adelle, and Clarkson for; Doc Francis, Sandy, Charlotte, and Jeanette against.

"Clarkson, you referred to what I did for you and Rosemary. At the risk of sounding like I'm calling in a chit, I need your help."

"Just name it."

"The way I've got this thing figured, I'll need one more vote if the committee reconsiders. If you could help on the inside with those others you mentioned, it might make the difference."

"I'll do it. You tell me what to say and I'll say it."

"I can't until I hear from Korea. Frankly, I'm not optimistic there. But I just came from Sandy's, and if I'm reading her correctly she's had some second thoughts about this whole issue. If, and I stress if because I don't know, she voted no last time, she might switch, given the chance."

"Sounds plausible," he says with I quick glance back to the blackened wasp nests. "Well, let me know."

I return to the office buoyed by his promise. Unless a prisoner of self-deception, I have made strides today. How else to read Sandy's disagreement with Charlotte over the future of the Society and her insistence on fairness? What other conclusion to reach in Clarkson's advocacy before the vote and willingness to lobby fence-sitters?

Throughout the day, thoughts of Natalie have intruded into my most concentrating moments. While walking, my mind drifts in a fresh nostalgia, enhanced by the springtime unfolding around me. The swiftness of our ascension from business associates, kindly put, to potential lovers confounds me. When I left her in the chill of her doorway, there was no talk of future but intense gratification in the moment.

32

On Sunday Allie and I attend St. Philip's. I scan the crowd as we stand, kneel, and sit, the mechanical rosary of the Episcopal Church. St. Simeons are everywhere. Margarite and John are here, regal in their perfectly pitched piety. Sandy and Edgar Charles slipped in moments after the service began. Clarkson Mills is absent, but I see Rosemary among the crowd up front.

Adelle is also present, a reminder of unresolved tension. I owe her nothing, as I have reiterated internally time and again since my evening with Natalie. Still, I brood. Was there some implied fidelity? Had I bound myself to her at some level of commitment violated by foreplay with Natalie? That sounds prudish for a reason: I am a prude.

My veneration of fidelity among competing virtues could, I am sure, be explained by time and psychotherapy. A harbored need for precision movement in the mainspring of my being will not abide the rust and corrosion of guilt from violated loyalties. Yet I felt not a pang of remorse while with Natalie. Amazing to me, I did not once think of Adelle during the entire evening, and what that says about the future of our relationship seems too obvious, regardless of Natalie. Telling Adelle will be uncomfortable, not to mention the potential for changing the tally on the committee. Would I keep her close just to keep her vote?

As we exit, we are approached by Doc Francis, whom I did not notice inside. He looks serious, and sad. He speaks first to Allie. His nasal brogue is distinct.

"Young lady," he says, pumping her hand with both of his, "I haven't seen you in a couple of years. You've grown up. Good luck up there at Princeton."

"Thank you, sir," she says. I cannot remember if she is aware of his membership on the Board.

He turns to me as Allie walks ahead. "I've had something on my conscience for a few weeks now and I need to clear it." His infamous halitosis is at full strength but I ignore it. "As you know, your daddy deprived me of one of life's pleasures when he defeated me for the presidency of the St. Simeon." I am about to respond but he charges on. "What you may not know is that I lost a brother in Korea. 1952. So you see, your pitch to the Board opened a couple of old wounds for me." He pauses and glares directly at me. "Just to make it official, I voted against that young lady back then. I'm ashamed to admit it now, but it's true and I wanted you to hear it from me. I apologize."

"I accept your apology, for myself and for her."

"Good. Maybe for your daddy too if it's not asking too much. Those fool friends of mine in St. Simeon nominated me and I couldn't back down. I knew I'd lose but when it happened I got my feelings hurt. I wanted to resign but my wife talked me out of it. Anyway, I'm sorry I didn't wake up in time to tell him to his face. And I'm sorry I took it out on you and your daughter."

"He'd understand," I assure him. "And as for Allie, you may get a chance to redeem yourself shortly. Keep your powder dry, as they say."

"I'll do that."

I run by the office, then home. Allie has invited Christopher over, Adelle is there, and Steven arrives just after I do. In no time, Adelle has whipped up an impromptu lunch from what I thought was an empty refrigerator. She's standing at the counter when I enter the kitchen.

"Thanks for handling things," I say. "You're good at this."

She smiles and nods acknowledgment. "I saw you and Dr. Francis chatting at church."

"The strangest conversation. He fessed up to voting against Allie and wants to bury the hatchet. I had no idea he lost a brother in Korea. Ouch."

"Can you beat that?" she says.

"I nearly passed out. If Dad wasn't already gone, the shock of Doc Francis apologizing would have sent him. He all but said he'd change his vote if we can get it reconsidered by the Board."

She slides a hot tray from the oven. "Let me put these rolls on. Then, we need to talk about something." She backs through the swinging door as I wonder what's on her mind. Natalie? Seconds later she returns. "What do you know about Florida?" she asks sternly.

"Well, it's south of here, shaped kind of like—"

"This is serious. The trip the kids are planning. Are you aware of it?"

"No. Are they going to Florida?"

"So Allie hasn't mentioned it?"

"Not a word."

She sighs. "Chris told me last week that he, Robert, and Chad are driving to Florida with Allie, Jenny, and Melissa for spring break and I don't think it's appropriate."

"Why?"

"Why?" she asks impatiently. "For openers, the roads are dangerous with all the college kids in God knows what state of sobriety. And you read about so much crime in Florida."

"Is that your concern?"

"Some of it, yes."

"And the rest?"

"Think about it. Chris and Allie are together all the time and now they want to go to Florida. I don't know if there's anything between Robert and Melissa but Chad and Jenny have been hot and heavy for over two years. I can just picture what will go on."

"I could be wrong," I say, "but I remember something about Chris going to Florida last spring. Allie said a group from her class went down to . . . was it Sanibel?"

"That's hardly the same thing. Those kids were all friends having fun. This is much different."

"Because he and Allie are so serious."

"Don't you think they are?"

"I don't know, Adelle. It's their business as far as I'm concerned. I trust my daughter and I'm beginning to think I trust your son more than you do."

"Then you are very naive. I would appreciate it if you would back me up on this. I've told Chris he can't go and if you tell Allie the same thing it will be easier on everyone."

"I have no intention of telling her that."

Her gaze is cold, disbelieving. She turns and strides to the swinging door. Moments later, Allie enters.

"What's Adelle in a huff about?" she asks.

"Florida."

"Chris said she nixed his going. I was going to talk to you about it."

"Ok, we've talked. If you want to go, you have my permission."

"Dad, can I tell you something?"

"Sure, sweetheart."

"I don't think Adelle likes me."

33

On the following morning, Charlotte Hines, her Royal Ampleness, is not at home. A velvet-voice servant predicts her return around noon. I leave neither name nor message. At Carter & Deas, the morning passes swiftly. At one, I return to Charlotte's, on foot. Dropping in on her is crass but time is short and the odds are long. The first question out of the butler's mouth is whether she's expecting me.

"What a pleasant surprise!" she says as she enters the living room where the butler has me parked. The sight of her bearing down in her outsized muumuu is not unlike watching a painted boulder roll downhill. I rise to meet her. Later, to her friends, she will casually mention the international phone call she had to end prematurely to see me; or the gala she was in the middle of planning when I presented myself "out of thin air."

"How distressed I was to hear of Michael Foland's passing," she says, settling into a large chair just wide enough to hold her. This is a classic Charlotte opening. Foland, a member of the church I barely knew, died the week before. Why she has selected this subject for conversation is unknown. "How is Diane holding up? I must call her."

"Who is Diane?" I ask.

"His wife."

"I didn't know he was married."

"They divorced years ago," she says, as if this information is properly classified as Charleston 101. "I had every intention of going to the funeral," she tells me as she lights a cigarette. I wait expectantly but she offers no explanation. "Don't you think," she says, and I brace for her first irrationality, "it is unfortunate the way they bury people in that annex across the street from St. Philip's?"

The cemetery is divided by Church Street. "I'm not quite sure what you mean, Charlotte."

"The whole point of being buried in a churchyard is proximity to the sanctuary. I was telling Bishop Burgoyne just recently that I thought there should be a moratorium on burials across the street."

Charlotte is an inveterate name-dropper. The bishop has just fallen and before I leave she will mention the governor and at least one of South Carolina's U.S. Senators. The bishop will be in select company.

"Well . . . ," I say, already sensing the testiness she evokes in a remarkably short time, "they ran out of room in the old graveyard. Over a hundred and fifty years ago."

She blows smoke toward the high ceiling. "Then they should be creative. That's what religion is all about anyway, isn't it? Creativity?"

"Of course," I say, lost.

"It's for that very reason, creativity, that Glen and I attend St. Michael's."

"I see," I reply. "I guess I didn't know how creative they are at St. Michael's."

"Oh, yes," she says decisively. "Those lovely bells."

With Charlotte, elaboration rarely leads to enlightenment, so I say nothing. She studies me for a moment, her eyes suddenly flaring in anticipation. "You'll never guess what Fritz told me the other day."

"Fritz" is Ernest Hollings, a U.S. Senator. The governor cannot be far behind. "I can't guess."

"The naval base is doomed."

Vintage Charlotte. Her thunderbolt, authenticated by an intimate at the highest echelon, has dominated the front page of the *Sentinel* for over four years. When a budget-cutting panel of experts recommended closing a score of bases and military installations across the country, the Charleston Naval Base surfaced on the death list. The loss of this sprawling magnet for the bi-monthly filings of government largess has occasioned the greatest outcry here. The government team presiding over the closure has been in place for months. As news, her revelation is not unlike being told, in confidence, that the Japanese bombed Pearl Harbor.

"Charlotte, it's been my impression that the base closing was decided upon some time back."

"That's what they wanted us to believe. I happen to know of some top secret negotiations that have been held to save it. But Fritz reports to me that it can't be done and I know exactly who to blame."

"Who?" I ask dutifully.

"The environmentalists. Those Sierra Madre people. They've tried to gut this country's defense system for years."

I nod as some alternative to laughter. "Does Fritz blame the environmentalists?"

"Oh, he's a politician, too diplomatic to actually blame anyone. But Carrol will back me up on this."

Carrol Campbell is the governor.

"But Carrol is also a politician," I cannot help noting.

"Regrettably, yes, and at a time when we could use a statesman like Strom."

Strom Thurmond is the other U.S. Senator and by floating his name she has trumped herself. "But we have Strom, don't we?"

"What can that possibly have to do with the St. Simeon?" she wants to know. "That's why you're here, isn't it?"

"Yes," I say, relieved to have strayed, however circuitously, to my mission. Progress is as unlikely as my hostess, billowing smoke upward and crossing her legs under the muumuu.

"Coleman, put yourself in our place. If you were a member of the Board, would you vote in favor of Pocahontas?"

"The Indian maiden Pocahontas?"

"What other Pocahontas could we be talking about in a discussion of Allie's attending the St. Simeon?" she demands, snubbing her cigarette with repeated jabs into the ashtray beside her. "Do you see my point?"

"Not entirely."

"The Indians were a proud people. Some today even suggest we should return land to them, which is absurd given how long we've owned it. But we wouldn't admit Pocahontas to the Ball, because we, the Caucasians who have built this great country and this great city are also proud people. And that pride is going to keep what we've built. Do you think the zoning board would give her a variance to put a tepee on Church Street?"

"Allie?"

"No, Pocahontas." Charlotte looks exasperated at my failure to follow. "No tepees are permitted because our race, yours and mine, has surmounted primitive constructions. Don't you see?"

"Well," I say, grasping the fringe of logic that is the only material Charlotte exposes, "I do agree that no tepees should be allowed on Church Street."

"Now we're getting somewhere. Once you permit tepees, you have to allow their occupants, so then what have we done?" She eyes me sophomorically, like the answer should vault from my lips.

"I suppose we've . . . allowed Indians to move into the neighborhood."

"Precisely," she says, pleased. "But our pride wouldn't allow that. Pride in being who we were and who we are. It makes all the difference. If you'll think about it from that standpoint, I'm sure you'll understand the Board's vote."

I rise. This has been every bit as ludicrous as I expected. I cannot resist leaving her with something to ponder. "Charlotte, what do think about allowing tepees at the naval base once it shuts down?"

"I have no idea what you mean."

"Then we're even, but thanks for your time. I'll be running along now."

Jeanette Wilson's gift shop is my last outreach. As I drive toward the market, I review. Charlotte is a bigoted no, as I knew before I visited. For her, the human race worthy of preservation lives south of Broad, she will never change, and tepees, slums or, for that matter, nuclear waste are irrelevant as long as they remain discreetly beyond her myopia. But with Doc Francis's stunning contrition yesterday, I have more cause for optimism. Charlotte stands as the sole implacable opponent, with Sandy Charles declaring a willingness to listen and Clarkson Mills firmly in my service. At this moment, Jeanette's support appears superfluous, but taking nothing for granted I will bring to my meeting with her the honed concentration worthy of the deciding vote. She is behind the counter, reading a magazine in the deserted shop, when I enter.

The Open Oyster sells commemoratives of an antebellum past unrecognizable to those who lived it but no less treasured by their descendants. In the idealized city found within this twelve-hundred square feet, stately homes along the Battery suffer none of the ravages inflicted by year-round exposure to the Atlantic's whims of nor'easters and salt. Colorful prints capture blacks selling flowers, but not captured blacks being sold like flowers. Here, even the Yankees find stylized redemption as innocuous villains, miniature soldier casts no more destructive than your traditional cross-state football rivals. A yesteryear that never was can be purchased for as little as $8.95 by those willing to settle for authentic reproductions of the lace doilies used in the lobby of the Charleston Hotel, razed in 1960 but elegant when it counted: 1860.

Jeanette closes Cosmopolitan as I close the door behind me.

"Would you believe," she says, "that you're my first customer this afternoon?"

"Would you believe I'm not a customer? I came to see you about my daughter."

Jeanette is my age. She has a way of looking at men that takes them all in, the kind of sizing up faculty found in veteran tobacco buyers. Her very shapely leg, crossed over one knee and exposed, begins pumping as she speaks.

"Allie walked by the shop last week. She's a pretty thing."

"Thanks. You should see her in a formal evening gown."

"Now Coleman, don't start in on me." She divides my name into two distinct syllables, so that it sounds like Cold Man. "I was no more comfortable with that whole St. Simeon business than the rest of them. I could shoot you for making us decide."

"I'm sorry, Jeanette. You know what old Harry Truman said about the buck."

Jeanette is unique. She married James, the best surgeon in town and a man we all assumed to be gay. Childless, they lead totally separate lives. He puts in marathon hours at the hospital and is rarely seen at social functions other than the St. Simeon while she never misses a tea or cotillion. Some believe her religious devotion to Charleston's peculiar gentility masks her true passion: men of all ages, sizes, and colors. Rumors gather around her like ducks around bread in Hampton Park. A particularly vicious one several years back had her in a rented house on Kiawah Island with three Greek sailors for an extended weekend. She is one of those women who look as though they were designed and built for middle age, and I cannot imagine her young though I have known her for fifteen years. When drinking heavily, she is quite aggressive, yet fanatically observant of her friends' marital boundaries, never to my knowledge risking her social rank by coming on to the husband of someone in a position to damage her. Until Elizabeth died, Jeanette's conduct with me personified decorum, in pointed contrast to her more recent sultry but discreet advances at the Cooper Club after four martinis.

Of one thing I am convinced: she voted with the majority as best she would have been able to determine it by the arguments advanced during debate. But for the aromatic spice of her rumored sexual peccadilloes she is a relentless "me too," unwilling to venture a centimeter beyond the crowd that gives life meaning outside her bedroom. How a woman could simultaneously exhibit such numbing social conformity with the devious lust attributed to her I have not figured out. Perhaps she has been maligned by the jealous, but her pumping leg and her "try me" look today say otherwise.

"That meeting surprised me," she offers. "Knowing your daddy was a past president, and knowing how close you are to the members, I assumed you would get what you were asking us for."

"I may ask again," I say, fingering a guide to historical homes displayed on the counter. She absorbs my information on the Lafayette exemption with practiced disinterest. Jeanette will attempt no independent analysis of its bearing on my request. She will await the pronouncements of those closest, then throw in with the winners. Her first question demonstrates her grasp of what I said.

"Lafayette was French, wasn't he?"

Dear God. "Very French," I confirm. "Without asking you to commit yourself, I was hoping the precedent for an exception would alter your thinking."

"So you're just assuming I was against you. Did Adelle tell you that?"

"Adelle has told me nothing. I assumed it because I lost."

"I think she has talked, personally. Sandy and Charlotte think so too. She's violated our agreement."

This is something that has worried me from the beginning, the assumption that Adelle's loyalty would run to violating the Board's injunction. "No," I insist. "Quite the contrary. I've been frustrated because I can't get anything out of her."

"Well, she'd better stick to our deal. Just because she took no part in the debate she has no right to reveal what's confidential."

No part in the debate? This squares with nothing, but arguing will only convince her that Adelle has given me a full account. "Of course not. But I swear to you she has played by the rules. If I leaped to a conclusion about your vote, I apologize."

A real customer enters the store, diverting her attention.

"All I'm asking, Jeanette, is a fair hearing if it comes back for another vote. Can I count on that?"

"Sure," she says, "we all want to be reasonable."

Returning home, I scan the mail. An electric bill, a solicitation from the Heart Fund, and a flyer hyping an art opening. The phone rings. Mr. Quan has just heard from his brother.

"The Children's Home is still there. They can give him no information about their files. Everything confidential."

I make a reservation for tonight.

"I will have the kitchen fix something special," he says.

"Speaking of something special, I won't be with Adelle."

"I understand," he says in a wry voice. "Mrs. Roberts is busy this evening."

"Something like that."

Natalie is ready when I ring her doorbell in North Charleston. A part of me has been apprehensive about this first private reunion, but she ushers me in casually, glad to see me but not awkwardly so. She offers a drink. Her scotch is my brand and I know she has shopped for me.

I make small talk. Her back is to me as she stands at the counter fixing herself what appears to be mineral water with a twist of lime. Instinct pulls me forward to nuzzle her neck, but I refrain.

"Any word from Korea?" she asks over her shoulder.

"Yes. I spoke to Mr. Quan just before I left home. Have you had dinner?"

Driving to the Red Dragon, we talk of the last few days. There is in her an unrushed exodus from the tightly harnessed personality I met. Emotions within seem to be undergoing a chemical reaction that will produce new substance, but it is yet too early to predict its form and properties. I see elements of caution, but not much, of relief, of longing, and even a touch of fear. Noticeably absent is any sense of urgency. She offers no explanation for our involvement, no theories of how or why, and solicits none from me. Somehow, what to me has come as suddenly as lightning from a cloudless sky she takes, on the surface at least, as a progression, if not anticipated at least not unduly skewed. I look forward to learning more of what is going on inside the relaxed woman sitting beside me.

Pham greets us near the door and shows us to a table, explaining as we walk that Mr. Quan is upstairs on the phone. Our food is brought immediately, the special off-menu fare he promised. We are well into succulent if unrecognizable dishes when he appears. At introduction to Natalie, he is formally polite.

"My brother called back. He forgot one detail."

"Speak freely," I tell him as he sits. "She knows the whole story."

"He left this number for the home. In case you would like to call," he says.

"I would," I say, taking the slip of paper he's offered. "I wonder what time it is over there."

"Afternoon," he says. "You may use my phone upstairs."

I return ten minutes later. He and Natalie are discussing the unlikely subject of Vietnam antiwar protests. "That was a waste of time. They're very nice, but the woman who answered speaks limited English. I think she said they have a policy of not discussing much of anything by phone. Understandable, since I could be anyone."

"Maybe you should go over there," Natalie says. "Didn't you tell me you were planning to take Allie for graduation?"

"In June."

"So, go early. Maybe she would like to visit the home where she stayed."

"It's a thought," I say. "Mr. Quan, why don't you come with us. You could visit your brother."

"That was suggested once before," he says in diplomatic deference to Natalie being seated now where Adelle was seated then. "I have been thinking it over. I would like to see him, and we are getting older."

"Great," I say. "Let's book it."

"Just a moment," he says. "As you Americans say, 'hold your horse.'"

"Horses, but go ahead."

"I have a proposition. I will accompany you if you will accompany me."

"Where?"

"Vietnam."

"You have been thinking it over."

Natalie asks, "You have family there?"

"My cousin has not been seen in Saigon for over three years. An old friend of mine thinks he made have moved to the country."

"What about the old friend?"

"Yes," Mr. Quan says, for the first time showing some vulnerability around the eyes. "A veddy old, dear friend. After so many years he is still a good friend. We shared great times in the old days and much danger during the war. Now we are old. Well," he says, business-like again, "will you come?"

He and Natalie stare at me expectantly.

"Why not?" I say, more defensively than decisively. I look to her. "Want to come?"

Natalie shakes her head. "Love to, but there are at least three problems. I have no passport, no money, and no time. I'm starting a trial next week that has been postponed twice."

"What about you?" I say to him. "Do you have a passport?"

He nods. "I visit Europe," he says. He is thinking. After a silence, he adds, "That is as close as I have come, until now."

"You look worried," I suggest.

"It . . . is not safe."

"Why, will they arrest you?"

"The danger is not of that kind. It is not safe here," he says, pointing to his chest. "Everything has changed in Saigon," he says. "The communists rename everything. Revolutionary themes. Veddy third world," he says, shaking his head.

"I'll keep you company," I say. "It's a deal."

Natalie and I return to North Charleston. She asks if I regret committing to Mr. Quan.

"No. Allie really wants to go. I owe it to her. Why wait until graduation when we can take care of some business now? Of course, I didn't bargain for Vietnam, but what the hell."

Natalie laughs and drapes her arms around me. "You realize what you're doing, don't you?"

"Yes. I'm taking my daughter to the land of her birth."

"And what else?"

"Nothing else."

"Yes, something else."

"Nothing else."

"You're going halfway around the world to avoid what you'll end up having to do anyway: sue your friends."

"Maybe," I say.

Allie is waiting when I return home at the thoroughly decent hour of 9:30. "Mr. Quan called," she says before I can remove my coat. "He says he's packing his bags and you'd know what that means. What does it mean?"

"It means," I say, smiling at her, "that if you're willing to take off a week from school you're going to get your graduation present in April."

34

In six days we will depart for East Asia, and now that I've made the decision to go I'm filling with anticipation. Not only does the lure of an exotic part of the world appeal just now, but the human dramas built into this trip assure it will be memorable for all of us. Life changing? That remains to be seen.

In addition to experiencing Korea's culture, we will be looking for an orphanage with records I'm betting no longer exist. And if they do, what do we expect to learn? And most important: assuming we learn anything, what will we do with the information? Allie has consistently said she has no interest in finding birth parents who abandoned her. But what if her file shows names and an address? What if it documents a compelling reason why her birth mother was forced to give her up? Would her curiosity get the better of her? What would I do in her place? The decision to seek out birth parents is fraught with risk on both sides. In satisfying her curiosity (longing?) is she ripping a scab from a wound eighteen years in the healing?

Each of us has a valid reason for this trip, notwithstanding the St. Simeon. Allie asked to go before the Ball became an issue and if I don't take her now I will be making this trip in June. Mr. Quan has not been home in fifteen years and, I suspect, would not go now had the door to his past not been opened by our recent conversations. That leaves me. The Korean leg of the trip I can handle and enjoy. Elizabeth talked of taking

Allie, so the only hesitation I feel is one vaguely related to the injustice of her missing what I won't. I agreed to accompany Mr. Quan to Vietnam because it seems important to him.

But each of us also rolls some dice. Allie stands to be disappointed by either the total lack of information or the revelation she is the offspring of a prostitute, drug addict, or who knows what. It has taken Mr. Quan a decade or longer to work up the courage to return to Vietnam. I think back to him pointing to his chest as the locus of his angst. And Vietnam brings me face to face with Philip's death and my own circumvention of the war that defined my generation. Maybe I can find a way to pay tribute to Philip while I'm there. Margarite's lament about him being forgotten hit me in a soft spot, and to bring her any solace would gratify me.

World War II's legacy of glory made rational discussion of Vietnam almost impossible, particularly between veteran fathers and apprehensive sons. John Huger, Philip's dad, was an avowed hawk, embracing the war as fervently as he traded stocks. Like so many fathers of that era, he viewed war as a chance for glory. His militance infected his son, a risk taker by nature. I, on the other hand, went quietly and thankfully to law school.

Philip would have made the perfect soldier in 1941, but this was 1968, and behind his gung-ho enthusiasm for combat, any combat, lay serious reservations about America's role in that war, as I learned in late night discussions with him after his orders came. When his basic training instructors diagramed the Battle of the Bulge or Patton's sweep into Germany, Philip questioned. "What the hell has this got to do with the price of eggs where we're going?" "They're playing on their home field," was another of Philip's simple yet murderously incisive analogies, a reference to our high school football experiences. "We're always tougher at home."

I saw in these and other common sense observations doubts that he hid from his parents and the other junior officers in his infantry unit. He never spoke publicly of his doubts. The peace freaks who began to blight campuses and infiltrate news programs revolted him. The patriot in him viscerally condemned anarchy, yet he seemed to be teetering on an intellectual edge where the war was concerned, and what came closest to sending him over that edge, to the side of the protesters and draft dodgers and antiwar zealots he despised, patriotism be damned, was his implacable dislike for and distrust of Lyndon Johnson. "I don't think," he told me late one night as the two of us did our absolute best to drain dry a newly purchased case of beer, "that my president is the kind of man that would worry much if I bite the banana over there." We were together the night Johnson announced his decision to retire rather than face a primary. Philip watched it with macabre satisfaction, almost as if this ignominious abdication was Philip's revenge for his mortal wound still seven months in the future.

Years ago, one of those change-your-life-in-a-day motivational speakers put to a group of us a time-management challenge. An all-expenses paid trip around the world would be ours, so ran his hypothetical, provided we could wrap up all pending business by that afternoon. "You will," he predicted, "find a way to get it done." I am about to put his theory to test.

I call Margarite and though it is early I have not awakened her. "If we hope to learn anything of Allie's background, we need to go to Korea," I say. "A long shot, as you know, but even if we come up empty on her history, it will fulfill Elizabeth's wish and Allie's wish for a graduation present." I think I startled her with my next question. "Where, exactly, was Philip killed?"

After several seconds, she wants to know, "Why do you ask?"

"Because we added Vietnam to our itinerary. I want to pay my respects."

Margarite, never at a loss for words, stays mum. A very long pause ensues. I wait. "Margarite?"

In a subdued voice: "John and I have talked about going. I just don't think I could bear it. We were told it was about halfway between two villages, one called Cu Chi and the other Duc Lap."

"Near Saigon?"

"Very close, perhaps thirty miles. Coleman, what will you do?"

"I thought I'd lay a wreath of some kind. Would you like me to take something?"

"Yes. Give me the morning to think of just what."

"Call me at the office. I can come by and pick it up."

My next task involves preparing Mother. She is far more worried about me than she needs to be.

"But dear, it's a communist country. A leopard doesn't change its spots. I won't sleep a wink the entire time you're gone. You cannot trust them for an instant. Suppose they won't let you leave? Suppose Mr. Quan is wanted for some war crime and you're with him." She is wringing her hands, uncontrollably nervous.

"I don't suppose Mr. Quan would be willing to go were he wanted for war crimes or anything else. The Vietnamese are wooing us as trading partners now. They have to behave themselves."

"Communists appear one way and act another. I won't sleep a wink."

Sarah's brand of xenophobia is as common as clover. I believe Allie's Asian features were so distressing to her because they evoked war memories of slant-eyed, buck-toothed Japanese in the army of the Red peril. While her assessment of those same features has undergone drastic revision ("She's positively lovely") the anathema provoked by communists, of any race, religion or country of origin, remains rabid.

"Don't forget a jacket," she says.

"Mother, it's a hundred and ten in the shade over there."

"Well, take one along anyway. You never know. You can't put anything past communists."

On my way to the office I stop by the office of Harry Porter, M.D. Harry is the best wheelchair-bound doctor in the country for my money, and he's gotten quite a bit of it over the years. He gives me the same shots he will give Allie this afternoon after school. My arm begins to throb before I arrive at the office.

The motivational guy may be on to something. Clients who "must" see me are convinced to re-schedule. Those unable to wait are referred to partners familiar with their files. In a few short days my calendar has been cleared of all but one obligation, one Harris assures me he will handle. After a stop by the travel agency and the bank for travelers checks, I am more or less, when packed, ready to go.

I have not heard from Margarite, who tells me, when I arrive at her house late in the day, that she cannot decide on a fitting memorial to be left at the site. "Just some flowers, I suppose."

"Let me pick something," I suggest. "What about the Corona bottle from Mexico. Philip would approve. It will be a little like having a beer with him."

"Perfect," she says. "I'll get it for you. Fix yourself a drink and wait for me in the Haiti room."

I pour us each an Old Granddad as she returns with the Corona bottle. Handing it to me she says, "This is quite thoughtful of you, Coleman. I assume you have other business in Vietnam?"

"No business, really. I agreed to accompany Mr. Quan on his first return home in many years. He is very apprehensive about going by himself for some reason. He has a brother in Seoul who will help us navigate a city none of us knows the least bit about."

I sit in a chair by the cedar box, painted jaguars near enough to gnaw my knee. Margarite takes a seat on the sleigh-bed. I'm shifting the Corona bottle from hand to hand as Margarite says, "You mentioned looking into Allie's background over there. Do you really hope to find something?"

I shrug. "We're both realistic. All we know for sure is that the orphanage is still there. Mr. Quan's brother located it for us. Eighteen years is a long time. I doubt anyone there was on the scene when we adopted. It could prove the wildest of wild goose chases. The odds are overwhelmingly against us finding anything over there that could bring Allie legitimately within the exemption."

She sets her drink down deliberately. "Just as I feared," she says. "The inquiry into her background is more than an orphan looking for her roots. This is related to the Lafayette exemption, isn't it?"

"Why not? I've been visiting board members."

"So I've been told," she says, stress in her voice.

"Those visits tell me this vote would come out differently if taken again. Sandy Charles was most sympathetic and almost any excuse would be good enough for her to change sides. Doc Francis all but pledged to support us. That leaves only Charlotte, who is hopeless, and Jeanette."

At the mention of Charlotte Margarite smiles drolly.

"What I'm saying is this." I shift the Corona bottle to the other hand. "If the sentiment among the committee has changed as I think it has, then one pretext will be as good as another to reverse the vote. It becomes largely irrelevant what we find, if anything, about Allie's background. The critical need is another vote, and you can arrange that."

Margarite stands, her clouding face an unmistakable barometer of doubt. "Coleman, do you want my honest opinion of your efforts with the committee?"

"Of course."

"You're wasting your time and a lot of money."

"I don't care about either."

"Then consider your image in the community. I can't bear the thought of you making a fool of yourself."

"Why? All they can say is no and they've said it once."

"And they'll say it again."

"So," I say, "you don't agree with my reading of the group."

"No," she says softly, reluctantly. "Not at all."

"You should know, Margarite, but I'm still going. It seems the only way. If I fail, I fail."

I watch as she paces behind me, striding the floor aggressively. I have the feeling I have angered her and she is about to explode. Suddenly, she stops in mid-stride. Wheeling, she glares down at me, through me. Her patrician voice is close to a guttural rasp.

"You are forcing me into the dishonorable act of violating my word."

"No," I protest. "I wouldn't want that. I'm doing this on my own. It's my theory and you don't have to agree. I just need you to reconvene the Board."

She circles me, coming back to the seat she left but leaning forward, squinting intensely. "You need more than that. You need to know who your friends are and I'm going to violate my trust to tell you. What has Adelle said about our meeting?"

"Almost nothing."

"I don't wonder. It wouldn't be a pretty account. Would it surprise you to know she did not speak in your behalf?"

"She implied she did, although Jeanette made some reference to her taking no part in the debate."

"Well, she didn't. Nor did she vote for you."

I grip the Corona bottle by the neck. "You said the vote was secret. Everyone on the Board said so too."

"Yes. I counted the ballots."

"Did you recognize her handwriting or what?"

"Coleman, it required no detective work. Don't you understand? The count was six to one and I voted with you. They all voted no."

The bottle drops from my hand and I am only vaguely conscious of it striking and breaking the glass tabletop. My eyes lower to a point at her chest and I utter a dismal moan. "Fool, fool, fool," I repeat until the word is on my tongue but not beyond.

"When I called you on the night of the vote to report the result I tried to think of a way to tell you that Adelle had . . . how should I put it? Betrayed your trust. I knew from our discussions you were counting on her and she obviously was not truthful with you."

"Obviously," I mutter lamely. "And what about Clarkson? He said he went to bat for me."

"He did, in his own fashion. He said he thought we were all making too much of a single exception and that dozens of them must have been made in the past. Sandy Charles also made quite the speech about what an outstanding girl Allie is and how we needed to be fair in dealing with her. I must tell you, from the tenor of the discussion I was optimistic. Now I wonder if they weren't all simply going on the record as having said nice things, assuming whatever they said would get back to you through Adelle, or possibly me.

"I was so stunned when I counted the ballots that I had difficulty talking. I think Adelle knew from the look on my face. She had counted on at least one vote from the group to hide hers and when she saw my reaction she must have known. She was waiting for me in the parking lot as the meeting broke up but I walked by her without a word."

"Six to one," I murmur, as though by repeating the score I will alter the result.

"I've felt horrible for weeks," she says, "knowing you believed that a vote or two would turn it around. I feel better now for having told you. I'm resigning from the St. Simeon as soon as the Ball is over."

"Don't do that, Margarite. It's not your fault."

"No, but I am sickened by what this has shown me. I want no part of it in the future."

"Well," I say standing, my legs a bit shaky and my arm throbbing from the shots, "I guess that's that."

"Is there anything I can do to help?"

I pause, my head down and my gaze focused on the fresh cracks in the table top. "Yes. Please call the Board together as soon as you can."

"But for what purpose?"

"To reconsider its decision. And if it won't reconsider, to discuss a response to the lawsuit I plan to file when I return from Vietnam."

Margarite recoils. "You're suing us?"

I lean over and kiss her gently on the cheek, and she, frozen in her surprise, does not move. "I'm suing the Society and I'll have to see about my grounds to sue individual members. I will not, I give you my word, sue you personally, no matter what my lawyer advises."

She takes a rather long pull on her bourbon as she turns her head away. "I don't blame you. I think we deserve it. Perhaps John and I should accompany you to Vietnam and boycott the whole ugly mess."

"As much as I would enjoy your company, you would have gone before now if you intended to go."

"You're right. I just can't face it. Even now." After a pause, she asks, "What should I . . . tell people?"

"Board members? Tell them the Board has some urgent business. That will be true, I promise. And Margarite, I will keep quiet about what you've told me with one exception. I'd like your permission to use this information to confront Adelle. If I can do so without exposing you I will."

"Feel free," she says. "She brought it on herself."

Turning to leave, I say, "And send me a bill for the broken glass."

She smiles. "I'm leaving it just as it is. It adds character and you can never have too much of that."

As Daniel shows me out, I sense my anger toward Adelle will follow the well-worn, indirect path that I recognize from past confrontations. My fuse is long and meanders. Walking down Margarite's slate walk to my car, I reflect on the wisdom of confronting Adelle later, after I have refined my approach to a razor precision. Besides, I need to pack.

But at the first traffic light I turn right when left would take me home and amaze myself by speeding toward her home at close to sixty miles an hour through a residential district, my hands gripping the wheel like it is her throat. I slow the car a house or two away to avoid the melodrama of squealing tires.

By the time I reach for the doorbell, I am fully cognizant that my anger has broken loose from a pit of lifelong restraint. It roams wild, unchecked and vengeful. Treachery has nourished it with a potent fuel, injected it with strength I do not recognize, empowered it with a white-hot energy that will do great damage whether targeted or abandoned to random gyration. I am shaking with rage, and the interval between ringing the bell and

Adelle's prolonged response is just long enough for me to arrest my sore arm's visceral desire to punch her face in.

"Coleman! Come in. I just heard about your trip. How sudden."

"Yes, very," I say walking in and turning from her to disguise my impulse.

"You seem in a hurry," she says. "Would you like a drink?"

"Yes, I would."

"Follow me to the kitchen while I fix it. Then you can tell me how this came about."

"Is Chris home?"

"No. He called from the club. He's playing doubles under the lights."

I cannot predict what my new monster will do. It is on its own, roaming and sniffing. In a real sense I will be as surprised as Adelle when it pounces.

"So," I hear myself say, almost casually, "how are the kids doing these days? Still going strong?" Evidently my monster has a gift for stealth.

"I assume so," she says, stirring my drink. "Chris tells me nothing but as you know they still see a lot of each other. He's beside himself about her leaving on this trip."

I accept the proffered drink and lean philosophically on the counter. "You know, I'm beginning to think there may be more to their relationship than I originally thought."

"Oh?" Her faces pinches in alarm before she can check it. "Why do you say that?"

"Allie talks to me. Some things she said recently made me realize that they have progressed beyond high school sweethearts."

"How far beyond?" she demands.

"Well," I say flippantly, "if you mean have they crossed over the big line I couldn't say. I was speaking of their future. She's planning trips to USC and he's going up to Princeton—"

"Chris has said nothing about that to me. He's not the student Allie is and I would worry about his grades if he's spending his first college semester on the road."

"Sure," I agree. "But tennis takes time too."

"He has no choice there. He's on a scholarship."

"Yeah, I guess you're right. Did he mention them working together in Alaska next summer?" Allie had expressed interest in this but had not included Chris in her plan. Apparently my monster is not without cunning.

"What! That's absurd. Chris . . . can't possibly stay on top of his game in Alaska. He'll be here on the summer circuit."

"Maybe it's not his game he wants to be on top of."

"Coleman, what a grotesque thing to say about your own daughter. And you insult my son."

"Why? I would consider Chris a lucky guy if Allie thought enough of him to let him that close." Her scoff is sickening and my arm renews its jabbing twitch.

"Allie is a . . . special girl, for sure. But there's just no future for her with Chris. They're too . . . different."

"Gosh, I don't know about that. They both love the outdoors, they each have a nice sense of humor, both smart—"

"Oh, you know what I mean."

"No. Tell me, Adelle, exactly what you're talking about. Because I think I'm finally beginning to figure it out." I am off the counter now, advancing toward her as she retreats, startled, until the fridge blocks her. "Spit it out, Adelle," I shout. "She's not white, is she? She's not the kind of woman you've got your heart set on for Chris, is she? She's not really, bottom line, good enough for him, is she?"

She eyes me coldly, unmasked. "No, if you must know, she's not. That may sound harsh—"

"What it sounds is ignorant and small-minded, like its source."

"I don't have to take abuse from you." She moves to escape her corner but I block her passage.

"Yes, you do. In the thirty seconds between now and the last time I walk out your door you'll have to listen. I know now why I've never felt comfortable with you. You are one of those rare people who can lie with impunity and go on about your business. How far would you have gone to prevent an Asian daughter-in-law? Any Charleston know-nothing, lily white from south of Broad, would be better, wouldn't she? You disgust me. You're not enough woman to carry Allie's riding gear. Have a nice life."

My monster carries me to the door. I am just about to congratulate him on our restraint when he grasps the knob and violently slams it behind us as, for the second time in an hour, I shatter glass.

35

We leave today at 1:41 P.M. My morning is spent at Natalie's office, niched in a drab walk-up on King Street north of Calhoun. In the reception area, a framed print of Matisse's Joy hangs above a small, efficient couch, and beyond this cubicle is her office, furnished in an essentials-only austerity befitting the limited budgets of both the attorney and her clients.

"I want you to sue them for me," I tell her before relating the events of the night before. She sits behind her desk, her head propped against her hand, scribbling notes on a legal pad. Her strokes in ballpoint are abbreviated, not shorthand but a personal hieroglyphic that concentrates a paragraph of my speech to a line or two on her page. Twice she raises her head to ask a detail, a clarification. When I reach the meltdown with Adelle, I watch for signs that she is celebrating the demise of her rival but she is unflinching. "And don't," I conclude, "tell me I told you so."

She looks up, unsmiling. "I can't possibly draft this before you leave. It will require at least a couple of days for research, maybe more."

"I assumed so. Do you think we have time to do this?"

"There are two ways to view it. One is to automatically assume time limits us and the other is to hand that liability off to them."

"How?"

"By waiting until the last possible moment to file and putting all our chips on the District Court judge. We ask for an injunction against them barring her from attending the Ball. The Society will have to hire counsel and they will have to bring themselves up to speed, which as you know takes time. They won't have much. If we get a favorable ruling, the burden of appeal shifts to them and we just might sneak in before they get organized. But if we lose locally, clearly the time liability hurts us. I'll have Susan research all this and draft a brief in advance so that if that happens we can shoot it to the Fourth Circuit without delay."

"I'll come straight here as soon as we get back," I assure. "If you draft it, I'll sign it."

"What does Allie say about this?"

"That newspaper coverage a few weeks back gave her a taste of what is now to come and she didn't care for it. But she says she'll go through with it. I think you've been a strong influence on her."

"I'm flattered, but I hope you won't hold that against me."

"I feel at peace with all but one thing."

"Which is?"

"That first evening at your apartment, you mentioned legal ethics. Now that I'm your client, will it prevent us from sleeping together?"

"Is that what you want?"

"You know it is."

"Me too." She stares in mock reproach. "We have some time to decide."

"Are you going to get Susan to research that as well?" I grin at her.

"I think I'll handle that one myself."

I lean over the desk and kiss her. "I wish you were going," I say.

"I wish you weren't."

I leave her still seated at her desk, her pen in hand and a legal pad full of notes before her. At the house, Allie is pacing, her luggage assembled on the side piazza next to the driveway.

"You're going to change, right?" she asks as I step from the car.

"I'll be down and ready in ten minutes," I say, breezing by her.

"Dad, don't forget to wipe the lipstick off."

Our flight from Charleston to Chicago is packed but smooth. Mr. Quan, already waiting at the Charleston Airport when Allie and I arrived, is glued to the window as we approach O'Hare. He has never been here, he tells us. Our collective mood is the brightly lit spirit of friends on holiday. Allie has brought along a new novel but is too excited to focus. We change planes, then head for Hawaii, a refueling stop. The sun has chased us all day, finally overtaking us in the Pacific, so that as we make our final approach in Honolulu, my watch indicates midnight in the east but the sun's fireball is just extinguishing itself in the luxuriant isles of Polynesia and beyond.

I glance at Allie, asleep now against her pillow and the edge of her blanket tucked child-like beneath her chin. I am reminded of her when she was young, perhaps five. Although we had disclosed her adoption from her earliest cognition, for a while she had no more grasp of its import than she would our telling her she was an Episcopalian or a Virgo. The mirror gradually informed her of what needed to be learned.

It was in those days that she advanced her first theory about how she came to be with us. She had had a dream, she said, in which a mother held her hand as they walked through a busy market, her mother pointing to things she could never afford to buy. At each stall in this fabricated and impossible image, the toddler would point to some object that drew her interest and the mother would shake her head. At the last stall, the child eyed a large doll. She turned to her mother hopefully, but the mother had released her hand and was gone.

Allie understood this dream as chronologically impossible, yet she clung to the imagery. As a reason to give her up, poverty proved the necessity of choice, the easiest to rationalize and accept. If she dwelled on the darker motivations, she didn't mention them to us. What she did mention later—and this surprised us—was the need to earn money to send her birth parents. In that she had never expressed interest in finding them, we puzzled at her logic: sending support to people she had no interest in meeting, and who conceivably may have forgotten she existed. She proposed this only once, but it did not strike me as whimsical, and her work ethic, always strong, seemed to find fuel from a source beyond my vision.

Beneath the goose-bumped exhilaration of returning to the land of her birth lies jeopardy to her infant image. Her mother holding her hand, walking through that market, their poverty-driven sacrifice—all of these are bedrock for her indisputable stability. She will handle whatever she finds here; of that I am convinced. But that does not lessen her peril. She has grown into womanhood convinced that she was at birth a valuable, God-kissed child whose abandonment could have been inspired only by the darkest necessity.

We may soon know. I close my eyes to summon sleep.

As we make our final approach into Kimp'o Airport, we get our first view of Seoul. Allie's childhood image of a small town is replaced by a generous metropolis spreading on either side of the Han River to the surrounding mountains. In the four days we have set aside for this portion of the trip, we will be lucky to see a thumbnail of the giant hand below. The terminal is immaculate. The people, so small and thin, are also immaculate. As we clear customs, Mr. Quan breaks stride to reach his brother, waiting on the other side of a blue cordon rope and bouncing on the balls of his feet in anticipation. His name is San, and while he is noticeably older than Mr. Quan, their smiles are identical.

At baggage claim, a porter ignores Mr. Quan and me to direct rapid Korean at Allie. She shrugs her shoulders in futile bewilderment, a gesture she will master in the next 72 hours. San Quan intervenes, speaking and gesturing. The porter listens, nods, then grins at her.

"What did you tell him?" she asks San.

"That you are Irish and came here to learn the language." He winks.

Soon we are speeding down a modern interstate toward the Kahoe-dong area, where San lives. He has done well. No apartment above the store for him. The house is in the traditional style, L-shaped, with post and beam construction, *ondol* floors, sliding doors. His wife, Go, greets us, then disappears into the sunken kitchen, where she is preparing a light welcome. San slides a door that opens onto a wooden veranda. From it, we take a visual tour of landscaped gardens. Even through the fatigue bearing down us, we are awed by cherry trees in full blossom. We freshen up, unpack, and look longingly at the mats we will sleep on tonight. It is mid-afternoon. No sleep now, San cautions. Our reward for remaining awake will be a memorable sleep tonight.

Like me, Mr. Quan has never been to Korea. He expresses his desire to see the country, to take in museums and landmarks, to tour palaces and shrines, to attend performances and shop the markets. He has said he wants to do these things with us. But time is short, and the years of separation from his brother pull him in ways we are not pulled. I suggest a day or so for the three of us to get oriented, after which he should follow his own agenda. He seems relieved at being let off the tourist hook.

Back in the car, we drive to Chong No, in the Old City, where San's enterprise is located. On the way, we pass an old, six story brick building set back from the highway. "That is the orphanage," San Quan says casually. Allie stares, but does not flinch. She has not committed herself to going, and I am prepared to make a separate effort if she opts out.

San has arranged a guide. Within the first hour, we receive an Orient comeuppance of sorts. Because Charleston is home to so much colonial heritage, with buildings, art and antiques dating from the pre-Revolutionary era, we tend to think of it as old and venerable. But the Geumcheongyo Bridge here dates from 1411, eighty-one years before Columbus discovered the New World and one-hundred eight years before Cortez landed in Mexico. Seoul itself is two thousand years old, begun when parts of Charleston were still under the Atlantic. When we are informed that the Jongmyo shrine to kings and queens of the Joseon Dynasty, one of the Three Kingdoms, dates from 1394, I eat another slice of humble pie. Confucian rituals are performed here featuring dancers and scholars accompanied by music that is five centuries old.

We attend a performance of Ganggangsullae, an ancient folk dance originally restricted to women due to Confucian restrictions on men. In it, performers in flowing robes dip and rise in pinwheels and conga lines, a full moon-inspired choreography representing various manual labors which women bore in Korea's agrarian society. The all-important lead singer dictates the pace, which begins slowly (*gin* rhymes with been), picks up tempo (*jung-jung*) until it reaches its quickest movements (*jajeun*). As I watch, I picture Allie on stage with them. She would blend in perfectly, another pretty face in the crowd, another graceful presence in the show. But me? With my pale skin and western features, my height and build, I would look as out of place up there as an Eskimo at a luau. Is that how Allie would feel at the St. Simeon? Is that how she has felt all her life? In the span of this performance, the concept of foreign has taken on new dimensions, and my admiration for how she has adapted soars higher. How lonely it must have been for her. I glance over at her. She appears engrossed in the pageantry, but these same thoughts must have intruded. Or maybe she is so accustomed to the estrangement that it no longer registers as such.

For the next two days, we absorb the fascination of the country and culture. I have never found Charleston's equal in gracious civility, but sections of Seoul come close. With each new sight and sound, my daughter's eyes and mind expand with the wonders of a heritage she begins not just to see but to feel. At a dance performance in the National Theater, she is swept away by the color, the elaboration of the costume design, the athleticism of dancers her age. At a palace of the Choson dynasty, she lingers for a full thirty minutes at delicately painted panels depicting a thousand years of history. In the markets, surrounded by vendors pitching her in Korean, she is reluctant, at San Quan's elbow in the narrow aisles and passageways. His Korean may or may not be perfect, but he seems to be understood.

We shop for clothes. As a clerk concentrates on credit card paperwork, Allie nudges me and silently mouths the words, "The eye operation." I look closely. There is definition in the upper lids, but no more than Allie's without surgery. "No," I say flatly.

I arise early on the third morning. Allie reports seeing the sunrise.

"So . . . ," I say.

"I'm going," she replies. "I can't come this far and chicken out."

Go sends us off with fried eggs over rice. San Quan will accompany us to translate, while his brother remains.

We make the trip to the home in silence. On the surface, her mood hovers between indifference and a what's-next-on-the-itinerary resignation, but below I sense she is guarding herself against the unknown, not unlike her fear of the dark after the hurricane. Not nervousness of the kind she exhibits in the warm ups to horse shows or soccer games, but a deeper anxiety that is unlikely to evaporate with the first jump or the opening whistle. As we walk from the parking lot to the entrance, she seems to me to be making a conscious effort not to hang back.

The administrative office is just to our left as we enter. A waifish woman with an alabaster complexion, a Mrs. Chou, greets us formally. She is not the woman I spoke with by phone, but her English is as limited, so San Quan's presence is felt. She ushers us into her sparsely appointed office. When we are seated, she folds her hands as if in prayer and asks how she can help. Her eye contact with Allie is less than she shows for San and me.

I explain, he translates. I mention the year of her arrival, the paucity of information arriving with her, and the curiosity natural to anyone in her place. Is it her curiosity, or mine?

Mrs. Chou smiles, nods, and replies in what seems to my ear to be elaborate explanations but which, when translated, enlighten us less. The home is little changed from the time Allie would have been here, she tells us, but that was of course before her time so she is only repeating what she has been told. Are there records? She will check, and leaves for fifteen minutes, returning with empty hands.

"I am very sorry," she says in English. Then, in Korean, she tells San that an era of records has been lost to moisture damage and she fears Allie's may be among that batch. She has checked with the senior nurse, who has been at the home for longer than anyone else. "Hana is the final authority," she says. "That year and the year after, to the best of her recollection. Would you like to see the nursery?"

Allie speaks for the first time. "Yes."

We are taken down a long, highly polished corridor to an elevator. At the third floor, it opens into a foyer from which we can see, for the first time, children.

"This area is new," she says, "but the nursery is old. It is our next project." She leads us through a complex of doors and halls until we arrive at what I reckon to be a corner of the building. "Here," she says.

Through a glass panel we see perhaps twenty cribs, a few of which are empty. At the sight of a toddler who will soon outgrow her need for a crib, Allie smiles. The toddler pulls herself up so that she is standing at the crib's head, looking at us.

"These are waiting for homes," Mrs. Chou says. "Not like the old days, when we had dozens. Again, I have been told this by others."

Allie is saying something about the light in the room when a nurse rounds the corner, an infant cradled in her arm.

"This is Hana," Mrs. Chou says. "I mentioned her."

The nurse looks at Allie. "Are you one of us?" she asks.

Allie nods.

"Ah," says the nurse, in English. "The records. Mildew. Would you like to come with me?" It is understood that this invitation has been issued to Allie only. Hana leads her through the double doors into the nursery, deposits her infant in a crib, and appears to be conducting a tour of sorts, stopping at each child. Allie is speaking now, then smiling as she reaches into a crib to pat a child's head or back. From what I can plainly observe through the glass, Allie seems quite relaxed and animated. Ten minutes later, they emerge.

"Dad," Allie says, "she asked how many came over on my flight. Do you remember?"

"Over twenty, as I recall. Maybe twenty four or five?"

The nurse nods, then stares at the floor. "That many?" she mutters, as if in disbelief. "And your age at that time?"

"Four months," I answer.

The nurse raises her head. "I keep a journal in my office. If you will wait, I want to check it." She disappears through a doorway down the hall.

"She's very nice," says Allie, but I sense heightened nervousness.

Mrs. Chou says something in Korean to San.

"The director says she is the mother of all who come here. That is her reputation."

When Hana returns, she wears a look I can only characterize as studied. She is focused on my daughter to the exclusion of those around her. "Were you the youngest?" she asks.

Allie looks to me as I think back to the Zarnells. "No, one younger," I say. "A boy."

Hana asks, quite softly, "Was there a mirror?"

In the instant before I can ask how she knows, the two women have come to some mutual insight that makes conversation impossible. Allie embraces her, the nurse returns that embrace, and San Quan and I stand there in awkward stupefaction.

"Are you her mother?" I ask at length. Allie is sniffling and her grip on the nurse has not slackened.

Hana smiles lamely. "No. But I took care of Soo Yun here, in her early months. Over there." She points to a crib. "Against that wall."

Allie dabs her eyes, follows the nurse's point, then says, "I love that mirror. How did you get it?"

"It was with you when we met. Your mother sent it."

"Did you know her?"

"No. I only met her. Twice. The last time was the day you left."

"Do you know her name?" Allie asks.

The nurse shakes her head. "I'm sorry. So long ago. I knew it once, but I have forgotten. She lived outside of Seoul. I never asked her where. I remember she was very young. She came here, to the home, to take you back. She missed you too much, she said. The rules of the home did not permit this. When I showed her a picture of your new family, she was at peace with her decision. She wanted you to have a good life in your new country."

"You haven't seen her since?"

Again, the nurse shakes her head, taking Allie's arm in hers as she does so. "I thought of adopting you myself," and her smile is broad. "I was unmarried then."

"And now?" I ask.

"Married to a U.S. Army major I met here. We have two children."

The nurse invites us to lunch the following day, to meet her husband and children, to see her home, to visit. "I will take you to the police station where I first saw you," she promises. I am explaining our scheduled departure when Allie makes it clear she wants to stay. It makes sense for her to do so. San and Go Quan will hover over her like a possessive uncle and aunt, and Hana will expose her to aspects of Korean life she may never experience otherwise. I spend part of that afternoon rearranging our flights.

36

That evening, the evening we leave Allie in the care of San and Go Quan, Mr. Quan and I depart for Vietnam. He and his brother have been discussing the return since we arrived, but San steadfastly refuses to join us. He has never been back, and pledges never to go. I don't think the younger Quan is surprised, only disappointed. And visibly apprehensive about the trip.

A flight attendant distributes blankets and pillows. At altitude, the cabin lights are extinguished, but here and there conical shafts of reading lights project from overhead. Mr. Quan's light is on, although he has nothing on his tray table to read. He seems trance-like, meditative in the Zen sense, but without its peace. His chair-back is straight, his arms firmly on the rests with his hands cupped over their ends and no slouch to his body, as though he is about to be electrocuted. In the harsh illumination of the reading light, tears glisten on a path downward. Feigning sleep, I watch him closer, unsure of what response to make, if any. He is staring straight ahead, unblinking. A passing attendant pauses, then leans over me to him, whispering.

"Sir, may I do anything for you?"

"Yes," he says quietly, not moving his eyes from their relentless stare forward. "Tea."

The attendant returns, placing a cup on his tray table. He nods faintly. Seconds later he sips. As his eyes maintain their fix on the seat ahead, his face tenses. His brow, smooth enough for a man in his early fifties, meshes into a rutted plain, the muscles of his chin and jowls contract into a perceptible relief sharpened by the overhead lamp so that the entire effect is one of severe stress, advanced aging. Yes, that is it. Whatever storm rages within has transformed him into a man ten years older than the one who boarded the plane. A tear traversing this new landscape is diverted by a canted crevice, invisible before. So dramatic is this mask that I am seized with panic. His body is still, frozen in its rigid uprightness.

"How's the tea?" I ask, sitting up. Nothing I can think of seems appropriate to say.

"Good," he says solemnly, mechanically.

"Well, then," I say with a meek attempt at cheer, "I think I'll have one." I hail an attendant, who seems visibly relieved to see me roused, as though I am a doctor arriving on the scene of an accident.

"Want to talk?" I ask.

"As I said, this trip holds dangers for me. But I have put it off too long."

"Yes," I say, fumbling my way toward him, "seeing so much change in what you left will be difficult. Do you have family other than your cousin and brother?"

For the first time since entering his catatonia, he turns to me, and deep within his eyes I see concentrated despair.

"No, no family now." He brings his drink napkin up, wiping his face and for an instant seemingly surprised at the moisture that is there. The attendant returns with my tea.

"I . . . used your bathroom once when Allie and I came to your apartment. All those people in the photographs . . ."

"Yes," he says softly. "That was my family."

"And you in the picture with the bride?"

He nods, turning forward again. "Mi Chon was my bride. She was veddy beautiful. I never hoped for a wife as good as her." His voice is weak, resigned, defeated. "For nineteen years she kept a perfect home, giving us children, seven children. Our culture is different. Our wives accept our need for other women. Often I would go out to pleasures in Saigon. I stayed late, sometimes all night. In almost twenty years she never once, not a single time, got angry with me. She loved me that much. Can you believe that?"

I sip my tea. "Not like America, that's for sure."

"We had to get out. After the Americans left, I told my wife that the communists will come for us. I had done much to help our government, but there was no one left to help me. I planned escape."

"How?"

"The only way. By boat. I could have gone by plane, possibly with my wife, but never with the children, my parents, aunts, uncles, nephews. Boat was the only way."

"Did you have a boat?"

He shakes his head. "I bought one, near Vung Tau. That is a city on our coast. Many rivers intersect there."

"Did it cost a lot of . . . what was your money called?"

"Gold. The currency was worth little to us and nothing to the communists."

"You didn't buy your boat from the communists."

"In a manner of speaking, yes. They knew about it. In those days, they knew everything. Everyone was trying to get in with them when the end came. You could trust no one. I paid a bribe to the communists to allow me to buy the boat, then to sail on it.

"We left Saigon after dark. It was important that no one see us go. There were forty-one of us in my family. The boat held sixty, so I arranged with another family to take space and help pay. My wife consulted our calendar. The stars told her of great danger. It was not a good time for a trip. She begged me to put it off, but I could not. The men I had bribed to let us leave were about to be transferred north and I would have to pay another large sum to the new guards.

"The other family, I forget their name, met us at the boat. The boat was not quite finished as had been promised but again, time was short and we had no choice. We put everything we had carried from Saigon on the boat. You must remember, we were leaving our homes after many generations and we did not expect to return ever. Mostly, we took clothes but some furniture and prized possessions like photographs."

"The ones I saw in your apartment."

"No," he says. "Not those. When the boat was loaded I had to settle my account with the guards. We had paid substantial gold earlier to get this far and now the rest was due."

"Expensive, I assume," and he nods.

"Yes," he says grimly, "veddy expensive. The guard, his name was Dong, called it 'half-go, half-stay.' That was his formula. His demands were veddy specific. We were to put all our gold in a box where it could be counted. Anything with gold in it, even wedding rings, had to be placed in this box. He warned of a search before the boat left; if he or his men found any gold hidden they would arrest us but keep the gold. We were required to fill this box and show him its contents. Our gold required two boxes. We had been saving it a long time for just such an emergency. Dong was veddy pleased. He divided out his half, quite fairly, and carried it to shore. Then his men searched the boat and everyone on it. They were thorough. With the women, they were more thorough. They found nothing."

"Could Dong be trusted?" I ask.

"In the weeks before I dealt with him, seven families from my region had escaped this way. I had a friend near Vung Tau, and he confirmed that the boats left with these families on board. It appeared Dong was reliable.

"At midnight we poled out of a river near Vung Tau. There is a great hill behind the beaches. Years before, the Americans built a giant concrete Christ. His arms spread to the sea. As we left the shore behind, I remember saying a prayer, though I am not a Christian. I hoped it would cancel out the bad news told by the stars.

"One of Dong's men guided us through the channels. When we reached open water, a small boat came alongside and took him off. He left us a chart. We must stay on that course, he said, because patrol boats along the way had also been bribed to expect us and let us pass. In three days we would reach Malaysia."

"Were you happy to leave?"

"There was no joy on the boat that night. We were leaving everything to save each other; to save our family. No one slept except my youngest daughter, Mihn, only three years old. My wife cried although it upset the children. She always obeyed the calendar, and she felt sure we would wreck in a storm or be boarded by the pirates that waited for those like us.

"Near dawn, we passed two patrol boats but, as the guard predicted, they made no move to stop us. The sun came up and the water was calm. We had worried over this because it was a season for storms. I steered but have little experience in boats. I was happy not to have to navigate in rough weather.

"Soon the women fixed breakfast. My wife brought me hot food that tasted good for these conditions. My family began to mingle with members of the other family and by mid-morning both families were singing songs of thanks to Buddha for our escape. Mihn awoke and came to sit on my knee as I steered. Everyone seemed in good spirits except my mother, who was seasick, and my wife, who thought the worst.

"I began to feel relief. As head of the family it had been my decision to risk escape. I began to look ahead to Malaysia, to our time in the resettlement camp. My wife came to me and tried to smile despite her fears. We talked about America and what our life might be like there. The sun rose steadily, the water remained calm, and there were no boats in sight. Mihn grew restless, leaning over the stern to wet her small hands in the cool water. My wife worried about her falling overboard so she carried her forward where the singing grew louder. Later, my father came to reassure me. He knew I had worried greatly about taking the family from the land of our ancestors. 'We will return in my lifetime,' he predicted. He was fifty-four."

He pauses. For several seconds it is as though he has forgotten a detail he is now struggling to recall. His eyebrows knit over the bridge of his nose. Then, something in his manner signals a shift within, an internal debate resolved. He takes a deep breath, exhales, and fingers the empty cup between his thumb and forefinger. He is fighting for control.

"So long ago," he says, with a finality that seems to end his account. I wait, and with another deep breath he resumes.

"Then the engine sputtered. Although the boat was new, it was an old diesel and I had feared its reliability. I turned to inspect it. Suddenly, the deck collapsed beneath my feet. Everything went white, then black. I woke up in the water, dazed. I was twenty-five meters from the boat. It was in flames. I could hear screams but I thought I was dreaming and did nothing. Then I swam as close as I could but the heat was too much. Before I could think clearly, the boat went down."

His head bows slightly, casting his face into shadow from the light above. I cannot take my eyes off him.

"I am a poor swimmer. I searched for something to cling to. As the boat sank, several loose boards stayed on the surface and I managed to reach one. It was large and I pulled myself on. Then I passed out. When I woke, it was afternoon and my face was blistered from lying in one position exposed to the sun. I was not near anything, the wreckage or the oil slick or anything. I tried to figure out what had happened. I decided the fuel tank had exploded and blown me clear of the boat." He pauses here, lowering his head as if suddenly seized with overwhelming fatigue. "They were all gone. All lost."

"I'm so sorry," I mutter ruefully, more to myself than to him. "The stars were correct."

"Yes, but I was not. The fuel tank was not the cause. That afternoon, I heard the sounds of a powerful motor. I thought at first the boat in the distance was my salvation, although just then living and dying were the same to me. I was about to wave my arm to attract its attention when I saw the yellow star, the communist flag. Suddenly, a new fear took hold of me. I slid into the water, holding the board, and watched as the boat slowed, then stopped.

"The first man to emerge from the cabin was Dong. I recognized him at once and my fear grew larger. Then, two men came up in wetsuits and scuba gear. They dived overboard, and in that instant I knew what had happened. A bomb planted in the boat had been timed to go off when we were out of sight of land. Dong's divers were below the oil slick, collecting the rest of the gold he had so fairly let us remove from the country." His voice is a whisper now, and over the incessant hum of the jets, his words are difficult to discern.

"I was going to kill him. I started swimming to his boat to do what I could when I realized how foolish it was. They would shoot me in the water like a shark or a porpoise. And, I remembered something else. More families from my region would follow us. Unless I reached shore, no one would know what became of the Quans. That, of course, is why Dong let us leave instead of demanding all the gold on shore. Spies would report to others like us that we had escaped and Dong's business would flourish."

"How were you saved?" I ask.

"A fishing boat two days later. I was delirious until we reached land. They put in at Can Tho, where I recovered from sunburn and dehydration."

Throughout his account his eyes have strayed only briefly from forward, as though the entire horror were running on a small screen mounted on the back of the seat before him. Watching those eyes, dark and blank, has been like standing on the end of a pier gazing out into night. But now, with the chronology of his rescue behind, a light appears, a glint, as though, from that same pier, distant running lights signal a seaward approach. His eyes narrow, and the running lights draw nearer. His voice firms.

"I returned to Saigon. Another family was preparing to leave. The head of that family I knew. I told him what had happened and that I wished to go with them. He would have cancelled their escape but I told him no, we could succeed. I was to be smuggled aboard his boat in a large basket under some clothes. This was to avoid the risk that Dong would recognize me. While he dealt with Dong, I would search for the bomb. There was confusion on deck with thirty or forty people moving back and forth to unload possessions so below I could be thorough.

"I found it almost at once, near the fuel tank where I assumed it would be placed. It was crude but effective, made of material stolen or captured from the Americans. I loosened it and put it in my shirt."

Involuntarily I draw back a fraction, as though distancing myself from the explosive he once carried. His glint has hardened, dropping the temperature within to a point near absolute zero.

"By agreement, my friend began a dispute with Dong over the split of the gold. His attention was diverted. I left the boat and hurried into the shack by the river that Dong and his men used as a headquarters. There, I planted the bomb under a sofa, well hidden. It took only a minute. I returned to the boat as Dong was insisting in a loud voice that the division was fair. He threatened to shoot my friend and have his family arrested. Minutes later, we sailed."

"Did the bomb go off?"

"Yes. Our spy who verified sailings stayed to see the result. Several were killed. Dong survived, but was severely crippled. Perhaps that is better. He crippled me in a way I cannot describe."

"You've done a pretty fair job," I say, reaching over to pat his forearm. "I had no idea. I feel guilty for pressing you into this trip."

"No matter. It was time. For many years my enterprise took all my time and energy so that I was too tired to think much. Lately, that is not so."

"I'm going to conduct a little memorial service for my friend Philip," I say. "Perhaps we should rent a boat and do the same for your family."

He shakes his head. "I buried them long ago. I will go to see our old house. That will be enough. I must think of happier times."

He reaches up to switch off the light. His seat reclines and eventually his head lolls toward me, his breathing spaced and deepening. His brow has returned to its familiar countenance, the lost years restored by this draining exorcism. High above the ocean, I dwell on his account. I try to visualize the conflagrant boat, the screams mercifully silenced by the life-snuffing hiss that must have accompanied its descent below the surface, his stunned helplessness at being forced to witness such ineffable tragedy. I think of Mihn, an angel only three, vulnerable to God's whim or Dong's greed, but vulnerable.

I have heard his story but I cannot grasp his loss. Like an immense reef arising from the sea it looms. I can cling to it as true but grab only a piece or fragment, the enormity of it such that only the arms of a deity could encompass it entirely.

Above, the night is clear and moonless. Stars litter the heavens in sparkling fenestration. Our jet wings us on, the undeviating pitch of the massive engines lulling us near the speed of sound. We could be encased in a cloud, so smoothly do we glide. Here, above it all, a perfect peace presides, surreal and infinite.

We land. Heat and humidity reach us before the luggage, saturating us instantly in a heavy blanket of sweltering thickness. The monsoon season is still a month away, but ambient moisture gloms my shirt to my skin. By comparison, Charleston seems like Vail.

As we enter the terminal, slightly built, wiry porters hustle about us jabbering in a cacophonous admixture of sing and song. Mr. Quan takes command, pointing out bags, shouting directions. In the cab he falls silent, gazing somberly out his window, and soon his head is in something of a constant, subtle oscillation, a continual denial or disbelief, either from evidence of change or lack of it. I ask him about the slogans printed on a whitewashed wall we are passing but he points a discreet, silent finger at the driver before saying, "Later."

We enter the city on a wide boulevard. Black and white TV images from the mid-sixties superimpose on pedestrians in cone-shaped hats and delta pajamas. Traffic inches along. Bicycles weave in and out with daring precision. Women carry, suspended from their shoulders, loads equal to their weight. As we near the center, aromas made familiar by the Red Dragon are mingled with odors of street refuse and sewage.

Our reservations are for three nights at a hotel franchised by an American chain. Here, quality is desirable for food and service but essential for air conditioning, still very much a luxury. At the entrance, uniformed porters engulf us and minutes later we enter the bracing chill of five-star air conditioning.

Behind a highly polished teak desk a striking woman in an *ao dai,* the long-sleeve traditional pantsuit, registers us. The clerk's apparent boss, a young manager in a European suit, prowls the length of the counter and rivets his eyes on us as we sign the register and accept our keys. An ancient elevator, equipped with a living operator, takes us to the fifth floor.

The next morning, I take a tour alone. I had not planned it that way, but when I knocked on Mr. Quan's door there was no answer. I waited half an hour, knocked again, and left a message. He either got out early, or never came home last night. I hope it was the latter. At any rate, I'm here mostly for him, and if he doesn't need the support he thought he did, so much the better. Perhaps telling his story on the plane was catharsis. In late afternoon, I'm in the hotel lounge, showered, changed, and, with a little salt and soy, hungry enough to eat the wooden table at which I sit.

In the middle of my cocktail, a very professionally crafted martini, he gets off the elevator, spots me, and waves as he approaches. He offers no account of the past eighteen or so hours.

"Dinner this evening is on me," he announces. "It may be unforgettable."

"May be?" I ask.

"If the restaurant still exists," he says.

We go out into the sluggish evening. Lights incongruously reminiscent of Forty-second Street and Times Square blink overhead as we walk the crowded sidewalks.

"Here, we are two blocks from the Saigon River," he tells me as we stroll. A septic smell of salt water and fish waft by, borne on a breeze which is no cooler than the air it displaces. "The street is called Dong Khoi. It means, 'Street of the General Uprising.' In my day, Tu Do—Freedom Street. You could buy anything here." He shoots me a knowing "for men only" glance.

We pass a club called Maxim's, which Mr. Quan says caters to an international crowd hosted by *tu san,* Vietnamese capitalists beginning to emerge openly in the city. "The ones who look unhappy are Russians," he deadpans as we pass. The canopied doorway is busy, and a band blares out as the door swings open. "It is not far," he says.

In mid-block he slows, seemingly reluctant to have answered the fate of the restaurant to which he is leading us. Then, smiling broadly, he accelerates. "It's still here."

He enters ahead and inquires of the maître d', who turns and disappears into the kitchen. Moments later, a wizened old man limps from the kitchen door, trailed by the head waiter. The old man approaches with the same restraint I observed moments ago in Mr. Quan, squinting as he nears. Mr. Quan advances. A brief pause, then both men enfold each other in fraternal embrace. Within seconds they are laughing, talking simultaneously and inspecting the changes wrought by fifteen years. The old man beckons aging waiters, who, upon recognition, abandon customers to join the reunion.

An hour later, our table resembles a cache of contraband from an international cuisine raid. Of the items I can identify, we are treated to giant shrimp, lobster Newburg, fried squid, conch, ginger duck, roasted pig, chicken in four distinct sauces, goat, and a medley of fresh vegetables. Unidentified are a murky soup, a shredded leafy something, and a sea creature who eyes me from the plate with almost the same intensity with which I am scrutinizing it. The spring rolls are the best I've ever had, provided I leave off a condiment popular around the table; a sauce that looks innocent enough but which would, in fact, take the ice off a Nova Scotia windshield. Veuve Clicquot champagne, plum wine, and a beer called Saigon Export wash it all down.

During this feast, Mr. Quan and Mr. Ngo, the old man, have held incessant conversation, while I remain contentedly ignored. Two waiters stand behind us, anticipating whims I don't have. Unforgettable it is. At the other side of the table, smoke from Cuban cigars is wreathing their heads as the years are compressed into paragraphs punctuated by laughter. I extend my thanks to Mr. Ngo, who asks me in very fractured English to return another night.

Mr. Ngo, I learn as we exit, has told him of a friend he wants to find. "In the Phu Tho sector. I knew it well. If she is at home, we may find her."

We alight on the sidewalk of the Phu Tho district as an evening crowd besieges street vendors selling food, as pungent as it is mysterious. We walk two blocks without slackening. Mr. Quan seems bent on a certain destination. At the window of a small jewelry shop, he slows.

"Wait here," he instructs, then disappears inside with a jingle of the entry bells over the door.

Nearby, a vendor tends a rickety wooden pushcart. I idle over. He seems reserved at my approach, at odds with a merchant's enthusiasm for a customer. Displayed on the dingy beige cloth overlaying the cart are cigarette lighters of distinctly American manufacture, old Zippos and others predating their modern disposable counterparts. I pick one up. On the side is engraved EHT. Near the lighters rest assorted rings. My eye is drawn to a large, substantial one: West Point, class of 1965. The name Boyd G. Fleming is inscribed inside; a name I silently wager is also chiseled into a black marble slab in Washington, D.C. The man says something to me, presumably a price.

The bells on the jeweler's door rustle and Mr. Quan emerges, smiling. I beckon him over.

"I'd like to own this ring. Offer him whatever it takes."

Mr. Quan engages him, shaking his head decidedly several times before turning to me. "He knows its value. It won't be cheap." A counteroffer later, it is mine. On my return, a Fleming may value it, and if not the USMA museum may suggest a display more appropriate than this tired street in this haunted city.

"She lives not far," Mr. Quan announces. "The owner has not seen her for some time. Let us hope her health is good."

We walk two more blocks. "Are you hungry?" he asks.

I shake my head. "After that meal? You must be joking."

"It is just as well," he says, indicating the aromatic stall we are passing. "Barbecued dog." He turns to read my expression.

The neighborhood is declining. Tin doors languish on rusted hinges, half concealing almost certain squalor inside. Mr. Quan seems less assured here and consults a map crudely drawn by the jeweler. At a rundown tenement, he checks it yet again before approaching an unmarked door. He raps and we wait.

We hear no movement within but the door swings open. A frail woman looks inquiringly out. Her silver hair is pulled straight back. It is a rich, luxuriant sterling highlighted by contrast against her dark skin, so that she could be a Mayan princess whose headdress had been crafted from the ore of a priceless vein. On top a tortoiseshell comb serves as a demur crown. For a moment she does not recognize him, but when she does, the Mayan sun rises in her eyes.

They speak for several minutes. He introduces her as Lily Nguyen. She looks doubtful, neither confirming nor denying the relationship I feel sure they've shared. He offers more words and gestures toward me. When he stops, she bows her head and steps aside to permit us to enter. The room is immaculate. A Buddhist shrine, a scaled down miniature of the one in Mr. Quan's apartment, lends a reverential aspect to what would otherwise be the mundane, if fastidious, appointments of her sitting room. Mr. Quan indicates we should be seated and that she will make tea. We are silent until she returns, carrying a tray with the spryness of a girl. She serves us. He apologizes for holding a conversation with her that is inaccessible to me, then speaks rapidly with her for thirty minutes. We leave as suddenly as we arrive, but even without a word of Vietnamese, I know he will be back.

We return to our hotel, where I place a call to Natalie. She has just gotten out of bed, she tells me, and the vision heightens my longing. I relate the events of my day, then ask about progress on the lawsuit. She has almost finished her research and will begin drafting the complaint that day. Before moving to more personal matters, I ask her to call Margarite.

"Tell her we return on the morning of the seventh and that it is critical that she gather the Board as soon as possible."

"You're going to meet with them again?"

"We're going to meet with them again."

I hang up, satisfied that all that can be done is being done. Still to be trod is that rural road between Cu Chi and Duc Lap, to an unmarked grave where the Army would say Philip gave the last full measure and where, in his own words, he bit the banana.

37

The road to Cu Chi quickly dissipates into a rural byway once we leave Saigon. Mr. Quan, driving a car borrowed from an old friend, assures me that it has been much improved over the two-lane pothole tarmac of twenty years ago. He has purchased since our arrival a lightweight jungle hat, resting on the seat between us, and a loosely fitting white silk shirt with a small dragon embroidered on the pocket. The countryside, green and pastoral with corn, languishes to either side. Iowa east.

"To understand what happened here," he says over the hum of the engine, "you must see the tunnels."

My arm is resting out the window and the wind is flapping my short sleeve and though it is not yet ten in the morning the air rushing by is hot and clammy, a devil's breath which, when augmented with the unobstructed sun, foretells a day of vengeful heat. Nascent beads of sweat form at my hairline and on my chest, trickling downward in erratic tendrils. Mr. Quan does not appear to feel the heat.

He glances at me. "Do you have fear of tight places?"

"Claustrophobia?"

"The fear of being confined?"

"Yes. No, I have none."

"Good," he says with satisfaction. "These tunnels are veddy narrow."

An hour out of Saigon we enter Cu Chi. The main road is paved and along it are parked trucks laden with produce and livestock, all pointed in the direction from which we have come. Mr. Quan is scanning the signs, he says for directions.

"I have not been in the tunnels since I was a young man, just after the French left."

We turn left onto a dirt road and proceed for about a mile. He slows, then stops, pulling a few feet off the road in an area worn to bare ground.

"I see nothing," I say as I climb from the car.

"Ah," he says. "By seeing nothing, you see everything."

He leads us toward a wooded enclave some hundred yards from where he has parked. A small sign peaks from the shade of mangroves. As we approach, from the deep shadow of the grove appears a man, a peasant. He and Mr. Quan exchange rapid conversation, then money. The peasant turns toward the deeper shadows within and we fall in, trailing. Fifteen or twenty yards from where we have met he stops, reaches down, grabs an iron ring and pulls upward, thereby raising a wooden door approximately two feet square. At the apex of the door's arc on its hinges he lets it go, and before the door strikes the ground, jettisoning dust from beneath, he has entered the hole revealed. He disappears momentarily, resurfaces with a lantern, and motions us into the earth.

A crude ladder descends. The peasant waits for us at the bottom, a dirt cell approximately eight by eight and too shallow to permit me to stand erect, although both shorter men do so with inches to spare. Three burrows branch off of this conjunction, so that I am immediately put in mind of the stark lobby at the orphanage with its three converging halls. This dirt lobby is ornate by comparison.

A phrase of Vietnamese. "We are to wait," says Mr. Quan as our guide disappears into the blackened yawn of one tunnel. Moments later, light flickers, illuminating the tunnel walls in a ghastly mustard yellow. I drop to my hands and knees behind Mr. Quan, who enters the orifice in the same duck wattle employed by the guide. He rapidly extends his lead, so that he has rounded a bend by the time I reach the light source, a candle mounted in a sconce that appears to be little more than a jagged metal shard thrust into the dirt wall. Light lures ahead, and my sense of urgency propels me faster. Having claimed to be immune from claustrophobia, I am beginning to wonder.

I reach a second candle, then a third. Ahead, I hear voices and redouble my crawl. Although the air is very cool here, I am sweating from the exertion of quick movement in a confined place. One salient reality of the tunnels has been driven home: the two Vietnamese are built for this clandestine movement and I am not. I see two pairs of legs ahead and when I emerge, panting, it is into a large room where both men are talking leisurely. Between them is a table, on which rests two candles and a large map.

"This is a command center," explains Mr. Quan as I straighten almost upright before encountering the ceiling. "The tunnels were built by the Viet Minh to defeat the French. Then, of course, they were employed against you . . . us."

I hover over the map, clearly the scheme of the labyrinth overlaid on a contour plat of the surrounding area. The network is quite extensive.

"Two hundred miles underground," says Mr. Quan, and although he must fully realize the role this complex played in the ultimate demise of his chosen government, he cannot suppress a certain pride in what we see here. "Only a direct hit by the most powerful bombs would destroy a section. They would rebuild it within hours." He leans over the map and traces a sector with his finger. "Notice how three tunnels lead to this spot. This provides alternate routes in case of destruction. The Ho Chi Minh trail worked on the same principle, which your generals never fully appreciated."

I survey the room. There is not much to see but much to marvel at, not the least of which is that this network would require me to spend months or years on my hands and knees to fully explore. Mr. Quan consults the guide, then explains air vents, ambush points, communications, logistics, and sleeping quarters. The guide injects something.

"He says he himself lived here for over two months without once coming above ground." I nod but make no reply.

Mr. Quan leads our exit, the guide trailing to extinguish candles as we retrace our steps. Patches of sky above the trapdoor are blue and beautiful, and I find myself climbing the ladder with alacrity. Mr. Quan and the guide exchange words as the door is closed. We are returning to the car when I stop and look back. We are ten yards from the entrance and I cannot see any trace of the hole from which I just emerged. The iron ring has been covered with leaves and the guide has vanished without a sound into the shadows of the mangroves.

"I thought you should see that," he says as we approach the car, baking in waves of corrugated heat rising from the roof and hood.

"Yes," I say. "I'm glad we came."

The road to Duc Lap stretches southwest towards the Parrot's Beak of Cambodia, less than twenty miles away. We travel a mere five minutes when Mr. Quan steers onto the shoulder, stops and shuts off the engine.

"This area was once a great producer of rubber," he says. "Few of the old plantations remain. For a time it was what the Americans called a free-bombing zone. No command approval was required to shell and strafe." He turns his head from the windshield to me. "This is about half way," he says gravely. "You have precise information?"

"No. Only that it occurred half way between Cu Chi and Duc Lap."

"Then perhaps this will do."

I nod and gaze around. Blue sky domes over us. Emphatically benign fields extend from irrigation ditches running parallel to the road's edge on either side. In the distance, a phlegmatic ox labors. Tethered to an antique plow held by a cone-hatted farmer, it surges forward a few yards before lumbering to a crawl. Each step taken by the massive beast appears to signal collapse. The farmer manifests no impatience. On the shoulder of the road ahead, two young boys are walking toward us escorting a cow. The smaller boy brandishes a willowy branch, occasionally touching the animal's flanks. There is much evidence of life here, and none of death, but then what did I expect?

Stepping from the car, I wipe my neck and face with a bandanna and stretch down into the back seat floorboard for the Corona bottle propped upright in my satchel. A single rose purchased at the hotel this morning wades in two inches of water, its bud opening cautiously and attar drifting upward in defiance of the oppressive gravity of heat. I put on my hat, a white, narrow-brimmed affair I wear on the boat.

"I will remain here," Mr. Quan says.

"Come with me. This won't take long."

"It is a private matter," he insists. An awkward pause, while he trusts his hands in his pockets, avoiding me by looking purposefully around, as though waiting for a bus.

"Please," I say. "It'll only take a minute."

He utters a barely discernible sigh of resignation. "Perhaps I can show us to shade," he says, leading along a ditch in the direction of Duc Lap. We pass the boys and the cow without speaking. Some fifty yards from the car the bank drops more precipitously into the ditch and from the side some green ferns grow, shading a dark loam beneath.

Together, we sit down. I splay my legs on the sloping embankment and begin to dig listlessly between them, my hands acting as scoops and the dirt cool between my fingers.

"Careful," says Mr. Quan. "Not all the mines have been found." I cut my eyes at him to confirm he is joking. He is not.

Inside, I am also digging, not to create a hole but to fill one. On the plane coming over I picked up the airline's in-flight magazine with its eclectic assortment of features designed to appeal to the broadest possible spectrum of travelers, from one-armed horticulturists to dictators flying into exile. An article on solid waste disposal established a thousand years as the durability of a glass bottle in a landfill. I didn't make the connection at the time, but it occurs to me here that the Corona bottle will "outlive" Philip by an astounding factor. This might not shock obstetricians or undertakers or others on speaking terms with the evanescence of organic things like people, but it gives me something to ponder. It reminds me that Philip will live on this earth only as a fragment of memory in those who knew him. In this landfill we call earth, over the span we call time, that amounts to little more than a vaporization.

Yet, in the years since his death, images of his face, his mannerisms, his slang, and a dozen other elements of his uniqueness have stayed with me, like light from a persistent star. Other memories, once equally valued, have long since begun their eclipse in that amorphous galaxy we call the past, each glittering event or relationship in its time a supernova but now, increasingly, a dead rock, a dulled, eroded particle on the verge of oblivion in the cold cosmos of longevity. Why is Philip's star rising in the east as these others diminish?

Because, I half-mutter when the hole is deep enough to deposit the bottle, Philip's memory echoes not the past but the present. Held at some precise angle or in a conspicuously revealing light, the neural lines and intersections of our time together comprise a map of sorts, a liminal path across a modern mine field. All I have to do is read it. I backfill around the bottle. The rose projects starkly from the earth.

"Doesn't look like a likely place to die," I say, glancing up to the fields before us. The ox has reached the end of its furrow and is turning our way.

"The South China Sea is also veddy peaceful . . . at times," he says.

"Yes," I agree. "After your account on the airplane, I'm reluctant to make too much of my loss."

"Not at all. You came to honor a friend. All life is precious."

I turn to his profile. "I'll bet that farmer out there plowed that same ground before the war—"

"And his father while the French—"

"So what's changed by Philip's death? Answer me that. We—you and me and our side—lost the war, you lost your family, I lost my friend, and this poor soul plows like always."

"My suggestion," he says. "Perhaps you ask the wrong question. Buddha does not instruct us to find meaning in death but in life. Death is veddy random, as you and I know from our personal experience. But life is not so random. Some communists will die in their beds of old age but it will not atone for their crimes. Your friend led a good life?"

I drop my head to stare at the budding rose. "Yes, he did. He was a great guy, a great friend. He was a better man than I am."

"That is a harsh judgment on yourself."

"It's true. The war came, he went where he was told. Did his job."

"And you?"

"Me? I dodged. Very legally, quite acceptably, but a dodge just the same." Odd, I think. I have never spoken these words to myself, let alone another.

"And now you feel guilt."

"I think it's been eating at me."

Mr. Quan leans back upon his elbows, his face partly hidden by the brim of his hat and his shirt dappled by elongated blades of sunlight slicing through the ferns. Very slowly he says, "Suppose . . . you had made the arrangements for your family . . . you had assumed responsibility for their passage . . . and you had been wrong. Do you have trouble imagining the guilt?"

"No," I say, almost whisper.

"Many times I have questioned my survival. I can find only one answer, and it is not perfect. It took courage for my wife and children to leave our home and climb aboard that boat. It took courage for your friend Philip to come here, to this place. But courage is also required of the one left behind, to face what they are now free of. If we face it well, we honor them in a way mourning and guilt cannot. I decided many years ago that too much grieving was a retreat into their deaths. What was demanded was courage in tribute to their lives. I have tried to live that way."

The delicate outer petals of the rose, tissue thin, bend away from the ripening center, peeling gently to expose the penultimate layer of anxious petals. Among the hard smells of tilled, manured earth wafts its perfume.

My eyes rivet on the bud, my mind conscious of Mr. Quan gathering himself to rise. He claps his hand on my shoulder, a jarring, comradely thump.

"My suggestion," he says. "Bury your friend. I will wait at the car." He leaves me alone under the ferns.

A formal benediction over my makeshift monument seems melodramatic and unnecessary. Philip seems as far removed from this place as I am. Nothing in the landscape, the fields, the air, the heat, the laboring ox, the indolent cow, the scrabbling peasants suggests or evokes him. Perhaps that is the tragedy of it. He died between two hamlets with foreign names in a country void of anything remotely connected to him save some global political strategy rooted in implacable opposition to a monolithic communism.

Yet here we are. Perhaps we are no part of this strange land but it is undeniably part of us and we can no more distance ourselves from it than we can our eye color. It is as real as any coordinate on the map of our personal journeys, Philip's ended, and mine? An area of the world that took Philip gave me Allie and, I think as I prepare to stand, possibly some insight as well.

I breathe deeply once more of the rose, then tamp the ground around the bottle. "Goodbye, old buddy," I say, then rise and brush off the seat of my pants before returning to the car, against which Mr. Quan is leaning, gazing at the plodding ox in the distance.

Back in Saigon, I shower with the frenzied intensity of a man exposed to excessive radiation. The suffocating tunnels of Cu Chi, the grit of the roadside near Duc Lap, the compost, fly-filled air of the farms yields to soap and water, then spirals down the drain with a gurgle. I towel off and fall naked on the bed, asleep instantly.

The following day is our last full one in Vietnam. We spend it sightseeing and shopping. Mr. Quan's narration tends toward what this building or that park used to be, so that after two hours we have seen Saigon as though on a recorded tour utilizing stale cassettes. And he is weary, falling asleep whenever he is not speaking or moving. For the past two nights he has renewed his old habit of prowling, perhaps today reminded that the tomcat he once was needs to spend more time curled up on the hearth.

My sleep that night is erratic and I rise early, packing and pacing. I am looking forward to our rendezvous with Allie in Athens, the only city that would bring us together for a flight home. In Mr. Quan's room there is no answer. I go to his door, rapping firmly. No response.

I'm at breakfast when he arrives, looking fit and chipper, smiling as he enters and greeting the hostess cordially. At the table, he declines a menu from an approaching waitress.

"Would you mind," he asks, "if I do not accompany you on your return?"

"You're staying here?" I ask.

"For a time. I have to explore some business prospects."

I smile. "You were with a business prospect last evening?"

He returns my smirk with a flicker of his eyebrows. "Saigon has changed but there is great opportunity here."

"What about your enterprise?"

"Pham can take care of things for a time. Then, a decision."

"I think I can handle getting back. You're sure about this?"

"No. But by the standards here I have become a veddy wealthy man. Perhaps it is time to address . . . other matters."

"I understand. I can manage."

"I will speak to Pham by phone. Then, if you carry to him some written instructions, I will be grateful."

At the airport I thank him for all he has done. He in turn thanks me, by which I think I grasp the change in him over these past few days. I am in line to board when he waves his last farewell, already striding confidently toward the exit. Soon, he is indistinguishable among the throng waiting for taxis.

38

In Athens, Allie and I board a plane for New York. We talk for hours. Her time in Korea has changed her in some way I will need to come to terms with, but not today. While she "fell in love" with Hana's children, the nurse told her all she knew about Allie's first months of life. Hana repeated the account of her birth mother's visits, trying to summon a physical description of a woman she met only briefly. In a lighter moment, Allie mentioned upper blepharoplasty surgery. "Very popular," Hana conceded, "but still surgery. Did you know those scars you have almost kept you from being adopted? While you are here we will visit Faith Stockdale. She is retired now, but I want her to meet you. It is my way of telling her 'I told you so.'" They talked of a reunion in Charleston.

Upon our return, I stop at the Red Dragon as Mr. Quan had requested. Pham's English is limited. He nods and smiles often, but we do not communicate easily. I give him his employer's written instructions and stay long enough to impress upon him my availability to help should legal problems arise.

Carter & Deas is unchanged. Within twelve hours of being back on U.S. soil I have a cluttered desk and calendar. Harris is glad to see me, asks the usual questions, and advises me of an appointment with Middleton tomorrow.

"We both need to be there," he insists. Cathcart has cut his fees again and a final negotiation session, with partners from the two firms sequestered at opposite ends of City Hall, has been arranged. "The city is enjoying this game," Harris reports. "They're using Cathcart as a bludgeon to get us cheap. If we're not careful this contract won't be worth winning."

The lawsuit Natalie has prepared will reopen Pandora's box where the Arts Center is concerned. I have not told Harris, although I must before walking into tomorrow's showdown at City Hall. Then, there is my unqualified disclaimer to the press, the legal equivalent of its political counterpart, "If nominated I will not run, if elected I will not serve." My plate will be piled high with crow to be eaten over disavowal of legal action "now or ever."

Natalie has prepared well in my absence. On the afternoon of my return I stop by her office to read the seventeen page complaint. I close her door long enough for a welcoming kiss before we turn to business. The suit is skillfully drafted, naming both the St. Simeon and the city as defendants. Pursuant to my instructions in a phone call from Vietnam, she has not named the Board members in their individual capacities.

"This is not a lay-down," I say as I finish reading.

Natalie looks up from the work on her desk. "Are you kidding? At best it's twenty-five, seventy five. It's the old state action problem."

As a lawyer, I understand. Cases dealing with equal protection, the constitutional guaranty at issue in a case such as this one, usually require a showing of state action, loosely translated as participation by the government in the denial of the right. Without such a showing, individuals or groups are relatively free to discriminate in their personal affairs. Because of the city's chartering of the Society, we have hopes of showing government sanctioning of the objectionable conduct. While the city gives the Society no funds and no tax breaks, the very act of authorizing its formation in 1766 may be sufficient to be deemed state action by the courts, many of which tend to go to substantial lengths to find it. If not, we will probably lose, according to Natalie, and I don't disagree.

"So, what do you think, counselor?" she asks.

"Damn good job. Very professional."

"Thanks. Now what?"

"I called Margarite before coming here. Everyone on the Board will be there tomorrow night. She said she had to listen to an exhaustive explanation from Charlotte about Roberts Rules of Order, of which she knows little, and some link she sees between reconsidering my request and storage of nuclear waste from the Savannah River power plant. She said Doc Francis seemed pleased, Jeanette changed her mind a dozen times, Sandy Charles had a meeting she couldn't get out of, then did."

"What about Adelle?" Natalie asks.

"Margarite didn't say, and I didn't ask."

"They know I'm coming?"

"Yes," I say, remembering the pause on Margarite's end. "Margarite assured me that she certainly has no objection, but she wanted to know what explanation she could give. I said to tell them you're an anthropologist doing research for National Geographic. She laughed at that, then said, 'But Coleman, they'll know her purpose.' 'Precisely,' I told her."

Natalie smiles vaguely at this account. "Should be an interesting meeting."

I look back to the complaint in my lap. "Want me to sign it now?"

"Please. Also, you need to sign the retainer agreement Susan prepared. It's on her desk."

"Is this the one that says we have to be ethically correct in our personal relationship?"

"Don't you think that would be advisable? At least until this is over?"

"I suppose you're right. I don't have to like it, do I?"

"Nor I. I prepared the outline of an appeal if the District judge turns us down, but my experience with the Fourth Circuit is limited. That might be a good time to bring in another firm. Then you and I can begin acting like the depraved people we wish to be."

"I can't wait," I say. "How about one more kiss before I sign the damn retainer."

On the following afternoon, Harris and I block off an hour together to prepare for the gunfight at City Hall. He is relaxed, confident, sliding into the chair in the main conference room with his natural ease. Clearly, he does not suspect that prior to squaring off against the city he will be waylaid by his own partner. I hate this.

Our staff has prepared duplicate briefing notebooks in blue vinyl binders. Harris opens his to the index, scans it, then flips to an exhibit. "Why don't we start with Camilla's spreadsheet, tab C," he says. I make no move to open my book. He looks up. "Coleman?"

"Yeah?"

"Tab C, you with me?"

"No."

"Would you rather begin somewhere else?"

"Yes."

"Fine. What exhibit?"

"This one. It's not in the books." I reach into my briefcase and extract a copy of Natalie's complaint. I slide it across the table. He picks it up, rapidly reads the style and first paragraphs, and replaces it on the table. Then he takes his glasses off, rubs his eyes wearily, replaces the glasses, and sighs.

"Oh, boy. Here we go again, eh?"

"The vote by the Board was six to one against issuing Allie an invitation," I say. "Margarite Huger supported me. The only one."

"Margarite's a neat lady," he says. "Has this been filed?"

"No. I'm meeting with them tonight. If I don't get what I want, I'll plunk it down first thing tomorrow morning."

Harris rubs his chin. "What are your odds?"

"Tonight or if the suit is filed?"

"Both."

"Better with the Board than in the courts."

Harris puffs his cheeks, his mind racing as I have seen it do so often when, in the middle of a trial, a quick tactical decision must be made. He is considering the safest way to defuse this bomb, and I am the bomb. "Who else is on the Board?"

I list the members, omitting only Adelle. He nods at each name.

"I can help with Sandy Charles," he says. "Clarkson surprises me."

"It shocked me."

He rubs his chin. "Charlotte will be hopeless," he says. "What about old Dr. Francis?"

I relate the St. Philip's rapprochement, including Doc Francis's expressed regret at his vote on Allie.

"I could call him," Harris says, "but it sounds as though he's come around. Better leave it alone."

"That's my thought too."

"Jeanette? . . . your guess is as good as mine."

"Adelle Roberts is a no," I say casually.

His eyes cut at me hard. "Adelle is on the Board? I had forgotten. Did you mention her a moment ago?"

"No."

"You're telling me Adelle voted against you?"

"I'm telling you the vote was six to one and she was among the six."

"But aren't you—?"

"We were. I'm seeing Natalie Berman, the woman who prepared this suit."

Harris lets out a subdued whistle. "It's a good thing this situation isn't complicated."

"It's bordering on fiction, I agree."

"So Adelle's pride got wounded and she took revenge?"

"No. Natalie came later." I relate Allie's relationship with Christopher and the meltdown with Adelle.

"So you're dating your lawyer now?" Harris shakes his head. "Careful you don't get your ass in a sling, partner."

"We've covered that," I assure him.

Harris rises, suddenly restless. He paces back and forth in front of the two framed prints on the far wall, both scenes of hunters riding to the hounds. He glances at his watch. "In thirty minutes we're due at City Hall," he says. "What do you suggest?"

"We have to level with them, don't we?"

"Coleman, if we go into this meeting raising the possibility—no, probability—that by noon tomorrow we'll be suing them, we're dead."

"We can't conceal it."

"I know. I'm thinking delay. Maybe Carlton can postpone this meeting." Harris goes to the small table in the corner, dials the conference room phone, and waits. Moments later he has Carlton Middleton on the line.

"Carlton, Harris. We've run into some glitches over here. Any chance of rescheduling this? I know it's short notice."

Harris listens, his face tensing as Middleton's voice, normally docile, rises. Harris moves the receiver from directly over his ear. I catch words and phrases of Middleton's diatribe.

"I understand, Carlton," Harris says. "Your office has been patient. Do what you have to do." He hangs up, holding the receiver for several seconds before turning back to me. "They're afraid they'll catch hell in the press if there is more delay. They're going ahead with the meeting."

"I'm sorry," I say.

Harris shrugs. He returns to the table and closes his notebook with a marked finality. He stares at the book a long time. The conference room is virtually soundproof and the silence permeates to the bone. At last he looks up at me, the faintest trace of a grin in the corners of his mouth.

"I guess," he says, "if it were my daughter I might feel the same way. You want me to call Sandy?"

"That would be great."

We stand. I am nearer the door and turn to leave. Harris picks up his notebook and chuckles.

"What's funny?" I ask.

"I love this business," he says. "Sure, I wanted this contract. But in something this big a lot of things are bound to go wrong. When you represent the city, you have to turn down work from everyone who wants to sue it. We'll be okay."

Harris Deas is my hero. We shake hands. "Thanks," I say.

"Good luck tonight," he says. "I'll call Sandy now."

I return to my office. I don't love this business. If I ever did, my zest for it has become ground down, with little more than a powered residue remaining. In the coming months I'll reassess my role here. If I stay, Harris will be a big part of the reason.

I have no appointments, my calendar having been blocked off for the aborted meeting at City Hall. I dial Margarite and ask if I can come by to give her an account of my trip. Five minutes later I am out the door.

As I turn onto East Bay Street, I reflect on how often I've come here in the past several weeks, almost as though the house is now part of my world again. I am half way up the walk when the door opens and Daniel appears.

The day is mild and he leads me to the side porch, where Margarite sits and iced tea waits in tall glasses. She offers mint, picked moments ago, she says, from a patch in the backyard. "I want to hear all about it," she says, crushing mint leaves between her thumb and forefinger before depositing the sprig into her glass.

I deliver an account of our trip largely as I repeated it to Natalie and Steven upon my return, omitting Mr. Quan's trauma on the plane but dwelling on passage through customs, where the Corona bottle had indeed prompted inquiry. At the description of Allie's meeting with Hana, Margarite's mouth rounds in a tiny doughnut of disbelief, then flattens and tails into a smile of profound satisfaction as Allie and the nurse embrace in her mind's eye.

I continue, "We—Mr. Quan and I—went to Cu Chi."

She tenses at the mention of that long dreaded village, and her hands unconsciously gather the seams of her skirt as if they were the lap bar of some fierce, terrifying roller coaster and she is bracing for the first Niagara-like plunge of the rickety lead car. She looks very old today, and were I not here she would probably be taking a nap.

I describe the tunnels, the bucolic hamlet of Cu Chi, the rutty road to Duc Lap, the cover provided by the roadside fern, the rose in the buried bottle, my silent benediction. She does not blink or move, other than to slowly release her stranglehold on her garment.

"A beautiful service," she says at last. "I'll think of it in just that way; a outdoor church service. You did a wonderful thing by going there, Coleman. Philip would be so pleased."

"I went for me, mostly. And not everything I've done has been wonderful. Part of my reason for coming here today is a guilty conscience."

"Why, what could cause that?"

"I lied to you about Mexico."

"What on earth for?"

"To protect myself; to keep up an image. I told you Philip and I concluded, very rationally, that we would leave to spare Adriana further trouble with her family."

"Yes, I remember that very clearly," she says, her face now a mosaic of curiosity.

"On what turned out to be our last night, I had arranged to spend the night with her. We were both virgins, as odd as that sounds today. She was taking care of a house for some people who were out of the country; watering plants and feeding two dogs. The house was called Casa de la Luna, House of the Moon. I'd helped her a couple of times and as we grew . . . let's say, more intimate, we decided that this would be the perfect spot to give ourselves completely.

"That evening, she went early to do her chores and to prepare herself for my arrival later. What I did not know was that Rodrigo, the brother, had been following us closely for days, reporting back to her family. About a block from Casa de la Luna that night, he stepped suddenly from a recessed doorway, directly in my path. Before I could react he pushed me into this doorway and my head struck the brass knocker pretty hard. I was stunned, but not too stunned to realize that he had put a large knife to my throat. He was very powerfully built. The blade of his knife was resting on my Adam's apple and his breath smelled strongly of *pulque*, a cheap and potent booze. He motioned to the house to let me know he knew where Adriana was, then spit out some Spanish with a little English sprinkled in, but I got the message. He kept saying 'nunca'—'never'—over and over and I knew he meant to kill me if I ever saw his sister again."

"How terrifying," says Margarite. "What did you do?"

"Returned to the hotel, shaking like a leaf. Philip knew what Adriana and I had planned, so when I started packing he caught me by the arm and asked what I was doing. 'The guy is crazy,' I said, 'and I'm not going to get killed over this.' Philip glared at me and said, 'Bullshit.'"

"Yes," she says with a wan smile, "he loved that word."

"He couldn't believe I was going to be bluffed out of my night with Adriana by a bully like her brother. He said we'd go back together and if 'Roddy-boy'—that's what Philip called him—if Roddy-boy caused any trouble we'd take him out. Philip had some brass knuckles and he put them in his back pocket and we returned.

"As we neared the house I kept expecting Rodrigo but we reached the door with no sign of him. 'Piece of cake,' Philip said as we waited for Adriana to answer the knock. Once inside, I told her what had happened and she got very angry and called her brother loco, but dangerous. And, she warned, he has dangerous friends. Philip told her he would take care of Roddy-boy, that she and I were to have our night and he would make sure we weren't disturbed. So, while we stayed inside, Philip went out to guard the door."

Here, Margarite, I must omit some details of those next three hours, not only because revelation would embarrass us both but because they are beyond my feeble powers of description, stored in a mental vault I rarely open even to myself. When I do, I tremble with those images of moonlight and Adriana in the smaller courtyard, the one away from the street. As we kissed longer and deeper she broke away, pulling me toward the house with her giggle and pointing to a mattress we took outside and spread by the fountain in the wall. I lay there waiting for her and after a while the door opened and she called the dogs to come inside and closed the door very softly, then came out from the shadows. The night was so mild and the moon so full I could see every detail of her naked body as she came to me, yet now all of those curves and creases are muted so that what remains is the glimmer of moonlight from the crucifix around her neck and the white of her teeth against the suntanned peach of her skin. The pomegranate tree in the corner near the fountain gave off a sensual musk, the aroma of ripe fruit clinging to the bougainvillea but so heavy it floated down onto the mattress and into her hair as she smiled down on me from her propped elbow and her crucifix lay on my chest, cold, while all else was warm. Later, lying close and staring at the moon, I whispered that life could not hold many moments such as this and she shushed me with a kiss while the fountain murmured pebble-splashed canticles in a language I had never heard but understood completely. And all that time, as the moon moved silently across the courtyard, as it flooded our mattress with beams that played upon the downy folds of her body and cast into the palest shade the clefts and creases I explored to bursting, Philip stood guard.

"Later that night," I tell her, "we heard a tremendous uproar outside the door. It took a few moments for me to . . . dress, and by the time I got outside the fight was over. I saw Rodrigo staggering down the street, but

Philip sat on the cobblestones holding his shoulder. He had been stabbed and there was quite a bit of blood."

"Stabbed!" said Margarite. "He never told us—"

"He was protecting me. Philip didn't like a fuss made over him and the cut, while deep, turned out to be not as bad as it first appeared. Adriana bandaged him, then went home. The next day she reported to us Rodrigo's broken jaw and the plans being made by his friends to get even. She begged us to leave before someone was killed.

"So you see, Margarite, Philip fought my battle for me. I owe to him my magical night with Adriana. And later, in Vietnam, he did it again. He was a far braver man than I, and it has taken awhile for me to come to grips with that."

"Perhaps," she says a little skeptically. "But Philip could be rash at times. And, there are many forms of bravery." She leans forward, her tone suddenly confiding. "In the weeks before he left we had some long talks—some of our best. He had great doubts about the war, doubts he didn't think he could share with his father. He told me that for a time he had considered refusing to go, but he didn't think he could face people. He was less afraid of being shot than being judged, if you know what I mean." She pauses, seeming to drift into another room with a distant glaze over her eyes. "Stabbed," she says softly. "I never knew."

I stand, newly weary from transcontinental flight, the tension of the meeting with Harris, the weight of confession. She gazes up at me with the skepticism of moments ago. "The part where she kissed you boys at the train . . . did that happen?"

"Just like I said."

"Good," she says with a dimpled smile. "That's so romantic."

39

"So this is where the bad guys live," says Natalie as we arrive in the parking lot of St. Simeon Hall. My lights converge on the stucco wall, where patches of missing mortar resemble giant jigsaw pieces. Then darkness, followed by the dutiful hum of retracting seat belts. She muscles her door, arcs her legs in a sitting pivot, knees together, and alights. With one hand she grips her slim briefcase and with the other, me, at the crook of my elbow.

I knock on the back door as I did in February. A chorus of cicadas serenade a frog hidden in the low boxwoods flanking us to either side. Again, light beyond the security peephole flickers, the handle rotates, and a trapezoid of light widens with the door. Before us, framed in the doorway, stands Adelle.

Her eyes dart to Natalie, so quickly that the flat "hello" intended for me is delivered to her. Natalie nods in acknowledgement while Adelle turns her gaze on me.

"Christopher tells me that Allie had a good trip," she says dryly. "I'm glad. Please come in." She steps aside as we enter. "The Board is waiting."

I lead down the hall, Natalie beside me and Adelle behind. Through the open door of the library, I see Margarite standing at the head of the table, gesturing to her still-hidden audience. As we enter, she pauses. I walk to her, shake her hand, introduce Natalie as Adelle slides into her seat at the table. Then, turning to them, I rest my hands on the table and lean forward.

"Some of you," I say, indicating Natalie, "may have met Ms. Berman. She is my guest." Natalie smiles, not without a twinge of self-consciousness, then sits in the chair Margarite has positioned for me, placing the briefcase before her.

"In five days," I remind them, "the Society will once more gather at the annual gala. My daughter has not been invited—an embarrassment to her and to us that I hope you will remedy tonight. I've met with each of you privately, so I have some feel for your views."

In the fleeting hiatus between sentences I survey them. At the opposite end of the table sits Charlotte, unmoving, her corpulent arms folded under her breasts and her head rigid, in a pose recalling clay Buddhas I saw in Korea and Vietnam. To her right at the far end, Clarkson tilts his coffee cup in its saucer, appearing intent on the parabola of the liquid against the sides as he swirls it methodically. Seated beside him, closer, is Sandy Charles, her face puckered in a preset affability and her eye contact emphatic.

To Charlotte's left coming back is Adelle, who manages to appear bored and anxious at the same time, looking at her watch and at Margarite, at Natalie, but not, I note with some satisfaction, at me. Then comes Jeanette, her head propped in her hand but her fingers fluttering against her temple and, as her eyes shift from me to Natalie, I can already see her peering from behind her drapes, wondering if the neighbors are watching as the sheriff comes up her walkway to serve the papers. Next to her, Doc Francis sits in replication of his distance at the last of these meetings, his manner aloof and his gaze directed across the table at a bookcase or beyond.

I clear my throat and look at Natalie. The releases on her briefcase snap open and she removes from within a stack of papers, each set stapled at the corners and laid perpendicular to the set below. She rests them on the table beside the case, closing it silently. Doc Francis does not alter his impervious stare but Jeanette's eyes would be no wider if I had rolled a live grenade into their midst.

"A clear majority of you voted against me last time, against Allie, and I think I know why. I've done some soul searching these past few weeks and I have a confession. If I'm totally honest with myself, I come to the reluctant conclusion that I too might have voted no. You see, I understand what it is we're clinging to here. It is nothing less than a sense of ourselves; a fundamental security in who we are, who we came from, where we live, how we relate. Those seem like simple things until we look around us, at the mess this country is in today. And because none of us are insulated from that mess, it's easy to conclude—I've thought it myself often enough—that some unseen conspiracy wants to invade and destroy a way of life we happen to think is special.

"Everyone here has some antique at home that he or she treasures. I might have a sideboard that's worth five times what your four-poster is valued at, but are you going to trade me that bed? No way. Because my sideboard doesn't remind you of your grandfather. You never crawled up on it to listen to stories or to be comforted during a thunderstorm. We treasure the things that take us back to a simpler, often happier time.

"'So,' we ask ourselves with perfect logic, 'why can't we keep one old relic like the St. Simeon the way it used to be, the way it's always been? Why, in a politically correct world full of strident voices, militant organizations, lobbies, factions, political parties, twelve-step programs, TV religions—why in a world that big and diverse can there not be one place where we can go to be among those who applauded us when we were eighteen, that told our parents how lovely or handsome we looked that night, that made sure we met all the people we would need and who would need us when those thunderstorms came along. And why can't that place be the same place, those people have the same names, run the same businesses, have the same aunts and uncles and houses and summer places and coats of arms and go to Clemson or Carolina like they have for generations.

"Why? . . . I don't know why, unless it's for the same reason you can no longer take a trolley downtown or a steamer to Europe." I pause to gauge the room's pulse.

"Coleman," offers Sandy Charles, "what you just said about the trolleys and steamers—isn't that the point? Everything changes, so why can't this remain? Doesn't its value go up because it does not change? I think that's on the mind of a lot of the members I've talked to." Clarkson looks up from his coffee cup and Doc Francis turns his head to me expectantly.

From behind, Charlotte says, "It's the open floodgate, Coleman. Many members have called me on this."

"I understand their concern," I say. "But a man named Darwin gave this whole question a lot of thought. Adapt or die would be his answer. Perhaps, by identifying very specifically what it is we're protecting—"

"We're protecting tradition," pipes up Charlotte, punctuating her declaration with a jot of her ample head. This momentarily unhinges me as her comment is not predictably inane.

"What time does the St. Simeon begin, Charlotte?" I ask.

"Eight-thirty."

"Every year?"

"Since I've been there, and that covers forty years."

"Suppose we change it to eight-forty-five. Would you say that changes the nature of the Ball?" Her face registers a mealy blank.

"What he's saying, Charlotte," injects Doc Francis, swinging his head toward her end of the table, "is that there are traditions and there are traditions. Which ones are important enough to hold the line on. That's the issue, isn't it?"

"Yes," says Jeanette unexpectedly, "but blood kinship is the glue that holds the entire thing together, isn't it?" She casts nervously around for approval, then once more at the stack of papers in front of Natalie.

"It shouldn't be," I say. "And it hasn't always been. Clarkson down there thinks, and I agree, that there must have been numerous exceptions made in the beginning—"

Charlotte interrupts. "But then it wasn't the tradition it is today."

"No," I continue, "but there was also Lafayette. I have prepared,"—and here, as I reach for the papers, a collective inhale deprives the room momentarily of oxygen—"a brief history of the Society's treatment of the French hero." I slide them to the center while they exchange looks for confirmation and the pin is replaced in the grenade.

"You will see on page four the exact wording of the exemption passed by the Society's leaders, your predecessors. It says, and I quote, 'Special invitations to the annual gala may be extended from time to time by majority vote to foreigners of royal descent or distinguished birth.'

"As you may know, I just returned from Korea. Our purpose in going went beyond this conflict with St. Simeon, but we learned things there I want you to know." I recount the highlights of our trip, the visit to the home, the reunion. Then, I play my trump, relating to them what I learned from Allie on the flight from Athens.

"Hana has been at the home for almost twenty-five years, and in all that time only one mother tried to reclaim her child. Thousands of children were abandoned or given up, but only Allie's biological mother came back to reclaim what she thought she could not live without. I can get an affidavit if you need one. When I heard that, the adjective that occurred to me was 'distinguished.' So my question to you, the Board, is whether you agree that my daughter is a foreigner of distinguished birth."

"That's a lawyer's trick," says Charlotte with unabashed nastiness, verging on a literal hiss. "It's got to be royal."

"No, it doesn't," counters Doc Francis. "Says royal descent or, Charlotte, o-r distinguished birth."

"Well, it's clear what they meant. To me, it's perfectly clear."

"But that's not what they said," adds Clarkson in his deliberate way. "I'd call it distinguished."

"So would I," says Sandy Charles. "It gives me goose bumps. What do you think, Jeanette?"

"Well . . . I'm just not sure . . . I'd like some more discussion. Adelle?"

"I have nothing to say."

"I have," says Charlotte. "I see good and well what is happening here. Everyone is afraid of being sued if they don't go along. I, for one, could care less. I won't be intimidated. And, if it makes everyone feel better, I will personally pay the legal fees to defend the Society. It's that important to me that we stand on principle."

"Then perhaps it's time to vote," says Margarite, rising at my side.

Clarkson speaks again. "I'd like to ask Miss Berman a question." As Margarite nods, he faces Natalie. "I know you would be Coleman's lawyer if it comes to that but I'd like to know if how we vote could make a difference, you know, in court."

Natalie steeples her hands on the table. "As you say, Mr. Mills, I would be Mr. Carter's attorney so I am unable to officially advise you. However, as a general rule an organization is liable for its illegal acts and directors such as yourself can escape liability by showing they did their best to reach the proper result."

"Thank you," says Clarkson. "That's what I thought. I suggest an open vote."

Charlotte turns on him. "Why not?" she demands. "It's clear as the nose on your face how it's going to come out. By all means, an open vote. I want to record my opposition."

Margarite looks serenely down the table. "Is there objection to an open ballot? Hearing none, I will ask for a show of hands on whether to extend an invitation to Allie Carter. All in favor . . ."

I watch as first, Doc Francis, then Sandy and Clarkson, then Margarite raise their hands. A full second later Jeanette follows as Charlotte resumes her Buddha-like fume and Adelle sits in downcast stillness.

"Thank you," I tell them. "You've done a great thing, and I truly believe for the right reason."

I reach for the back of Natalie's chair as she rises. Over her turned shoulder I make fleeting eye contact with Adelle, whose malice lances out like twin stilettoes. We are just out the door when Margarite tugs at my sleeve. With a furtive look over her shoulder she slips me an envelope. On it is engraved Allie's name. "I had a hunch," she says.

Natalie and I walk to the car without speaking. In a perfect world her presence tonight would not have affected the outcome, and I choose to believe it did not. I crank the car and head toward home. At Church Street I idle in the driveway.

"Well, we did it," I say. "Thanks for all you've put into this."

"How is she going to react?"

"Tonight? I suspect with relief. The idea of court, newspapers, thrusting herself into the limelight—none of that appeals to her. I'm feeling some of that relief myself."

Inside the front door I call to her. She answers upstairs, saying she'll be right down. Natalie and I are seated in the den when she enters.

"The Board changed its mind," I say. "That envelope on the sideboard is for you."

She gives a quick glance over but shows no emotion, seating herself on the sofa nearby. "Was it ugly?"

"Very civil," I say. "Natalie's presence helped, but I think the result would have been the same."

"I think so, too," Natalie says.

"I guess Adelle will hate me now," Allie says.

"That is Adelle's problem," I say. "Your problem is to come up with a dress in a few days."

"I have to call Kenny," she says. "I asked him to find me a horse show this weekend, just in case. He entered me in a show in Greenville."

"He'll understand."

"Natalie," she says, "would you like to help me shop for a dress?"

"I'd like that very much."

"Cool," she says, rising. "Well, I have homework to finish."

She turns, passing within three feet of the engraved invitation as she mounts the stairs to her room.

40

Tonight, we will attend the St. Simeon, as Carters have done for almost two and a half centuries. Sarah, whom I have not seen since our return from Korea, is coming over for an afternoon meal before we dress. I have offered to send Steven to Sullivan's but she insists on driving herself into town.

Natalie reminds me that with Allie's invitation, she is the sole uninvited guest at the Church Street gathering. I need no reminder, but she is teasing. "I hate dancing," she says. "Besides, it's a cultural thing; not my culture." One side of my brain says she is right, but the other side and a goodly portion of the rest of me would like to take her anyway. Perhaps another year.

I am preparing the grill for steaks, glancing at the clock as it is now almost three and Sarah was expected at two. I instruct Steven to call his grandmother while I fine-tune the marinade. He reappears on the patio, reporting no answer. Odd.

Allie is making potato salad. In jeans and a sweat shirt, she stands in the kitchen peeling spuds and, but for her styled hair purchased at the cost of a morning at the salon and for a sum equal to the interest payment due the World Bank by a medium size developing nation, could as easily be awaiting a horse show as the Ball. Christopher is circling the kitchen, cola in hand, tickling her periodically and laughing as she brands him "a perfect nuisance."

"Steven," I say, "I'm getting worried about your grandmother. Try her again."

"I just called," he replies a bit testily.

"Try again. It's not like her to be this late."

Mid-April heralds the barbecue season, and if I stand accused in this life of any failing, the want of any fidelity, should I be indicted, as the Nicene Creed expresses it, for having "left undone those things which we ought to have done," there cannot be numbered among my crimes the neglect of barbecue season.

Spring comes to my neighbors in accord with the timeless dictates of biology. The prodigal sun returns from its winter solstice, the ambient air temperature pushes the mercury in outdoor thermometers roofward, the setting on Mother Nature's turf blanket is raised to warm phlegmatic bulbs, birds nest, bees pollinate, weeds rouse.

Not so here. The Carter patio obeys the laws of an aberrant botany. Let the patios to either side be shaded in new verdure, let their dogwoods shower down the snowflakes of falling petals, let their magnolias molt, live oaks live, quinces jell, tea olives triumph—let the entire raiment of spring be spread upon their boughs and branches and the Carter patio will remain in remiss hibernation, refusing every order, enticement or blandishment save one: the lighting of the grill.

Hovering over my charcoal, a man who cannot boil water on his best day in the kitchen becomes the living embodiment of Monet and Pasteur combined. On a pallet of olive oils and vinaigrettes he deftly gauges the delicate chemistry of dills and tarragons, thyme and teriyaki, so that when the coals reach their optimum embered radiance, he lovingly spreads his creation upon filets and chops, red snapper, tuna, lowcountry shrimp, London broils, Vidalia onions, green peppers, cherry tomatoes. At that moment, when the first searing aromas waft over my sun-kissed flagstone, the Carter azaleas soar to their peak, Confederate jasmine lean to absorb the fragrance of hickory smoke, red-throated roses open to sing out alleluias to the pagan god Grill.

I am increasingly concerned about Sarah, as Steven reports no answer. Leaving Christopher in charge of the charcoal, and the women in charge of food preparation, I ask Steven to drive me out to the island to check on her.

"Call me on the car phone if she shows up," I instruct.

Traffic is heavy with tourists, so our path to the Cooper River Bridge is littered with Buckeyes and Badgers, New Yorkers and Hoosiers. The connecting bridge, the Ben Sawyer, opens just as we approach, and in the ten minutes we idle a lone sailboat, red trimmed and sails furled, motors serenely through the watery lacuna.

Sarah's car is in the driveway, heightening my alarm. Before Steven has come to full stop I am out, headed for the door. I have not covered two steps when I hear a thin rasp: "Praise the Lord!" I glance in the direction of the voice, to the trash bins. There, forlornly on the floor of the enclosure, sits Mother, imprisoned.

"I've been calling and calling," she says as we advance to her rescue. 'I've never seen so little traffic along this road. And on a beautiful spring day."

"Mother," I ask, springing the bolt, "how long have you been in there?"

"Well," she says, beginning to hoist herself up, "what time is it?"

"Three-thirty," answers Steven.

"Oh, my. I came out to empty the trash about one. Oh, my. I called until I got hoarse. I've had this cold and I guess my voice didn't carry very far." She straightens with great effort outside the cage, leaning on my arm.

"Steven," I say, "perhaps we should award this round to the raccoon and dismantle your trap."

"There's nothing wrong with the trap, Dad."

"It's a fine trap, son." He turns with a puff of exhaled breath and begins unhooking the cable linked to the bolt.

I guide mother toward the house, propping her up until she regains her legs. "It's a good thing," I say, "that this didn't happen late at night. No telling how long you might have been in there."

She stops abruptly, looks up, and begins laughing in her self-conscious way. "I saw one living thing the entire afternoon," she says, the sparkle returned to her eyes. "You can't guess."

"Ralph," I offer. "He seems fond of the trap."

"No. The coon. He came right up to the fence and looked in at me. I can't imagine what he was doing awake in the middle of the day."

"Maybe with your calls for help he couldn't sleep." She cocks her head to consider this. "That's a joke, Mother." She pats my hand affectionately.

"Have I spoiled the day?" she wants to know. "I'm packed and ready."

"Not at all. But ride in with us. I'll bring you back tomorrow."

"Yes," she agrees, "that would be best."

By the time we arrive back at Church Street the coals are a redemption red, just right for Monet/Pasteur's magic. Steven leaves, returning in ten minutes with Amanda Smathers, his honey-blonde date whose loveliness is destined to make strong men weak and weak men quail.

The next two hours are spent in backyard ritual. I lounge indolently on a cedar chaise, my culinary chores ended and the warmth of the afternoon working the balm of contentment into my shoulders and neck. On the trellis leading back to the rose bed, a swallowtail butterfly flits among the honeysuckle, honoring one trumpet, then another with her flirtations. In the magnolia, a cardinal cheers us from a lofty branch, calling to an unseen mate. Sarah, fully recovered from her ordeal, initiates a chorus of compliments on the food as we echo her praise and pass the credit around like the plate in church.

I stand and stretch. "The limousine, ladies, arrives at eight-thirty. I'm going to run Natalie home."

Steven looks up from his third ear of Silver Queen corn. "You didn't rent a limo for me, Dad."

I arch my eyebrows indignantly. "That is because I like your sister more." Allie projects her tongue at him and he, careful of his grandmother's line of vision, scratches his forehead with his middle finger.

Natalie gathers her things and says goodbye to Mother, Steven, and Amanda. Christopher and Allie escort us to the car. Standing in the driveway, Allie reaches for her hand. "I'm only going because of you," she says. "Thank you for everything."

"Yeah," chimes Chris. "I'm really glad I got you involved."

"You called her?" I say, narrowing my eyes at him as Natalie grins.

"Well, yeah, sure. My mom's not very happy with me but someone had to do something."

"I guess you're right," I say. "Someone had to do something."

At Natalie's, inside her door, we linger in an enduring embrace. As I rest my chin on her head, I whisper my thanks. "I'm not going next year without you," I confide.

"We'll see," she says, smiling with her perfect teeth and leaning back to look at me full face. "You southern boys want to take your 'best girl' and tonight that isn't me. I'm not even jealous. Allie belongs there; I don't."

"You northern girls can be pretty understanding; something I wasn't until recently and if it weren't for you—"

"Go home. Have fun tonight and call me tomorrow."

"Count on it," I say. "How about Arliene's?"

"Perfect," she says, leaning close.

Back at Church Street, I open a small drawer in my dresser. An envelope rests there, the word "Allie" written in Elizabeth's distinctive script. I decided on the flight back from Korea that if the Board did the right thing, I would share it on the day of the Ball. I feel Elizabeth would approve. I have never read it; the envelope is sealed. That it will prove emotional is a given. Too emotional with everything else going on today? I will leave that up to Allie.

I knock on her bedroom door. She peeks out, then closes it to put on a robe. "Mom wanted you to have this," I say, handing it to her. "She left it up to me as to when to give it to you." She studies her name, perhaps as a way of avoiding eye contact. "If it's too much for today . . ." but she waves me off, closing the door.

Dearest Allie:

This is the letter I never wanted to write. It means I will not be there to tell you these things in person. Now that my illness has moved from fear to dread to finality, I must, as they say, get my affairs in order. Funny how we think we have forever to say the important things until something like this reminds us how brief forever can be.

I cannot say when I felt a compelling need to adopt internationally, but it began long before your brothers were born, and even before your father and I married. If pressed I'd say late in high school. Senior year? Nor can I exactly say why. It must have been rooted in all that homogeneity of the Scotch-Irish and Germans so prevalent in Kansas. Three girls (not good friends) got pregnant the summer before our senior year, and they were all so thrilled, beaming really, with the family likeness they saw (or thought they saw—so many babies look alike at birth). I remember thinking that if I ever got married and had kids, I'd like a baby that was, well, different. But then I was different. Not much Scotch-Irish in this girl; maybe a bit of German. Whatever the genetic makeup, I had a serious move-along gene that couldn't wait to leave Topeka for somewhere, anywhere, more exotic. The idea of raising a child of another culture fed that need for the exotic.

Of course back then I had no idea we would adopt from Korea. I doubt I could have located Korea on a world map in those days. To be honest, I pretty much forgot about the whole thing in college. Too many other things (and boys) to think about. Then I began dating your father and along came Josh and Steven and the longing came back. For a time I didn't trust it, thinking international adoption might have been one of those teen fancies, like starring opposite Paul Newman in a movie or dancing with Rudolph Nureyev. But no, the urge was still strong, even though we could have more kids the old fashioned way. So I started getting serious.

The agency I contacted, Open Arms, pointed us to Korea, where there were so many infants available. I say "us," but really it was me, because your father, God love him, wasn't too keen on the whole idea. He is a traditionalist if ever one walked the earth, and as you know from his mother, your grandmother, he comes by it honestly. Most true southerners do. He wanted a daughter, but in his heart he wanted a traditional daughter. You shouldn't stress over that—in his heart he also wanted a traditional wife, and look who he married! Between you and me, he has more rebel in him than he admits. He talks a good traditional game, but his actions often tell a different story. And he adores you, as you know.

The hardest part of nearing the end is knowing I won't be there to cheer at your high school graduation, to shop with you for your first Charleston cotillion, and to meet your Mister Right when and if you find him (and you will). This letter will have to do. I've asked your father to give it to you at a special occasion of his choosing. Thought of recording a video message, but I fear it would remind you of what we all wish was avoidable. When you read this, think of the day we spent on Folly Beach, right after you got your braces. We walked to the pier while we talked ourselves blue. I treasure that walk. Think of me as I was then.

I have often wondered about your birth mother, as I know you have. That same walk on Folly Beach was the last time we discussed her, speculating on what kind of person she was, what compelled her to place you in the care of Korean Social Services, whether you have biological brothers or sisters, and how much of your fate was influenced by the Asian preference for males. I guess we may never know. As I told you that day, and repeat now, I have a feeling she is a good woman who gave you up to give you advantages she could not provide, for whatever reason. Who knows? One day you may meet her. If you do, tell her about me and about how much joy her gift has brought to our family.

I spend hours each day (when I'm not loopy from all these drugs) thinking of you, Josh, and Steven, but mostly you because a girl needs her mother most in her high school years. But I will be there in spirit, your faithful cheerleader, as I have been since that day at Kennedy Airport when the flight chaperone put you in my arms. As you know, I'm not much where religion is concerned. I suppose if I was ever going to lean that way, now would be the time. And I do think about it, because I'm not ready to die and would love to believe there is hope. But the absence of a God doesn't mean there are not forces in the universe beyond our sight and imagination . . . destinies, for lack of a better word. With billions of people on the earth, and millions of orphans needing homes, you were destined for us, and we for you. I know that with absolute certainty. That same destiny will carry you far. Wherever I am, in whatever form awaits us, I will beam with pride at all you are and will become.

Lying here in this stupid bed for months has given me the time and the peace (yes, peace) to crystallize my feelings, and here I come to what I need most to say: you have justified my life. My wish for you is to find someone or something that justifies yours.

I love you. Mom

By 8:00 I am having my annual tussle with an impossibly difficult white tie. These outfits, I suspect, are a lingering legacy from the

Marquis de Sade. Finally, I stand back, fully penguined, turning right and left before a full length mirror. I pick up my white gloves from the bureau and go downstairs.

Chris has left to dress and escort Adelle, reminding me on his way out not to forget to bring my daughter. Sarah soon descends in a powder blue gown set off by silver pendant earrings and a matching silver necklace she wears only to the St. Simeon. Steven arrives again with Amanda, in a sleek black satin, low cut, that halts conversation for a moment.

Promptly at 8:30 the limo pulls up in front. "See to the ladies," I instruct the boys. "I'll check on Allie." At the second floor landing I pause at her closed door, then rap softly twice.

"Sweetheart, the car's here."

"Coming, Dad," is the muffled reply from within.

I turn the handle and crack the door. She is standing near her vanity, giving her hair its last finite adjustments. In her hand, tilting in synch with her head, is the pearl-backed mirror. "Ready now," she says, reaching to the bed for her clutch and wrap. She turns to me, arms spread in exhibition. "Well?" she demands, but I can make no reply.

Her gown is a long, white silk affair that flows and ribbons over her litheness like a meringue of cloud. Held by spaghetti straps across the shoulders, it glitters with a diagonal band of tiny iridescent beads tapering to the hip, where a silk flower blooms. In her ears, diamond stud earrings catch the overhead light and around her neck is the elegantly simple diamond choker I recognize as Elizabeth's.

"And look what Chris gave me," she says, offering her lower leg through the slit up the side. High heel sandals display her pedicured toes, around the second of which, on the right foot, is a silver ring.

"As long as it stays on your toe," I say.

She crosses the room and takes my arm. "You look exceedingly handsome, father," she says coyly. "Shall we go?"

The green canopy is in place and yawns before us as the limo pulls to a stop. The door opens and we uncoil from its leathery plush. After a short walk to the hall, the ladies stepping carefully to avoid hems, we arrive at the entrance doors, opened with a flourish by two uniformed cadets in full dress swords and sash.

The foyer is round, reminiscent of Monticello on a smaller scale, with one giant chandelier suspended overhead and tall mirrors on the sides to enlarge its aspect. Waiting there is the receiving line, consisting of the Board and spouses. Margarite grins broadly as we approach. It is a measure of her natural grace that she looks much the same in everyday life as she does now, bejeweled and done to the nines. She greets Mother warmly, then extends her hands to clasp Allie's.

"Our guest of honor," Margarite says with obvious pride. Then, leaning forward, she says in stage whisper, "And thank you for your patience with all us old fossils."

We greet John, Margarite's husband, followed by Doc Francis, his wife Katherine; Sandy and Edgar Charles; Clarkson and Rosemary Mills; Jeanette and James Wilson, the surgeon; Charlotte, her royal ampleness, who coldly turns us over to Glen, her long-suffering husband, as I smile at her gaily in the best of spirits; and finally, Adelle, stoic and polite. Chris is beside her, deliberately harnessing his enthusiasm in deference to his mother.

"Chris, where's your cap?" I ask as we shake hands. He winks, then turns to Allie, telling her where he'll catch up to her.

We enter the main ballroom amidst the crush of familiar faces. Allie is on my arm, while Steven ushers both Amanda and Sarah behind. From the night of the vote I have anticipated this moment, when we would stroll to our table under the indirect but appraising eye of the membership. I have played it over in my mind, knowing the Board's decision has spread through this crowd like a rock on a windshield. In my worst moments I envisioned smartly turned backs, the coldest of shoulders, unrequited greetings, sharply and pointedly diverted gazes. In calmer reflection, I considered the prospect of a routine assimilation, with no-big-deal greetings from closer friends and a benign tolerance from others. Whether Allie has labored in such speculations I cannot say. Doubtless neither of us anticipated the reality.

As we progress, an aisle of sorts forms as guests take a step back, reminding me for an instant of the day at Kennedy Airport when the crowd of waiting families parted to admit those first dazed orphans. Then, from somewhere on the left side, clapping begins, muted by the white gloves but discernible and building as we progress. Allie smiles imperceptibly, like the queen of some exotic land, and nods faintly in acknowledgment. To be sure, I see in my peripheral vision some reluctant participants and a few resigned to observation only. Some engage in intense conversation as a way to avoid witness, but they cannot shut out sound.

We reach our table. Chris joins us as the orchestra, immured beyond its clandestine curtain, strikes up an old waltz, as all the music here tends toward. Three Dog Night derives few royalties from St. Simeon.

But already I have told too much. As a true and loyal member in fair standing, observant of our sacred secrecy, I cannot reveal what we did, who we saw, how we danced, or what we ate at the champagne breakfast, just as Allie will tomorrow decline to be interviewed by Scott Edwards for the *Sentinel,* citing the long-standing tradition of silence in the organization of which she is a part. In good conscience, I can reveal only what we did at the end, when the Ball was technically over and we were, very technically, no longer within the Hall.

Steven carried Sarah and Amanda home while Allie, Chris, and I lingered. As stragglers weaved toward the door, I motioned to the kids to follow me. An aging fire escape leads to the roof and the door at the top has not been locked since Beauregard.

We climb single file skyward, Allie trailing to preserve the dignity of her gown. The door gives and we step out onto the flat tar surface. A balustrade surrounds the edge, added for aesthetics and too low to serve safety.

There is no moon tonight, rendering brighter the canopy of stars overhead. Allie, pulling her wrap closer, holds Chris's hand as they walk to the far end to look out at the skyline. There is a breeze, warm and gentle enough to float leisurely a balloon released into the night air. Perhaps, I think as I study their silhouettes, that is part of what tonight has been about. There will follow her graduation, of course, and departure for college, but I sense here, on this roof in April, the string tied to that balloon slipping through my fingers. It drifted over us seventeen years ago, released into an uncertain sky on the far side of the world by a special woman we will never know and pulled in by Elizabeth, whom I miss tonight more than ever. It falls to me, her father, her only father, as she likes to remind me, to send it on its way.

Fly, sweetheart, fly.